KINDLING

Kindling: Scorched Earth series: Book One
Copyright © 2024 by Sandra Macek.

Published by Snowy Wings Publishing
www.snowywingspublishing.com

Cover by Okay Creations (www.okaycreations.com).
Interior by Key of Heart Designs.
Interior images by Jukov/DepositPhotos and Freepik.

ISBN: 978-1-958051-73-3
Library of Congress Control Number: 2024909061
Also available as an ebook.

SCORCHED EARTH SERIES: BOOK ONE

KINDLING

Humans had their chance; welcome to Plan B.

SANDRA MACEK

TURNER, OREGON

To creators everywhere.

THE RECKONING CALL

In the darkest hour, when human destruction of the natural world reached its zenith and all the mistakes of the past became irreversible, the Creator spoke. The Divine's voice reached into the mind of every soul upon Old Earth. To them the Creator said,

This land you have destroyed, I made for you.
Face now the great cleansing of your greed.
All children conceived yesterday will be my New Order.
They will lead this world as I reshape it.
Females all, they shall be revered and protected.
I have touched their minds, and they shall bear my mark.
They will hear my voice while you cannot.
Keep them safe, for they shall be the last human-born for forty years.
No other human conception shall occur, natural or through science.
Humankind shall shrink to near extinction for my hand to remake.
From these chosen few, a new race shall emerge, join with you, and flourish.
They will be legion.

This is the Call. Blessed be the words of our Creator.

PROLOGUE
CRANE ELDER

In the past...
January 4, 2108; 593 years ago
Montreal, Quebec, United Countries of America

In the morning darkness, Crane Elder trudged beside her nephew, Jon Jr., weaving through refugees as they made their way along the new seawall. Old Montreal was nearly gone now. The St. Lawrence River rushed past, flooding south like black ink spilled upon the land by a rising sea.

Her nephew was the unforeseen joy that even her pessimistic grandmother could not have imagined when Crane decided to marry at nineteen. It saddened her to remember their disagreement that day.

"You won't be happy as a soldier's wife, *mon coeur.*"

"*Mamé*, he's not just a soldier, he's going to be a doctor."

"A doctor and a soldier? You'll never see this man!"

"Of course I will. I'm going to be a midwife. We'll work together, just like you and *Pépère.*"

Her grandmother had hung her head. "A doctor and a nurse are not the same as two farmers.... You're sure about this?"

"*Je l'aime.* With all my heart, I love him."

"Well, I hope you enjoy delivering other women's babies, *mon ange,* because between the army and the hospitals, you're never going to have one of your own."

Her grandmother had been right, not only about the demands of military life, but also about children. When miscarriages and failed procedures gave way to resignation, she thought her life would be forever void of babies. But nature abhors a vacuum, and the arrival of a cherished nephew became a gift from God.

"Careful!" Crane pulled Jon toward her before he could trip over the outstretched leg of a man turning in his sleep on the sidewalk. The air around them stank of unwashed bodies and rotting trash. Ahead of them, a figure rose from the shanties near the entrance to the Cadillac metro station.

Jon pointed. "The professor, Tante."

She hurried forward. "*Bonjour,* Monsieur Williams. Please, don't get up." She gripped his elbow and held out the bag of day-old bread from the Army canteen.

"*Bone-jur,* ma'am." The Texan touched two fingers to his stained hat. "Much obliged. I'll get my wife—"

"Oh, no need." Crane looked into his haunted eyes. He was young, maybe forty, but the perilous migration from Houston had aged him. "How is Camila? Have the contractions started again?"

Her nephew tugged her arm again. "Tante? The train." He pointed to the arrival board.

"She's well, thank ya. You better run, ma'am."

"I'll see you tomorrow. And please, make her eat something," she called over her shoulder as she raced for the train.

Moments later, the brakes of the metro car whined as they approached McGill. The car was nearly full at 5:45 AM; most seats held American migrants, fast asleep.

As the doors whooshed open, a few people dressed in scrubs pushed past them to board. Crane recognized their haggard looks and knew her face would look the same in thirteen hours after her shift in maternity.

What passed for her nephew's holiday break was already over—they walked the familiar tunnels, back to their routine in which Crane and her husband helped get their nephew off to school while his parents were at work. Emerging into the McGill University Health Centre, they headed to their usual bench to wait for Crane's husband.

Jon Jr. worked his jaw and fiddled with his cuff. "How long?"

Crane checked her watch. "It's almost six. Your *oncle* should be here in…there he is."

She immediately recognized the man moving toward them from the ICU. Captain Jon Elder Sr. smiled, and Crane's chest squeezed from missing him, just like her grandmother had warned her all those years ago.

"*Bonjour. Comment ça va?*" She kissed his cheeks.

"*Ça va.* And how are you this morning, Jon? Ready for breakfast?"

Jon shrugged. "*Ouias.*"

Crane rolled her eyes at her nephew's lack of enthusiasm. "How was your shift? Did you have the meeting last night?"

Her husband's eyes tightened. "I did."

"And?"

"I got it. A field command…and a promotion, if I do well in

specialty training."

"That's great! Congratulations." She squeezed his hand, noticing the pinched expression at the corners of his eyes. "What? What's wrong?"

"It's in Fermont—the training *and* the work."

"Fermont?" Jon Jr. jumped to his feet. "Fermont Compound? That's like a million kilometers away!"

"1,200 actually."

"No way!" Jon Jr. shrugged off his bag. "*Merde!* I'm first year at Brebeuf! It was impossible to get in—my parents will never let me keep going if you aren't here. It's not fair."

"Hey, Jon—" Crane took a step toward him, but her brain started to buzz, like a sugar rush. The room spun. She leaned against the bench and clutched her temple. "I'm sorry…I…"

She peered up through her fingers as the buzz grew to a painful roar in her head. Was she having a stroke?

Someone screamed.

She focused on her husband—reached for his outstretched hand. He was clutching his head too. She heard a thud and watched her nephew fall sideways onto the bench, smashing his face on the armrest.

"*Tante!* What's happening?" He rocked back and forth, clutching his head in both hands.

Crane ignored her own pain, pulling her nephew's hands away from his face so she could squeeze his bleeding nose. "Pressure…apply pressure."

Her husband fell to his knees in front of them, groaning.

People shouted nearby. A group ran screaming toward the exit. Others fell on the floor, holding their heads.

She tried to speak, but all she could do was huff a few breaths. Slowly, the painful buzzing faded. The stillness was replaced with words—they filled her mind.

This land you have destroyed, I made for you.

Crane jolted, startled by the voice.

Face now the great cleansing of your greed.
All children conceived yesterday will be my New Order.

She sat up, confused. The voice was inside her head!

They will lead this world as I reshape it.
Females all, they shall be revered and protected.
I have touched their minds, and they shall bear my mark.

"Crane?" Her husband's hand crushed hers. "What…"

They will hear my voice while you cannot.
Keep them safe, for they shall be the last human-born for forty years.
No other human conception shall occur, natural or through science.
Humankind shall shrink to near extinction for my hand to remake.

"Oh, God…" Crane swayed.

From these chosen few, a new race shall emerge, join with you, and flourish.
They will be legion.

Crane breathed deeply, shaking her head, disoriented and chilled to the bone.

Her husband groaned next to her. "Oh my God."

"Oh, no. Oh, God. Jon, it's okay…it's over." She pulled a rag from her pocket. Her nephew's lips and chin were smeared with blood. "Here, keep squeezing."

"What was that?" her husband asked. "Some kind of biological attack?"

"I don't know. I…I feel okay now. Shaky, but not hurt. You?"

"I heard a voice," her nephew interrupted, "in my head."

"Me, too." Her husband stood and pulled them both up.

"The voice said we ruined the Earth and new people are coming."

Crane checked her nephew's pupils. "They look fine to me—"

"Let me see." Her husband repeated her examination.

Jon Jr. pushed his hands away. "I'm fine. I want to go home."

"Is your nose still bleeding?" Crane asked.

He tipped his head back, wiped away the blood. "Only a little; it's fine. Can we go home? I want to see my *maman…*"

"First things first. I think we're okay.…" Her husband's voice trailed off as he scanned the room. People cried nearby, some quietly, some almost keening.

"How is this possible?" A sliver of ice ran down Crane's spine. She gently pried her hand from her husband's grip. "It's okay. It's alright now."

"Yeah, I think so." Her husband straightened. "We're okay, but we weren't alone in whatever that was."

An emergency siren sounded then. Small red lights started flashing from devices mounted on the ceiling. It made everything worse.

Her husband placed a hand on their nephew's shoulder. "We're fine, and your parents are strong people, so they're likely also fine. What's important right now is to help these people—make sure they're okay, too."

Crane cleared her throat. "We can do that, right? It's what we do—take care of people."

Her nephew's skin was pale. He wiped blood from his fingers before resolutely shoving the rag in his pocket. "*Oui*, I'm fine—had worse on the soccer field."

"Okay, then. Let's get ready." Crane grabbed her nephew's bag and handed it to him. "Your parents will be proud that you helped, just like we are."

"Wait a second." Her husband raised one finger. "I...I don't know what that was, but..."

Crane bit her lip. "But...it changes everything. Well...." She rolled her shoulders. "We better get started."

600 years later...

1
MERCY

I've studied dozens of events just like this one, so I can read the signs. Our society is splintering and war is coming. And yet I spend my days living in the past, metaphorically speaking. I'm a historian—a completely useless profession as it turns out. My expertise in history impresses no one, helps no one, as we prepare for civil war.

Even my famous family name is useless. I'm not like my American ancestors, John and Abigail Adams. I don't have the skill to fight, the ability to strategize, or the tact to negotiate, yet somehow, I find myself on the fringe of a group ready to do *all* those things. I'm not that kind of Adams—I'm a student of their courageous acts, born in an age that needs their valor.

I'm not like my Chinese ancestors either, though I resemble them. Their hands were rough with the calluses of survival, while mine are as soft as a baby's.

My best friend Eddie sits in the seat of the magRail car next to me. She picks at her skirts, nervously shredding the hem. A sudden deceleration has me gripping her hand.

"Ow!" Eddie yelps. "Mercy, not so hard."

"What now?" My father peers over my shoulder to see out the window behind me.

I crane my neck to look.

A large crowd of people lines the roadside. Their voices rise like a great swarm of geese, calling shrill commands in disjointed song. New Juneau, our small city, looms behind them—a fragmented collection of eco-friendly habitats and repurposed buildings. As we approach, I see that the crowd is two separate political groups.

"What is this?"

"A demonstration," my father answers.

Eddie hisses. "A protest, more like." Her face contorts into a grimace. "It's fine. Ignore them."

On our right, Pilgrims with their arms interlocked form a long rope stretching toward the train station. Their neat, black SciCorps uniforms remind me of a braided whip, uncoiled and alive with menace. A gust of wind hits the people near our vehicle, and I watch the movement articulate down the rows like a pulse. The black gem between their eyes, the extra-sensory organ that marks us all as praenex, appears like punctuation on their angry faces. *No mere sapiens here!* they seem to say. The words of their chant reach me.

"Birthright, take flight...True sight, take flight...Our fight, take flight...Take flight!"

On the opposite side, Terrans press together singing a tune

not quite discernible above the SciCorps chant. They're a mix of praenex and sapiens. I recognize some friends from school in their plain tan jackets and trousers, a few Farmers from Alberta, and even some Couvies with their colorful clothing and ornate rings. Altogether they're a smaller crowd—a clutch of loose confetti. I half expect them to blow away in the next breath of wind off the bay.

"Pathetic and wasteful!" Eddie slumps back; her restless hands continue their attack on her helpless hem. "They should all be on their work rotations."

I wonder again about how serious and troubled she seems after just a few years as a cleric in the Legion, as if her newly gained knowledge has radically changed her perception of the world. Can knowledge do that? I study constantly, but it doesn't change me. I'm the same old Mercy, just with more useless facts stuffed in my head.

"Papa? A protest? When did this start?"

"How long have you been buried in those history books?" Eddie mumbles.

"I...." I shake my head, unsure of what to say. When I first met Edelweiss, Eddie's full name, she was an extremely rude girl with a snobbish brother. Though her albino skin and slender features give the impression of frailty, she's strong like the sturdy white flower she's named after. Once I got to know her, I downgraded her from *extremely rude* to *strikingly frank*. Now I love her like a sister, and like a sister, I worry when she's out of sorts like this.

My father nods. "Ignore them, as Eddie suggests. They're not here for you. They can't know about your role yet. The four of you'll be together soon, and then you'll know what to do."

"My role? I don't understand, Papa."

He glances at me, his bushy eyebrows furrowing together, obscuring his gem. "I'll explain more, but not here. We're almost to the station."

I turn back to the serious faces outside as we inch through the crowd, our automated magRail car slowed by the crush of people. I wish I were back in the library, safely ensconced in my cubby with some ancient tome and my tablet. Alone. Quiet. Unseen.

The car hisses to a stop in front of the station where Eddie and I are to meet the Legion's delegation and their foreign guests. My nerves jangle because I know I'll see our spiritual leader the Gran Bozan and her entourage for the first time since my failed ascension to adulthood. The memory brings a stab of sadness, and I shove it aside for another time.

"It's a lot of people," I murmur. The protesters have followed our vehicle and now clog the steps up to the station.

"Councilman Adams!" Someone calls my father's name.

The car rocks suddenly, and I yelp in surprise.

Eddie squeezes my hand, still entwined with her own.

"It's Councilman Adams!" Voices rise to a new peak as the crowd presses in. The car bumps back and forth as dozens of hands press the plastic separating us from the horde outside. A fist pounds on my window.

I can't breathe. My skin starts to prickle as my heart races. "I don't think I can handle this."

Eddie blows out a breath. "Give me a second...." She closes

her eyes and inhales deeply, and then I feel it—the compulsive need to move away from her. I'm fighting my own urge to lean back when the people outside go quiet and start to step away. The car stops rocking.

"Very good." My father leans in. "Can you clear a path?"

"Well enough, if you can draw their attention."

He grunts in agreement.

I sling my heavy book bag across my shoulder and try to find my courage.

"It's going to be okay, Cricket." Eddie opens the door and climbs out. Her steps are slow at first, then the path clears like she's Moses at the Red Sea. A second later she's striding toward the station, her satchel swinging wildly, her skirts swirling in the hot wind.

I shuffle across the seat and climb from the car. I want to catch up with Eddie where she waits like a boulder in the stream of people flowing out of the station. The path before me is walled by an undulating human mass. It's a corridor of safety leading to my future. I take one step, then another. It's not so hard. I'm focused on the stairs ahead when I'm suddenly blocked by a black uniform. I pull up short, but it's too late.

"Ugh!" I huff as I slam into a soldier. "Sorry...." My apology dies in my throat as I look up to meet their cold amethyst stare. The soldier's arrestingly handsome—their smooth mocha skin contrasts with white teeth set in a strong, clenched jaw. There's both anger and something more in their eyes—desperation, maybe, as they stare back at me.

The soldier draws a deep breath and I realize they're straining against Eddie's will. They bare their teeth, then hide them behind tight lips, struggling to stand in my way. "We're leaving." They growl and take a deep breath before continuing. "All of us. It's the only way." Their voice is low and clear now, meant just for me.

A chill slips down my spine. "I...." I glance back to the car. "You've got the wrong person." I glance at the soldier's arm and realize they're an officer. "You want to talk to my father, Lieutenant." I point behind me to where my father has emerged from the vehicle to speak with a group of protesters. As I move to step around the officer, their hand shoots out and grabs my upper arm. They squeeze hard and I wince.

"No. I mean you, Mercy Adams." Their nostrils flare as their expression hardens. They squeeze my arm harder—hard enough that my knees start to buckle.

My instincts scream at me to run and hide, but I force myself to stand still. It takes all my strength to tear my eyes away from theirs and stare at their hand clenched around my arm.

With a sharp indrawn breath, they slacken their fingers and release me. Their brow furrows in confusion, maybe even surprise, at their own violence. They shake it off and straighten. "We're leaving, we Pilgrims, and we *need* you with us, you and the others. Join us, and we'll leave Scorch as a unified people, to start again."

"I...I have to go," I choke out, and quickly brush past them.

"Mercy Adams!"

I keep moving but chance a look back. At first, I think they're going to argue some more, but then their expression clears and they straighten.

"Divine grace with you." They raise their palm to me.

"Peace with you, Lieutenant…"

"Naveen. Caesar Naveen."

I nod automatically before rushing up the steps.

I focus again on Eddie, waiting a few meters away. As I reach her, my father catches up and together we push into the station. My father points toward a bench in a quiet corner. I slide onto the seat.

Eddie squeezes my knee as she presses in next to me. She's focused on my father, who squats close in front of us so others can't hear.

I close my eyes and rub absently at the bruises forming on my upper arm. I think back to the serenity of the last hour's drive in from the countryside. I imagine the views out the magRail window—the gleam of an Alaskan spring sun, the glistening fields of solar panels, the soaring wind turbines. I try to forget Caesar Naveen.

"Mercy?"

I open my eyes to see Eddie's wide with concern, her albino skin a bit whiter from the strain.

"Are you alright?"

"I'm fine, just tired, I guess."

"Well…." She tips her head toward my father.

"Cricket, you can't wander into your thoughts now, you've got to be ready for this mission."

Despite my father's indulgent smile, waves of fear and worry ripple like the heavy bass of an invisible drum. I rub my gem, the rough patch of skin between my eyes, to dispel the sensation, then quickly brush my brow to hide my tell.

My father huffs and I know I'm fooling no one.

My brain's buzzing with all the warnings my parents have spent the last 48 hours drilling into us. I'm not so null to have expected a relaxing weekend camping under the stars, not with the increasing tension as the conference approaches and more citizens take sides, but I didn't expect a mission briefing either. My mother was so exhausted that she went home early, just one of the signs that her illness is worsening. I say a silent prayer for her.

"Listen, Cricket. Try to remember everything we've told you, eh?" His eyes are fierce with conviction as he turns to Eddie. "I don't know why you two and the others should lead this mission, or why I don't see myself there with the other leaders, but my gift assures me it's true. I see the four of you, though barely adults," he says with a sideways glance that makes me shrink in my seat. "This is *your* mission, and yours alone."

My father's not precognitive, but his gift is similar. He sees the truth and always knows when he's on the right path. It's made him a brilliant scientist, a leader among his peers. It also means that I can't ignore his prediction that things are coming to a head. Soon our society will have to choose—go on trying to save the planet or evacuate. There aren't enough of us to successfully do both. The fight's going to be brutal, and apparently, I'll be right in the middle of it. Right there with my friends.

"Eddie"—my father turns to her, and I'm temporarily

relieved to be out of the spotlight—"how well do you know the leaders who arrive today?"

"I don't work with the Gran Bozan directly very often, but I know her, and all of her staff. Recently we've had a…*project* that brought us together. I know her team. I know what to do and who's who."

"Okay, that's covered then," my father agrees. "I don't know much about these foreigners, these *Spherans*, as they call themselves, except that they arrived just in time, offering a Terran alliance."

"Arrived from where?" I ask.

"Somewhere in South America, which explains how they kept themselves secret—it's a long way from Alaska. I don't know…I just don't know." He rubs his temples. "It's a blind spot. I'm sorry."

My stress ratchets up a level at the worry in his voice. "But they're not sapiens, they're praenex like us, right?"

"Hmm." My father shakes his head even as he agrees. "But we're all *human*. We're all creatures of will." He gestures toward the protesters outside. "And for the first time, we're about to learn what it means to live in a praenex society divided in purpose. We have to decide how much to trust these Spherans."

"I've been thinking about the timing. Strategically, it's to their advantage to appear to be aiding us, entirely at their own risk. It creates a debt, doesn't it?"

My father lifts his chin. "It does at that."

"They must need something from us."

"I agree." My father jabs his finger at me. "I think you'll find out *what* only when it serves them. They're skilled at keeping secrets. Be cautious, but hurry. Time's running out. The conference is about to begin."

He grips my hand as if he can push his strength into me. "I've got to go. Remember everything I told you, and don't trust anyone until they've earned it."

I focus on his gem and know the usual comfort I get from its solid black surface—no sign of the disease that plagues my mother.

"And let Van be the sapiens that he is, both of you. Let him use his size and strength to protect you and the other praenex when he can, just as you protect him with your cleverness. Trust yourself, Mercy. Draw what you can from your histories but remember this above all else: family is the most important thing, both the family you're born to"—he gestures toward Eddie—"and the family you make."

"Yes, Papa. I'll not fail you." I squeeze his hand to make my point, and know he feels my self-doubt as real as his own urgency. I reach into my bag and pull out a book, like it's any other day, waiting in the station and reading.

"Goodbye, then. Divine blessings on you both."

I watch him stride for the door. The noise outside increases as he joins the people walking out of the station. It transforms into a buzz in my ears and his image shifts out of focus like a mirage. I grip the book in my lap, try to steady myself, knowing that a vision is about to overtake me. The world shifts and I'm gone, my mind traveling to another time while my body waits behind.

I'm kneeling on a cold floor. It vibrates with a familiar, mechanical hum. I'm in some kind of transport. I feel…loss…dread.

Movement draws my eye. Another officer walks toward me. I don't recognize them, but I'm not afraid. They kneel next to me and hold out their hands. "Doc applied a wound patch. He thought you might want this."

I reach for the bundle they hold. It's a perfectly folded strip of red fabric. I rub the hem between my fingers, puzzled, and then lift my arm to let the fabric unfold. My nose fills with the rusty stench of blood.

There's only one person who wears a red sash like this. It's the Gran Bozan's, our spiritual leader. The sash is sacred, symbolic, and covered in blood. A tendril of ice forms in my stomach.

"Mercy." My name is whispered like a plea. Beneath my knees the deck presses into my flesh and I know that when I rise the pattern of the steel will remain on my skin like a temporary tattoo. It's then that I feel it—a body, warm but fading, rests against my knees.

"Mercy!"

I flinch as a bloody hand closes around my wrist.

2
VAN

The loadmaster is a wee wean of a soldier, even for a praenex. They're looking away, tapping their stylus in the air like they're counting the crates stacked all around the staging area. Their tidy black uniform is crisp and clean. They remind me of a newborn foal, all sleek and fresh. I walk slowly, so as not to startle them.

I clear my throat and let my bag drop noisily to the ground. "Pardon me."

"Oh!" They jump anyway. "God's grace!" Their eyes scan up my tall frame until they're practically leaning backward to see my bake.

"Lieutenant Sylvan Elder reporting for transport." I inch back a pace and remind myself that each step in this trip brings me one step closer to Mercy. I just need to fake patience until we're back in New Juneau.

The loadmaster's skin is nearly as dark as mine, and shiny with perspiration. I watch their Adam's apple bob a few times before they stutter out a reply. "*You're* Lieutenant Elder?" They scrutinize my face, stopping on my smooth forehead.

Alberta Farms maybe be filled with sapiens, but the airfield is entirely run by praenex. It must still be odd to this new loadmaster, my lack of a gem; only my eyes broadcast my emotions. I keep them neutral now, despite my embarrassment. At eighteen, I'm old for my rank compared to the praenex in the Terran Army Corps. With their fast growth and wicked cleverness, they'd be majors by my age.

"Aye, Private. Ye've met my father General Elder, I presume. He's in charge of this here mission. 'Tis some resemblance, don't ye see?"

"General Elder? The giant…." They swallow hard and open their mouth like a bird in the nest but nothing comes out.

"Aye, the giant sapiens who's in charge of this whole mess." I motion to the crates piled nearby.

"Of course, I mean…I should've recognized you. It's just Elder's such a common name among you…"

I shift my weight. They're not the first sheltered praenex I've met, but possibly the least tactful. Course, I've a bit of a reputation for direct speaking myself.

"Right on that. My fifteen siblings alone make up a fair share of Elders in my neck of the Farms, though I'm likely more than my share by mass." I flex my arm.

Their eyes lock on my bicep, which is about the same size around as their torso. They're frozen in place. Even for a private, they look pretty green. It's probably their first month in uniform.

This is taking too long, making impatience hum through me.

I don't really want to scare this poor kid, though, do I? I sigh. "So, where do ye want me, Private?"

They stare for a moment like a deer in the headlights, and then, with a shiver that ripples all the way down to their tiny black boots, they focus back on my face. "Oh, um…you're in transport two." They point to the small plane nearby and we both take a juke.

"Well that's craic." I heft my bag onto my shoulder. "Maybe I can strap myself on top like. Not sure I'll fit, elsewise."

The wee loadmaster doesn't say anything, and when I turn back, they look like they're considering it.

"Well now, don't get your kex in a bunch. I'm just slaggin' ye. Thanks for the information, I'll be goin'."

I stride across to the retractable steps and tuck myself into the small cabin. A blur of movement catches my eye, just as I feel the cool, wet press of a dog's nose into my palm.

"Hey there, Cousteau." I bend to scratch behind the dog's ears and get my chin licked in reply. I glance down the aisle. "Aye, what's got ye worked into a frenzy?"

My best friend TJ, our SciCorps Navy pilot, pauses his pacing to give me a sarcastic head wag. "Nice to see you too, Van."

"I'm takin' the first row." I toss my bag on the floor, push up the wee armrest and swing myself around to sit. At 193 centimeters and 105 kilograms, everything in the praenex world feels miniature to me. When I stretch out my legs, my boots are in the cockpit.

"Comfortable?"

"For now." I blow out a slow breath. I hate waiting as much

as the next bloke, but growing up sapiens in a praenex world taught me how to appear relaxed when everything inside me screams for action. Maybe it's the closest thing I have to a natural gift—this ability to wind in my emotions while my body hums with restraint.

"Gah!" TJ grumbles as he trips over his dog. "Cousteau!" He points to the space opposite my seat and the dog obediently moves to sit there. "Stay."

TJ's comm rings keep buzzing like a swarm of bees. He pauses to check and then ignores it, before spinning to pace again. This time when he passes my seat, I stick out my foot. He lurches off balance, knocks awkwardly between the seats and lands on his butt, narrowly missing Cousteau.

"What the—" TJ kicks his feet free of mine and sits up. "Some friend you are! I know you're terrified of the conference, but you don't have to take it out on me." He rubs a hand through Cousteau's fur absently before resting back on his elbows.

"Terrified?" I shake my head. "Why for all of Scorch's red dust would I be terrified?"

"Because you're completely intimidated around other praenex. I know you, brother. I can see behind that mask of yours—you're afraid."

"Mask? What in the hell are ye carryin' on about? I'm not afraid of praenex folk!"

"Oh, don't worry—nobody else seems to notice. You've got them fooled. I think it would do you a world of good, my friend, if you could trust that you're just as good—no, better!—than any praenex man for one particular praenex woman we know and love. Then you could just…get on with things."

"Stop weaving cloth, yer talkin' nonsense." I hold out my hand. "Besides, yer worryin' the dog."

He harumphs but takes my hand and lets me pull him up. "For my part, I don't want to be late."

TJ's typical praenex—kinetic, empathic, and bright as the sun reflecting off the Hudson Ocean. Add to that his savant-like tech skill and ye get one sneaky bastard. A good guy to have as a friend. And he's punctual. Always punctual, the praenex, which makes waiting for the planes to be loaded even more trying. Must be why he's lashing out with such blather. Me, not as good as a praenex man…. Me, afraid of a small praenex woman…. It's ridiculous.

"Hate to be late. Hate to be late." He's moving again.

"Aye, then we won't be late." I stretch my long limbs and try again to get comfortable in the tiny seat. "Ye know you'll make up the time in the air, brother."

TJ moves to the open hatch. "By God, your father doesn't travel light, does he?"

I hear it too—the sound of folks and vehicles outside on the tarmac as they traipse past to the lead aircraft. "Naw, never light, my da. Won't go any faster with ye watchin' either. Why don't ye sit for a bit? Meditate or some such thing, yeah?"

My da is General Elder, chief botanist, Alberta Farms council leader, and force of nature. Lucky me. It's from him, I'm told, that I get my well-honed survival instincts.

TJ resumes his pacing, Cousteau jumps up to follow on his

heels. I feel bad for the dog, I really do. It's time for a distraction. "Hack anything craic lately?"

"*Hack* and *craic*? Sometimes I don't even know what you're saying. Is it English? Is it Gaelic?"

It's something I get from my fair and freckled mam, who can trace her ancestry all the way back to Tánaiste Sean O'Brien, who convinced 100,000 Irish folk to leave their flooded isle and rebuild their country here in Alberta Farms all those centuries ago. My expressions carry the lilt of that lost isle, a place I'll never see. I hold that uniqueness close to my heart here on Scorch, if only to remind me that such a cool, wet place existed.

"Ye ken my meanin' well enough. So have ye lifted anything interestin' lately?"

"No!" TJ scoffs. "All the chatter's about the same thing. I'm starting to get bored...." He stops pacing and tips his head to the side. "I just had the strangest feeling."

I sit up. I know from experience that things are about to get interesting. Many of our best adventures start exactly like this. "The strange kind of feelin' only praenex get, is it? Did it warn ye not to tell me anythin' about the chatter ye hacked?"

TJ swivels to meet my eyes. "On the contrary. It urged me to tell you everything..."

That's new. I wait, but he just keeps pondering.

"So are ye gonna share it, brother?"

"It's about a secret transmission," he answers. "It's encrypted, but, you know, that's to be expected."

"Aye, sure 'tis. I mean, all the secret transmissions that *I* intercept are encrypted like." I roll my eyes to the ceiling.

Apparently, I'm supposed to know everything about tech espionage. Me, a sapiens Terran Army Corps officer from the Farms. Sometimes really smart folk can be incredibly dense.

TJ stares at me for a moment, then shakes his head. "What I mean is the interesting part is *who's* excited about it and exactly *what* they're trying to figure out."

He smiles like he just explained everything, and I itch to knock him on his praenex butt again, best friend or not.

It must show on my bake because he holds up both hands. "Okay, okay. The *who* are astrophysicists, telecommunications experts, even some strategists. *What* they're trying to determine is the transmission's *origin*. They don't seem to care so much what it says, just where it came from."

"Aye, that's odd."

We're interrupted by a commotion outside the plane. "For all that's holy, what now?" TJ's out the door with Cousteau at his heels before I can lift myself up.

"Van Elder!"

My da's voice has me shooting out of my seat and crashing my head into the low ceiling—my height a frequent hazard in the praenex world. I curse under my breath. "Aye, sir, I'm here." I rub my head as I swivel toward the door.

Suddenly he's filling the doorway, his massive arms filled with crates of produce. "Make room, lad. Change of plans." He places the crates delicately behind my seat, then unceremoniously shifts me out of the way as he exits the small plane.

"What's all this?" I follow him out and see for myself that the long procession of cargo has changed direction and is headed my way. The wee loadmaster stands to the side tapping their stylus in the air again. A delirious TJ trips back and forth between the planes, Cousteau on his heels, his hands in his hair, trying to convince the small army of porters—my multitude of brothers and sisters—to stop.

My da heaves another crate on top of the others at the base of the stairs. "Somethin's wrong with the air conditionin' controls in the other craft. It's a blasted oven, sure to turn into a freezer once we're airborne."

"Ye want I should take a juke at the controls?"

"Naw, I've got it sorted. The troops will ride in that plane, and the cargo here. If we stay below 5,000 feet, everything should be fine."

I shake my head at the logic. I get it because I get my da—the botanist *and* the general. The only thing more important than his vegetables is his sense of duty.

TJ approaches, his hands gesturing wildly in the air. "Stop! Make them stop. We don't have time for this, we don't have time!"

As sapiens we sympathize with the praenex obsession with timeliness, we just can't adopt it.

"Lieutenant Commander, wind yer head in, lad." My da makes TJ's title sound like both an insult and an order at once.

TJ snaps to attention, his nose in the air. He may be SciCorps, and we may be TAC, but a soldier's a soldier.

"Sir, if you will, please explain why the cabbages, tomatoes"—he says *toe-mah-toes* in his flyboy accent—"and other assorted vegetables cannot remain in the malfunctioning aircraft while the troops remain in relative comfort aboard my aircraft…sir?"

"Men before vegetables?" My da's eyebrows shoot up.

If I laugh now, it'll only encourage my da and irritate my best friend, so I bite my lip and study the sky as if my life depends on it.

From the corner of my eye, I see my da's chest expand, and expand some more. He shakes his head side to side, as if TJ's uttered the most ridiculous idea ever spoken on God's good Earth.

A line of children, big and small, form a train of crates and robotic carts winding behind my da like an eager snake. My siblings—some dark-skinned like me and my da, some lighter like my red-haired mam—are good soldiers, good farmers. Their circular Terran insignias glint in the sun like a row of blinking beacons. Cousteau barks excitedly, his tail wagging wildly as he weaves in and out of the long line of wee giggling soldiers.

An hour into the flight, my da drones on about heirloom tomatoes, having used the excuse of old age (forty!) to commandeer the co-pilot seat in our temperature-controlled aircraft. I stare out my window at an endless sea of green grass covering what once was solid white tundra. It should be a frozen beauty, but our world is sick—fevered with heat, polluted, and forever changed. *Earth.* The old name chews like seed cake in my mouth, rich and dense. Now it's *Scorch*—the way yer throat feels on the hottest days when the wind brings ash from the south and even a mask can't stop the grit from coating yer tongue.

We did this, we sapiens, before my Irish ancestors left their devastated isle for the new fields of Alberta. Even before the praenex arrived six hundred years ago. Now our mixed population is dividing into two camps—fix or flight. We Terrans hope to heal Scorch and start over. Our symbol is a perfect circle, the Earth of old. But for each one of us, there are two Pilgrims now, those like TJ, who believe it's our destiny to launch ourselves into space, to colonize another world.

Hundreds of years ago, statisticians reckoned that we wouldn't have the numbers to do both. We don't have the resources either. The colony ships alone need a right massive population just to operate; if any of us stay behind, it drastically shrinks the chance of success for both groups. Choices will have to be made. What started as whispers of forced compliance has built into an open debate. Should folks be forced to leave? Distrust returned to our planet and with it, a massive split. Though ye can still find Pilgrims in Alberta Farms and Terrans in New Juneau, SciCorps, our dominant government and societal group, is almost entirely Pilgrims now.

TJ keeps busier than required piloting our plane and rejecting a constant stream of incoming calls on his comm. He's supposed to be on holiday, but after an argument with his da—who also happens to be a SciCorps Admiral—he quietly changed his plans to help me out. He hides his emotions pretty well. Only our years of friendship allow me to see the impatience in the tilt of his head. My da lecturing from the co-pilot seat isn't helping. TJ's gem is almost parallel with the ceiling now. If his nose gets any higher, he'll be piloting us blind.

"You'd know these things if ye had a partner and wee ones. A person has no greater motivation than their children." My da pounds his massive fist on the armrest of his seat, and I know what's coming.

"This"—he points to his own circular insignia—"this is a symbol of more than my dedication to remain on Scorch, to heal her. 'Tis my commitment to extend the race. To teach my children how to bring us back from the brink of extinction. So, tell me, lad." He points at TJ now. "When are *you* goin' to marry? Huh? I suspect that space travel won't mean a thing once ye watch yer children play on the grass of this sweet land?"

He pokes the rocket insignia on TJ's SciCorps uniform, and I'm too cowardly to speak up lest I draw my da's attention.

"Sweet land? *Scorch*?" TJ mumbles.

I can't help but roll my eyes. *Eejit!* Now the lecture will begin anew.

A year ago, if my da had put the question of marriage to *me*, I would've simply answered; Mercy and I had plans—or notions anyway. But now I'm not so sure. When her petition for adulthood was denied, I felt like the world shifted. At fifteen, she was the typical age for a praenex to reach majority; she'd finished her PhD, heaped up more than the necessary credits through her work. I hadn't even considered that we'd have to wait.

"Ask Sylvan how 'tis. He'll tell ya."

I look up and they're both twisted around to stare at me. "What?"

"Aye, tell him, son." My da nods at TJ.

"Tell 'im what?"

TJ smiles and twists even further. "Tell me *how it is.*"

I roll my eyes. "I dunno what yer goin' on about.... Shouldn't ye be flyin' the plane?"

He reaches back and hits the autopilot button. "Plane's covered, so tell me."

My da smacks his palm on the armrest. "Tell him about yer Mercy. Tell him when ye first knew she was the lass for you."

I suck in a breath and hold it.

My da turns to TJ. "He was helpin' her over a fallen tree—"

"A mud puddle!" I can't help but correct him. "It was mud, not a tree. Where do ye get this stuff, Da?"

"Oh, sure now. Sorry. He took her hand and felt a jolt of recognition."

"A jolt of recognition?" TJ looks at me.

"I don't wanna talk about it." I swivel in my seat and stare out the window. I can just see the tail of the lead plane among the thin clouds.

My da's voice rises. "It was like electricity, or—"

"Energy?" TJ suggests. "Like a physical thing or just emotional?"

My da nods so hard his seat shakes a little. "Physical! He was overcome with the urge to kiss her—"

"You kissed her?" TJ's voice squeaks.

I blow out a breath. "Naw! I didn't kiss her."

For me, it's always been Mercy Adams. Even the prettiest, smartest girls at Alberta Farms were for my mates, never me. I didn't always understand it—why her opinion mattered most, why I couldn't relax in a room with her until I was standing at her side.

"What happened? Why didn't he kiss her?" TJ asks my da.

"She read his mind, and she made a *disgusted* face."

I turn forward and throw my hands in the air. "It wasn't *disgusted!* It was…" I search for the right words. "Never mind! Besides, they can't read our minds, Da. The gems don't work on us."

"So they say." My da shrugs.

"So, she looked repulsed?" TJ asks.

"Sick?" my da offers.

"No! Scared, okay? She looked shocked out of her bleedin' mind… Why're we even talkin' about this?" I slump back into my chair. With each of their questions, my nervousness over seeing Mercy again mounts.

TJ shrugs. "I don't understand. You'd been friends forever, so why was she scared?"

"She was twelve! Okay? She was barely old enough to understand—"

"Twelve is old enough for praenex," TJ interrupts.

My da nods. "Many praenex marry at that age. Ye grow so fast."

I stare out the window again. The lead plane's a little closer now.

TJ's quiet for a minute. I can tell he's thinking. Remembering. That's never good. "This explains so much. I remember—that was the year you started ignoring her. She kept asking me why you were mad at her. Then you stopped hanging out with us when we were all together." TJ looks confused. "So what changed? I mean, all of a sudden last year you were back together. Inseparable. You were promised, right?"

"I don't wanna talk about it."

"It was at her birthday party last year," my da tells him. "His mam made him go, even though he complained. At the party, he shook Mercy's hand, and she was breathless—"

I sigh. "Ye really need to stop tellin' my stories, Da. Yer gettin' 'em all wrong."

"Well, then *you* tell me," TJ pleads.

"Ye told me she was breathless!" my da insists.

"No, not breathless… she gasped." I turn from the window to look into their eager faces. If I reveal too much, they'll know how nervous I am, but if I ignore them, they'll just keep gnawing on this. I grit my teeth. "I shook her hand and the jolt ripped through me, just like before, but this time she gasped. She felt it too." I shrug.

TJ leans toward me. "And that's when you kissed her?"

I squirm in my tiny seat. "I don't wanna talk about this—"

The proximity alarm screeches. The autopilot decelerates so hard I strain forward into my seatbelt. The cargo squeaks and groans as it shifts behind me. My da's arms flail as he struggles to regain his balance.

"Mayday, mayday!" The voice of the first plane's pilot blares from TJ's panel.

A crate of cabbages slams into the back of the seat next to me. Cousteau yips and jumps out of the way.

"Here boy!" I shove him between my knees to brace him.

TJ's corrects course, frantically trying to keep us away from the now smoking plane ahead. "Captain, status report. We see smoke from your aft engine."

"Affirmative. I can't shut it down. I'm going to have to land her."

At that moment, a puff of orange fire erupts from the side of their plane—a small explosion. We watch in disbelief as the lead plane makes a rapid descent to the green fields below.

"Hold on to Cousteau!" TJ shouts, diving after the smoking plane.

"I've got him!"

TJ follows the smoking plane, slowing slightly to increase our distance. "Prepare for emergency landing." TJ's voice is calm but commanding.

Da responds immediately, bracing himself against the console.

We watch helplessly as the smoke thickens. It looks like they'll make it when suddenly there's another explosion on their wing, making our plane rock in its wake.

"We've lost comm." TJ's relentless in his pursuit of the now barely controlled plane ahead. "They're at 100 meters...50 meters..."

The damaged plane hits the grass hard and lists to the side as it skids along the field. A plume of grass, dirt, and fire erupt into the sky. The plane plows through the field before coming to a stop at an awkward angle.

TJ wrestles with the stick to control our landing. Our own

rough impact feels like a sock to the gut as our gear hits the uneven turf.

Finally we stop. My da's up, his bulky form filling the cabin. "Open the door!" he demands, and seconds later he's down the stairs, Cousteau with him.

I run to catch up, TJ close on my heels. Even meters away the heat presses against us, but my da doesn't slow.

His gloves are on and he's at the door, twisting the release handle as TJ and I reach him. He pulls down the retracted steps but doesn't wait for them to hit the ground before vaulting up them. He disappears into the plane, into the smoke.

Before I can follow, soldiers begin to stagger from the craft, some dazed, all coughing. Cousteau dances around them, yipping.

I do a quick count. "That's ten, everyone but the pilot!"

We help the soldiers into the grass a safe distance from the smoke still spewing from the side of the plane.

"I'll triage here," TJ tells me. "Get the pilot—get them out!"

Normally I can run like the wind, but my legs feel like anchors as I rush to help my da and the pilot still inside. The twenty meters feel like twenty thousand. I reach the stairs when my da emerges, balancing on the steps, waving his arms to clear the smoke, coughing hard.

"Their leg's stuck between the console and the seat!" he shouts. Smoke rises in wisps from his singed hair. "I'll try to move it, and you pull them out!"

"Okay!" I leap up the stairs behind him and into the smoke beyond, grabbing a fistful of his jacket to guide me. It's only steps to the pilot's seat where they sit unconscious and bleeding. I can't tell if they're breathing—there's too much smoke.

My da climbs onto the crushed equipment and uses the back of the pilot's chair as a handhold as he positions his feet. With one foot on each side of the panel that's crushing the pilot's legs, he arches his body in a bridge along the ceiling, barely fitting in the tight space.

"Ready?"

I bend into the pilot, slide my arms under their thighs, and dig my shoulder into their chest. My hope soars as I hear a quiet moan. "Hold on, Captain, I've gotcha… Ready!"

At first nothing changes, then my da's grunt becomes a roar and the chair begins to tip as the metal frame bends. The pilot's leg swings free suddenly, threatening to tip us both into the side of the listing plane. I react by instinct, closing my grip and lifting them free. They're lighter than I expect—the praenex always are. With a few lumbering steps, we're at the hatch.

"Hurry, Van. Hurry!" my da shouts.

We're almost clear. I'm on the steps with the pilot in my arms when the plane explodes. The force throws me through the air. Somehow I manage to twist so I won't crush the pilot. My back hits the grass in a graceless thud as the pilot's helmet slams into my chin.

My ears ring, but nothing hurts, not one bit. I know it will; the adrenaline's blocking the pain for now. Between the weight of the pilot and the impact, I'm well pinned. I swivel my head to see my da facedown next to me, so close I could touch him if I could move my arm.

TJ rushes to us, bringing a couple of soldiers with him. They pull the pilot off me. "My da!" I try to shout, my voice raspy. "Help my da!"

TJ shouts something. The soldiers immediately rush to my da's side. Cousteau is there already, barking encouragement and licking my da's face.

For a moment, I can only watch and wait.

Then my da's arm moves. Then his knee. He coughs.

With a sigh of relief, I watch him push to his hands and knees.

"Good lad." My da pats the dog's head and heaves a huge sigh. He turns to look at me, his eyes scanning for injuries. He nods. "Good lad."

I turn to TJ, expecting to see relief, but instead he's rigid with anger. A small muscle flexes at his jaw. His eyes narrow in resolve, and I follow his stare back to the burning plane.

A perfectly round hole mars the fuselage exactly where my da would've sat, if he'd flown in the lead plane as planned.

TJ waves toward the plane. "That was no accident."

My da coughs. "Huh. I guess that explains the problem with the air-conditioning." He collapses back into the turf.

I rest my head in the grass and look up at the clear blue sky.

Someone just tried to kill my da. But who? And why?

3
MERCY

Current year: 2701
Wednesday, 1 PM
New Juneau

"Mercy!"

Eddie shakes my arm and jars me back to the present. Away from my painful vision. Away from blood and death. If I linger on these thoughts any longer Eddie will press for answers. She knows I have visions, but she's patient enough to wait for me to tell her about them. Usually. But right now, she's casting out tiny ripples of irritation that prick my senses, and I don't want to test her.

I slouch like I'm bored and find the place I left off in my book. The business-like bustle of the station continues around us. It's an odd kind of serenity to be bundled within this shell of normal activity. The emotional hangover caused by my vision is fading fast, just like the noise of the crowd outside. It's an effort, but I try to act normal, to shield my thoughts. I don't want to tell Eddie what I saw until I understand it better. *If* I understand it better.

I settle in to wait for the train. I can't get interested in my history book. I consider pulling out the collection of letters Van sent me—his annual gift, sent ahead instead of given in person. I wonder again why he did that. Is he expecting to not see me much? To not have time alone? The gift itself is also odd, a selection of what we historians call *Dear John* letters. Is that significant in some way? Or did he just know that I would be intrigued by these letters, those from his famous ancestor, Crane Elder, in particular. Hers were so filled with sadness, so revealing in their rare, unscripted glimpses of history. Almost the opposite of my future-sight gift, they're glimpses of a sad and poignant emotional past.

"Do you think Van's forgiven me yet?"

Eddie stops fidgeting.

I can feel her eyes on my face.

She's quiet for a minute, assessing me. "Yes, I do, though for the hundredth time, only *you* think it's something to forgive."

I don't reply. I can almost hear her counting to three in her head—reaching for patience. When she turns back to me, I find the courage to look into her eyes.

"Van truly loves you, Cricket. He doesn't doubt you. It's still the four of us against the world." She huffs. "Even more so *now*, I guess."

The four of us. Four against many. Me, Eddie, her brother TJ, and Van, my fiancé…or boyfriend, rather…or maybe just friend. I'm not sure. Anyway, we've all been friends forever. Our parents are diplomats, our planet's leaders. As children, we were thrown together, a small band of misfits. Our parents dragged us to these conferences, and, looking back, I guess no one truly knew what to do with us, so they dumped us together and left us alone. Now that I know what our parents are capable of, I sometimes wonder if it was strategic. After all, it didn't take long for four bright and bored children to see things in terms of "us against the world." It served as a primer for where we are now. Among us, we represent four of our five main societal groups. But that's not accurate any longer either—now we know there's a sixth group, these Spherans we have a mission to meet today.

We spent weeks at a time together, for years. Even now that we're grown, we still gather at the conferences. We'll be together soon, and this year we have assignments. Eddie and I will meet the Legion's delegation coming in by train today—we'll see these mysterious Spherans any minute now. And Van and TJ are bringing Van's father in from Alberta Farms. We thought TJ was going to miss this go round, but luckily for us, his plans changed at the last minute.

I check the time and watch more commuters gather near the platform. I set my book aside and pass a hand over the bench seat and breathe in the familiar railway scent of lubricant and sweaty humans. "This is ironic."

"What is?" Eddie doesn't bother to look at me, intent on the crowd.

"This. Sitting here. On this exact bench where I sat last year, waiting for the same train. Who would've thought one wooden bench could change so much?"

Eddie lets her head loll back to thump the wall. "Mercy, the bench hasn't changed...." She throws me a quick glance and then shakes her head.

She won't state the obvious—the bench hasn't changed, *I have*. A year ago, I was full of confidence and excitement, sure that I would win my majority and have Van's proposal, that by this time we'd be married and awaiting our first child—keeping pace with our peers. How naïve I'd been.

On Scorch, our journey to adulthood is a guarded one—guarded by the almighty Legion of the Praenex—the order to which Eddie now belongs. They control our aggressive, year-round schooling, teach us to leverage our unique gifts, prepare us to be productive citizens dedicated to assuring the survival of the human race. Then they judge us, one child at a time, to determine when we're ready for the adult world. My friends are all adults now. But not me.

Last year, Bozan Rumesa Kahinu didn't approve my petition. The influential cleric reported that my tests revealed no awakening purpose, no truthful understanding of my gifts. "You see only a piece of yourself, Mercy Adams," they'd said. "An adult in our society must grasp the whole, no matter how difficult to accept."

And what is there to grasp, I ask you? What are my gifts? An annoying, compulsive habit of quoting history, and small, ineffective glimpses of the future. Glimpses that, like so many gifts, have their quirk of capturing only an intense moment of emotion, and none of the useful surrounding whats, wheres and whens. I'm a girl obsessed with history who sees the future. No doubt the Creator has a sense of humor.

So I lived another year, had another vexing birthday come

and pass, still a minor: unable to marry, to make my own home, to set my course. And Van's comm, full of pity at first, became more and more strained until now we hardly speak. In a few hours he'll be here for the conference. I'll see him for the first time in months and I wonder, will I know what he feels for me?

I shake myself. I have to think of something else. Anything else, or I'll fall into a swirling, sucking eddy of despair.

I turn my attention back to Eddie. "What's a Spheran anyway?"

"I don't know. Some delegation." Eddie flicks her hand in the air. She's busy scanning the crowd again. For what, I don't know. A spiky edge of annoyance pulses under her boredom.

I try to distract myself by watching the pop banner—the huge electronic display on the wall, counting our global population, sapiens and praenex, one birth, one death at a time. The banners are everywhere. Public buildings. Street corners. Our personal tablets. If you stare at the banner long enough, you'll see it change—a baby is born, a person dies. I squeeze my eyes shut on that morbid thought.

I know all about the origin of the banners, but their roots go back farther. After the wars and pandemics of the late twenty-first century led to the Collapse, the planet's population dropped to three billion. The banner started in 2108, just after the Call. It recorded massive loss of life to suicide, murder, and war. Some governments stabilized. In the forty long years following the Call, the population continued to decrease as the human race endured the Great Death. As promised, not a single sapiens birth occurred. Then, on Feb. 22, 2372, for the first time in Scorch history, the banner sustained a positive floor—a number from which our population would continue to grow and never again dip below. The following year, the world celebrated the first Addition Day.

Today the banner is still. Stuck at 223,149. I fidget restlessly. Suddenly annoyed by the mismatched music selection piped into the station. Jazz, then a waltz, some tribal bit I can't even place, followed by rock-n-roll. I've tried to explain time periods, trends and styles to the Aesthetics Committee more times than I can count, but they always simply thank me and never make a change. Of course. Our society doesn't have any professional musicians. New music, it turns out, doesn't contribute much to human survival, so we just regurgitate the old, and badly at that.

I wonder if that's what's causing Eddie's restlessness too, the horrible music selection, which is now a polka. Eddie can barely keep her seat.

"Doesn't this schizophrenic music make you want to scream? As a musician, I mean." Eddie can play just about anything. This noise must make her crazy.

"I'm not a musician. That's just a hobby," she huffs. "Why're we talking about this?"

"Because of the music!"

"What music?" She seems sincerely perplexed.

I wonder again why she's so distracted. "Eddie?" I touch her arm and she jumps.

"God's grace, Cricket! If it bothers you so much, post about it or hush up."

I do, quickly, but I know it's just another post in my rant

about music genres that no one really wants to read. At least it helps me ignore her harsh words.

"I don't remember reading anything in history about a group that called themselves Spherans. Where in South America do you think they're from?"

"I don't know." Eddie makes to stand up, then quickly sits back down. She does it again, and this time when she sits, she drums the bench on each side of her knees.

Goosebumps rise on the backs of my arms; I rub them away. I clear my throat. "Some subculture? Maybe sphere refers to the Earth insignia—maybe they're a radical scavie group—"

"I don't know!" Eddie grits her teeth and rolls her neck.

"Okay, what's wrong?"

"Nothing! Or…something…I don't know. I—My comm's buzzing." She snaps her hand open to activate her holocomm device, revealing the image of Bozan Kahinu aboard the approaching train.

"Omag Gran!" Rumesa shouts Eddie's title. "We're in danger. Clear the station!" Rumesa's image shakes as they turn away and shout more instructions to the people in the train around them.

"What's happening?" Eddie shoots to her feet and I do too.

"There's no time! Put me on the panel and get them out!"

Eddie moves quickly, entering commands to send the comm to the wall panel in the station even as she races to the front of the platform.

I look around, not sure what to do. A few people, mostly praenex, mill about waiting for the train. Others sit patiently in clusters of chairs.

Bozan Kahinu's image appears on the large screen—their dark skin shiny with sweat. "Citizens, leave the station immediately!" they demand.

The crowd stares in disbelief.

"You're in danger! Evacuate!"

No one moves. They stare at the screen like they think it's a fiction vid, not real-time. I watch, frozen in position near the bench. At the front of the platform, Eddie's shouting and pointing, but still no one moves. We're a motionless herd.

I look down at my discarded book on the bench, then glance to the wall on my right, see my fingers pull the fire alarm before I think to do it. Sirens blare, but I can still hear my heartbeat in my ears, fast and steady.

Eddie's jumped up onto a bench now, doing that thing she does—pushing her thoughts into the room. The pulse of fear, the desire to flee hits me like a physical blow as everyone around us finally reacts—rushing for the exits, urging the children on, helping those in need. In typical praenex fashion, there's barely a sound besides the alarm and Eddie and Rumesa's shouting.

Then a roar builds in the tunnel, and I watch, still frozen in place, as the engine appears, approaching at a dangerous speed. This is the end of the line; the giant rubber bumpers are just around the corner.

Eddie leaps from the bench like a slow-motion silhouette against the flash of steel as the engine passes the platform and plows into the barrier beyond. It sounds like an explosion. My chest shudders from the shock wave and I'm thrown back on the bench.

Eddie's body flies through the air toward me, her arms spread wide, her face contorted in horror.

I struggle up and rush to her, finally acting. The sound of multiple crashes echoes down the tunnel. People scream all around us. Eddie struggles to sit, and I help her to her feet. Her mouth and nose are bleeding, but she shrugs me off and pushes toward the nearest passenger car.

It's badly jarred—sandwiched between the cars ahead and behind, but I can see that all the passengers had converged to the center—no doubt due to Rumesa's instructions.

Praenex clerics trip through the doors, followed by a small group of strangers in odd clothing. It's all too new and pressed and matching like an Old Earth advertisement. One child wears a coordinated hat and jacket. This must be the Spheran delegation. They join the surge of passengers stumbling toward the exits.

Behind them, surrounded by guards is Gran Bozan Li herself, our spiritual leader. Automatically I raise a hand in greeting, then quickly pull it back down to my side. Should I rush to help her? Where is Bozan Kahinu? Do they need help?

Everyone's shouting instructions now. From behind me comes the shrill trill of whistles and the pounding of feet. Soon police in stark black uniforms rush into the station. How did they arrive so quickly?

Eddie jerks next to me, her shoulder knocking into mine. Her face is frozen in a hypnotic stare. I follow her gaze to a Spheran man standing in the center of the delegation, their intense gaze fixed on her. Their connection is almost visible, humming just below the din like a virtual tether.

"Eddie?" I feel her next jerk to my core.

She breaks the stare and rushes toward the far wall. "It's going to explode! I've got to seal off the tracks!"

She's running toward the emergency door controls when two streaks of color—two children from the delegation—break away from the group and scurry into the crevice where the emergency blast door will seal the platform from the tracks. The boy's hat gets knocked off as he squeezes in. It glides across the floor toward me.

"Wait! Help them!" I grab an officer's sleeve as they pass me, but they shrug me off, intent on their job of moving the passengers to emergency vehicles outside. Across the room, Eddie activates the controls that start the huge steel door rolling shut.

You cannot wander into your thoughts now, I hear my father say. I take off running, arms pumping, knees high, across the few meters that separate me from the children I must save.

"Mercy, no!"

Eddie tries to push her control on me telepathically, but I resist. I reach the hat and throw myself into the blackness of the apron, grabbing blindly into the dark. At first I find nothing, then two small hands slip into mine. I tug at the same moment Eddie pulls at my waist, pivoting to throw me away from crash. All of us go sprawling across the station floor like a snapping human chain just as a blast of fire and debris erupts behind us.

My ears ring. I lift my head from where it rests on my forearm and notice that all the hair on my arm has been singed off. I fan away smoke, roll to my hands and knees, and slip in a trail of blood as I scramble over to Eddie. My cheeks tingle and sting as I face the fire burning in the tunnel. Eddie's taken the worst of it—she shielded me from the debris. The blast door screeches to a close and the heat is gone, just like that.

"Eddie!"

She groans and pushes herself up on bloody hands. "I'm okay."

The children pull at my arm, silently urging me to move. Sirens continue blaring. Police whistles trill.

When we're finally on our feet, Eddie leans heavily on me, her tall frame making it hard to keep my balance. "Come on, we've got to get out."

We're among the last ones left in the station. The children cling, but when I move toward the main exit, they balk.

"This way," the little one insists, pointing tiny fingers toward an emergency side exit down some stairs to our left. "Please!" Their eyes are desperate, and I feel their plea as much as hear it.

Eddie is losing consciousness. I can't tell how badly she's hurt, but when I look back toward the exit, toward the police and injured passengers, I have a sense of something wrong, something sinister at work and I hear my father's words again.

Trust no one until your trust is earned.

I turn aside and let the children lead us down the stairs, through the door and into the hot, windy world outside. We huddle at the base of the outdoor steps. Eddie is heavy like a tower of antique tomes against my side. Her nose continues bleeding and she's barely conscious, her breath coming in ragged gulps.

"Oh, Eddie. Where exactly are you hurt? Why did the train

crash? What's happening?" I lean her back against the cement wall.

"Just need a minute…to rest." She looks at the children. They're crouching next to us, heads together, gem to gem, trying not to cry. "The man?"

I shake my head. "I only saw them."

"Oh, okay." Her head swings toward me like it's falling off her shoulders. "You did good, Cricket. So courageous."

I try to laugh, but it comes out like a squeak. "My God, Eddie. What now?"

But it's too late to get her suggestion—Eddie passes out and I catch her in her slow slide down the wall. I sit so her head rests on my thigh. Using the corner of my shirt, I wipe the blood from her nose, and once she's clean enough, I lean back against the cool concrete to rest my head and try to decide what to do next.

MAY

Small symbols can have great meaning. Deputy Mayhem Forge understands this fact—she's put her faith in it. As she pulls off her gloves and rubs a fingertip gently around the smooth outer edge of her new insignia, she knows the risk she's taking. The style is new: in the background is the Earth of old, like the Terrans' emblem, in the foreground, a rocket, like the Pilgrims', both encircled in a gleaming ring of gold. The design embodies synergy, neutrality, and hope.

Pinning it to her shirt, she steps away from the mirror and pulls out a chair to sit while she laces her shoes. A run is just what she needs. Her dog, Piper, gets up from her cushion in the corner, stretches her back and yawns hugely, revealing an impressive set of teeth.

"Well, Lady Piper, have you rested long enough for a run?" May gives Piper a scratch behind the ears, and then carefully picks the loose hairs from the many rings covering her fingers.

The dog shakes, sending a cloud of white fur into the air like angels from a milkweed pod.

"Oh, Ava will love that," May laughs.

"Hiya." Her uncle Arson rubs his whiskers as he emerges from his bedroom and heads for the teapot. A sleep wrinkle crisscrosses his face, making him look older than his twenty-nine years.

"Good afternoon, Sheriff. Late shift last night?"

"Yep. Ava had garden duty this morning, so I got to sleep in for once. You goin' for a run?" He studies her over the rim of his steaming mug.

She knows the instant he sees the pin.

His eyes narrow, his posture straightens. "What's that?"

May looks down at the small pin and shrugs. She walks over to the velvet-lined tray on the counter and starts removing her rings, one bejeweled finger at a time. She places each one delicately in the tray, admiring the diamonds and other gems that sparkle up at her, hiding each ring's true purpose.

"It's nothin'."

"Listen here, girl—"

"I'm not a girl." May's voice echoes in the quiet kitchen.

Piper whines and hurries back to her bed in the corner.

"I'm nearly twenty. An adult. So don't tell me how to live my life."

"Your life *is* my life!" Arson shouts back. He puts his cup down and moves to stand directly in front of her, gently grasping each of her shoulders. "*Mon bijou.*" His voice is quieter. "We're family. We stick together. That pin—"

"This pin says that I think there's another way, that we don't need to take sides. That Terrans can stay, and Pilgrims can go, and that's what I think *should* happen. Neutrality. Compromise. *Tu comprends?*"

Arson runs a hand through his hair and stares at the ceiling. "And how can we survive divided, huh? How can Terrans start again if the other half of the world runs away? Your parents—"

"Are dead," she interrupts. She's heard this argument so many times before. Why would it end any differently this time? "I appreciate the life you've given me. I know you were barely more than a kid yourself when you took me in, but you're not my father. You have your own kids to raise—"

"I might not be your father, but you're my kin just the same. You're mine just as much as your *maman* was mine. My big sister. Her husband…like a brother to me, my best friend." Arson blows out his breath and picks up his cup, takes a slow drink. "Sure, I promised to look after you if anything ever happened, but it's more than that. I promised myself to help you find your way without 'em. To make it possible for you to be—"

"What *they* wanted? What everyone *expected?*"

Her uncle points at her. "To be whatever it is that you would've been had they lived, but now…." He points to the pin. "Now you're ready to do what? Leave the Verge? Follow that boy to God knows where? For what?"

"That *boy* has a name—"

"And it's *LeRoux!*" His shout booms through the house, startling them both.

In the short silence that follows it feels to May like the whole world is holding its breath.

Arson clears his throat. *"Je m'excuse.... The name LeRoux....* It may as well be *Enemy,* or have ya conveniently forgotten who his folks are?"

"Sins of the father?" May steps closer to the door. "Here we go again. You're wrong about him. TJ is a good man. If you'd just give him a chance—"

"He'd what? Huh? Explain to me why I should be a Pilgrim like him? Why I and all the rest of us Couvies should climb inside little stasis pods and go to sleep while he and his people decide the future of the human race?"

"He's not like that. He's not a separatist—"

"You'd like to think that he's a pacifist, that he's fair. For God's sake, May! He's a pilot. He's not just an heir apparent. He's not just SciCorps. He wants to fly the damn ship!"

For a minute they both absorb that truth.

"I keep telling you, you're wrong about him," May grumbles and heaves a sigh. "He's not a mindless soldier who follows orders, and he's not a tyrant."

"No, he's a *LeRoux* and a Lieutenant Commander, and last time I checked they *give* the orders. And his next order may just be to take you away from here, like it or not. Forced conformance."

May shakes her head. "Like I keep saying, you're wrong about him, but you're right about one thing—I *am* going..." She drops the last gaudy ring in the tray, leaving only the plain comm rings she always wears, and whistles for Piper. "...for a run."

As she shoves the screen door open, Arson catches it. "You

can't run away, ya know. *Écoutes-tu?* No matter how far ya go, this place'll always be home."

May glances over her shoulder before stepping down from the porch. Remembering what started the argument, she touches the pin on her shirt. "It's not a revolution, Sheriff. It's a pin."

Arson grimaces. "It's an insult's what it is." The screen door slams as he goes back into the house.

Ten minutes into her run, May reaches the edge of the sea cliff. This is the verge, the true edge of the world after which their settlement was named. Hundreds of years ago, before the San Andreas disaster reshaped the western coast, this was an inland wilderness. Remarkable only in its isolation. Quiet. Today the sky is a clear blue bowl holding in the ocean all the way to the horizon. Crashing waves echo in the briny breeze that carries the scent of salt and sun. Soon the ship will come, May can sense it. But still she feels caged. Trapped by inaction when she really wants to fly.

Casting her eyes to the northern sky, she strains to see the station and colony ships hovering in skydock above the Alaskan range. On clear nights they're visible—those ships the LeRouxs control—winking like stars. One day they'll leave the planet, and May wonders what her perspective will be—the ships disappearing from her sky, or Scorch shrinking away from a porthole?

Piper gives a yip of warning before a whinny sounds behind

her. May turns and the mustangs emerge from the brush just a few meters away. The big brown stallion stares at her, then prances nearer to the cliff's edge, tossing his wild mane in the salty breeze.

She feels it then—his frustration with the sea. His hunger for more beyond this edge. To their right a prairie spreads like a gold and green carpet away from the water, inland as far as the eye can see.

She smiles. "Wanna race, big guy?"

The stallion focuses on her again and shakes his head as if considering.

May doesn't wait. With a shrill cry of delight, she bolts away, jumping and running as if for her life, knowing it won't be enough. Not nearly enough. Piper is right on her heels, keeping pace, ears flat, serious.

May's lungs burn, but it's only seconds before the rhythm of hooves pound the ground behind her. The snorts and neighs of the approaching herd grow louder—and she pushes harder, ignoring the pain, focusing solely on the next leap, the next flat run.

Soon the stallion's big eye is level with her head, just a few meters away. May keeps pace for a moment, pushing herself harder, before he throws his head back with a loud whinny and surges away from her.

In seconds the whole herd passes by, their dust coating her skin, stinging her eyes and clogging her throat. She slows, panting heavily until she finally stops and sinks to her knees, elation vibrating through her like electricity.

Piper yips and whines, turning happy circles around her, glad to be part of the game.

The herd is a cloud of dust and noise far in the distance now, racing east into the unknown. As her joy subsides, a deep longing takes its place. She wants to go with them. She wants to see it too, like her parents did. To travel, maybe even scavenge. To find something more on God's great Earth than the Verge and its wait-and-see.

But the ship is coming. She can feel it. She rubs a finger absently across the rocket at the center of her pin. The ship is coming. And when it comes, every choice she has will be at hand.

4
VAN

Current year: 2701
Wednesday, 4:30 PM
New Juneau

"Watch out!" I grab my da's sleeve to pull him away from the robot medic flying across the lobby of the emergency room.

"God's grace! What's happened here?" My da shifts the pilot he's carrying. Fresh red blood has seeped through the field dressing we applied earlier to the pilot's head, but their eyes are open, if dazed.

"I dunno, but I'll find out. Beg pardon!" I block the path of a passing nurse. "We have injured—"

"Over there." The nurse points to the end of the queue that's formed along the wall.

"Wait!" I hold their arm to keep them from immediately moving on. "What's happened?"

They give me a puzzled look. "Aren't you from the train accident?"

"The what now?"

TJ nudges me aside, but the nurse is off again, and we're left to figure it out. He taps into his comm. "System's down. I can't get anything."

An alarm sounds and red lights trip along the hall leading back to the treatment rooms.

"Oof!" I'm pushed aside by a robomedic answering the code. Other personnel rush down the hall like moths drawn to flame.

I point to the empty chair at the end of the queue. "Da, sit there with him, would ye? TJ, take the others and I'll try to get help."

I find another nurse. "We have new wounded who need assessment."

"Hold on." They key commands into their tablet. "K12 will assist." They point to a robomedic heading toward my da.

"Thank ye. I—" But the nurse is already gone.

As I stride back, I scan the scene. Most of the folks waiting seem to have minor injuries—cuts and abrasions showing through torn clothing, a few head wounds and quite a bit of coughing. A sanitation robot cleans a smear of blood off the floor closer to the corridor. Most of the noise and confusion comes from folks searching for their people, more of them arriving all the time.

"A medic's on the way," I tell my da as I squat next to his chair. "I dunno anything more."

Quiet crying has me turning my attention to the praenex child in the next seat. An older man leans heavily on their shoulder, resting with eyes closed.

"Well now, why're ye cryin'? I'm sure yer da will be fine."

The child sniffles and sits a little straighter. He nods. "It's just that he's stopped talking. He was talking a few minutes ago, but not making any sense. Now I can't even reach him telepathically."

"Well…" I take another look at the man. He's deathly pale. I reach over to check for a pulse, and he shifts, sliding lifelessly off the child's shoulder to slump against me. I grab his head and feel the massive lump at the base of his skull. It's sticky and warm.

"Holy—"

The K12 robomedic is still checking out our pilot. I grab its arm. "Check this man!"

The robot complies, its numerous diagnostics arms quickly scanning vitals. Almost immediately a red band appears around its middle and the code alarm sounds. "Code red. This patient needs immediate care. Code red."

"Aw, hell!" I shove the robot aside and scoop the man into my arms. "Da, I'll be right back." I turn to the child. "Come on then."

I rush awkwardly down the corridor following the red lights. The man is light in my arms, but the corridor is narrow and clogged with folks. Even without a man in my arms, I'd be struggling to avoid knocking into folks moving through this crowd, big as I am. The robot soon outpaces me and leads me to a medical bay swarming with nurses and doctors responding to the code. I settle the man gently onto the bed and back away, noticing for the first time the trail of blood that's run down my shirt and pants, across the hall and back toward the waiting area. The sanitation robot is already cleaning it up.

The child is there, staring wide-eyed from behind a nearby

curtain.

I grab a nearby nurse. "Can ye help this wean? Their da...." I point into the medical bay.

They grimace, wiping at their arm where my bloody hand smeared it. "I'm just an admin."

"Please just take them back to the waitin' area, could ye now?"

The admin nods and reaches for the child.

"Hang on a tick. Where's the boss?"

"The boss?"

"Aye, whoever's in charge."

"He's in a meeting with the authorities."

"I need him."

"I can't disturb him, I'm sorry."

"What d'ye mean? We've had a serious crash. My pilot's badly hurt and there's been an attempt on my father's life—"

"Then you'll be happy to know the police are already here investigating the train crash. As soon as the investigators finish with the Gran Bozan, I'm sure you'll be next. Our doctors will help your—"

"The Gran Bozan?" I lean closer. "The GB is here? She was involved in the crash?" My stomach goes cold. Our spiritual leader, our top councilmember, was also attacked?

The admin sighs, snatches a washcloth from a nearby cart and hands it to me before taking one to clean her arm. "Yes, the whole entourage. Do you have any idea how much paperwork goes into caring for a councilmember?"

TJ pushes into the space next to me. "I'm Lieutenant

Commander LeRoux. My sister, Omag Gran LeRoux…Eddie! They call her Eddie. She was meeting the GB. What's happened? Is she hurt?"

The blood drains from the admin's face. "I'm sorry. I didn't realize.… I thought you knew."

"Thought we knew what?" TJ demands.

"We're havin' comm issues," I tell the admin.

"Everyone is." They turn to TJ. "Your sister's here—a minor concussion, some scrapes. The others are being treated. Perhaps we can sit—"

"Others?"

"Please come with me." They motion toward an office.

"We don't need to talk. Just take us there!"

They peer around TJ to where Cousteau's hiding. "That dog—"

"Stays with me." TJ's voice is flat with finality.

"Let's go!" My shout startles the others nearby and the voices around us ebb for a moment as folks turn to stare at us.

"Fine." The admin hands the child over to a nurse and we rush down the corridor and through double doors marked ICU. I haven't a baldy notion how the admin moves so quickly. They turn in front of us and spread their arms indicating two rooms, one on each side of the hall. The door to our left is open.

TJ's sister, Eddie, stands next to the bed with her back to us. I recognize the sleeping patient—it's Bozan Rumesa Kahinu, the *aeterna*. Fluids drip from bags into a tube in Rumesa's arm. They look grim and focused, even in sleep. I know that aeternas are natural novus, just like my friends, but there's something about *this* clone that always raises the hairs on the back of my neck. It's like my lizard brain understands something the rest of me can't. Eddie once told me that Rumesa's the most gifted cleric alive. Precognitive. Telepathic. Even clairvoyant at times. And a councilmember to boot. It must be strange to be so much.

Eddie's standing still. Probably praying. The fingers of her right hand lace through Rumesa's creating a ying yang pattern—ebony and albino. A machine beeps out Rumesa's heartbeat like an eerie melody.

TJ seems frozen beside me. I lower my voice to a whisper. "Divine grace."

Eddie turns and lets out a huge breath. "Hey, Van. Hey, bro."

Is she okay? There are bruises, some scrapes, a little blood around her nose and on her shirt, but her hands are clean, and she looks steady. She's okay. The tightness in my chest eases just a wee bit.

"Sis?" TJ crosses to her.

She lets go of Rumesa's hand to face him. They embrace, gem to gem, their hands cradling each other's heads gently as they silently connect. "Where have you been?"

Even from across the room, I can hear the tremor in her voice.

"We had some trouble."

For a second, I feel the familiar twinge of envy I always have when I see them like this. I know it's a twin thing, but I can't help wishing that *I* could feel that connected to someone. I came close once with Mercy, but now…. Now I dunno.

I need to find the GB, but I'm torn about leaving them. Cousteau whines, turns a circle and curls up in a ball right on the threshold, as if to say *leave them with me.*

I turn to the other door and nod to the GB's two acolytes guarding it. "First Lieutenant Sylvan Elder." I flash my ID. "Requestin' to see the Gran Bozan, if ye please."

One of the acolytes reaches for the door handle. "She's expecting you."

I enter and my heart goes wump in my chest. Mercy is here…right here by the door. Her violet eyes are round, her face is smudged with soot and scratches, and her dark coppery hair is a bedraggled mess. And still she's the most beautiful girl I've ever seen.

My heart stalls—sputters out and stops, and then starts again at a gallop. I'm supposed to say something, do something, instead of standing here like an eejit, but I can't remember what.

I'd forgotten how tiny she is. I feel like a giant in comparison. I flex my hands, oddly large like my da's. I always notice things like that when I'm around her.

Oh, melter, I was supposed to offer my palms, that's what I forgot, but it's too late now.

She stares at me with a question in her eyes, her perfect lips parted but silent.

I shove my hands in my pockets and rock back on my heels. Then I look at her arms, crossed over her stomach. They're covered in sticky brown smears. Her shirt is filthy too. Dried blood.

"My God! Are ye hurt, too, Mercy?" I pull my hands out of

my pockets and reach for her, stopping short, unsure what to do.

"Sylvan."

Not *Van*, but *Sylvan*, my formal name. It's all she says before turning her eyes to the others in the room.

Folks are watching us. The Gran Bozan, a nurse, and off to the side, a police officer.

"Forgive me." I bow my head to the GB. She's reclining in a chair by the bed—her forehead bandaged, more blood on her gown, her vibrant red sash twisted and stained. Her eyes show strain, but also pride and determination; despite her condition she's alert and watching everything.

"Lieutenant." Her eyes are intense, like she's looking *into* me.

I shuffle my feet, bumping into Mercy. "Sorry." Heat rushes to my face. "What's happened?"

I startle when a small hand slides into mine. I look down to see a praenex girl, gem gleaming black between violet eyes wide with wonder. She must've been hiding behind the door. "And who are you then, lass?" I kneel down to get on her level and notice how elaborately she's dressed, like in a fashion vid.

"I'm called Nairobi, *pronoms fem*, and here is Fez, *pronoms mascu*." She points to boy now emerging from behind the door. "We're Spherans, and we've never seen a person as big as you before." Her voice sounds like bells, and I'm amazed to hear such maturity from such a small person, praenex or not.

"Ah, but I'm not so big," I tease.

Her face falls in uncertainty.

"Wait until ye see my da, lass. He's not quite my height perhaps, but ten kilos bigger. I'm but a wee kitten by comparison."

Her grin's my reward, as the boy shyly steps up to meet me. He's dressed oddly too—like someone's going to take his picture.

"I like your face." He bravely reaches out and runs a fingertip down the smooth bridge between my eyes.

I've no gem, only the smooth skin of a sapiens.

"It tells me what my gift cannot—you will be our friend."

I like them. I like kids in general, but I especially like these strangely garbed kids hiding among this powerful group of adults. "And what's it mean—yer 'Spherans', did ye say? Is that some new sport I need to try?"

The girl, Nairobi, giggles and is about to answer when the GB interrupts.

"Enough for now. First is first. I'll tell you what's occurred."

The GB recounts their travel to the conference including Bozan Kahinu's precognition of danger and the ensuing crash.

Mercy adds details from the station point of view and describes their covert arrival at the hospital with the kids. Her voice is sweet and soft, just like I remember.

I'm tempted to close my eyes and just float on that sound for a minute—let it heal the pinch in my chest that never seems to go away. Already the knot behind my ribs is easing. I sigh and shut my eyes, just for a second.

"Lieutenant?"

The GB's voice pulls me back to the present. I open my eyes to find everyone staring at me, except Mercy. She looks straight ahead, her mouth a tight crease. I've embarrassed her, and I've missed what was being said.

The police officer speaks then. "I'm Commander Vi Garcia, *pronoms neutre*. I'm in charge of the investigation." Commander Garcia holds out their hand to shake, the old-fashioned sapiens gesture.

Mercy tenses next to me, and I'm instantly on guard as I shake hands. Like Mercy and Eddie, Garcia wears the circle-rocket insignia. They're neutral, seeking consolidation of Terran and Pilgrim viewpoints. Their fingers are covered in gaudy rings, very unlike the residents of New Juneau. Suspicious, I focus on their face. Though their eyes are a deep shade of amethyst, their gem matches their brown skin perfectly, not a trace of black pigmentation, nor the pale edges that indicate the Trade disease. Garcia's a healthy null from Vancouver Colony, the Verge. What's a soldier from the Verge doing in New Juneau? Is that what startled Mercy?

Introductions finished, I recount our events, from the switch of cargo and passengers, to the crash, and our escape in the remaining plane. I don't exaggerate or omit anything of consequence—the praenex would sense any bit of either.

"My da agrees it's clearly an act of sabotage, but he's more focused on what to do now.... He's heartbroken about his vegetables, wiltin' out there on that hot field."

Something close to a smile flits across the GB's face.

I straighten and try harder to ignore the familiar scent of Mercy's shampoo, the warmth of her small body next to mine. "My concern is different. It appears we were targeted, my father specifically, Your Grace. It was an attempt on his life."

TJ and Eddie join us then. We squeeze forward into the

hospital room.

Eddie smiles at me, but it doesn't touch her eyes.

Still, I feel better, more complete, like I don't have to watch my back. It's always this way for the four of us. Our friendship binds us, makes us stronger.

Commander Garcia clears their throat. "Excuse me, Your Grace, Lieutenant. The investigators onsite at the station found similar signs of sabotage on the station's failover mechanisms. It's early, but it would appear that the first responders witnessed removing victims at the scene were an organized group engaged in kidnapping the delegate, ah…" Garcia refers to her tablet. "Dr. Varela. Two clerics are also unaccounted for. Based on the timing, the arrival of the actual police and your guards' diligent protection probably prevented your own kidnapping as well, Your Grace."

The room is silent as we all take this in. Mercy's exhaled breath fans across the hair on my arm. I shiver.

Finally, the GB nods. "The ID tracking system?"

"Nothing yet, Your Grace. It appears the system's tracking software is temporarily offline," Garcia explains.

The implications of this statement hang heavy in the air. Few have access and knowledge enough to hack into the system, and anyway, why would they? This kind of deception is unprecedented in our peaceful society—we have low privacy, sure, but low crime too. I rub the tiny implant in my left arm and wonder at the small freedom of being invisible, if only for a moment. Something occurs to me for the first time then—if I were intent on committing a crime, how much would anonymity help me?

TJ's comm buzzes and startles us all. He doesn't even look at it before declining the call.

I turn toward Mercy, whose brow creases around her gem. She's always been observant; I know she noticed. I try to catch her eye, but she won't look at me. The knot in my chest tightens a bit again.

Garcia's comm buzzes next. They snap their palm unit open and read, and then lift their eyes to us. "There's been a break-in in the Hab."

Mercy flinches, her fingers running quickly over the comm in her palm. Her home is in the Hab. "My parents…they're not answering." Eyes wide with worry, she finally focuses on me. "What if they're targets too?"

Mercy's parents are scientific leaders and councilmembers. My hand is at her back before I even think. In my peripheral vision, Eddie and TJ shift position. We move as a group toward the door.

"Wait!" The GB's tone stops us. "Lieutenant Elder, Lieutenant Commander LeRoux, you must stay here and guard these children. Like you, they're central to this crisis. You must not leave them to others. This I can see."

The GB closes her eyes for a second, then looks directly at me. "There's more at play than the conference or the Spheran delegation. I have a mission for you, and you'll need this information, so wait a moment and listen, all of you." She pauses to scan our faces. "One week ago, SciCorps received an encoded transmission from an unknown source."

I send TJ a short meaningful look—could this be the same transmission he told me about?

TJ shakes his head slightly and I look away. He wants to keep it secret, and this room is full of perceptive people. Already there's a question in Mercy's expression. She wonders what we know.

The GB continues. "Within four hours of the transmission, all SciCorps projects were suspended. The only two exceptions were the colony ships and information systems. All their resources are now dedicated to these projects...and all SciCorps credits have been pulled from the global bank into inactive reserve."

There's a collective gasp—my own control wavers. "That's more than half of our global wealth, removed from global use. Our economy will crash."

SciCorps is our science and technology branch. Originally they were part of the four-part government—a balanced system of the Legion, SciCorps, Alberta Farms, and Vancouver Colony—but over the years they've gained power. Now they control pretty much everything. TJ and Eddie's parents, the *other* LeRouxs, lead SciCorps. Talk about a challenging home life.

TJ steps toward the GB's chair. "I don't know anything about this. What're they doing?"

"We don't know, Commander. There's a lot to consider, but I do know that here and now, in this moment, it's imperative we protect these children."

I look at the kids I've been called to protect, fear and anxiety ripe in their eyes, but it's a fight with my nature to let Mercy go to the Hab without me...to go into danger alone.

TJ exhales loudly. "My father...." His eyes shift to rest on the

GB. "I know you all suspect him, but we should check…that he's safe, that is. That the targets are not broader. He's here for the conference too."

"Of course." The GB nods. "Commander Garcia, please send someone to Admiral LeRoux's quarters."

Mercy vibrates with energy at my side.

Eddie grips my shoulder. "Van, I have her. She won't be alone."

Garcia steps in front of Mercy. "I'll join you."

"Come with, or don't. I don't care, but I have to go!" Mercy's voice rises, stronger than I've ever heard it. She squares her shoulders and faces the GB. "If this is our mission, as you all say it is"—she waves a hand at the adults around the room—"then stop treating us like children and let us go."

The GB waits a moment, then nods. "You're right. Enough time wasted." She rises from her chair, chin high, her face regal despite the bloody bandages and sooty gown. "Dr. Mercy Adams, you know everything there is to know about revolutions. Go and be the spark we need now."

Mercy scoffs. "Yesterday I was studying revolutions. Today you're talking about igniting one."

"*Igniting.*" The GB nods. "Yes, it's an apt metaphor. Trace any great inferno back to its origin and you'll surely find the innocent kindling from which it began."

Mercy looks up at me. "Did she just call us kindling?"

"Aye, let's hope when this is done there's more left to us than a pile of ash."

The GB clears her throat. "It's time. Commander Garcia will

go with the—with Dr. Adams and Omag Gran LeRoux, and help if they can, but let us be clear, all of us. This is the Culmination. War is upon us."

As Garcia follows Eddie and Mercy out the door, Mercy doesn't even look back. I lean out to watch them stride away, down the long hallway.

"It's going to be okay, Lieutenant." Nairobi squeezes my hand, and I'm glad for the distraction.

"Aye, I'm sure it will, lass." My mind is a jumble, and I'm not sure if it's because of me and Mercy, or the possibility of civil war. In this moment, in this place, I selfishly can't rightly tell which is more important.

5

MERCY

I could navigate these corridors blindfolded, but I've never tried it sprinting before. People hug the walls when they see us coming. Some call my name. My book bag thumps against my hip, slowing me down. As we leave the public areas and go deeper underwater into the private apartments, my ears pop. The coolness of the sea permeates the space, a natural protection from our too-hot world. My raspy breathing and rapid heartbeat blend with the light, quick footfalls of Eddie and the Commander behind me.

As we turn the final bend in the habitat's maze of white tunnels, I expect to see the door to my parent's apartment—my home, crisp and clean and closed. It takes a few seconds for my brain to process the scene before me. The hall is lined with police—it looks like the whole department turned out for a look at this rare sight, a crime in New Juneau. I have to slow down to move through them. I brush past one of my neighbors who's talking quietly and quickly with two officers. Beyond them, my door teeters, wrenched on its hinges. A cluster of police examining the damage. The whispers of curious neighbors stop as I pass.

The squeak of Commander Garcia's comm reaches me. "Miss Adams, wait."

I turn to look at them, but I don't stop moving forward. I can see that they're surprised by all the people too.

Just before I cross the threshold, an officer holds out an arm to stop me. "Sorry, I can't let you by."

"This is my apartment." I twist to squeeze past them, my lungs heaving from the run.

"I'm sorry." The officer holds my arm, then seeing Commander Garcia behind me, straightens. "Commander, they're still working inside."

"Alright, McNamara." Garcia turns to me. "Let me check with the team, and then I'll come right back."

"This is my…apartment. I need to talk…to my parents," I wheeze, unable to catch my breath. There's a funny buzzing in my ears and the hallway tips a little. I lean on the wall just as a huge shiver runs up my back and radiates down my arms. "This is my apartment."

Eddie murmurs something I can't make out. I think she's talking to Garcia. Her arm soon slides around my waist. "Mercy, we're going to wait here for a minute while the commander finds out what's going on."

Why does Eddie's body pressed along my side feel so warm? Why is her breath even, while I'm gasping?

"I need to…talk to my…parents."

"I know, Cricket. Just a minute. Try to settle down now. Breathe slowly."

I hold my breath and let it out in one long stream. After a few tries, I think it's getting better. I'm staring at the sharp plastic shards protruding from the door jamb when Garcia's face appears ahead of me.

"Okay, I'm going to let you both inside for a few minutes, but you have to stay where I say. Do you understand?"

"This is my apartment." I reach out to touch the torn door jamb.

Eddie catches my hand. "Don't. You'll hurt yourself."

"I need to talk to my mom."

"Maybe you better stay out here." Garcia shifts in front of me.

Eddie squeezes my hand. "No, it's okay, I've got her. She'll be fine."

Garcia shakes their head. "I think she's in shock."

"She'll be fine."

"I'm fine. I just want to talk to my dad."

Garcia stares at me for a minute. "Okay, she can go in, but only long enough to answer some questions and grab a bag—she can't stay here tonight."

The plastic shards catch my sleeve as I brush by, tearing the fabric of my shirt. "Oh, no." I finger the hole.

"Come on, Mercy." Eddie presses my back gently.

"I tore my shirt."

"I know, we'll fix it later. Let's keep moving."

Inside, the galley is a mess. Kitchen debris—scraps of food, utensils—litters the floor. A little tendril of steam or smoke floats out of the pot on the cooktop and is quickly sucked into the overhead fan. The counter stools are overturned, the back of one is broken. My mom would hate this. I need to clean it up fast. I bend to grab the stool.

"Miss Adams." Commander Garcia extends an arm to stop me.

"Doctor." A cold, clammy chill dampens my skin.

"Excuse me?"

"Doctor," I repeat, "or Mercy, if you please. Not *Miss* Adams."

The hum I noticed in the hall builds in my ears again. Some small part of my brain knows that I need to snap out of it and deal with this, or Garcia's going to make me leave, but all I can think about is picking up the mess before my mom gets home.

"Impact here."

I turn to the opposite wall where an officer scans a hole where something punctured the wall. It almost hit an antique painting—my father's favorite snowy landscape from a long-ago place called Michigan. It's tipped to the side, and it seems imperative that I straighten it.

"Please don't touch that!" Garcia pulls my hand away.

"I think she's in shock," the other officer says.

"Wouldn't you be?" Eddie lays a hand on my shoulder. "What happened here? Where are the Adamses? Why would anyone target them?"

Garcia blows out a breath. "We don't know. A personal alarm

was tripped in this apartment at 14:40." Garcia runs a hand across their face and cocks their hip to one side.

I'm detached from everything like I'm watching a vid, like I'm not here in person. And yet I desperately want to straighten the painting.

"We weren't aware that this unit *had* an alarm." Garcia glances at me like I should say something.

I raise an eyebrow. "This is my apartment."

They shake their head.

I try harder. "Um, they just installed the alarm. I didn't ask why."

"Well, when the police arrived the door had been wrenched open but, as far as we can tell, no one saw anything. Most of the neighbors had already left for the conference, but we're talking to a few who hadn't." Garcia looks around the apartment, nudges one of the stools with their toe.

A wave of possessiveness passes through me, but I tamp it down. What does it matter that this is my home? Without my parents, it's just another place.

Garcia scans the splintered doorframe. "Forced entry. Several signs of struggle."

My nose fills with a rusty stench, like from my vision. I know what it is now. "I smell blood." It's my voice, but I don't know if I said it aloud, or just in my head.

Eddie grips my hand.

Aloud, I guess.

I turn to see an officer redirect the forensics robot scanning my kitchen. I glance at Garcia. I'd recognized them as the officer from my vision at the station the moment they entered the hospital room, but I'd avoided looking more closely, nervous about the vision, about the nameless body at my feet. A shiver rips through me, and I force myself to look at them now.

Garcia's gem, though the same size and texture as mine, perfectly matches their warm caramel skin, not a smidgen of black pigmentation, yet no signs of illness either. It's not disease; Garcia's a natural born null—a praenex so strongly mixed with sapiens that they have no gifts. What's a null doing here in New Juneau?

"You're a null." Apparently I've lost my filter.

Their nostrils flare. But a shout comes from the end of the galley, so I never get to hear how they would have responded.

"Here!" An officer points to the underside of the counter which the robot has spotlighted. "It's wiped clean except here, under the edge."

Garcia checks the robot's scanner results. "Lab grade disinfectant and human blood. ... Dr. Parker Adams's DNA."

Eddie hugs me tight, like she thinks I might float away. "They'll be okay. We'll find them."

I push away from her, and she winces. It's then that I notice the blood seeping through her pants near her hip. "You're hurt again!"

"It's nothing."

"Let me see." Garcia pushes me aside. They don't wait for Eddie's permission, but peel Eddie's waistband down and lift the corner of her shirt to reveal a small, clean cut oozing blood. "This isn't from the crash.... This is surgical."

"It is. It's nothing. It opened while I was running—just a little soon for exercise."

My attention is riveted not on the bloody cut, but on the yellow and purple bruising across her side. Eddie's hip is a monstrous mass of color. "What's all that?"

"It's nothing to do with this."

"I know, it's healing. That's not from today." I didn't think my blood could feel any icier, but it does now.

Eddie pushes Garcia's hands away and covers herself. "I keep telling you, it's nothing."

I simply stare until she gives in.

"Fine. I'll tell you later, but it has nothing to do with this. I promise."

"I'm taping that," Garcia insists, and I like them a little more.

They grab the medical kit another officer hands them and pulls out a roll of tape. "You can have it stitched later." Garcia pushes at Eddie until she cooperates.

I watch Garcia's capable fingers, their rings glinting and sparkling in the artificial lights—not plain comm activation rings like mine. Theirs are covered in beautiful, elaborate markings and jewels.

The buzzing in my head quiets, and my mind feels more connected to my body.

Finishing the first aid, Garcia sits back on their haunches thinking before they stand. "Now, what I want you to do is take your friend into her room. Get a change of clothes. Personal items. Pack a bag."

Eddie nods. "My things are here too—we traveled together

recently."

"Okay. Get them. Touch as little as possible." They turn to me. "Do you have a place to stay tonight?"

"She does," Eddie answers for me. She's already heading to my room.

I turn back to the painting of peaceful snow. "It's my father's favorite." I hear his voice in my head. *Family is the most important thing.* I look at another framed piece on the wall, a photograph of my grandmother's family from when she was little. My grandmother stands clutching a book in her tiny hands while my great grandmother, a beautiful blonde woman with smiling eyes, hugs her from behind. My great grandfather stands triumphantly behind them, hands on his hips. His straight black hair and almond-shaped eyes proclaim his Chinese heritage and I recognize his broad, smiling cheeks as the source of my own.

I run a finger over the frame's edge before my gaze moves to the right, to a small family photo of the three of us. It's new. My father took it recently and hung it with great care. Suddenly I know what he was trying to tell me. *The most important thing.*

"We're ready." Eddie holds up two small bags—the two my father brought back for us when he dropped us off at the station. "I removed the extra books from yours."

"But…" I think about the bag and wonder where I'll be taking it. Eddie must know the weight will be an issue. Turning to Garcia, I point to the new portrait and ask, "May I?"

"Go ahead." They reach over and gently remove the picture from the wall for me.

"Thank you."

"Don't go far," Garcia reminds me.

My parents are missing, so where would I go? But then I know, like all the haze in my brain has disappeared. I know that I'll go anywhere.

"Only as far as needed," I tell Garcia.

I clutch the frame in my hand and nod. As far as needed.

CRANE ELDER

In the past...
April 6, 2108; 593 years ago
Fermont Compound, Quebec, UCA

It didn't matter that most of the autopsy shift was via video conference, Crane Elder still felt like no amount of scrubbing could truly get her hands clean. Cataloging the dead was gruesome business.

"I'm Lady Macbeth," she mumbled to herself, slamming the disinfectant soap back into the soap basin and rinsing her reddened arms to the elbows.

With 20,000 suicides a day, every nurse, even midwives, had to do their part in helping to identify the cause of death—suicide, virus, or natural causes. Sites around the United Countries of America relied on nurses like her at Fermont and other compounds for instructions on processing their dead.

"Ugh!" she breathed as a final shiver ran down her spine. She did her part without complaint; she knew better than to complain, but as a midwife she was more accustomed to greeting new lives, than accounting for lost ones. She kept her head down and her comments neutral. As a result, her peer ratings were higher than she expected, but not too high to arouse attention. Just the way she liked it.

"Do you think it's truth?" Elsa asked in her thick Swedish accent as she joined Crane at the sink.

If Crane knew better than to complain, she also knew better than to hope.

"No." Crane shook her head. "Don't get excited, Elsa. You know the rumors are seldom true. We haven't had a new arrival in weeks. It's done. There're no more women to save—no more babies to shelter."

"I'm sorry for you, my dear. Sorry that hope has left your heart. You have a sadness that even the praenex cannot change."

A popular writer coined the term *praenex* after The Call. She speculated that the new people God promised would be "the leaders standing out in front of humankind's violent destruction." And just like that, the praenex became Earth's last heroes.

Crane looked in the mirror at her friend's sad face. "I—" Her comm buzzed in her pocket. "Excuse me." She moved over to her locker before checking her device. Reading the short message, her heart gave a little jump.

"What is it?" Elsa stepped up behind her.

Crane juggled her tablet as she shoved her arms into her uniform coat. "I've got a new assignment in maternity."

She looked at Elsa, astonished.

"I knew it!" Elsa slapped her on the back. "*Lycka till!*"

"Don't get excited—"

"Someone has to! Go!" Her friend shoved her toward the door.

Crane couldn't help her smile as she took the steps two at a time. She ran in short bursts, slowing only when someone passed her, so she was breathing hard when she made it to the processing office.

"I've a new… patient," she heaved, trying to catch her breath.

The intake nurse looked at her like she was crazy.

She found the name on her tablet. "O'Dell, Phoebe." She bent with her hands on her knees and breathed slowly through her nose.

"Oh, so you're the lucky one. She's right through there. Phoebe, *pronoms fem*." The nurse pointed through the glass wall into the waiting area.

Crane saw her immediately. A sickly young woman, barely more than a girl, sitting in a wheelchair—ghostly and thin. Her hair was clean but stuck out in random tufts around her head. She sat with one bony hand resting on her protruding belly while she tried to straighten her thin medical gown with the other. Knitting needles and yarn were piled on her belly. Crane glanced at the chair next to her new patient. A neat pile of tiny knit hats towered precariously on the seat.

"What's with the knitting?" Crane asked the nurse.

"She's says they're for the praenex. I think she means *all* of them."

Crane looked back at the young pregnant woman, knitting quickly now, a peaceful smile on her face. Her lips were moving, but she didn't seem to be speaking to anyone nearby.

"Who's she talking to?"

The nurse chuckled. "Not talking…listen." She flipped a switch to activate the speaker connected to the waiting room.

Phoebe's voice sang through the speaker, sweet and gentle, with an edge of southern twang.

"Oh, I'll dance, I will sing and my laugh shall be gay
I will charm every heart, in his crown I will sway
When I woke from my dreaming, idols were clay
All portions of love then had all flown away…"

"What is that all about? Never mind, this is just bizarre. Where did she come from?"

"Word is she just strolled right up to the gate at Sugar Grove Station in West Virginia and asked if she could get some help. Apparently, she even offered to do some chores in exchange for food and a bed. Command thinks she walked over a hundred kilometers down out of the mountains. Skinny thing, dressed in rags."

Crane winced. "That's unkind. Everyone's poor now."

The nurse shook her head. "They had to burn her clothes. I helped with her intake—we had to cut her hair before we could wash it."

Phoebe sang on through the speaker. Crane's throat tightened as she listened to the sad melody, made even more poignant by the southern lilt in Phoebe's voice.

"Oh, he taught me to love him and promised to love
And to cherish me over all others above
How my heart now is wondering misery can tell
He's left me no warning, no words of farewell."

Crane cleared her throat. "Husband?"

The nurse pursed her lips. "Dead. European front. Drafted six months ago…. That's where your husband deployed too, isn't it?"

Crane took a deep breath and blew it out slowly. "Yes. Well…Well…" She struggled through another breath. She'd had no word from her husband in weeks. The Army would only say that his mission was classified. She cleared her throat and forced her thoughts back to the moment. "Well…the hair's going to grow back a beautiful color." She tried to smile.

The nurse nodded. "Orange as a pumpkin, and that's what it looks like she's carrying too. You ever seen a belly that perfectly round?"

"Once or twice. Um, when did she arrive?" Crane watched Phoebe through the glass as she finished the song and smiled softly, leaving the nurse's station oddly quiet.

The nurse flipped off the speaker. "Yesterday."

"Yesterday!" Crane turned to the nurse.

The nurse nodded. "The C.O. there didn't want to take any chances. They put her and a medic on a plane and worked it all out with us mid-flight."

"Homo novus?" Crane discreetly crossed her fingers.

The nurse nodded again. "Confirmed by ultrasound, Homo sapiens novus, or praenex as we call 'em, but read the file. You got her because she's high risk, poor thing. Brain aneurysm."

"God, that's terrible!"

"Yeah, you're going to be watching her closely. We can't afford to lose either one." The nurse sighed.

They watched together as another nurse talked to an elderly patient sitting near Crane's new patient, Phoebe O'Dell. As the nurse helped the patient stand, their bag fell to the floor, spilling papers and toiletries everywhere.

Phoebe lurched out of her wheelchair and scrambled down to her knees, talking avidly. She held her belly with one hand and picked up items with the other, the whole time talking to the elderly patient and the nurse with a huge smile on her face.

"Uh, what's she doing?" Crane took one step toward the waiting room.

"Not again. Wait, she'll be fine." The nurse rose to come around her station. "She's kind to a fault is all—some kind of southern charm, I think. She keeps trying to help everyone, or do things herself, like no one's ever done a thing for her, you know?"

They watched as the nurse inside the waiting room dealt with the situation. The silent drama was almost ridiculous. The elderly patient, nearly panicked by the sight of a sickly pregnant woman crawling on the floor, urged Phoebe to leave their stuff. The nurse, a horrified look on their face, tried to pull Phoebe up from the floor. Phoebe would have none of it—she worked tirelessly until all of the patient's things were back in their bag.

When she finished, Phoebe awkwardly stood and straightened her gown. She shook the nurse's hand, waving off a final plea, then bent to kiss the elderly patient's cheek before finally waddling back to her wheelchair and scooping up her knitting, a happy grin on her face. Her lips started moving again as she began another song.

"Oh yeah," the nurse said to Crane, "you're going to have your hands full with that one."

6
MERCY

The heat that scorches our planet—ozone baked and environmentally corrupted—drove the architects of New Juneau to build my underwater home. Though too warm for many of the original fish and plant life, the water is always cooler than the air, so we use it as a sustainable source to cool our living quarters, kitchens, and recreational space. While some still prefer to live above the waves, I've always loved the quiet, pervasive peace of our underwater habitat. A world that, until today, felt safe.

Leaving my family's quarters, I keep pace with Eddie as we navigate through the myriad of tunnels to meet our…team? Crew? Group? I'm not sure what we are now.

The cafeteria is almost empty, so I easily spot Van and TJ, Cousteau curled between their feet. The children have changed into typical clothes—cargo shorts and vintage T-shirts. Nairobi's braids are gone, replaced by a simple low ponytail, like my own. Fez's fancy jacket is gone too; his black hair is neatly combed.

Their faces and hands are scrubbed clean. They raise their heads from prayer as Eddie and I approach. They could pass for Hab kids, until you look them in the eye. Their irises are the deepest purple I've ever seen.

Behind them, large oval portholes offer a view of the peaceful blue sea of our filtered bay. As a child I could sit for hours and watch the fish drift by. While I long for that serenity, today it's too important to stay focused on finding my parents. I can't get distracted.

"Why're we here?" I ask.

"We're waitin' for orders…. Eat somethin'." Van holds out a chair for me. He used to do things like that all the time.

I slouch into it and consider the food in front of me. Eggs and burnt toast.

Fez shifts onto his knees in the adult-size chair. "Van Elder burnt the toast."

Eddie snorts. "That's no surprise." She slides into the chair next to me. "He always burns the toast."

"Aye, I like it dark. Goes better with this." He swings his chair around backward and straddles it, as he holds out a golden straw.

I press my hand to my knee under the table to stop it from bouncing. He remembered my favorite treat. "A honey stick, for me?"

He shrugs.

I break open the straw and taste the golden liquid, but it doesn't taste like I remember. It doesn't taste like joy. I set it aside.

"What's that?" Nairobi asks, pointing to the pop banner hanging on a nearby wall.

I answer automatically. "That's a population monitor. It shows the number of people in the Legion of Scorch."

TJ interrupts my explanation. "If you stare at it long enough it changes…because someone dies."

I scowl at him. "Really? Macabre today?" I turn to the children. "It also changes when a baby is born."

Eddie squeezes my wrist to get my attention. "Mercy, do you want to tell them about your parents?"

"Aye, what happened? Sure is we've been waitin' a while to hear." Van crosses his arms and leans toward me.

I'd forgotten the way his accent stirs me, like a whisper of breath tingling down my neck to raise goosebumps on my arms. The thought brings a flush of embarrassment to my cheeks, and I can't find the words. All I manage is a squeak. I motion for Eddie to go ahead. I only half listen as she fills them in.

To steady myself, I flip open my comm and update my page with information about my parents' disappearance and to ask for help in finding them. I set my Prayers Needed flag to Yes.

Eddie continues talking. When she gets to the part about the blood, Van squeezes my hand and I jump.

"We'll find 'em, I swear it. We'll put the pieces together and we'll find 'em, I promise."

I pull my hand away to steady my knee again. "Maybe someone saw something…I just posted about it."

"Is that wise?" TJ asks.

I shrug. "How long do we have to wait here?"

Van checks his comm. "Not long. Just a wee bit longer."

My knees are both bouncing with impatience now. I blow out a breath and look around for a distraction.

I'm curious about these Spherans. The boy, Fez, spears a piece of broccoli and holds it up to his sister. She grimaces and goes back to poking at a pile of black rice.

Van notices. "Well now, what's wrong with ye two?"

No one wastes food here. Reminded, I nibble on my toast.

"Nothing's wrong." Fez puts down his fork of broccoli. "We just haven't had this kind of food before."

Van chokes a little. I thump him hard on the back and he winces, shrinking away from me. "Gee, thanks."

I point to Fez's fork. "It's broccoli. It's similar to cauliflower. It's a member of the cabbage family."

"Oh, I don't like cabbage." Fez pushes away his plate.

"Well, you'll have to eat it now, it's on your plate," I insist.

At this he looks truly downcast.

"Don't feel bad, lad," Van chimes in, "it's super food."

Nairobi crinkles her nose. "It doesn't smell super."

"Well, 'tis. All the food here is super. Take that rice, for example." Van points with his fork. "That rice was invented in the twenty-first century by an American scientist. He spliced regular rice with barley to create a genetically engineered plant that emits almost no methane. It helped slow climate change, it did."

Eddie scoffs. "For all the good it did them."

I just stare at Van, temporarily distracted by his uncharacteristic history lecture.

He sits back, smiling at me while he chews. "What? I can't know history too?"

I shake my head. "So where is this magical place without broccoli anyway?"

"Terra Faire," Fez answers, then shoves a huge fork full of broccoli into his mouth. He scrunches his eyes shut and pinches his nose as he chews.

TJ's comm chirps.

I sigh. "Finally."

We wait while he reads the holoscreen cradled in his palm.

As he reads, Eddie and Van get calls too. Everyone's reading orders. Except me. Nobody calls me.

I check my comm anyway. Nothing.

TJ speaks first. "Father's safe. He's denying any role in the attacks, and he seemed genuinely concerned about our safety—well, mine and Eddie's anyway. But...he's back at the Space Hub."

"The Hub? But he was just here. We saw him two days ago." I look to Eddie for confirmation, and she nods.

"Apparently he took the tether this morning," TJ continues. "Something about meeting mother to bring her to the conference."

Eddie scoffs. "Impossible. She would never leave her command for such a 'pointless event'—her words, not mine."

Van clears his throat. "I've orders to take the lot of ye and the kids to Vancouver Colony...quiet like."

My response is automatic. "No way. The Verge?"

"Ye always wanted to go..."

"This hardly seems like a time to go exploring. No, it's out of the question, really. I have to stay here."

Eddie snaps her comm shut. "My instructions concur. The Gran Bozan expects to have more information on the missing citizens soon. She'll relay them there."

"My parents aren't in the Verge."

My friends exchange glances.

TJ fidgets.

Van lets out a long breath. "We're used to takin' orders, 'tis fair to say. They want us—all four of us—in a Terran stronghold as soon as possible."

"The Hab isn't a stronghold?"

Eddie touches my hand. "The Hab is neutral. We need to get to the Verge."

I have a strange feeling, like this isn't real. Maybe none of it. As I scan the faces of my friends—destined cleric, genius pilot, and powerful soldier—I can't help feeling out of place. What do I have to do with any of this? My shoulders seem to fold in on me and suddenly I'm struggling to keep my chin off the table.

"Mercy?" Eddie jolts me out of my self-pity. "What's wrong?"

Van's forehead crinkles. "Cricket?" He tips his head to the side in question.

I slowly exhale. How can I explain this to them? I look down at our plates…

"In Old Earth history, during the Golden Years, citizens paid large sums of credits to eat food prepared by professional chefs. The food was as pretty as it was delicious, and the chefs prided themselves on presentation nearly as much as taste." I don't dare meet their eyes—I know what they must think of me and my stories. "On the plates, they placed colorful vegetables, lacy leaves and fancy fruits, on which to present the food. There was no intention for this to be eaten—it was only decoration. They called it *garnish*, and it always went back to the kitchen as waste. No one gave it another thought."

I wait in the silence, staring at our now empty plates.

Nairobi tugs on Van's sleeve. "Is it true?"

"I've never heard it, but if Mercy says so, then 'tis true, lass." He dislodges her little fingers from his shirt but takes her hand in his.

Nairobi shakes her head. "Such waste."

I'm startled when Eddie squeezes my wrist hard. Waves of anger and maybe even hurt pulse from her.

"You…are…not…garnish!" Eddie whisper-shouts.

When I look at TJ, he seems just as upset, but unlike Eddie, whose eyes are boring into me, he won't meet my gaze.

"Cricket…" Van reaches for my elbow.

While I long for his touch, I don't want his pity. I stand so quickly that my chair overturns and smacks on the ground with a loud clang. Cousteau zips out from under the table and yips in surprise. TJ whistles and tries to calm him.

Other diners look at us.

"Sit down," TJ commands, and I realize I'm making a scene. "The tracking system could already be back online. This is a small crowd and although no one suspects anything yet, they could easily count the people here and be confident that the system record is two children shy.… Our friends, the Spherans, have no

ID implants. We're trying to keep a low profile. The four of us plus two untagged kids—it wouldn't take much to connect the dots."

Van rights my chair and I sit. "How is that possible? Every citizen has a tracker, they're integrated with the comm, the network—everything."

Fez lifts a hand. "We don't have implants, but we're still important. Each of us plays a part." He sounds so much wiser than his size suggests, even for a praenex. "Our teacher, Dr. Cairo Varela, he's to meet with Dr. Parker Adams about important scientific discoveries. Omag Gran Edelweiss Renee LeRoux will cure a disease. First Lieutenant Sylvan Elder will see us safely to Vancouver Colony, where Lieutenant Commander Tern Journey LeRoux will work on secret transmissions."

I feel a pang at the mention of my father. Did he ever meet the Spheran teacher to talk science? What kind of discoveries have they made? Something ozone related?

It's so odd how official Fez's predictions sound, like he's reading a report or something.

"My, that's grand, lad." Van leans back in his chair and rubs his hands up and down his massive chest. "And what about you, little man, and Nairobi? What role do you play?"

"We're ambassadors." Nairobi grins, and I do too.

"Okay, time to get serious." Van leans in and keeps his voice low. "How are we gettin' to the Verge without bein' noticed?"

"I have some ideas—" TJ's interrupted when a small group of SciCorps soldiers enter the cafeteria. They stop short when they see us, and then continue on to a nearby table.

I finally find my voice. "We shouldn't talk here. Where can we go without being monitored?"

"*Trust no one?*" Eddie asks, quoting my father.

I nod. "Exactly."

TJ's comm buzzes. "Uh oh. I was afraid of this."

"What?" Van asks.

TJ looks over his shoulder at the SciCorps troops. When he turns back to us, his face is grim. "They're looking for us."

As if on cue, an officer enters—it's the lieutenant from the protest who stopped me, Caesar Naveen. The one strong enough to resist Eddie's mental manipulation. They head directly for the SciCorps troops—a security team, I think. The soldiers stand and after a brief conversation with the lieutenant, they start toward us.

My urge to hide is so strong that I'm under the table before I even think to move. I startle at a rustle behind me and swivel to see Nairobi and Fez huddled under the table too. I scoot closer to them and hold out a hand. They clutch it and squeeze it tight. I put a finger to my lips and they nod.

As I look out at the room from under the table, Van, TJ and Eddie stand to form a barrier between us and the SciCorps police. The men can't see us past the tablecloth and my friends' legs.

They're talking now. Van and TJ mostly. Cousteau sits alert and ready at TJ's heels.

"Where are the others?" the officer asks.

"Well, hello to you too, Naveen." Van's voice is as cold as I've ever heard it.

"I'm not messing around," Naveen answers.

"Aye, we'd never think that now would we, TJ?"

TJ mutters something I can't hear.

Naveen pauses and shuffles one foot before clearing their throat. "Stop stalling and answer the question."

"Alright. What others?" TJ asks evenly.

"Mercy Adams and the two children."

So they remember me, but did they see me, or are they just assuming? All I can see is legs and feet at this point, there's no way to read Naveen's face.

"It's just us," Eddie replies. I feel her pushing her thoughts on them too.

"I feel your thoughts, witch," one of the SciCorps soldiers sneers as they take a step forward. "You can't trick us."

"Shut your mouth, Private!" Naveen snaps at the soldier.

TJ's feet step closer to Naveen's. "That's right, best leash your dog, Naveen, unless they want a mouth full of teeth. No one talks to my sister like that, and you know it," TJ snarls.

I shudder, glad he's on my side. The way they square off, I think my friends know Naveen. The familiarity gives us an advantage, but it's small comfort.

"Enough!" Naveen's voice rises. "As I said, step away from the table."

I sense the moment my friends choose their targets, watch their stances shift slightly. It's three against four, but I've no idea if the troops know just how outmatched they truly are.

Cousteau stands too, and a low warning growl reverberates from his throat.

The children shake next to me. I wrap my arm around them, pull them close, and squeeze my eyes shut, hoping they understand my instruction to mimic me. When I look again, their eyes are closed tight.

"Step away," Naveen says again.

Eddie's voice is deceivingly sweet. "Of course." She takes a step, her layered skirts floating gracefully, then one of her feet disappears.

The next thing I know, one of the SciCorps soldiers hits the floor hard. From that point on it's like watching half a dance—just legs and feet—as my friends defend us.

TJ's legs are tangled with one of the soldier's—the mean one, I think—and I realize they must be wrestling standing up. Abruptly, the soldier drops to their knees. Their eyes roll back in their head and they slide the rest of the way to the floor. Cousteau jumps out of the way, before prancing back to TJ's side.

Van's still fighting the other two. The air fills with grunts, curses, and the snap of fists hitting flesh. One soldier tries to move away toward TJ and sets Cousteau barking wildly.

"Ah, no ye don't, Naveen!" Van snarls. Suddenly the lieutenant's feet are dangling in the air next to Van's shins.

"Van, stop messing around!" Eddie says.

With a loud crash, Van dumps Naveen onto the table, causing it to shake and shift around us. The other soldier he was fighting thuds to the floor unconscious.

As Naveen scrambles off the table. Plates and silverware shower the floor in a cacophony of noise.

"Knife!" TJ shouts.

Van grunts in surprise. A lifetime seems to pass in the seconds before the next sound—the splat of blood on the stone floor.

Van's roar sends a chill down my spine. I slap my hands over my ears.

"Don't kill him!" Eddie's shout is muffled in my head.

Even through my hands I hear the unholy crunch of bone as Naveen falls to the floor, their arm twisted at an awkward angle. They land with their cheek pressed to the cold floor, their face turned toward me where I hide like a coward under the table. They peer at me with a shocked expression—at the pain or at the strangeness of finding me here, I can't tell. I pull my hands away from my ears and lean toward Naveen, drawn by their pain, their need.

"Mercy," they whisper, before their eyes slowly roll up into their head and close.

The tablecloth rustles and Eddie's face appears. "Come on!"

I scramble out from under the table and follow her, the children clutching my hands. When I can tear my eyes away from the carnage left in our wake, I see the guys are already leaving the cafe ahead of us. TJ has his hands wrapped around Van's bicep. Red blood oozes between his fingers.

Van curses under his breath—his face is damp with sweat, but he keeps up with TJ as we hurry down the hall.

A young woman jumps out of the way as we round a corner. She covers her mouth in horror.

"Soldiers!" Eddie warns, before shoving us all into a crevice near a maintenance room.

I stare at the woman. She stares back. I know her from laundry duty, but I can't recall her name.

Please, I mouth. I point to my pin. It matches hers.

The woman considers for a moment, and then straightens her back and looks away, just as the soldiers approach. She steps into their path, away from us. She says something I can't hear and then points down the opposite hall. Without hesitation, the soldiers continue the way she pointed and disappear around the corner.

When she looks back at me, I press my palm out to her and nod my thanks. She nods too and raises her hand briefly before tucking a strand of hair behind her ear and hurrying off.

Van is breathing hard. "Where now?"

"I know just the place." TJ waves us to follow him. "Come on, into the lion's den."

7

MERCY

Current year: 2701
Wednesday, 6:30 PM
The Hab

Admiral Yuri LeRoux's quarters are unremarkable except for two things: the size—probably twice the size of my family's home—and the heat.

Cousteau takes a quick survey, and then jumps into a chair, curls up, and shuts his eyes. The children giggle and settle in to pet him.

"Gah!" Van pulls at the neck of his shirt. "Why the blessed inferno?"

TJ and Eddie seem puzzled too.

"I don't know, but we've more important things to worry about." TJ nudges Van toward a chair at the table, his hands still wrapped tight around Van's bicep. "Med kit?"

I dump my bags and grab the first aid kit from the cabinet. I try not to throw up when TJ pulls his hands away from the oozing stab wound. I press a gauze pad to Van's arm and look away.

TJ goes to the sink to wash his hands. "You need a few sutures, courtesy of our friend, Naveen."

"*Yer* friend, Naveen, not mine. The bastard. Just hurry." Van turns to me then.

I must look as bad as I feel.

He reaches for the bandage and pushes my hand away. "We've got this, Cricket. Go on, now."

TJ returns and takes my place. "So, Mercy, how do *you* know Naveen?"

Van's head snaps back to me so fast, I actually startle. "Um, I don't, not really. They spoke to me at the protest earlier. Wait, how did you know I knew them?"

TJ stills for a moment, and I realize that he didn't know, only suspected. TJ's coyness always makes me uncomfortable, but I've never had it aimed at me before. I don't like it at all. "Oh, I see, you didn't."

Van straightens. "They spoke to ye at the station? When?"

"On the steps. It was nothing—"

"What did they say?" Eddie interrupts.

"Um, Pilgrim stuff mostly, and—"

Eddie steps toward TJ. "I was projecting on that crowd. They shouldn't have been able to approach her."

"But they did. We know they're strong...." TJ shrugs. "At least they didn't touch her."

"Well..." I cringe, embarrassed, but not sure why.

"They touched ye?" Van stands, like maybe he's going to go back and find Naveen and break their other arm.

I take a step back. "I..." My hand instinctively circles my

upper arm to rub where Naveen squeezed it.

"They hurt ye?" Van lurches forward, but TJ steps in his way.

At the same time, Eddie reaches for my sleeve and raises it to show the faint purple finger marks encircling my bicep.

Van's indrawn breath is audible. "Aye, they're a dead one."

"I'm fine." I push away Eddie's hand.

Van takes another step, this time toward the door.

"Hey!" TJ pushes him back, then wrestles him into the chair. "She's okay, Van."

Eddie sighs. "Mercy, maybe you should just tell us the whole story, start to finish."

I do, shrinking a little when I explain how Naveen squeezed my arm and I just stood there and took it.

Van rounds on Eddie. "How did ye miss all this? Where were ye?"

"I was controlling the crowd with my mind, okay! It's a bit consuming." Eddie throws her hands in the air. "I'm not a bodyguard."

"I don't need a bodyguard," I say, but no one hears me; they're too busy arguing amongst themselves.

"She coulda been hurt a lot worse!" Van shouts.

"Hey!" TJ interjects, refereeing. "It's a mission, we can all be hurt." He points to Van's arm. "And now we know Naveen is all in, which is *not* good. A part of me hates to say it, but so far SciCorps looks like amateurs trying to learn how to fight a civil war as they go—"

Eddie snorts. "They're StupidCorps."

TJ shakes his head. "Thing is, they learn fast. I wouldn't be surprised if Naveen's cafe stunt earns them a promotion. An officer that driven, you know what they're like when they get a bone in their teeth," he says to Eddie. "Truth be told, despite everything, I'd rather they were on our side."

"Well, they're not, and good riddance, I say." Van thumps a fist on the table. "Pickin' on little girls…"

"I'm not a little girl." None of them look at me.

Van continues his rant. "Knife fights…it's just…it's just…it's so damn hot in here!"

I throw up my hands in frustration. "Look, will one of you at least tell me what's up with this Naveen? Why are they so driven? How do you all know them and I don't? What's going on?"

Eddie looks at TJ, shrugs. "You know them best."

"But you saw them in the hospital, you stayed with them," TJ argues. He pauses, then looks back at me. "I met Caesar Naveen at the academy. We were friends, and their parents worked for our parents. I think your circles just never crossed."

Eddie exhales. "Naveen's young—only sixteen, but they've already lost their parents to the Trade."

"That's terrible." I think about my mother and wonder if she's getting her medicine, or if the disease will accelerate during her abduction.

"Yes," TJ agrees, "and their parents, they were fanatical Pilgrims. They worked as technicians on the life-support systems on the colony ships. They built some of the practical components that'll see us through the long journey. They were brilliant, really. Our parents trusted them, encouraged their work. Caesar and I…after a while we were more than friends, but after their dad died things changed. They changed. When their mom passed too, our parents took Caesar in—"

"Can ye get to the point? I'm about to combust in this damn heat." Van uses his shirt to wipe sweat from his face.

"Anyway, I left for flight school shortly after. I expected our relationship to change then, but it got really twisted. I think Naveen resented me for, well…I don't know, probably for a lot of things."

Eddie nods. "Living in our parents' household, their parents' political views…it galvanized Naveen. I could see it happening when I visited. Now Naveen's even more invested in leaving. They're a hardcore Pilgrim, no middle road."

I nod, understanding a little more. "Caesar Naveen wants to use the things their parents built. I mean, personally. They want to do it in their own lifetime." My conclusion is met with silence. "Thank you for telling me."

Eddie's comm beeps. She opens her mouth to reply but pauses when she sees who's calling. "Ah, not good timing.…" She swipes a command on her holocomm and the callers appear on the nearby wall panel.

"Your Grace, Bozan Kahinu, divine peace with you." She holds her palms up and out to them.

We all quickly mimic her action—Van with one hand.

The leaders on the screen repeat the motion. "The Creator's hand in yours, Omag Gran," the GB says. "Are you safe and well?"

Eddie turns to look at Van as TJ prepares to stitch him up.

Van waves a hand. "Aye, well enough."

As TJ prepares the suture device, my stomach rolls.

Eddie's unfazed. "We had some trouble, but we're okay. We're at my parent's apartment in the Hab. The children are with us."

I can't hold my tongue any longer. "Is there any news on my parents?" Hope flutters in my chest.

The GB exchanges a look with Bozan Kahinu, who has moved from the hospital bed into a large chair, tubes still attached to their arm. The GB's bandages are smaller too—only a patch at one temple—and her hair is back in its orderly bun. Still, she appears older, her gem duller at the edges.

"No, but we're taking their disappearance seriously. I'm sorry to be curt, but we have other news. The conference has been cancelled."

We all gasp. The bi-annual conferences are our main political and social forum. Their feeds are posted live and the ratings determine which thirteen citizens will constitute the council. We're a social media government. Without this forum, the issues of our society will have no organized voice.

TJ speaks first. "Then they've won. They got exactly what they wanted." He continues wrapping a bandage around Van's arm.

Bozan Kahinu shakes their head. "No. The conference is merely the public face of our actions. A tribunal has formed and met. Our purposes are served."

I'm confused. "Tribunal?"

"The Legion, Alberta TAC command, and Vancouver Colony officials conferred an hour ago. Our earlier inclination to make for the Verge has been confirmed." The GB rises slowly from her chair, reaching out a hand to Rumesa to help them up.

I step closer to Eddie, sensing her anxiety, and slide my hand into hers. Immediate warmth and assurance wash over me, and I wonder who's more comforted, me or her. The others press forward too, even the children, who until now had been keeping out of the fray. We're a unit now, a bit rag-tag, but united. We wait for what happens next.

The GB clears her throat and stands straighter. "Omag Gran Edelweiss Renee LeRoux, by the power granted me by the Supreme Order of the Legion and with the Creator's hand to lead me, I hereby promote you to the station of Bozan, effective immediately and entailing all the rights and responsibilities therein. How say you?"

My heart has either stopped entirely, or it's beating so fast I sense no rhythm. My best friend, my inner voice, my sister always, is to be *Bozan*. At 18, no less. I can't recall any time in history in which this has ever before occurred.

Eddie's albino face, always truly pale, is nearly translucent now. A blue vein trips at her temple, her lavender eyes stare at the screen.

I squeeze her hand and she jumps.

Her whispered question is barely audible. "Why is this? Why now?"

The GB inhales deeply, clearly weighing her response. "Rumesa has seen what must come next—the four of you are central to the story that shall unfold. You and these children. We're not merely at the point of civil crisis.... This *is* the

Culmination. From here, humankind shall start on its new path, whether on Scorch or on pilgrimage, we shall know before a year has passed." She pauses long enough for everyone to take this in.

I look at Van, who stares unseeing at the floor. The children whisper to one another as they both reach for his good hand. He closes it automatically about theirs. Cousteau circles around TJ's feet.

I've always considered the Culmination more a myth than anything. It's the future, after all, something I see only in bright glimpses, not concrete facts like history. The prediction of a time of culmination, when all of the Creator's plans from the Call to the present day come to a head, is fantasy to me.

Eddie straightens and blows out a narrow breath. "I accept this promotion and offer my thanks for your faith in me. I promise to keep the Creator's will as my guide in all I do."

I feel something new radiating from her now—anxiety still, but mixed with determination and a steadiness that's difficult to describe. It's foreign to me, yet a solid thing. An awakening...of *power*.

She must sense my astonishment as she turns her head slightly and smiles at me, just a tiny tip of the corner of her mouth.

"Good." The GB sits again. "You will represent the Legion in Vancouver Colony. We'll not always have a means to speak, but as Bozan, your decisions will be wise and binding. You must leave quickly. Prepare yourselves and be underway."

Rumesa raises a hand to us. "Peace with you." The screen goes dark.

TJ draws Eddie into a hug. "Sister—Bozan."

Her eyes close briefly as she smiles.

Cousteau prances excitedly around them.

"Fair play, Eddie." Van's congratulations are brusque, but sincere.

He pauses only a moment before dropping the children's hands and moving to the wall. "It's downright *hot* in here." He moves his hand over the vents, back and forth before stopping in front of one. He begins to pry at the panel. "Protests… Knife fights…" He's mumbling, sometimes cursing. "Bozan at 18. No childhood for us." His sarcastic laugh is laced with anger. He yanks at a corner of the vent.

"Take it easy on that arm." TJ shifts toward him but stops. He looks at me and shrugs.

Van ignores him, pawing at the panel like a man possessed. "God…blessed…Caesar…Ramrod…Naveen!" He's pulling with both hands now.

The rest of us just watch helplessly.

When we were younger, Van was always in motion. Constantly energized. He recharged through *more* action, not by rest. In the last few years, I've watched as he's gained a rigid control of himself. At times I was afraid that he'd erupt and his wave of energy would sweep us all away like a tsunami.

That's how it feels now as I watch him pulling relentlessly on the wall panel, grunting and sweating while he grumbles under his breath. He's waging war with the wall. My body has tightened in response. I don't need my gem to understand the emotions pouring from him. His stress is contagious.

"Now the Verge," Van grunts. A bright red line soaks

through his bandage. "What's next?" he shouts at the panel. "The God blessed space station? HUH!" He grabs ahold and leans back, bracing one foot against the baseboard to leverage his full weight to pry open the panel.

Nairobi whimpers. TJ moves first, crossing to Van and laying a hand on his good shoulder. "Van—"

Suddenly the panel breaks free. TJ jumps aside as the momentum sends Van sprawling on the floor still clutching the square of plastic. An avalanche of black clothing tumbles from the duct. We all stare.

"I think you found the problem with the ventilation." Eddie's voice, tinged with her usual sarcasm, breaks the spell and I let out my breath.

"Aye." Van makes his way to the pile of clothes and gear spilling from the wall. "What's all this now?"

Cousteau wades into the heap and drags out something in his jaws.

"Uniforms." TJ takes the jacket from Cousteau. "Black police uniforms."

I reach for another piece—a helmet with a tinted visor. "Why're these here?"

The children's voices reach me then, as they talk to one another excitedly in a foreign language that I've never heard before. A chill runs down my spine and my gem contracts. Something is very wrong.

"Portuguese, I think," TJ whispers to Eddie.

I kneel before the children and touch their shoulders to get their attention. "Fez, Nairobi, what's wrong?"

Fez looks at me, and then scans the rest of us with his big violet eyes. "The bad men at the station wore those uniforms. When our teacher saw them, he pushed us toward the dark corner and told us to hide."

Van grips TJ's shoulder. "And now we find this here, hidden in the air duct of yer father's apartment. Ye know what this means."

"But he's our father—"

"And he always will be." Eddie interrupts her brother as we stand. "He's never hidden his agenda from us. He always lectured us on his mission—to evacuate this dying planet, to start the pilgrimage." She grabs her brother's elbow. "You know this, that the Creator's voice has always been clear to him, preparing him for the journey."

"Preparing TJ too," Van adds.

TJ's quiet for a moment. "That's true. When I see the future, I see myself surrounded by stars, not fields. All my skills, my training… I'm a pilot—"

"And a tech geek," Van offers.

"And a language freak," I add, hoping to ease the tension.

"Yeah, okay, I get it. You know me well, but like my father, I've always been honest about my motives."

Eddie's head falls. "Yes, you've both been honest, but I didn't think he would ever stoop to this—kidnapping, risking human lives to force his position. If he's behind this, then he even endangered your life with that plane crash."

"Nah, TJ wasn't supposed to be there. He changed his plans last minute to help me with my da's transport."

TJ nods. "Yes, but my father didn't know that. This explains his sincere panic when he realized I was with you."

"Aye, but gettin' back to the point, this kind of espionage—it's a prelude to war. There hasn't been a civil war on this continent in…"

"Over 800 years," I offer.

Eddie spreads her hands wide. "How could he do this?"

"*All men will be tyrants*," I murmur.

Van tips his head to the side. "Winston Churchill?"

I shake my head. "Abigail Adams." My body's finally relaxing. I move to lean a hip on the arm of a sofa. "She believed that the checks and balances in government could keep any one man from turning to his nature, the true nature of all men—tyranny."

Eddie considers this, her eyes cast to the ceiling now. "With SciCorps' seclusion of funds from the global bank, the other communities will be crippled. SciCorps holds all the cards—commerce, the tether, even the population."

TJ nods. "Between the tether, the Hub and the SATO Space Station, nearly half the population is either off world or steps away."

I rub my temple. "But that's been true for years. What's changed now?"

As if our thoughts are perfectly timed, we turn our gazes to the children, quietly listening to us.

Nairobi rolls her shoulders back and lifts her chin as she's seen Eddie do a number of times now.

I would laugh if I didn't feel like I might throw up.

Nairobi points her tiny finger at TJ's chest, at the rocket

insignia emblazoned there. "You wear this symbol because you want to leave, you want to find a new home for our race."

"We are Spherans," Fez says.

"No one in Terra Faire needs any symbol," Nairobi explains. "We are, each one of us, tied to this planet, to healing her so she might thrive once more. What will you do now? Will you stand by us, or will you take flight, Tern Journey LeRoux?"

TJ startles, his face drains of color as he considers this direct and life-changing question, then his body stretches as if awakening. He flicks open his palm to activate his comm. His fingers fly across the small display hovering there, then just as quickly he closes his fist, deactivating it. "I've resigned my commission at SciCorps."

I shake my head in disbelief. How do I fit in with these people? These powerful, decisive, important people? These friends. What can I possibly offer them?

"There's more." TJ sounds almost reluctant.

The look he gives us makes me hold my breath.

"They're trying to trace us…me, Van, and even Eddie. While the system is down, we're safe independently, but whatever contacts we have, it's too risky to use them to get out of here."

"This is bad." I rub at the goosebumps rising on my arms.

Van shakes his head. "So how're we going to get to the Verge?"

"And how are we going to rescue my parents?" My voice is louder than I expected.

Eddie stabs a hand toward the ground. "Don't panic! You'll just worry the children."

"Well, what do *you* think we should do?"

"What we always do." She looks at each of us in turn. "We're going to take a minute and ask the Divine to show us the way."

Her jaw's firm, her eyes blaze. Even if I disagreed, which I don't, I'd go along with praying just to avoid her glare.

"Okay." I hold out my hands.

The guys move closer and we stand in a circle, hand in hand, and close our eyes. Before we begin, the children break our holds and wriggle into the ring.

Settling again, I concentrate on the breathing around me. I focus my prayers not on what I want or need, but on what I have. My blessings. My life. My friends. My family. I call up my mother's face. She's laughing at something I said. My father is there too, smiling as he kisses her cheek and reaches for me. The sensation of warmth surrounds me. It's like I'm floating, like I'm at sea, moving gently with the ebb and flow of the waves, and then the waves turn to stars. I sense the cosmos swirling around me, like I'm at the center of the Creator's love—a force surrounding, supporting me. At that moment everything is connected and anything is possible.

"Van, what do you feel?"

Eddie's question hovers at the edge of my thoughts. I peek at Van.

He takes a deep breath. "I feel the land, the farm. My thoughts kept going back to comforts." He smiles out of the side of his mouth. "I'm a farmer first, a soldier second. Community. Family. Friends. Us. That's my center." He sighs and runs his hand through his hair. "I was thinking of the first time we exchanged gifts at a conference."

"That's odd," TJ says. "My thoughts were much the same, only even more focused on us. On our history. Our bond, and our gifts."

We all open our eyes and look around the circle now.

Eddie rolls her shoulders and sighs. "Yes, me too. I kept coming back to us. I saw the three of us time and again, hovering around Mercy, laughing over her presents for us. Years' worth of presents…"

Eddie looks at TJ, then at Van. No one speaks.

I look at the ceiling trying to think, to connect the dots that the Creator has given us. When I drop my gaze, they're all staring at me.

"What?" I'm pinned by their stares. A little spike of adrenaline streaks through my veins, sending hot-cold needles prickling along my skin. My vision goes a little grey around the edges. I realize I'm holding my breath and let it out in a whoosh. "What?"

TJ clears his throat.

Eddie grimaces at him, then rolls her shoulders. "You'll have to do it, Cricket. The three of us can't, so you'll have to."

"Have to what?"

"Get us outta here." Van's voice is quiet, like he didn't really want to say it.

"Get us…" Now *my* voice is a whisper. "Me? Get us…How am I supposed to do that?"

8
MERCY

If there's one thing I know, it's praenex history. Culmination lore began in 2139 by a third generation praenex girl who would later become the first Gran Bozan, founder of the Legion. She was psychic and foretold of a time six hundred years in the future when all of the Creator's plan for reshaping the world would converge in a great culmination of events. So many of her other predictions came true that most people believed her. But as time passed and her predictions became exaggerated, they took on the sound of myth.

As I watch TJ check Van's sutures and replace his bandages, I wonder if I'm seeing a casualty of this myth. It all seems so surreal. I'd like to take over the wound care—my technique is better than TJ's—but I don't want to embarrass Van by fussing. He's going to be embarrassed enough when he finds out what I've arranged.

The guys have both changed out of their uniforms. Van's

simple black T-shirt pulls tight against his massive biceps. His muscles flex as TJ works.

He catches me watching and it's my turn to be embarrassed. I look away, prickling heat rising to my cheeks.

"How'll ye mask our transport?" Van asks TJ. "Won't the mag shuttle record passengers?"

"The system's still offline."

I lean in. "What if it comes back online?"

TJ glances at me and grimaces. "I can't afford to activate the program I have in place for disguising our IDs. Not yet. We might need it later and the longer it runs, the sooner someone'll figure it out."

"So what then? How're we gettin' there? A plane'd be too noticeable…"

TJ busily ties off the bandage and avoids the question. Van ducks his head to try to catch TJ's eye, then gives up and rolls his eyes. His neck reddens and I get a sinking feeling in my gut. There are limited ways to leave New Juneau and he especially isn't going to like the one I chose.

"There. All done." TJ snaps the med kit shut.

"Will somebody please tell me how we're gettin' to the Verge?" Van's voice grumbles through his clenched teeth.

I can barely stand still. Working up my courage, I blurt it out. "I know a fisherman—"

"Oh, hell." He turns away, rolling his shoulders and neck.

His curse sends a chill through me. Still, I can't change what needs to be done, so I straighten my spine and suck in a breath.

TJ shakes with silent laughter. "It's so *sapiens*, your

seasickness."

Van growls and clenches his fists before turning back to him. "So *novus* of ye to point it out!"

"Don't worry. The captain told me they've got medicine onboard to help you." I flash a brittle smile that threatens to crumble at the slightest movement.

Van continues shaking his head. The redness on his neck spreads upward to his face and I know he's remembering the last time he was seasick.

In front of me. Well…on me, a little.

"It wasn't so bad!" I insist.

TJ tugs my sleeve and shakes his head. I'm making it worse.

Eddie joins us. "Mercy, you've got to leave behind some of those books. You're carrying too much."

"But…" I lower my eyes, pull my satchel around, and start the difficult process of deciding which books to keep, and which to let go.

Eddie drops a bag at Van's feet. "Don't even think about taking off."

My head whips up. "He wouldn't do that." I'm not sure, so much as desperate. He can't leave. He just got here.

Van's silent.

I reach out to touch his arm but stop short. "You wouldn't do that, would you?"

His shoulders slump as he lets out a long breath. "No, of course not." He won't meet my eyes.

A few minutes later, TJ helps me balance while Fez mounts the tandem bike behind me. My heart pounds in my chest. Each of us carries a small satchel in addition to our own backpacks. It's hard to juggle it all, but the children don't complain. They smile and giggle in excitement—it's just a big adventure to them now that they know we'll keep them safe.

TJ hacked the bike kiosk; I hope the people whose accounts he used won't mind. It's only a short ride through the business district to the port. The bikes'll be checked back in before they notice.

With Eddie and Nairobi riding another tandem, and TJ and Van on their own bikes, we start off. Cousteau keeps pace with TJ in the lead. When TJ signals, we spread out so we don't look like a group. It's past dinner hour, so the streets are quiet. The people we pass on the well-lit streets are in a hurry—they're satisfied with a short nod in greeting. My heart still in my throat, I wave to neighbors I see on their way home to the Hab, my smile a little lie I'll have to live with.

Halfway there TJ signals and abruptly stops behind a small maintenance building. His face is a mask as I pull up and dismount, but the frown lines at the corner of his mouth tell me there's trouble.

"What's happening?"

TJ motions us all to come closer. I huddle closer with the others. "I set an alarm to tell me if SciCorps' search parameters change to cross our path. Troops will be here in less than ten minutes to search the square and surrounding area. They have our exit route covered at the moment but should be moving on in about twenty minutes. We've got to hide until it's clear."

Eddie gestures with both hands. "Stay calm. There has to be a good place around the square. The lights create pockets of darkness and there're sheds and kiosks all around—"

Van interrupts. "They'll search those—"

While they argue, I ponder solutions. Hiding is about evading capture. How do we hide? What have others done? As it often does, my brain sinks into history. Animals evade capture all the time—evolution provides them with all manner of camouflage. How do people evade capture? What's our camouflage?

"Mercy!" Eddie's voice is a harsh whisper.

I look up and realize someone's asked me a question. "Uh, what?"

Van exhales. "What're ye thinkin', Cricket?" he asks.

I look at their earnest faces, still not sure why they trust me with any of this. "Um, I was just thinking of George Washington—"

"George…. Okay, never mind." TJ huffs.

"Wait, let her finish." Van gestures to me. "Go on, Cricket."

I take a deep breath. "Washington learned his spying skills during his early career as a British officer. Later as an American general, he developed a vast spy network. Twice his spies' information helped him avoid assassination attempts by the British. All of his spies were good at one thing—hiding in plain sight." I pause, not sure if this is worthwhile.

TJ nods. "Go on."

"During the revolution, Hercules Mulligan was a favorite

tailor of British officers stationed in the colonies. John Honeyman traveled as their butcher during troop movement. They both succeeded and survived by blending in and passing the time doing normal things all while staying within earshot of British officers."

Eddie meets my eyes. "What're you suggesting?"

I look at TJ. His gaze is locked on something behind me, thinking. With a jolt, he meets my eyes. "I think it could work.… What do we do?"

"First we've got to spread these bikes around and shed some of this luggage."

Everyone grabs a bike and quickly parks it away from the others in places people would normally leave them before entering the square for some evening relaxation. We stow bags beside benches and against bike tires.

As we gather again just off the square, there are a good number of people sitting around the fountain or on benches, enjoying the late-day breeze. There's also a small class spread out on a patch of grass listening to a lecture and watching a vid.

"Now what?" Van asks once everyone's back.

"Eddie, you're a student in that class." I point to the group on the grass.

"Okay," she agrees.

"And for divine grace, sit away from the screen," TJ whispers. "In the glare you're like a luminescent fish."

She crosses her eyes at him and sticks out her tongue.

"Van, you're working that kiosk, helping the volunteer hang bikes and secure hover boards.… Use the ladder to disguise your height."

Van considers for a second. "I can do that."

"TJ—"

"I get it. I can find my own job."

I feel a tug on my pant leg. "What about us?" Nairobi asks.

I smile at her. "See those children with the sidewalk chalk by the fountain? I want you to go make friends and tell them your teacher has invited them to hear a story about the statue in the center of the fountain."

"But our teacher's not here," Fez pouts.

"Mercy's our teacher," Nairobi tells him. "Right?" She looks at me with big eyes.

"Right."

"Ready Hercules?" Eddie jabs her brother in the arm.

He scoffs.

"What about Cousteau?" Fez asks, fear for the dog clear in his voice.

TJ hunkers down so he can meet Fez's eyes. "Oh, don't worry about him. He's a genius at hiding. Aren't you, boy?" he asks Cousteau, giving him a quick rub around the neck. TJ stands and signals Cousteau with his hand. "Hide!"

Cousteau takes off into the shrubbery and it's like a sign to the rest of us, we all spread out.

I watch as the children fearlessly run ahead, directly into the group of children. Their parents smile as they sit chatting on the rim of the fountain. I follow more slowly.

Van strides across the square like he's late. I can't hear what he says to the awe-struck volunteer at the bike booth, but his gestures and easy smile quickly win him a smile. He grabs an apron and puts it on. With the booth's desk and awning partially concealing his size, he looks like any other worker as he hefts a used bike onto the nearby rack.

Eddie skirts around the square and I lose sight of her temporarily, only to watch her reappear and slide gracefully into position next to another student on the grass. Even in the shadows, she's a striking woman. The lecturer—a male teacher I vaguely remember from a botany class—stutters in his presentation and pauses when he sees her. As if she can hear my thoughts, she flicks up her hood to conceal her face. The lecture continues.

I've no idea where TJ went as I take up position in front of the fountain.

"Come on," I hear Nairobi say, and just like that I'm surrounded by children eager for a story.

"Hello." I smile and try to relax. "Tonight, I'd like to tell you the story of Arturus Samuelson." I motion behind me to the statue at the center of the fountain, just as six soldiers enter the square. They pause on the path exactly where we were standing just minutes ago, then quickly spread out and start searching.

I clear my throat and try to settle my nerves. "Vancouver Colony, as you know, dates before the Call. A wealthy, powerful man by the name of Arturus Samuelson was called by the Creator to create a safe place for pure-hearted sapiens to retreat."

A soldier stops to talk to the volunteer at the bike kiosk. Van's back is turned; he's on a ladder, busy loading hover boards into overhead slots in the shed behind the booth. The volunteer shakes their head at the soldier and the soldier moves around to the shed. They say something to Van and Van waves at the empty space around him. The soldier peeks inside, nods and moves on.

I let out a huge breath and take another. "In 2098, just after the start of the Second Pandemic, as the United Countries of America closed its borders, Samuelson bought a whole town and military base north of Vancouver from the government. People around the world flocked there—many Californians, but also foreigners given special permission to enter the UCA."

The soldiers approach the class slowly, listen, and then pass on. I feel lighter, hopeful. Maybe this will work.

Directing my attention back to the children, I pose questions. "Can anyone tell me the countries that made up the UCA?"

Hands shoot up. I point to a curly-haired student with brilliant violet eyes. "Mexico, the United States, and Canada."

"That's right." I nod. Nairobi's waving her hand insistently. I call on her.

"Did they get the virus?" Nairobi asks. "The people who joined Samuelson?"

"No. Samuelson's grandchild, Levi, was a brilliant doctor. They were part of the team that developed the vaccine. Levi later became the leader of the colony. Does anyone know the other great act of Arturus Samuelson?"

I call on a tiny serious-looking child kneeling right in front of me. "He saved people from the earthquakes," they say.

"That's correct. Arturus had a calling from the Creator just like his grandchild. He convinced many still living on the western shore to join him at a centurial retreat just days before the San

Andreas disaster. He saved many lives. After the faults and sea level changes reshaped the western coast, Vancouver Colony became a mountainous, coastal town and gained its nickname, *The Verge*."

My eyes continue tracking the soldiers as they gather back at their starting point. They turn and look up the path just as Naveen strides up to them, arm braced in a tight sling.

I tip my face away and pull the elastic band from my hair. There are several other women with long dark hair gathered in the square. I try to blend in, wishing only that I had a hat to conceal my face.

From the corner of my eye, I watch Naveen asking questions. The soldiers keep shaking their heads, then one of them points up at a dark streetlamp. A worker balances on a tall ladder, tool belt hanging loose, hardhat and protective glasses concealing their face, a neckerchief loose around their jaw. Naveen shouts something. The worker stops working but leaves their noisy tool running. They strain to listen to Naveen's shouted question, eventually pocketing another tool to free their hand. Even from this distance, their annoyance is clear. They wave a hand in a sweeping gesture to encompass the illuminated square. Naveen turns a circle to scan it before looking back up at the worker. Naveen shouts another question, to which the worker simply shrugs and resumes working.

Naveen throws their good hand in the air, checks their comm and waves the troops to follow them back up the path toward the residential area.

I look back up at the worker and focus. They point at

something and I think I recognize one of the signals TJ uses with Cousteau. I scan where they're pointing just in time to see a furry tail disappear into a bush. It's TJ! The utility worker is TJ! I laugh despite myself. I can't believe it worked.

I look down at the children and realize I owe them just a little more for helping me. "The statue of Arturus you see here was made by a group of New Juneau residents two hundred years ago. They spent over five thousand leisure credit hours across two generations to procure the supplies and complete the bronze. They remind us that while we all work together to save our planet and increase our population, a time will come again when artists, musicians, writers, and performers will live among us—not just as a leisure pursuit, but as a way to rebuild our culture."

I smile and the children do too. I hold up my hands, palms out. "Thank you for listening to my story tonight. Divine peace."

"Divine grace with you." They thrust out their palms toward me.

As the group breaks up, I take Fez and Nairobi's hands and move back to where we left our tandem bikes. Eddie appears almost immediately, carrying our bags.

"Mercy, you really need to lighten this load." She balances my bag on the rack and heaves my book bag into my arms.

"I already left books behind."

"Well, maybe a few more? We have a long way to go."

"Exactly! What will I read?"

She shakes her head and moves over to her own bike to get ready to leave.

Reluctantly, I open my bag and select two volumes I've nearly memorized. "Fez, will you put these on the bench please?"

He takes the books, balancing them against his chest and bending his back to keep them steady as he walks over to the nearby bench.

A small hand slips into mine. "Don't be sad," Nairobi says. "Someone will find them and take them home to read. It'll make them happy, like a surprise gift." She smiles up at me.

"You know what, you're right. And the bonus"—I hold up my bag with one hand—"it really is much lighter."

Van and TJ join us, already on their bikes.

"Nice work," TJ says.

"Did you see Naveen?" I ask. "They didn't know it was TJ."

"Bloody Naveen." Van rubs at some bicycle grease on his hands, his fists flexing on Naveen's name.

TJ ignores him. "Yeah. Based on the questions they asked me, they're intent on finding us, but also the children. Let's go. It's another ten minutes to the dock. Stay spread out and follow me." He takes off as Fez and Nairobi settle behind me and Eddie. Van picks up the rear and we wind our way downhill toward the sea.

At TJ's shrill whistle, Cousteau darts out of the dark right next to TJ far in the lead. His head is forward, his ears back as he runs full out alongside his master's bike.

I'm on the brakes most of the way; the road is clear but steep. Motion activated streetlamps flick on and off as we travel, making me feel like a flashlight beam is tracking us from the heavens above. An Alaskan spring moon adds a silvery glow to the unlit forest to our right and casts steep shadows down the dark alleys and streets to our left. Soon we're maneuvering through the storage buildings and unadorned streets leading to the docks, quiet in the lengthening night.

My skin starts to prickle when the piers come into sight. Our boat sways in the distance, waiting. The dark water caressing its sides is tipped with white. A rough sea. In the last stretch, the warm air of the colony mixes with the cool breeze off the sea, creating pockets of chill. Just as we pass through a cold spot, TJ's bike disappears behind a large stack of shipping crates at the entrance to a pier.

Fez whimpers.

"It's okay." I try to keep my voice to a whisper. "We'll be there soon. And then we'll get to the Verge and start planning our rescue mission. We'll get my parents back."

"And our teacher too." Fez squeezes my waist harder.

"And your teacher too."

I brake around the final turn and my feet hit pavement wet with sea spray. We awkwardly dismount. Eddie grabs my bike and leans it against hers off to the side. Nairobi has both hands wrapped around TJ's leg, her eyes the size of saucers. It's a spooky place, and we're on the run. The children are keyed up, and it's starting to rub off on me.

I startle as I hear the screech of brakes behind me. I step out of the way just as Van slides to a halt and jumps off his bike.

TJ sinks down to ruffle Cousteau's neck. "Scout!" He gives his dog a hand signal. Cousteau eagerly slips silently into the shadows. Shadows that seem to grow and move now that I'm standing still.

My heart's pounding again. Adrenaline like icy tendrils spikes through my system, making goosebumps on my arms and legs. We're so close, but my instincts are tripping with fear.

"I'm scared." Fez clutches my hand and pulls me toward Nairobi and TJ.

"There's nothing to be scared of." Eddie looks over the tops of their heads. "Right?"

I open my mouth to answer.

"There's someone near." Fez stares off into the distance, concentrating on something I can't feel. "They...*He's* on a mission. He's worried he won't find us." He shivers and looks right at me.

"He's here!" Nairobi shouts, just as a huge dark hand reaches out of the shadows and smothers her scream.

MAY

May Forge knows what outsiders think when they first see her—they see the camouflage; amber hair glinting with gold, lavender-blue eyes, and the inconspicuous nova gem that blends perfectly into the tan skin of her forehead. Her gem's not black, like the praenex in New Juneau, because DNA's a tricky thing.

Why can't the praenex outside of the Verge see that? For all their clairvoyance, for all their gifts, they've failed to see a simple truth—that looks are only skin deep. That a gem of any pigment is still a gem. To judge a person by their packaging is like saying you understand the ocean because you know it's wet and large and salty, when really it's what's underneath that matters. May's fellow Couvies—the praenex of Vancouver Colony—understand this. They know that DNA keeps secrets.

May hurries along the cobblestone street toward the chapel, her dog Piper at her side. The urgent call came in nearly twenty minutes ago. She's late. The people she's rushing to meet aren't fooled by her pretty face—they know that what's inside her makes all the difference. She gathers her braids, coils them into her fist, and squeezes out more water into her towel. The wet mass has already darkened her shirt, which sticks to her hastily dried skin. Her feet squeak in soggy sandals. As she approaches the old strip mall, she pulls a pair of thin gloves from her pockets and slips them on. With a single command, she sends Piper to wait in a spot in the shade.

The metal door handle is cool in her grip, the early evening sun casting shadows into the surrounding concrete lot.

"May!" Her Aunt Ava rushes to catch up with her. "You're late, too." It's a statement, not a question.

"I was in the shower."

"I'm just in from the farm." Ava scrubs her dirty hands together and gives her shirt a sniff. "Ugh. Chickens."

May smiles and hands over her damp towel. "Here."

"*Merci.*" Ava takes the towel and rubs it across her face, then starts on her hands. "I saw Arson just as I was leaving. You two had a fight, *non?*" Ava looks at the pin on May's shirt.

"More a loud discussion, really. I can't stay here, you know. I've already done all I can to be what he wants me to be. I've taken his vocation. I live in your house. But I can't be this…this…*caged* forever."

May jerks back from the entrance and shakes out her arms. She paces away and then back, winding her hair into a tall, twisted knot she secures with a pin.

Ava watches her. "It's getting worse?"

May turns to her aunt—the woman who's been a mother to her for the last twelve years. She sees the empathy, the understanding in Ava's gentle lavender eyes, feels her aunt's support as their hands touch and hold.

"I feel like I'm going to jump out of my skin. I know it's all in my head, but sometimes I can't breathe. Or…more like I have to keep *moving* to breathe, as if my lungs can't do it alone—I need to walk into the wind to fill them." She hangs her head. "It sounds crazy."

"*Ma chèrie*, it doesn't! Not crazy. It sounds…compelling." Ava tips May's chin back up so their eyes meet. "He'll understand when the time comes. You have to be true to yourself. Come on." She pulls May's hand. "We'll be missed by now."

They enter the makeshift chapel quietly and give their eyes a moment to adjust to the dim light. The walls separating the store units were removed long ago to create one open space. Benches full of praying people fill the room, spreading end to end in unbroken rows.

"So many!" May whispers.

Ava moves to the last open bench. Usually May would do the same. She'd take the last seat at either end of the two queues before quietly reaching out to touch hands with her neighbor to join the linked group, but today she's filled with urgency—a kind of energy she can't quite control, like she's an old-fashioned timer wound all the way, just waiting for someone to let it go.

She moves around the edge of the group to the area at front where she knows she'll find her grandmother. A hundred or so people have silently linked hands in this human chain already. Her Grandma Dixie sits in the front, middle bench, her eyes closed, her hands clasped in her neighbors' on each side. Her face is drawn in concentration, her shoulders slumped. She's the silent center.

May looks around and finds a folding chair. She quietly lifts it and carries it to the space directly in front of her grandma, careful not to disturb her grandma's meditation. She knows that even the smallest interruptions will detract from the energy flowing through these souls into her grandma's gift, into her vision.

The vinyl seat cushion squeaks as she sits, but a quick look around tells her no one noticed. May closes her eyes and clears her mind of all the clutter she's been dealing with for the last few days—files away the fears, the insecurities, the doubts. Tries to even out the nervousness. Everything else can wait. This is about the call. Her grandma needs her now, needs May's energy to see her through whatever this vision will be.

With a final deep breath, she removes one of her gloves and places her hand on her grandma's knee.

"Oh, no!" May feels the wave of energy like a tsunami as it rolls through her fingers, but there's nothing she can do to stop it. Her hand is frozen in place.

Her grandma's gasp echoes through the congregation—a hundred quiet exclamations as the jolt of electricity passes through them like synapses firing in quick succession.

May grimaces and tries again to pull away, but in that instant her grandma's hand closes over hers in a vise-like grip. She opens glassy eyes to stare directly at May.

"They're coming. The ship." Grandma Dixie's whisper is meant only for May. The Culmination…it's about to begin."

May opens her mouth to ask what she means, but Grandma Dixie's eyes roll back in her head and she faints dead away, collapsing onto the bench.

9

VAN

I fully get that praenex are freaks about water. Their cities cling to the sea. They live on it, under it, like at the Hab, they sail on it, and of course they swim in it. The Creator knew what they'd need after the thaw in a world filled with water and built them with increased lung capacity. I've heard Pilgrims argue that this *improvement* is also suited for other low oxygen environments, like a ship in outer space. Like it proves that the Creator meant for them to leave Scorch.... If ye ask me, Pilgrims try too hard.

Aye, water's fine—I like it as much as the next bloke. I've always liked the views of the Hudson Ocean, a short trek east of Alberta Farms. Still, while I like the salt air, I'd much rather open my window to the scent of tilled earth, taste it on the air. Or watch smoky tendrils of fog weave through my folk's crops in the stillness just before dawn. Waves crash, but fog whispers.

So, Eddie was right when she guessed that I might bolt. I'm not proud of it, naw. I just hate sailing. Loathe. Despise. Detest, and greatly dislike it. Within a minute of hearing Mercy's plan, I had a list of loyal Terrans in my head who all could help me get to the Verge without even gazing at the water. But thank the Creator, Mercy's faith convinced me to stay. If I'd left, my friends would be facing this alone.

I'm frozen in place because of Nairobi. I dunno how to free her from the large sailor crouched behind her, smothering her scream. I'm about to act anyway when Cousteau appears out of the shadows. Tail wagging, he circles once and then sits next to the stranger holding Nairobi.

"Captain Souza!" Mercy breathes.

"Shhh! Quiet, my friends," the sailor whispers. Their voice is low and rough. Aged. The whites of their eyes flicker in the deepening darkness as they turn their head to look directly at Nairobi. Their gems nearly touch. "You're safe now, but soldiers are about." Souza pats Nairobi's shoulder and releases her.

As they straighten, I can make them out more clearly. They're older, maybe fifty. Though shorter than me—all praenex are—Souza's heavily muscled shoulders and chest strain beneath their uniform. It occurs to me that they're the sea-going equivalent of my da. It's the first time I've ever thought a praenex to be like my da, and I soften a little. Maybe I could trust this man.

"Captain, this is—"

"Introductions later, Cricket," Souza insists. "My crew've been waiting, we've got to hurry and get out of the port before full dark. Climb up," they say, motioning to the crate we've been hiding behind.

I notice what I hadn't before—the massive crate rests on a

truck used to move goods from ship to shore along the pier. The side toward us is open. Souza's already helping the kids in. Mercy and Eddie go next.

"When we get to the ship, you two carry the children," Souza instructs the women. "From a distance you will look larger, like men."

I peek around the corner of the crate and see that two other piers are active with folks transferring cargo in both directions.

"Ye usually work this late, do ye?"

Captain Souza smiles. They have one of those huge smiles that stretches from ear to ear, full of teeth. "No, but the soldiers don't know that."

"The other ships?"

"Let's just say I owe a lot of favors come the next scavenge run."

"Will they talk?"

Souza's smile vanishes. "We're a loyal group. Not a Pilgrim among us." They look TJ up and down. "Not 'til now anyways. Now let's go!"

TJ steps up into the crate, and I help Souza maneuver the truck up the pier. They pull and I push. It feels like forever, but finally we stop.

TJ's the first one out. Souza hands him a small wooden crate and points up the gangplank to the deck. "Go!"

The girls jump down and hold out their arms to the kids. Souza and I grab crates and TJ scoops Cousteau up under his arm. We follow the others aboard. My feet barely clear the gangplank before I hear the scrape of metal on wood as it's drawn up behind me.

We're on a sturdy sailboat, energy efficient and graceful, not that that will help. The deck is already rocking.

"Well done!" Captain Souza's grin is back. "Welcome aboard, friends."

I move clumsily to Mercy's side as she introduces us.

"Everyone, may I present my dear friend and philosopher, Captain Souza, *pronoms mascu.*"

Souza presses palms with everyone else, mussing the children's hair affectionately, patting a delighted Cousteau on the head, and then holds out his hand to me in a traditional sapiens gesture.

We shake. His white teeth gleam in contrast to his weathered ebony skin, a shade darker than my own, and the corners of my mouth turn up when I realize my teeth are probably gleaming like that too. His grip is strong and rough in mine—the hands of a working man, a man of action. We're alike, me and Souza: men who aren't afraid to sweat. I realize that holding his handshake steadies me as well as the rail might. He seems anchored to the deck, like part of his ship rather than a traveler on it.

"Let's get you all settled, shall we?" He releases my hand with a short nod. "You've a long journey ahead."

He turns to the crew awaiting orders nearby. "Take us out! I'll see to these passengers."

"Nice boat," I say, turning a wobbly circle in the cabin area assigned to us. Four bunks line one wall, the other holds a booth. The ceiling's so low, I have to crouch to keep from banging my head. A couple of extra wooden stools hang from pegs on the wall. I pull them down. "Much bigger than I thought it'd be."

"The *Dewey-Locke* is a three-mast gaff topsail schooner." Mercy takes us through a short history of sailing vessels.

I let her carry on, enjoying the story like it were just any old day, but when she pauses for air, I reach out, stopping an inch from touching her arm. It's time to get back on track. "Cricket."

She blushes and looks at the floor. "Sorry. I'm just…nervous…and worried, I guess."

"Aye, that's understandable for sure, but now we've got business. Everybody sit." I need to keep my mind off the motion of the ship, so I take them through a quick assessment of the Terran Army Corps. TAC has been my focus for a while now.

The kids seem torn between listening, playing with the dog and investigating every damned nook and cranny in the cabin.

"More reserves have been activated in the last two weeks than in the whole of my four years. Now it makes sense. TJ?"

"Activities at Tether Base and the Hub have been stable for years, but SATO Space Station has seen a big influx of resources as the shipbuilding accelerates."

"What's the status on the Pilgrim ships?" Eddie asks.

"The Pinta is just over half complete. She'll be deep-space worthy in about a year, then completely finished in eighteen months. With crew, she'll hold 40,000—the true lead ship."

"40,000!" Mercy's whispered exclamation echoes in the small space.

Cousteau whines and TJ quiets him with a hand signal. The kids move to stand on either side of my chair and I notice that someone set a bucket nearby. I grimace and push it aside.

Eddie lets out a long breath. "40,000 sounds like a lot, but it's not the largest. Legion intel shows the Santa Maria will carry 60,000 when she's ready in a few years." She rubs her gem and I know she's worried about how many of her folk will be onboard, or whether she'll be called to go with them.

I do the math. "Well now, that's just over 45% of the global population. It's more than reported in the public scripts."

"Yes," TJ agrees. "The public only gets the passenger capacity. SATO withheld the crew complement."

"Clever," Eddie says.

"Will so many go?" Mercy asks.

We're quiet before TJ answers, "The planet *is* dying…"

It's not a fact anyone can dispute. We have hope, but so far no one has been able to solve the ozone crisis and rebuild the ice caps. Folks like Mercy's parents have made it their life's work, and we're closer, but they need more time.

TJ exhales. "Based on what's happening now, I think forced conformance is a real possibility. It's one of the things on which I disagreed most with our parents. They're willing to do what's necessary to assure successful evacuation and colonization. I'm not."

Fez shuffles next to me. "Dr. Varela says the Pilgrims will give up if Dr. Adams can make a break-in."

"*Breakthrough*," Nairobi corrects him. "Dr. Varela's going to help." Her smile falls. "Except he can't now because we can't find him."

"We'll find him. Aye, and Mercy's folks too. So now, let me tell ye 'bout The Verge. This colony we're 'bout to visit? Well, she'll surprise ye. The folks there're nulls—that's the not-so-nice name some call 'em because their gem and novitas lobe are dormant-like—"

"Dormant? How can that be?" Fez interrupts.

Mercy clears her throat. "Remember the story I told you at the fountain? About Arturus's grandchild, Levi?"

The kids nod.

Mercy sits back in her seat. "After the Call, at the birth of the first praenex, Levi Samuelson began a large project. With their colony's leadership behind them, Levi increased their residential capacity to twice its original size.

"In 2117, about 6,000 nine-year-old praenex girls, about two percent of the first generation, expressed the desire to live by sapiens traditions. Brym Elder convinced the council to let them leave Fermont Compound—"

"Oh!" Nairobi interrupts. "We love stories of Brym Elder— we have many we'll share with you, too!"

"Ye do?" I ask.

"It's impolite to interrupt a story," Fez scolds her, his little brows scrunching around his gem in disapproval.

"I'm sorry," Nairobi says shyly, "please go on."

I like these kids. I grin at Mercy and wave her on, but it's Eddie who picks up the story.

"You see," Eddie continues, "from the first generation, those women made families with sapiens, their children marrying and having sapiens-novus children, over and over through the generations until they became natural born nulls—their praenex biology and gifts suppressed by years of genetic inbreeding with sapiens."

I scoff. "Ye make it sound so unclean."

"That's not my intention," Eddie insists, her nose high, her shoulders back. "It's simple biology."

"Fair enough." I let it go, distracted by a sudden wave of nausea. "So now the Verge is unique like. Their leaders play a role in our global government, they lead the Preservation Corps crews—the scavies, who saved everything we need, from nuts and bolts to bolts of fabric and hulkin' industrial machines. I've seen them myself, covered in ghostly tarps like hibernatin' beasts in gigantic warehouses east of the Verge's power fields. They're filled to burstin' with centuries of supplies, and provide valuable resources to our society.

"Some say the Couvies are more sapiens than the sapiens of Alberta Farms, though of course I beg to differ, but they do embrace culture, music, and art in ways farmers can't find the time for. Aye, ye'll see new and interestin' things. A right adventure for ye two."

I glance at Mercy and Eddie and realize they're another pair up for an adventure in the Verge. I wonder what they'll think of the Couvies' city and the folks themselves.

"And they'll help us find our teacher, and Mercy's parents?" Fez asks.

"They'll try. They're brave and loyal. They'll test us, our resolve, our dedication, but only because once they set a course, they're fearless in their actions."

"I've piloted many scavenge runs with them," TJ adds. "I've yet to see better soldiers in a crisis."

"You make them sound like warriors," Eddie observed. "And that's what we need now, I suppose."

We're quiet in the moment that follows. Worry returns to Mercy's eyes as she stares at a fixed point on the wall. Suddenly she startles.

"Divine grace!" Mercy grabs up her bag and begins pawing through it. "The photo. I almost forgot."

She pulls a small, framed photo from her bag. I expect her to show us, but she doesn't even look at the image before unclipping the tabs on the back and pulling apart the frame.

"Here! I knew it!" She holds up a small data chip. Her face animated. "*The most important thing!* My father hid it in the photo for me to find."

"What is it?" I ask.

"I don't know. Information, I guess."

TJ takes the small piece of plastic from her fingers and examines it. "Data most likely. We can review it at the Verge, but if it's so important he'd hide it like that, best to keep it hidden still." He hands it back to her.

Mercy carefully puts the chip back in the frame and flips the picture over. "He would save us all, if he were here." Her head hangs low over the photo in her lap. I wanna reassure her, but how? Touching her now seems too self-serving. Besides, keeping my stomach takes concentration.

Nairobi whimpers quietly, Fez circles around to comfort her. I throw Eddie a pleading look, spreading my hands as I shrug. I dunno how to comfort them all. Even Cousteau seems at a loss as he stretches, circles, and lies back down under TJ's chair.

"Right," Eddie says, "this is all too serious, but we've something completely different to achieve this hour as well. Gifts!"

The children raise their brows in question.

Mercy perks up. "That's right! You see, every conference, just before Addition Day, we give each other gifts," she explains to the kids. "Oh!" She snaps her comm open and spreads her palm wide to increase the size of the hologram display. "See this book?" She uses a finger to turn a few pages for the kids. "This is the gift Van gave me this year."

She turns to me and smiles. "It's wonderful, by the way. Thank you."

I smile back for a second, so relieved, then look at the floor. The book is sad, yet meaningful. I wasn't sure it was right.

"I'll start," Mercy offers, as she pulls open the flaps of her weathered bag and takes out three small onion paper scrolls.

I look at my friends and know their excitement is reflected in my own eyes. Mercy gives us visions—her glimpses of our futures.

She smiles shyly as she passes them out. "Here. My gift to you is, well, my *gift*," she giggles.

I'm relieved to see her relax and let some of the stress go. The boat tips and my momentary relief is forgotten as I swallow back a wave of bile inching up my throat.

"I'll go first!" TJ's already unrolling his tiny scroll. He reads the page, then looks up at Mercy, his eyes wide with joy. "A captain's chair?" he asks in disbelief. "On a starship?"

Mercy laughs again. "I didn't see the setting clearly, just the chair with you in it—older, more serious, but at the same time, happy."

TJ rises and moves to her. He places both hands on the sides of her head as she mirrors the gesture and their foreheads meet. "*Merci.*"

"*De rein.*"

I'm so jealous of their easy affection, I could crush something. Would that I could cross the cabin and touch her so casually.

A crinkling noise distracts me—Eddie unrolls her scroll as TJ sways back to his chair.

She reads it, and her hands fall to her lap. She sighs.

"What's it say?" I ask.

Eddie hands me the paper.

"*A red sash.*"

We all stare at Eddie, waiting. When finally she lifts her head, her eyes shine with unshed tears. "Thank you."

Mercy simply nods.

Nairobi tugs my sleeve. "What's it mean?" Everyone hears her whisper in this small space.

I lean toward the kids. "The Gran Bozan wears the red sash. It means Eddie will lead the Legion one day."

"Oh..." They both look at Eddie, awe clear in their tiny faces.

"We don't have *bozans* in Terra Faire," Nairobi says.

"And now we can say we know the president of the bozans!" Fez adds.

"Careful now," I warn them, "We don't want her to start havin' delusions of grandeur."

"Thanks, Van." Eddie rolls her eyes and gestures to my scroll. "What's yours?"

I'm about to answer when TJ's comm buzzes. We all stare at him until he flips it open to check. "It's nothing," he says, ignoring the caller again.

"That's gettin'…" I can't find the right words.

"Annoying?" Eddie offers. "Frustrating?"

"Worrisome?" Mercy suggests.

"Okay!" TJ holds up a hand in surrender. "It's father, and I don't want to deal with him right now. Van, open your gift!"

Slowly I roll the page open to see the words "*three sons.*" It's more than I can handle. I look at Mercy. She's angled away, shy-like. *With you?* I wanna ask, but it's too much. I know I have to make a joke or everything will be too much. I aim my best roguish smile at her. "Three sons will make a fine little army—nothin' to my da's, but it's a start."

She blushes and TJ and Eddie laugh, breaking the tension. The kids giggle.

"I'm sorry we've nothing to gift you," Mercy tells them.

"Oh, but we do." I pull my gifts from a pouch in my bag. "My gifts for Eddie and TJ are enough for everyone." I throw a pouch to TJ.

"Dried apples?" he asks.

"Pears."

"Pears? Really?"

I nod. "And for you, Sister Eddie...." She snatches the pouch I throw from midair. "Yer favorite."

Eddie grins. "Strawberries. Thank you."

"I'm sorry they can't be fresh—"

She crunches on a handful of dried berries. When she sees us staring, she reluctantly empties the pouch onto the table next to TJ's dried pears.

We bow our heads in silent prayer, then devour the snacks.

"I'm next," Eddie says around a mouthful of strawberries.

She hands me a small package, about the size of my hand. I undo the laces and fold back the fabric to reveal a small, lacquered world map. "Wow."

"It's Old Earth, before the melt," she clarifies. "I thought you'd enjoy seeing it without the great storm—plus all that extra land. It came in through a scavie tray. A friend set it aside for me. She estimated circa 1982."

"Aye, the Golden Years, grand. Thank ye."

"You're welcome. And for you." She tosses her brother a cube.

TJ lifts the lid and presses a button on the device inside. Instantly the ceiling is covered with an image of the night sky.

"It's a star chart." TJ taps commands into the device as the image zooms in, refocuses, swings about.

My stomach flips and my head reels from the swirling motion. I once again feel the methodical sway of the ship that I've been trying so hard to ignore.

"Maybe you should turn it off for now—Van's going green." Eddie's voice carries little sympathy.

TJ shuts it down. "Thanks, and sorry, man."

"No harm done." I swallow down the hiccup of acid in my throat.

"And for you…." Eddie turns to Mercy beside her on the bench. She lifts Mercy's ponytail and wraps a long blue strip of soft fabric around the base before tyin' it underneath.

"How do I look?" Mercy asks, swiveling her head back and forth to move her dark copper hair.

I swallow hard. Clear my throat. Try to find words.

Eddie thumps me on the back. "Swallow your tongue?"

Nairobi saves me. "It's beautiful. I hope I'm as pretty as you when I'm an adult."

And just like that, the joy drains from the room. I can't look Mercy in the eye again. Technically she's not an adult. If she were, well, things would be different now for sure.

Nairobi seems to know immediately that she said something wrong. She pulls on my hand and shakes her head as if to say, *what did I do?* I smile at her and squeeze her hand. "Nothin', lass."

"My turn." TJ opens his bag and hands Mercy a pouch. "It's amazing the sapiens' interest in jewelry. We're always finding more at every scavenge."

Mercy holds up the long silver necklace. "It's amazing," she sighs. "This shape?"

"It's an *icicle*," TJ explains. "Water frozen in animation as it drips from a structure, like a building, or a tree."

Mercy spins the pendant and the tiny diamond and blue stones cast wobbly rainbows around the room.

I squeeze my eyes closed, but it doesn't calm my gut one bit.

"I love it, thank you." When she takes his hand across the table and presses it to her cheek, I look away.

Jealously is ridiculous and doesn't help my current state of nausea either. TJ laughs when I sigh in disgust.

"And for you, sister mine, this...." The statue he hands Eddie is pure white marble—cold stone that looks fluid and alive.

Eddie reaches for it, cradling it in her palm.

"It's a mother and child," Nairobi offers, leaning in for a better look.

"It's the Madonna and child, from the Old Earth Bible," Mercy corrects her.

Eddie's silent. For the second time today, she seems overwhelmed by a gift.

"If you don't like it—"

"No, no!" She interrupts TJ and shakes herself. "It's not that, it's just—I've got to tell you all something that's going to upset you."

"The secret you've been keeping?" Mercy asks.

I have no idea what they're talking about and I'm not sure my spongy, seasick brain can handle much more.

"Yes." Eddie scoots out of the booth and stands, feet braced on the swaying deck. She lifts the hem at her waist and hooks a thumb into her waistband to reveal a stretch of skin from hip to bellybutton. A small bandage rests in the middle of a large angry bruise—a surgical site, I realize.

"By God!" My head smacks the ceiling as I stand. "Damn!" I rub my head.

"Spherans don't approve of swearing," Fez says. "Do it again please."

Nairobi elbows him in the ribs.

Eddie covers her skin and sits. "It's not as bad as it looks—not painful, I mean. And it was my choice."

"What was?" TJ's voice is ice. His hands are fisted on the table and a muscle ticks in his clenched jaw. I know that look well. He's trying not to break something. "What've they done to you?"

Eddie exhales a long breath. "Since my birth, Bozan Kahinu has said that I'm different. It seemed obvious at first—I'm the only albino praenex ever born—but last year, the tests made everything clear." She clears her throat. "My blood has a property unseen in other praenex. It inhibits the buildup of toxins that cause the cancer, the Trade, that kills us all."

She's quiet. Waiting for us to catch up.

"Your blood's a cure?" Mercy asks.

"Not directly—at least not yet. For now, the doctors believe my natural resistance to the Trade is a genetically transferable mutation only.... My children'll be immune." She swallows. "*Are* immune."

"What?" I sit back down, harder than I mean to, and the stool wobbles under my weight. I'm not sure if I'm swaying or the boat is, but everything seems to be moving. "Children? When did this happen?"

"How many?" TJ asks. He glances around at our stunned

faces and clarifies. "How many surrogates?"

Eddie stares at her lap. She closes her eyes then slowly raises her head to answer her brother. "48 surrogates, 29 healthy babies so far. All being raised by two parents, in healthy homes throughout the Legion Enclave."

Mercy shakes her head. "Egg donation doesn't cause that kind of injury. It's not even an external procedure. What happened?"

Eddie picks at her skirt. "Hyperstimulation. My ovary got all twisted up. There were some complications, but I'm fine now. And I'm done…for a while, anyway."

"Or just done, if that's what you want," TJ says, the vein on his forehead pulsing.

The ship lurches and so does my stomach.

"I'm sorry you were hurt," Fez says, pushing forward to stand eye to eye with Eddie where she sits. "But now I know you'll cure us."

"I don't see how." Eddie places a hand over his on the table. Her smile, though weak, betrays an inner strength.

"We have the cancer," Fez says. "The disease you call the Trade, Nairobi and I, like many Spheran children, have it."

I'm too stunned to move. "Naw, that can't be right. Yer kids!"

The ship lists suddenly and I'm overwhelmed with sickness, both mental and physical. I look closer at the two young faces and see what I hadn't noticed before—the pale edges bleeding into their dark gems, so tiny in their little faces. A lump rises in my throat. I swallow hard, fight it down.

"How can this be?" Mercy asks. "Praenex live long lives—50

or 60 years even—and some nulls even longer."

"How can ye call that long?" We've had this argument before, and I never win. "At its height, sapiens life expectancy reached 92 years."

"That was only Japanese women," Mercy argues, then grimaces when I glower at her.

"Regardless, 60 years isn't enough."

Eddie clears her throat. "It's the Creator's work, Van, that's why we call it the *Trade*. The Creator gave us fast growth, strength, our gifts, and robust immunity—we don't suffer from your colds and flus. We don't need your immunizations. We all know how we'll die, and once the Trade appears, we even know roughly when. It's as the Divine intends."

"Then how do these kids get sick so young?"

Nairobi answers. "We're opposite to the nulls Bozan LeRoux described. Our ancestors didn't breed with sapiens—"

"You mean you practiced the *aeterna-sui rituali*?" Eddie asked.

Nairobi frowns. "Well, some did, yes, but that's not what I meant. You see, our first generation included *male* praenex. In the Sphere, we're all praenex."

"That's incredible," Mercy whispers, then turns to Eddie. "Did you know about this?"

She shakes her head. "I did not."

My stomach does a little flip. I try to focus on the conversation. They're talking about a sphere. What *sphere*? First generation male praenex? Do I know anything about all of this? It's getting harder for me to follow anything, dizzy as I am. Fresh air above deck might help. Before I can decide, Fez continues.

"Our ancestors made a mistake and now we're in danger." Fez moves closer to Eddie. "Dr. Varela thinks in 50 years our people will die of the cancer before they can have babies. Our community will fade away. Unless you can save us."

It's too much now—the ship's rocking, the kids' cancer, Eddie's legion of babies, raised by others. With the next pitch of the ship, I'm out the doors and up the steps. My vision wavers as I reach the side. Seawater sprays my face, but I don't care. With one last lurch, my stomach empties into the dark blue ocean.

CRANE ELDER

In the past...
July 19, 2108; 593 years ago
Fermont Compound, Quebec, UCA

The persistent buzz of Crane's comm woke her from a deep sleep. She shivered against the cold air that never seemed to leave the cement walls of the massive 1970s compound in which she lived and worked. Originally designed as a windbreak against seven months of ruthless Canadian winter, the structure now served as a haven from an equally ruthless Scorch.

Crane came awake fast and reached for her device, but when the chill came again, she knew there was trouble. Would this be the call she was dreading...was her husband dead? Killed in action some six thousand kilometers away in a land she'd never seen?

She cleared her throat. "Elder."

"Where is Phoebe O'Dell, Nurse Elder?" Dr. Laurens's voice held her trademark annoyance.

"Excuse me?"

"She had an early appointment this morning and she's not here."

"Oh, um…" It wasn't about her husband. Crane ran a hand through her hair, trying to readjust her thoughts. "Did you check her quarters?" She shuffled to her cinderblock-cell-of-a-closet.

Dr. Laurens's long exhale ruffled through the comm receiver. "Of course. So, you don't know where she is?"

"No, but I'll be ready in five minutes. I'll find her." She disconnected without saying goodbye.

It wasn't the first time Crane had been roused from bed to search for her patient. Phoebe sometimes lost track of time and Crane would find her outside, curled up in a hammock with a book, her comm left behind in her room, or singing quietly under a shade tree in the courtyard garden. But already this time felt different, wrong somehow.

Just yesterday, Crane had submitted a Potentially Significant Incident, a PSI, predicting a 28-week gestation period for the novus humans, a full twelve weeks earlier than sapiens pregnancies. Dr. Laurens had immediately rejected the PSI, but Crane's peer rating skyrocketed anyway, pushing her into the top twenty for the first time. Maybe that was why Dr. Laurens was so testy this morning.

Crane was dressed and ready in under five minutes, an edge of panic pushing her faster. What if she'd been right and Phoebe was about to give birth? She was rushing to leave when she accidentally smacked her forearm on the counter's edge.

"Ouch!" She rubbed the red welt. Of course she'd hit the exact site of her surgical implant. It was still sore. "Wait a minute…." She smiled up at the ceiling tiles. "If this works, I will never complain again about this God-forsaken invasion of privacy!"

She crossed to her tablet and pulled up the ID implant tracking software. "Computer, locate Phoebe O'Dell."

The computer churned for a moment. "Phoebe O'Dell is out of transmission range."

An icy sensation prickled across Crane's cheeks. "At which location did she exceed transmission range?"

"Phoebe O'Dell was last recorded at checkpoint eight."

"At what time?"

"At 06:00 today."

Crane scooped up her tablet and flipped open her comm just as her nephew, Jon, emerged from the guest bedroom, his hair sleep-rumpled.

"What's wrong, *Tante*?" He rubbed his eyes and stretched.

She'd forgotten he was visiting. What kind of aunt was she? "Jon, oh…I nearly forgot. Never mind, you can help!"

"What?"

"Phoebe, my patient you met yesterday, is missing. She passed through Eight more than three hours ago. She's close to her date, Jon, I can feel it."

Jon was fully awake by then, already reaching for his boots. "I'll get dressed and follow you."

"I feel terrible. It's your vacation—you'll want to sleep in."

"What does that matter? Go!" He waved her to the door as he ran back into his room.

Crane dialed security as she ran. The long halls of *Le Mur*, as the locals called the behemoth of a building, were nearly empty. It was half a kilometer inside from her apartment to gate eight. By the time she reached the checkpoint, a small group of soldiers were already there, taking orders and spreading out into the unpopulated area outside Eight. They had some of Phoebe's clothes for the dogs to sniff, and some were already straining at the leash to get started.

Crane answered a lieutenant's questions but got no answers to any of her own. She stepped back from the group, noticing for the first time how warm it was compared to her apartment. The air was thick with the moisture of a coming storm. She took off her hoodie and tied it around her waist. None of the soldiers approached her. It was clear they weren't interested in her civilian opinion. She closed her eyes and thought of Phoebe, alone outside the compound's walls.

"If I were Phoebe, where would I go?" She inhaled deeply and blew out a long breath. The air was fragrant with a mix of melted tundra, coming rain, and human habitation. Phoebe would've hated the last part. "If I were Phoebe O'Dell, West Virginian mountain girl, nature lover, and God's faithful servant, where would I go?"

She opened her eyes and immediately focused on the lonely road, still covered with mist in places, winding its way up the northwest hill like a black velvet ribbon sinking into a cushion of verdant foliage.

"Of course!" She looked around, but all the soldiers were gone. She dialed her comm.

"Did you find her?" Jon asked.

"No, but I think I know where she went. You know the old road leading north into the hills?

"Rue de Sommet."

"Yes! I think she's gone up the mountain. I'm going to head that way now."

"I'm only a few minutes behind you. Wait for me."

"No, I'll jog, you run. You'll catch up. Stop for a med kit, I didn't think to bring one."

"Okay."

"And a blanket. Maybe two."

"Okay."

"And—"

"*Tante*, go! I've got this. Phoebe needs you."

"Thanks, Jon." She hung up and started to run.

Jon Elder Jr. was her only nephew. At fourteen, he'd already earned a place at a prestigious science academy in Quebec. As she pushed herself faster up the gentle slope, her calves already burning, Crane thanked God that he still came to visit sometimes. Jon was a competent kid, and a strong athlete, he'd follow, and he'd bring what she needed.

"Phoebe?" She called as she ran. At the point where the grade pitched higher, she came to a small washout from recent rains. She looked across the gap at a bright patch of red color on the other side. Blood had pooled on the gravel and started trickling down the rough embankment in a small line of rainwater like an earthy vein. She followed the trail upward and saw another splotch of red, and another, leading away up the road.

"Phoebe!"

Crane picked her way down the crevice quickly, not caring as she scratched her palms and fingertips on the wet stones. Her boots dug into the mud and her belly scraped the jagged pavement as she pulled herself over the other side.

"Phoebe! Where are you?" Crane stopped when she heard a chuffing sound.

"Here! I'm here!" Phoebe's high voice came clearly through the mist.

Relief rushed through Crane. She rounded the corner just as a fine drizzle started to fall. When she saw what lay ahead, her panic returned.

Phoebe sat in the wet grass, her knees high, her hair and skin damp as she huffed and panted. Her labor had begun. Blood and mucus pooled on the ground between her feet before trickling away in a slimy rivulet down the hill.

"Phoebe!" Crane scrambled the last few meters and sank to her knees at Phoebe's side. She rubbed the mud from her hands before touching Phoebe's face. "How long?"

Phoebe grimaced. "I dunno. A few hours maybe? I'm so sorry—"

"It's okay. How many minutes between contractions?"

"'Bout two, I think." Phoebe moaned as another contraction ripped through her.

"Don't push! Let me check you. Are you hurt?"

"No. I'm so sorry, Mother Crane. I just wanted some fresh air, a little exercise—I had this burst of energy all of a sudden."

"Why didn't you take someone with you?"

"It was so early. Everyone was still sleepin', I didn't wanna be a bother. I felt fine 'til…it musta been that last climb. My belly hit the edge and when I stood again, my water broke. I woulda called but I forgot my comm. I'm so sorry."

"Hush, now, it's alright." Crane did a quick exam. "You're ready. You can push with the next contraction, but I've got to call it in."

Shifting back on her haunches, she dialed Jon.

"Did you find her?" His voice was breathy, like he was running.

"Yes. Come straight up. We're just to the other side of the washout. Can you call Security and tell them?"

"On it."

Crane hung up and texted Dr. Laurens, excited, and little smug—the first novus human was about to be born, just as she'd predicted.

Somehow Crane knew it would be Phoebe, she just *knew*. She'd been there when Phoebe got moved to the top of the high-risk list. Through it all, Phoebe'd been so serene, so reassuring to all of them, instead of the other way around. She'd pat Crane's hand and say in that sweet southern voice, "Everything's gonna work out, now don't you worry."

She was doing it even now.

"Now don't you go worryin' none, Mother Crane," Phoebe smiled up at her through messy hair damp with sweat and rain. "God's got a plan for this one, yes ma'am. Ain't nothin' gonna get in the way of this sweet child and all the Almighty's got planned for her. Nuh uh."

She squeezed Crane's hand, her grip growing stronger as she pushed and chuffed to bring her baby into the world—the *new* world, the world of the praenex.

"*Tante* Crane! Ms. Phoebe!" Jon slid to a halt beside Crane just as a new contraction started and Phoebe groaned loudly. He shoved the med kit and one blanket at Crane and quickly unwrapped a second blanket for Phoebe, but instead of covering her, he hugged it to himself awkwardly.

Crane slid her blanket under Phoebe's feet. "Lift her up!"

Jon stared at Phoebe's frail and half naked body for a second, and then rolled his shoulders, set his teeth, and slid his arms under her to lift. Crane shoved the cloth underneath, moved back into position and prepared the other supplies.

Jon unfolded his blanket and gently spread it over Phoebe's chest and arms. He moved slowly, tentatively, like Phoebe might break if he went too fast. "What else can I do?"

Crane glanced up at him. One of his hands rested on Phoebe's shoulder, the other bunched in a fist on his thigh. His hair was a dripping blond mess and his lips had started to turn purple despite the warm temperature. "Pray, Jon. You can pray."

He nodded, bent his head, and scrunched his eyes closed.

Phoebe exhaled loudly. "Hold my hand, Jon?"

Crane saw a blush rise on her nephew's pale face, but he took Phoebe's hand and let her squeeze his as she pushed.

A few moments passed like that—the three of them bracing through the contractions.

"Here's the head. You're doing great, Phoebe! One more push now."

The rain picked up to a gentle patter. Thunder rumbled far away over the mountains. With a final push, the baby girl arrived in silence. Crane checked her quickly—she was breathing easily and her skin was a satisfying pink. She held the healthy, squirming newborn in her arms, wholly unprepared for the reality of this little soul despite the weeks of waiting, despite dozens of ultrasounds and so many exams.

"Is she okay? Is my baby girl alright?" Phoebe tried to sit up, but only managed to lean on one elbow.

"She's amazing." Crane held the baby up for Phoebe to see as she cleaned the infant's face and dealt with the cord.

"My God," Jon whispered. He stared at the baby's unfamiliar facial feature for the first time. The nova between the newborn's brows had a sheen and depth of color they could only have guessed at from the ultrasounds. "It's like a perfect gem."

The textured black square stood on its corner right between the baby's delicate eyebrows. At the sound of Jon's voice, the baby opened her eyes.

They all gasped. The infant's eyes were a vibrant shade of amethyst, unlike anything Crane had seen before.

"Beautiful girl," Phoebe crooned and held out her arms. "Let me hold'er, please."

Crane snuggled the baby into Phoebe's arms and relaxed when the quiet baby exhaled a huge sigh.

Jon laughed and moved in closer, hugging Phoebe's shoulders, using his body to shelter the pair from the rain. "She's more…so much more than I expected." He looked up at Crane with wonder in his eyes. "I can't explain it. She's…" He shrugged and laughed again. Thunder rumbled, closer this time. "She's…"

"She's ours, the world's," Crane said.

Jon smiled. "Yeah, but also *mine*. I can't explain it…. Somehow, she's *mine*. I feel it here." He pressed a fist to his heart. "I don't understand…. I just *feel* it."

Phoebe grinned and wiped at the rain rolling down her face. "Well, ain't that somethin'?" She cooed at her baby as they stared at each other, and then she offered a finger for her daughter to grasp.

The newborn took hold and sighed again.

"What a wonder." Phoebe shook her finger and the baby

gurgled in delight. "With you this world is a cup just filled to the brim. Gonna run over with gifts from God. I think that's what I'll call 'er, Mother Crane. Like brim, but with a 'y' to make her unique."

Crane nodded in agreement, a single tear tracking down her cheek, lost in the rainwater. *Brym.* The name was perfect.

Phoebe rocked back and forth. She lifted her chin, and as Crane had seen her do so many times before, she began to sing.

"I know dark clouds will gather 'round me
I know my way is rough and steep
But golden fields lie just before me
Where God's redeemed shall have their sleep."

The baby watched her mother with a singular intensity, as if she understood the poignant words. Phoebe sang on, the old-fashioned folk song accompanied by the tinkle of rain upon leaves and stones, and an occasional bass of thunder growling in the distance.

"I'm going home to see my mother
And all my loved ones who've gone on
I'm only going over Jordan
I'm only going over home."

The last sweet note hung in the air. Phoebe pulled her baby close and planted a soft kiss on her forehead. "You take care of her now, Mother Crane. For she's somethin' precious to this world and ain't nobody I trust better'n you to see she gets loved."

Phoebe held the baby out and Crane reached for her automatically, confused by Phoebe's words.

The instant the baby left her arms, Phoebe collapsed back in a violent spasm.

Jon caught her just before her head hit the ground. "What's happening?"

"She's having a seizure! Try to hold her." Crane put the bundled baby down on the corner of the blanket and turned back quickly, but Phoebe'd already gone completely limp. She stared blankly up into the clouds.

"*Tante!*" Jon shook Phoebe by the shoulders. Rain ran off his head and into Phoebe's slack mouth.

"Jon, take the baby. Keep her dry!" Crane waited until Jon released Phoebe's upper body and scrambled over to pick up Brym. She positioned herself at Phoebe's side and checked for a pulse. She found nothing. She started CPR and mouth-to-mouth. Her knees sunk in the mud. Blood from the birth ran together with the rain to fill in the dips around her knees. Crane ignored everything.

Moments passed inside the rhythm of compressions and breaths. One small part of Crane's mind tracked Jon's quiet sobs—rocked back and forth with him as he swayed in sorrow, clutching the baby close to his neck. She kept up the compressions, kept pushing her breath into Phoebe's lungs, praying for a miracle, but she knew in her heart that Phoebe was gone.

Crane checked again for a pulse, found nothing. Her hands shook as she gathered Phoebe's hands and kissed them, pressing them one last time to her cheek before resting them across

Phoebe's heart. For a minute she and Jon sat in silence and allowed their grief to run free. Then Crane angrily wiped her tears and swallowed against the lump in her throat. "God damn it! Why?"

Jon sat back in the grass, weeping openly now. He curled his shoulders to shield the baby from the diminishing rain.

Crane shook her head. "It must have been the aneurysm. There was nothing I could do." She straightened Phoebe's legs and covered her with the blanket, and then she moved around to sit beside Jon. Her bloody boots stirred the wet grass, filling the air with the smell of summer rain and fresh forest—a smell that Phoebe would have called "God's perfume." The thought pushed a smile through Crane's grief, and she wrapped her arms around her nephew as she looked down into the baby's face.

Brym gazed up at her and Crane's own sadness reflected in the baby's eyes.

…Ain't nobody I trust better'n you to see she gets loved.

Those were Phoebe's last words. That was it—the only moment Brym would have with her mother. Just like that, Brym Phoebe O'Dell became the first Homo sapiens novus ever born, and the first orphaned.

10
MERCY

Even on the water, it's too warm. Rising from my morning prayers, I stretch my legs and watch as we approach the bay, dark and cruel with rocks. What would it have been like in its natural state before the melt, covered in snow and ice? From the ship, the deep etched passage looks like the yawning mouth of a great rocky beast trying to cool itself by swallowing the ocean. I can sympathize.

What can possibly happen next? In a few days, my world has utterly transformed. I can feel the shift. I am living history. I sense more than hear Captain Souza approach. He leans next to me, his elbow on the rail.

"*We sail within a vast sphere, ever drifting in uncertainty, driven from end to end.*"

"Thomas Aquinas?" I guess.

A grin splits his face, white teeth flashing. He shakes his head. "Pascal."

It's our old game of *name that quote*, usually conducted in a hushed corner of the library, or over a noisy dinner table, rather than the deck of a ship. It reminds me that my parents' trust—my trust—of this man runs deep.

He walks around me, silhouetted against the approaching cliffs. The sun behind him rings his wiry black hair like a halo, his circular insignia dull in shadow. "Searching for pirates, Mercy Adams?"

"Oh, wouldn't that be a treat," I sigh.

"And who would you wish for? Blackbeard? Jack Sparrow?"

"My favorite pirate?"

He nods.

"The most successful one of all, of course. Hsi Kai commanded over a thousand ships, controlling the South China Sea for years. It took the combined forces of China and Portugal to stop Kai, and even then it wasn't in battle."

"No?"

"The emperor of China offered an alternative."

"Prison?"

I shake my head. "Retirement. He allowed Kai to keep her treasure and live quietly until the end of her natural life."

Souza's smile flashes, but quickly disappears. "You like her because she was a woman in a man's world."

I turn to face him. "I like her because in her retirement from crime, she found a way to save the 70,000 people who served with her. A nonviolent solution for violent souls."

Captain Souza chuckles, but when he meets my eyes, a softer expression replaces the mirth. "What troubles you, Mercy Adams, is that for once the answers lie ahead, instead of behind in some history lesson, yes?"

I look away. If this friend of my parents, this philosopher I've sailed with since I could stand on deck can sense this about me, I'm fooling no one else. Still, I can't find the words to answer.

"Your parents'll be alright, Cricket. Coral's too kind to leave this life, and Parker…well, Parker's too stubborn. Whatever task the Creator has put before you, the Creator and this young man, you'll see it through and find them. You'll see."

His hand on my shoulder helps me find the words. "What if I fail?"

"You must have faith."

I blow out a breath and run my fingers through my hair, accidentally loosening it to the wind. I wrestle it back into a ponytail as I mumble, the elastic clenched in my teeth, "Faith?" My hair secure, I try to explain. "I feel like all I *have* is faith. Nothing else. No plan. No path except the next step before my feet. How can I know what's right, what's real, with no proof that each step forward has led in the right direction, instead of farther down the wrong path?"

Captain Souza doesn't answer right away. I can see my words, my question, reverberating in his head. Suddenly his eyes shift to capture mine. "*Faith is different from proof; the latter is human, the former is a Gift from God.*" He smiles, tamer this time.

"More Pascal?"

He nods. "Come, it's time to take the next step."

As he walks away, Eddie and Van emerge from below deck. Van yawns and rubs his face, then leans down to greet the children where they sit tying sailor's knots. He seems better, whether it was the vomiting (again) or the medicine, I don't know, but his smiling expression looks happy, if a little taut. His bandage has been changed too. I think he must have slept well enough. The ball of anxiety in my stomach eases just an inch.

Last night it was decided that Eddie and TJ would alternate rem cycles so that at least one LeRoux is always awake. Eddie forced herself into an early rem—another skill I don't possess. I'm hardwired praenex, in deep rem 12 hours and up for 36. I have little control over sleep.

Eddie and Van have awakened just in time to dock at Vancouver Colony. The boat's auxiliary motor roared to life only moments ago. While Van's clearly sleepy, Eddie appears entirely too alert. It's her first time here, too. Van and TJ know the Verge well, but Eddie joins me in uncertainty.

"Good morning," I call.

Her eyes zero in on me as she strides across the deck, her skirts billowing, her white-blonde hair catching bits of wind.

"Good grace, but you're a fright this morning, Eddie." I take an involuntary step back as she reaches me.

She doesn't answer me. Her too-knowing eyes take me in, top to bottom, before she focuses on the approaching marina. When she looks at me again, I wonder if she sees how small I truly am, how ill equipped I am for any of this, but when she speaks it's not about me at all.

"I sense…" She lifts her nose, closes her eyes and inhales, as if scenting something in the salty air. "Deception. Trepidation. Reluctance. Annoyance—"

"Okay!" I nudge her arm. "I get it. We're not exactly welcome here."

TJ joins us, bouncing on his heels, pulling at his cuffs and shirt tail. "How do I look?" he asks me, brushing the front of his shirt.

"What's wrong with you?" Eddie asks. "You're acting like… like you're here to meet a date or something."

He rolls his eyes at her.

"*Are* you here to meet someone?" I ask.

TJ huffs and shakes his head. "Listen to me." He grabs Eddie's shoulders and turns her to face him. "These people have odd ways, but they're often smarter and wiser than you'd expect. Don't"—he tilts his head toward her for emphasis—"*don't* try to force your will. Trust them. Trust me. That's all I can say."

"What do you mean by that?" Eddie shakes loose from his grip and raises a hand in the air for emphasis. "I'm not a child, TJ. I know how to be diplomatic." She flicks his gem before storming off.

TJ scoffs and rubs his gem. "Just…don't be too much, well, *you*!" he shouts after her.

"And you." TJ smiles at me. "You be exactly who you are. And keep an eye on her." He grabs my head in a fierce grip and crushes a kiss to my forehead.

I shove him away, exasperated by his mood swings. "Why're you saying all this? Why don't *you* keep an eye on her?" My voice hitches up an octave. I clear my throat.

"I've already said too much."

"You haven't said anything!" I screech, but he's already turned away, answering Captain Souza's call to help secure the last sails.

The small pier is nearly empty when we arrive. A few men, bearded and dressed in rugged clothing, wait to help the schooner's crew secure the ship. A slender person—barely more than a teen—waits for us, a furry white dog at their side. Their hair, an amber mass of loose coils and numerous rope-like braids, whips in the wind around a scornful face with suspicious eyes. Their clothes are an odd mix of styles and colors, patched and inconsistent, yet somehow beautiful at the same time. They raise an odd-looking hand in greeting as the ramp is lowered to the pier, and I realize they're wearing gloves.

TJ and Van push past us with the children and Cousteau close on their heels. "Good luck!" Van shouts to me, and they're down the ramp. That's all I get by way of greeting from him this morning. Somehow it's worse than nothing.

"May!" TJ shouts as he rushes toward the stranger. He's moving so fast that at first I think he's going to run right into them, but he suddenly pulls up short. A heartbeat passes, and he gives them a silly flourishing bow. At that crazy angle, he's almost pushed off balance into the water by the dogs jumping over each other in greeting, yipping with joy.

The stranger's serious scowl transforms into a delighted grin, and in that moment, their true beauty is glowingly apparent. They bow back and with a high whistle, send the dogs racing off to the beach.

TJ says something in a foreign language, grabs them by the shoulders and kisses each of their cheeks. The stranger chokes back a laugh as they answer in the same language.

"More Portuguese?" I ask Eddie.

"French. We're in the Verge, after all."

TJ speaks some more and the woman finally does laugh—a deep, confident sound—then gives him a little shove as he passes. Further up the pier I notice a group of young people playing some kind of sport in the small beach area down by the marina. Children watch from a low stone wall. Behind them a lonely marina building bears a worn and listing banner. Though the letters are bleached from years of neglect in the weather and sun, I can just make out the words. *Happy Addition Day.* Not for the first time I feel a pinch in my gem. What a joke we've all become.

Further upriver I can just make out the shape of the hydroelectric dam that powers the Verge. With my eyes on it, for just a moment, I can feel the deep bass hum of the machinery like an organ of Scorch, pumping life into the village it supports.

On the pier Van introduces the children and shakes the woman's hand. I'm relieved he doesn't kiss their cheeks like TJ did. I let out the long breath I've been holding. Van shoves his packs more securely behind him and grabs the children's hands to race after TJ. The people on the beach shout a welcome as they approach—old friends reunited.

"Let's go." Eddie pulls my hand.

I turn to Captain Souza, waiting to say goodbye.

"Keep safe, Mercy Adams," he says as we touch palms, "and may your soul feel the glory."

"May the Creator bless your next journey, Captain."

At a hiss from Eddie, waiting on the pier, I nimbly descend

the ramp and approach the stranger, my best friend by my side.

They don't offer their hands. "Welcome to the Verge," they say, their voice rich and a little raspy like singers of old. On their lapel they wear the neutral insignia, the circle-rocket pin like mine and Eddie's. I'd heard all nulls are Terrans. I wonder what else I've heard wrong. They lower their sunglasses to peer at us, revealing eyes the bluest shade of violet I've ever seen, almost sapiens in color. Their gem is barely noticeable—just a bump on their tan face.

"I'm Deputy Forge, *pronoms fem*. I'll be taking you up to your transport." She pops the chewing gum in her mouth, pushes her glasses back up and points toward the cliff wall some distance off from the marina. A steep set of weathered steps is carved in the rock, numerous switchbacks working up the wall.

"We're climbing that?"

Eddie clears her throat and gives my hand a little squeeze. "I'm Bozan LeRoux and this is Dr. Mercy Adams, *pronoms fem*. We're pleased to meet you." Her voice is the trained, authoritative one she learned from the Legion. I resist the urge to rub my head as a wave of cold intimidation pushes its way through my gem.

Deputy Forge's eyebrows shoot up at the mention of Eddie's new title—so the people here weren't *that* well-informed—and her stance wavers slightly as she studies Eddie's pale skin and graceful figure. I watch the two women square off. They're about equal in height, several centimeters taller than my 158. I recall my own reaction to Eddie this morning and I'm impressed with the deputy's confidence—she's braver than me.

The schooner parps its horn in farewell, breaking the standoff. The deputy shrugs, pulls off her gloves and waves a hand in farewell. Her hands are covered in elaborate, jeweled rings that cast prisms of light in the bright sun.

I'm mesmerized by the play of light and feel a shift in my perception, and then I see it, the vision.

Deputy Forge lies in a bed. Her pale face is wet with perspiration, but her smile as she reaches out, is more happiness than I've ever seen. Someone places a squirming infant in her arms.

"It's a girl, mon bijou." A man's voice. Somehow familiar.

Deputy Forge takes the infant and kisses her face. The baby has wisps of yellow hair, and between her vibrant violet eyes, a gleaming black gem. From behind me comes a laugh. Another woman bends down to peer at the infant. It's Eddie! She reaches out a finger for the baby to grip. Tears of joy run down her face—

"Mercy?" Eddie shakes my arm gently.

I startle. "I…Oh, I'm sorry. I…" I rub my hand down my face and try to come back to the present.

"It's fine," Eddie assures me. She moves closer to the deputy, blocking me so I can have a moment of privacy. "She's just—"

"Having a vision." The deputy shrugs, like it happens every day. In the Verge. With a bunch of nulls.

I'm trying to put it all together when the deputy steps around Eddie and looks me straight in the eye. "So, *où en sommes-nous?* Are you going to tell me what you saw of my future, or keep it a secret?" She snaps her chewing gum and cocks one hip, waiting.

Eddie stiffens. "Mercy gives her visions as gifts. It's a tradition—"

"It's alright. Remember what TJ said?" I give Eddie a pointed look.

She sniffs and turns aside.

I decide to be direct with this bold Couvie woman. "I saw you with your newborn baby. A girl with golden hair and violet eyes."

The deputy stills. Her neck moves like she's trying to swallow something too big. She clears her throat. "Oh, well, if that's all—"

"It's not. She was beautiful. Remarkable, really.... Her gem was the deepest gleaming black."

Deputy Forge inhales sharply.

Eddie mocks her. "Oh, well if that's all—"

"It's not." I give Eddie a shame-on-you look. "You were there, too. And you were delighted."

"Huh." Eddie raises one eyebrow, but that's the limit to her reaction.

Deputy Forge resumes chewing her gum. She blows a small bubble and snaps it, her face turned as if she's staring at Eddie behind her sunglasses.

I suspect this woman has been putting on a show for us. She seems far too comfortable around our strangeness, mine and Eddie's, than I'd expected a Couvie to be. We haven't seen the genuine *her* yet. She's no doubt more—impressively more—than she first appears.

Before I can ask her why she seems so unperturbed by our gifts, she heaves a sigh and straightens her spine. "I think you best call me May.... Come on then. The Culmination awaits, they say." She turns and strides away, not offering to help us with our packs.

Halfway up the steps I'm breathing hard. I'm in good shape for flat land, but not for all this climbing! We don't have this many stairs in all of New Juneau. I risk a glance behind me and see Eddie's stony face beaded with perspiration. At least I'm not alone.

"Aren't you glad you left a few more books with Captain Souza?" Eddie asks, reading my thoughts.

"Not really." I stare at May's heels in front of me and focus on not slipping. I count the steps as I think about my lovely books…I feel like I'm leaving more and more of myself behind. The pain in my calves is excruciating. After a while, I make myself *stop* counting the steps. It only makes the climb worse.

Adding insult, May's fluffy white dog rushes past us, still full of energy. Finally, we reach the top and move out onto a grassy patch bordering an area paved in uneven stones. Rusting, dead vehicles litter the lot, parked this way and that. Trash and debris cling to flat tires on crumbling rims; rivulets of rust paint the surrounding concrete.

May strides on, weaving around obstacles. There's no fatigue in her gait as she skates across the stones without tripping once. When she glances back at us, dragging along at her heels, she's fighting a smile.

I can't smile at all. Garbage is everywhere! I've never seen anything like this outside the vids. We step over it, around it, through piles of it. No praenex could tolerate this…except the nulls, I guess.

May's back to her unfriendly demeanor as we stop in front of the only operable vehicle, an open-top, rugged truck parked at the end of the lot. She gestures to the cowboy reclining against the car. "This is Sheriff Arson, my uncle, *pronoms mascu*."

Arson—a criminal fire. I've read about the unusual naming customs of the Verge—the *sins of man* nomenclature—but this is the first I've encountered. Is it a fitting name? Despite the relaxed, slouching stance May's uncle has the same kind of harnessed energy I've come to recognize in Van, ready to spring to action when needed. Even with the hat and sunglasses, his resemblance to his niece is evident in the amber hair, shot through with streaks of blond, curling at his tanned neck. His face is sharply attractive, with a shadow of beard and a crooked nose. This is clearly a man of strength and action with an abundance of confidence.

The moment I think this, one side of his grin kicks up and sets off a spark inside me. A weird prickly feeling fizzes in my middle. It must be the climb that's made me a little crazy. Surely not hormones or attraction. My cheeks are just heated from exertion. I couldn't possibly be blushing like a shy schoolgirl. Surely not.

"Hiya." He nods to May.

"Sheriff, may I present *Bozan* LeRoux and Dr. Adams." Her emphasis on Eddie's title indicates the promotion will be news to the sheriff.

The sheriff tips his hat, again not offering us his hands. His many rings of sleek metal and gleaming stones glint in the sun. He pulls a frayed toothpick from between his teeth, tosses it to the ground, and nods. "*Enchanté*." His voice is low and smooth, like a rare taste of chocolate.

I shift to stand a bit behind Eddie, which only seems to make him smile more.

"Well, I guess we best deliver you on then. If you'll have a seat?" He sweeps an arm toward the truck.

I get a good look at our transport for the first time and freeze in place. "Is that a halocarbon vehicle?"

"Sure. Used to be a regular Jeep, but we converted it a few years back. Added the proper exhaust pipes and such. Wanna see the engine?" He moves away as if to open the hood.

"No!" The chill tingling through my limbs is different now, and the heat of anger starts to replace my shyness. "Don't you know what happened with those engines?"

He stands a little taller and steps back to me. I can't see his eyes through his dark glasses, but I've got his attention.

"Oh, I see," he drawls. He shakes his head and kicks a bit of blowing trash. "Look, this is *one* car, a very efficient car, I might add, that runs basically on garbage. It's not gonna make any difference to the ozone—"

"The UCA banned halocarbon technology in 2090. Disputes over halocarbon technology caused the embargo that escalated in war between India and China. Some believe that *that* war spawned the Second World Plague. The catastrophic escalation of ozone depletion as a result of industrial halocarbon energy is cited as the single most significant factor leading to the Call—the end of the world. The technology was destroyed." I'm breathing hard again. My mind is racing at pace with my heart. Eddie moves closer to me, her body a shadow of heat—strong, ready. "How can you even *sit* in it?"

He's quiet for a moment. May shifts slightly toward Eddie; her dog follows. Arson takes off his sunglasses and gives her an almost imperceptible signal. She steps back, and then his nearly blue eyes zero in on me.

"Well, it's easy," he drawls. "Ya see, I turn my derrière like so, then bend my knees…" He pivots gracefully until he's seated in the driver's seat. "And just like that, I'm sittin'."

He spreads an arm along the back of the seat and smiles at us. A dangerous smile filled with charm and challenge, betraying his beauty as the weapon it is.

"Now you can join us.…" He motions to May and she jumps into the back seat; her dog follows. "Or town's just up that way, 'bout five kilometers. You'd make it by chowtime. So what's it gonna be, princess?"

MAY

With the morning argument with Arson still sharp in her mind, May wasn't sure if her uncle's mood would've improved by the time she reached the old lot with their guests, but his customary "hiya" had loosened the cord of tension in her gut.

Now, as they bump along alone on the old road toward the inner gate, her sides ache from laughter. "I can't believe you said *derrière*!" she laughs again.

Her uncle grins as he stops in front of the gate. "I thought it was a nice touch."

As the gate slides open to reveal the real town—glass, wood and steel interwoven with lush vegetation—he continues more slowly down the now smooth avenue.

"It was so ridiculous. And the way you flirted!" May fake gags, pretending to stick a finger down her throat.

Her uncle grins harder. "I'm harmless as a man deeply in love with his wife can be."

"I know that, and you know that, but…I thought the bozan was going to belt you at one point. She's a fighter, that one."

"Ya think?"

"Yeah, I think. The albino thing is…I don't know, *unsettling* maybe? She's very…intense. And Mercy Adams…. She looked scared of her own shadow. I just don't see how she's going to fit. Anyway, I still can't believe that they bought it."

"People see what they expect to see." He shrugs. "And no need to mention the flirting to your aunt."

"Ha! We'll see." May reaches over and gives his hat a little nudge forward over his sunglasses.

"Girl, I'm drivin'." He pushes his hat back in place, but she can tell he's forgiven her for their earlier argument. For now anyway.

"You think they'll be okay walking on their own?"

"A bozan witch and a precognitive historian?" He laughs. "Sure, they'll be fine. Looks like the guys found the elevator just fine," her uncle adds as they arrive at the public works office. With a short bark, Piper jumps from the back and races ahead to greet the team assembled there.

"May!" TJ calls and waves to her from across the lawn where he and Van wait in a spot of shade. His dog, Cousteau, springs up from the grass next to them as Piper reaches their group.

She turns to her uncle expectantly. His sunglasses shield his eyes and for a moment she's afraid he'll try to hold her back. Her pulse is pounding in her ears now, a familiar prickling returns to her skin. TJ's playful Old Earth Parisian kisses on the pier had rocked her. Only a monumental effort to stay in character prevented her from sitting down on the pier with her head between her knees. His effect on her was even worse than last time.

After a few seconds, her uncle lets out a long breath. "Go on then. But remember, we all got a part to play. That boy included. So keep your head. *Comprenez-vous?*"

May shifts her weight to one hip while she thinks about it. With a short sigh, she nods.

Her uncle's mouth ticks up on one side, then he tips his hat and stalks away to approach his crew.

"Peters!" he shouts to a waiting officer. "If one lick of that trash reaches open water, you're gonna need a wet suit, son!"

"Yes, sir!"

She turns away as the soldiers rush off to start their task of keeping the junkyard ruse from getting away from them, literally. They had a lot of garbage to collect and stow, and she didn't want to get dragged into helping.

"May!" TJ calls again. He takes a few steps toward her and motions frantically with his hand.

"Hey!" She waves and starts across the lawn, pulling off her gloves as she goes.

When she reaches them, she can see that Van is still a little green. "How you doin'?" She squats down on her haunches to look him in the eye.

"Fine, just fine, lass. Aye, I love the water, as ye know well. All that salt air and gentle rockin'."

"Ha, yeah."

Cousteau nudges his wet nose into her hand and whines in

greeting. She ruffles his ears and pets him for a moment, stealing time to prepare herself. She shoves her gloves in a pocket and wastes a few more seconds on Cousteau.

Van clears his throat awkwardly.

When she feels TJ's stare like a heat lamp on the top of her head, she mentally braces herself and rises to face him. "And you, Tern Journey? *Ça va?*"

He finger-combs his pale blonde hair before holding up a palm to her. The hint of a smile creases one corner of his mouth. "It's been too long, *Mayhem Rose.*"

He's waiting, his violet eyes locked with hers, and even as her mind is screaming stop, she knows it's too late to prevent what happens next. She reaches up and presses her palm flush against his. The surge of energy she's been feeling for weeks spikes like electricity and it's all she can do to keep her hand in place.

A muscle flexes in TJ's jaw as he rides out the pulse of shock.

The buzzing in May's ears grows to a roar. She breathes deeply as their connection ripens to an indescribable mix of pleasure and pain. It's almost more than she can handle, more than she *wants* to accept.

TJ shifts his attention to her lapel. His eyes widen a fraction. "What's this?" With his free hand he traces the rim of her new insignia. "There's a rocket ship on your chest."

The heat between their palms grows warmer and May braces against the excitement pulsing through their connection. "Don't get too excited; there's an image of Scorch as well."

TJ's eyes shift to hers, the victory they contain has May stepping back.

TJ shifts with her, refusing to break their bond. "You're coming with me to the stars, into what's beyond. You really are."

"No, now hold on a minute."

"This emblem says everything—a Pilgrim symbol? You've never conceded that much before, you wouldn't unless you'd decided to come. Why are you still resisting? Is it your uncle? I can talk to him—"

"No! Don't." Panic raises goosebumps down May's arms. "I mean, there's nothing to talk about. I'm not going anywhere, except on whatever mission this mess with the Adamses turns out to be."

May's heartbeat thuds behind her ears. She reads in TJ's eyes what neither of them can say aloud there on the grass. When the corner of TJ's mouth ticks up in a lopsided grin, she tries again to step back. When he curls his fingers down through hers in a gesture of familiarity, she knows she's lost. When he leans in to brush her lips with a feathery kiss, she knows she's found.

Her future lies away from this place. And it lies with him—this beautiful Pilgrim who wants to leave Scorch entirely, and to take her with him. Not just away but beyond the reach of this world.

"I *like* your new pin, *ma deuxième moitié*." His whisper in her ear sends goosebumps down her neck as the spark between them ebbs to a low undercurrent. She finds herself craving just a few moments alone together, just a sliver of privacy.

When he pulls back and their eyes lock, the mischief she sees in his face says that he knows her thoughts completely.

11
MERCY

When we reached the town—tired, mad, and a bit shocked, actually—a man brought us in off the road to this dingy, smelly room and left without a word. No water. No soap.

By now, I can tell that Eddie's tired of my rant on environmental history, but I can't seem to stop. For the last five minutes she's been catching up on posts—I think she's completely tuned me out. I peer over her shoulder to see the virtual screen hovering in her lap—her rank's just shy of the top 100, pretty impressive for someone so young.

In our social media government, the top 100 citizens are part of the Advisory Council. If it happened, if Eddie became an advisor, she'd have other responsibilities, but even as it is, everyone expects her to make regular posts. I flip open my comm to see what she's writing and find a short post, no video, about her promotion and suspicions about why the Legion felt it was necessary. That's good, it will get people thinking. We've all agreed not to post anything specific about our location, but all of us have running posts on the conflict that's evolving.

Eddie closes her comm and sits motionless, like an alabaster statue, albeit a dusty, slightly disheveled one.

I'm still seething about our treatment here—I can't seem to stop. I can wait in this ugly little room for eternity too, so long as I get to tell somebody just how many mistakes they're making here. I huff out a breath and it turns into a cough. It would be nice to have some water.

I rub my sweaty neck and contemplate how six hundred years of praenex habitation could have come to this. What do we truly offer to the world? Our immunity to disease? (Except the one that kills us all.) Our novus lobe and all its gifts? If the nulls live in a more sapiens manner, *are* more sapiens, what will they think of me and my friends? We're odd even by novus standards.

"I've changed my mind. Let's just go."

I turn on my heel, but a sound from the corner has me turning back. Deputy May Forge steps through a door followed by an old woman, shabbily dressed, their hair uncombed. Their expressions are angry, even mean.

"So, these are the *guests* I've been hearing so much about." Like everyone else, the old woman doesn't raise their palms in greeting.

"Mayor Henderson, may I present Bozan LeRoux and Dr. Adams. Guests, may I introduce you to Mayor Henderson, *pronoms fem.*" Deputy May's purpose seems to be introductions more than law enforcement. I shift my eyes to the mayor.

After a beat of silence, I decide to jump right in. "Divine

peace with you, Mayor. There truly are a number of troubling things I'd like to discuss with you about what we encountered on our way here."

"Oh?" She moves toward the table at the center of the room and with a huff, lowers herself into one of the chairs.

Eddie and I are forced to turn to follow her. "Yes," I continue. "The halocarbon vehicle, for example, is simply intolerable. In addition, we encountered copious amounts of trash—"

"Litter," Eddie interjects. She's an angry statue now, arms crossed, head high.

"—yes, *litter*, along the walk. In several cases we saw environmental hazards—an old kitchen appliance and some kind of fuel tank—along the side of the road. Chemical stench and rust leaching into the water and air. This simply will not do."

Mayor Henderson doesn't seem at all alarmed. She waves to the deputy who begins pulling items from a small storage cabinet. "You were saying?" the mayor asks.

"Yes, um, the trash receptacles along the buildings were overflowing in the small section of town we saw before being brought here—"

"You must be hungry after that long walk." At the mayor's signal, May plops two plates of congealed brown food onto the table. "Have a bite."

Eddie leans over slightly, sniffing a plate. "Is that canned meat?" she asks, her lip curled.

I can't believe what I see. "Are those *plastic* plates?"

The mayor's fist slams the table and I jump. She shoots to her feet, much quicker than I expected based on her lazy gait. "Now look here!" she growls, bending over the table, her angry face close to ours. "This is the Verge and this is *my* place*!* I run it as I see fit. *C'est compris?* We've been living on our own for nearly six hundred years. Surviving, thriving, without those rules you *novus* shroud yourselves in. Recycle this." She starts walking around the room, gesticulating wildly as she rants. "Reuse that! Environmental reengineering. Refuse filtering…. Our little world doesn't need to worry about that—if *ever* we gain that kind of population again, let *them* worry about it. In the meantime…"

She stops directly in front of me and points a finger at my chest. "Nobody comes into *my* place and tells *me* what's what! Especially not one lonely…" She pokes my breastbone.

"Bossy…" Poke.

"Novus…" Poke.

"Minor…" Poke.

"Girl!" she shouts.

A tremendous crash sounds behind her. People and dogs pour into the room and rush us—Van, TJ, Sheriff Arson, even the children, whom I'd almost forgotten by now. Eddie grabs my shoulders from behind, steadying me, giving me strength. Van and TJ reach us, grab on like I'm a life raft. The children wrap their arms around my legs. The dogs circle everyone, barking.

The sheriff and deputy stand straight behind the mayor, who's fuming now, fists clenched, barely restrained.

My diplomatic ancestors would probably have a plan if they were here, but I'm not one of those Adamses. No clever tongue comes to my rescue. I don't know what's going to happen. Are we going to fight? I've never struck a person in my life and I'm willing to bet Eddie hadn't either until yesterday—not off the training mat anyway. Van, well, Van's going to annihilate them if it comes to that.

God, I hope it doesn't come to that.

"She's not bossy," Eddie says in her clear, even voice. "She's brilliant."

"Aye, and she's not *alone*." Van squeezes my hand.

I'm infused with new courage. I stare back at the mayor and wait.

And wait.

CRANE ELDER

In the past...
August 28, 2108; 593 years ago
Fermont Compound, Quebec, UCA

Crane sat beside Elsa catching up on daily logs before the evening feeding. She loved her new workspace. The conversion of several of *Le Mur's* public spaces was complete. What had once been severe industrial design had been transformed into warm, welcoming nurseries filled with color and soft fabrics.

The town inside the walled city had also come to life, as if the news that thousands of praenex babies now called Fermont home had inspired skeptics to rejoin the human race. Crane even found that she no longer stiffened at the sight of soldiers making their rounds—they'd become an assuring presence as the small city welcomed more families and settled into an economy centered largely on the praenex.

The nursery around them was hers to manage. At this hour it was a hive of contentment as the fast-developing infants—sitting up and playing at only two-and-a-half months—were watched by several other nurses and several parents free from work or training. One nurse had begun to prepare for the meal—the babies were already eating soft foods. Others simply supervised and changed the occasional diaper. Their pod contained forty infants, all on the same 36/12 hour cycle—the unique sleep pattern of the praenex. With the babies wakeful for thirty-six hours followed by twelve hours of nearly comatose REM sleep, their sapiens caregivers were constantly challenged to adjust. At first they tried to "fix" the pattern, but it had quickly become clear that it was nothing the novus infants could control. It was just how they were wired. Their parents accepted the help of the nurseries, and the nurseries instituted shift rotations that kept the staff from falling over exhausted.

Crane's nursery included her own adopted child, Brym O'Dell Elder, the firstborn praenex. Crane was thankful for the time she could spend working, but also at last being a *maman* at the perfect age of thirty-two.

"I'm finished," Elsa said, shutting down her tablet and preparing to stand. "If that post doesn't improve my rating, nothing will."

Crane laughed. "Why do you care so much? It's a pointless popularity contest."

"Easy for you to say, you're getting more popular every day. Pretty soon—"

A crash in the dining area interrupted Elsa. A second later, a baby screeched. After the slightest pause, the whole nursery erupted in wails as all the infants began to cry at once. Their angry, fearful cries were unlike anything Crane had ever heard from them before.

Nurses and parents jumped into action, but when Elsa stood to help, Crane grabbed her sleeve. "Wait, where did it start?"

Elsa blinked in confusion. "Uh, in the dining room, I think." Elsa tipped her head toward the tables where a single nurse sat on the floor comforting a crying infant.

"Come with me," Crane said, a sickening feeling growing in her stomach.

They hurried to the feeding area to find the nurse and crying infant surrounded by spilled food and broken dishes. A wet, tangled tablecloth in the mess explained what'd happened.

"Oh my, can we help?" Crane asked.

The nurse's back straightened and they twitched, surprised by Crane's voice. Slowly they turned to face Crane and Elsa as they bent to pick up some of the mess.

It was Allison, a nurse Crane didn't really like. She smiled at Crane and Elsa with a blankness in her eyes. It sent a chill down Crane's spine every time. But a funny feeling wasn't a reason to reject an experienced and qualified nurse like Allison. Instead, Crane had requested Allison for her own team, so she could keep an eye on her. So far, they'd had no issues, except maybe that Allison was considered reserved and stand-offish by her teammates. Again, not a reason to criticize her work.

Allison kept her smile in place. "We're fine, thank you. No harm done. This little one just got a grip on the tablecloth before I could stop them."

Elsa looked at Crane and gave an almost imperceptible nod, before scooping the baby up into her arms. Together they soothed the child while discreetly looking her over. There it was.

A sharp red mark on the girl's thigh. When Crane passed a soothing fingertip over the little welt, the baby snuffled, stopped the worst of her crying, and stared into Crane's eyes.

"I'll be right back to help," Crane said loud enough for Allison to hear. To Elsa she whispered, "I'll check the vid."

At her tablet Crane accessed the video recording of the pod. As she suspected, none of the items from the table hit the child. It wasn't until Allison bent over the infant that the crying began. Crane reversed and rewatched the footage, but Allison had carefully blocked the camera's view of her hands. Cruel *and* sneaky. Crane fought down the impulse to rush back into the dining room and give Allison a few hard pinches, maybe a punch to the jaw—see how *she* liked it! She closed her eyes and breathed through the impulse. Violence would solve nothing, and maybe make even worse whatever meanness Allison had working within her.

Crane sent a quick command and crossed to reception to meet the security personnel. The pod watched in silence as she led the guards through to the dining area where they spoke quietly to Allison before escorting her out. Allison mumbled under her breath and shot Crane one last angry look as she crossed the room. The babies sat alert and quiet now, tracking Allison's movement, their violet eyes full of intelligence.

Crane looked for Brym among the sea of infants and found them sitting in a pile of pillows and toys, staring at her, waiting patiently for Crane's gaze to find them. Brym tipped their head to the side, then smiled at Crane.

Crane felt a jolt of shock move through her. *They know.*

Somehow, they know the pain the other child experienced. Crane lifted her chin and nodded back to her child. After an eerie pause, the noises in the room returned to normal and everyone went back to their tasks.

Crane sat with her tablet once more. She accessed the PSI reporting tool and clicked New. The empty form for PSI 4218 appeared on her screen and she began to type. *Clear evidence of telepathic activity observed in Pod 12...*

12
VAN

Mercy once told me that it makes her sad to watch me play sports. That she can see something Scorch has taken away from me, some divine talent gone to waste. Right now, standing next to her, holding her small hand in mine, it's all I can do not to use that God-given strength to crush these folks into dust for making her afraid.

What would Mercy think if I took one shot—at the sheriff maybe? Just a fast jab to wipe that scowl off his face.

I see the moment Mayor Dixie makes her decision—her shields fall away and she shows her true self—the compassionate leader I've come to know. Her uproarious laugh still startles me.

"*Bon!*" She raises both fists to the ceiling. Her smile is genuine as she slaps Arson and May on their backs. They're laughing too.

I exhale. "It's okay now, Cricket."

I nod at TJ and he pulls Eddie aside and talks quickly to her. With my free hand I pat Cousteau to quiet him down. There's nothing I can do about the children, who jump up and down like little beans, clapping and laughing.

"Okay now." I try to get their attention. "I know, that was craic, but let's settle down now."

Momentarily distracted, I'm surprised to find the mayor in front of us, just inches from Mercy's face. "Dr. Mercy Adams"—she holds her palms up in greeting—"welcome to the Verge."

Mercy hesitates, lines of confusion pinching the skin around her gem. Slowly, she lifts her hands. "Divine grace with you." Her voice is small, unsure.

Dixie smiles more gently and laces her fingers through Mercy's in a familiar gesture usually reserved for family. "Peace with you, *petite sœur*. You'll have to forgive our artifice." She lets go of Mercy so Arson and May can also greet her. Then the whole process repeats with Eddie.

When we arrived earlier, after a quick stop at the beach, TJ and I brought the kids up the modern elevator hidden in the marina building and caught the tram into town. During the short drive, I thought about my own climb up the cliff steps nearly six years ago. My own test at the Verge. How they tested my friends might have been necessary—but I don't have to like it.

"We're stubborn in our ways," Dixie explains to Mercy, "that much is true, but it was all a test of your conviction...and your hearts. From the start, Vancouver Colony has been a shelter for people dedicated to preserving the best parts of humanity. Right or wrong, we've always had a fundamental distrust of praenex superiority. Maybe even more than sapiens do." She gives me a sideways glance. "We've held ourselves apart, and we protect what we've built here from all but the most trusted outsiders. Our trust must be *earned*, first by showing a commitment to planetary citizenship—environmentalism, if you want to call it that. We tested you, and your friends, and you passed."

She turns to the rest of us as she removes her costume's jacket to reveal a casual uniform. "And you all, you did exactly right." She musses the children's hair, and tosses a couple treats from her pocket to the dogs.

In the Army, you learn to do a few things by rote. Make yer bunk. Eat what they give ye. Watch yer back. And salute a senior officer.

I flex a stiff hand to my forehead. "General Henderson, ma'am." I wait.

"We try to keep that part to a minimum here, soldier." She returns my salute. "Now come here! It's so good to see you boys." She squeezes me and TJ in an awkward hug. "It's Dixie, or Mayor, if you must, but that's it during off hours. There'll be plenty of time for titles later."

I'd forgotten how strong she is, her arms like bands of steel around me. I don't know why I wasn't expecting this warmth— the Verge's been good to me since the start. Yet her strength and absolute trust sets free something I was holding tight inside. I can breathe a little better as I release her.

"Mayor Dixie, we appreciate your help and hospitality." TJ's posture looks as relieved as I feel, but his pinched mouth tells me he's nervous.

I shake my head at his formality.

Dixie points a bejeweled finger at his chest. "None of that, now. We could argue for ages about who's helping who, but it's best we just get on with things. Let's walk and talk. *Allons-y!*"

She motions to Fez and Nairobi. They scurry out of door, racing with the dogs, a happy and excited pack. The rest of us follow.

Mercy's forehead is still wrinkled. "But, the litter, the rusted vehicles—"

"All for show," Arson interrupts, reaching for her shoulder.

I push myself between them. "Aye, every piece of trash's tagged for collection, I've done the collecting myself, so I know. The car lot's normally covered—they think of it as a sort of museum."

May chuckles and bends toward Mercy. "Normally *you'd* be part of the crew to put things right, but I suspect that's someone else's job today."

It must be theirs, based on the look May exchanges with her uncle. I'd offer to help, but I'd rather not leave Mercy when she's shell-shocked by our ruse. And that showoff Arson doesn't deserve my help.

Dixie waves us on. "That's right. We've no time to waste."

My stomach picks that exact moment to growl loudly.

Dixie smirks. "Let's get some real food and then we need to be on our way." She checks her comm. "We have less than an hour before the tracking system comes back to life. TJ, I've a special project for you and May."

Sheriff Arson steps up behind us, making me wary. He's not exactly pro-TJ, and that makes it hard for me to completely trust him.

"Nice costume." I swirl a finger to take in his odd clothes. "If yer ready to ride off into the sunset, I'll fetch yer horse.

He grins and says something to TJ in French. I don't know a lot of French, but I know enough to know his comment was laced with sarcasm and that his curse would thrill little Fez.

TJ laughs once, a tight, artificial sound.

The tension between him and May's uncle makes me glad that Mercy's an only child—I've always had her family's approval. Still, I have to clench my teeth to keep from saying something. Arson's always a little too smooth—one of those suave men who always says the right thing to a woman, always has the perfect comeback. He gets under my skin fast, and I'm not looking forward to him spending time with Eddie and Mercy. Not at all.

TJ waves at me and grabs May's hand. They walk ahead with Dixie, exchange a few short words and then run off ahead of our group.

"Hey, Eddie—"

She holds up a finger. "Just a minute, Van. Mayor, wait..."

Dixie keeps right on marching.

"*Please.*" That's Eddie being diplomatic. She speeds up to keep pace with the mayor and asks, "The tracking system, that was you?"

"Not initially. We're still working out who started the hack, but since we knew you all needed some cover, we decided to extend it a bit. Come on." Dixie waves us on.

The late afternoon sun shines high over whitewashed buildings and the now spotless street. Further down the road toward the bay, a large group of folks rushes back and forth, pushing large, wheeled receptacles in an almost parade-like procession. Some of the children stop and wave back at us before rejoining the cleanup activities.

I've seen this large gate before, so I know the surprise that's coming. Fez and Nairobi run ahead with the dogs, and when the gate slides silently open to reveal the town—the *real* town—Mercy gasps.

"Aye, it's really something, isn't it?"

She looks at me like she'd forgotten I'm here.

The sheriff chuckles behind me. "We're pleased you approve, *mon petit grillon.*"

"Oh…I think my head's on swivel." Mercy gives a breathless laugh. "Look at all the wood and glass—houses, offices…are those shops?"

"All three. Even Alberta Farm can't top this lane," he says, shooting one quick glance at me.

I ignore his slight and try to see the town through Mercy's eyes. Trees, shrubs and flowers are everywhere, woven in with the natural architecture of the buildings—hanging from ledges, spilling from pots and some growing right along the road, which is paved in pale stones, even and neat. It appeals to my farmer's instincts; I can't deny it.

Mercy's smiling now, her eyes round. Falling in love with this place. It's a familiar look I used to see loads more, only it was directed at me.

How lame am I? I'm jealous of a town.

"It's like a garden." She does a little spin. "Like Paris of old, only more tropical."

Arson slides between us. "I'll show you around. There's a café—"

"Well now." I intercept his reach for Mercy's elbow and stare him straight in the eye. "That's nice of you, Sheriff Henderson, sir, but it'll have to wait. We've got a meeting. Besides, I'm sure yer wife is expecting ye home to help with yer little ones."

"Well, then…" Arson flashes a crooked grin, takes Mercy's hand, and kisses it with a little bow. "*Enchanté. À toute à l'heure.*"

I roll my eyes to the heavens and rock back on my heels. Arson's a buck eejit if he thinks that'll work. I know Mercy, and flirting with her's as useless as a chocolate teapot.

Mercy giggles and her cheeks flare. "Oh, goodbye."

"Come on then, Cricket." I steer her away and have to force myself to slow down so she can keep up. We catch up with the others on the steps of the public dining hall in an old hotel still used mostly as designed. "Aye, you'll like this place. I've eaten and slept here countless times. It's elegant, filled with music and old art."

"Oh, there's music now." She pulls me toward where Eddie stands listening to the performers playing at one end of the wide veranda.

Music is the last thing I want, my body flush with the urge to fight that lecherous flirt Arson. I pace away and find old Cherie sitting on a bucket in her usual nook, praying and handing out ripe fruit, her freshly gathered wildflowers fanning around her like a wreath. She winks at me and salutes, her hand thick with rings on arthritic knuckles. The tension leaches from my limbs like water drawn in by thirsty roots. I'd forgotten how this place, with its many gifts, affects me.

"*Bonjour, madam.*" My smile splits my face as I take a knee in front of her. I'm sure I look ridiculous—a huge sapiens kneeling in front this tiny novus *grand-mère.*

She grins and waves me down to kiss both wrinkled cheeks. Her French is fast and fluid and I can hardly keep up.

Before I know what's happening, my hands are filled with flowers.

"*Bon! Pour votre petite amie.*" She waves toward Mercy on the other side of the veranda. "For your girl!"

I dig in my pocket for credits, but she waves me off with a smile and goes back to her prayers.

On impulse, I bend and gently kiss her again. "*Merci, Cherie. Je vous ai manqué.*" My pronunciation is poor, I know, but her cheeks turn red and her eyes sparkle, and that's what matters. I *did* miss her—I missed *all* of this, this remarkably *sapiens* place.

When I turn around, Mercy and Eddie have moved away from the musicians to rejoin our group and everyone is watching me with Cherie. I must look like a ten-year-old, reaching into Grandma's apron pocket for a sweet. Heat rushes across my face again. I try to slide my hands into my pockets, but they're full of flowers. A strange shyness overtakes me and I can't seem to look at Mercy.

I take a big step to rejoin them. "Hey, could you hold these for a minute?" I shove the flowers into Mercy's hands before she can answer. I bend to tie my boot. When I stand back up, I turn to Eddie to ask about the music.

Dixie clears her throat and announces, "I've had an update

from the Council." She pauses to exchange nods with a couple exiting the building and signals us to follow her through the hotel lobby and into an empty meeting room. TJ and May stride in behind us carrying black computer cases. We make room for them as Dixie continues. "SciCorps is pretending these attacks simply aren't happening. They say they're not behind any of it and that there must be some reasonable explanation. They have, however, officially acknowledged they have the Adamses."

She pauses a moment to squeeze Mercy's arm. "We think they're safe. SciCorps claims the doctors agreed to an urgent request for scientific collaboration and immediately joined the delegation returning to the Hub, but they refuse to allow any contact with them on the pretense that they're sequestered in their urgent work and cannot be interrupted. The two clerics who were missing were found wandering around Tether Base with no explanation of how they got there—looks like they were drugged, but otherwise unharmed."

I scoff. "How did SciCorps explain the blood in Mercy's galley, or the kidnapping of the Spheran leader?"

"They claim to know nothing about either of those events." She stops and looks at TJ. "Your father's adjunct reported a break in at his apartment and claimed that whoever broke in stole supplies and left some uniforms behind. Those garments are being held as evidence by the police. The four of you are wanted for questioning."

Everything starts to fall into place in my mind. "They're trying to make us look guilty. They know we're the ones who entered, took supplies. They're trying to frame us for the rest!"

Dixie nods. She's watching Eddie, who's keeping quiet.

TJ hisses. "We walked right into that."

May rests a hand on TJ's shoulder. "They're desperate. It's sloppy. They didn't think it through. They weren't expecting General Elder to arrive at the complex so quickly—"

"Or at all. The plane he was supposed to be in was hit *on purpose*. They thought he'd be dead by then." I clench my fists and grind my teeth.

We're all quiet for a moment, staring at the floor.

TJ breaks the silence. "I guess they don't know how he feels about his cabbages."

I snort at his joke and my tension eases just a hair.

Flowers begin to slip from Mercy's hands.

I watch them scatter at my feet and automatically bend to pick them up, but when try to return them to her, I realize the flowers are the least of my worries.

Mercy's hands have gone slack, her eyes are blank, her body stiff. Her pupils constrict to tiny dots, barely visible in her bold purple irises.

"Mercy!" I reach for her hand.

"Don't touch her!" Eddie blocks me. "She's having a vision. Just...don't touch her."

I fill my lungs and hold my breath—realize that everyone else is too. Of course Eddie's right. We've been through this before, but it's still hard to watch and wait.

Mercy flinches suddenly. Her eyes go wide and her mouth opens in a silent scream as she collapses.

I catch her and ease her down just as she makes the most

unholy keening cry I've ever heard. "Mercy! Mercy, it's over!" I cradle her in my giant arms and wait.

Her crying turns to quiet sobs as she buries her face in one of my hands. Her tears wet my fingers and slide down my arm. Slowly she quiets.

"There, now." Dixie reaches out to tuck a hair behind Mercy's ear. "She's alright. Let's give her some air."

Mercy struggles loose of my arms. Her pupils dilate as she sits up.

"Oh, God." She shudders. "Oh, Creator help us."

"What did you see?"

Mercy looks at me, then scans the faces around us. "The Verge, under attack...." She swallows hard, lets out a shaky breath. "Bombs."

"Where?"

She looks up at me, clenches her jaw. "Everywhere."

<hr>

We're all subdued after hearing the details of Mercy's vision. Bombs in the distance, in the valley. TJ shouting May's name. Folks running in panic, then an explosion in the street just meters from where we stood on the hotel's veranda.

Dixie leads us to a dining room on the other side of the hotel lobby. Our group has fractured into couples mumbling in low tones. Eddie holds Mercy's elbow while she talks non-stop into Mercy's ear. Mercy nods repeatedly.

A meal together is a good idea. It'll help us pull together, and yeah, I'm still starving.

Arson's deep laugh resonates behind me. He joins the girls, and points to a nearby painting and they turn to it. I know for a fact that Arson can tell them every detail of every famous piece here or anywhere in the Verge. The artist cowboy. As if he needed more appeal.

I growl to myself, pick a chair and flip it around backwards so I can straddle it. I'm hungrily looking over all the dishes coming out of the kitchen when TJ appears at my side.

He stops short when he sees my face. "You okay?"

"Aye, but I don't wanna talk about it."

"Okay…I still can't believe they walked from the bay." He points after the girls disappearing into the bathroom.

At least Arson won't follow them there.

"Not that they aren't tough, I just can't believe that they didn't see through the ruse," TJ continues.

I cross my arms along the back of the chair and rest my chin on my forearm. "Do you really think he said *derrière?*"

TJ snorts. "Hey. Don't be so angry, you knew they'd pass. Those two don't know how to fail."

"Oh sure, you mean like the last time Mercy faced a life-changing test?"

He grimaces, remembering what I can't forget: her failing to pass to majority. Before he can say more, his comm chirps. He immediately bypasses the call, then flips open his display and stabs in a few commands. "There, it's off. I'm done."

I roll my head to the side. "Yer not done, and ye know it. Ye've gotta face yer da."

TJ shakes his head. "By all that's holy, how am I going to make all this work? SciCorps, my parents, the Verge, us?"

"You aren't. It's not meant to *all work*, that's why it's called war."

"We don't know that!" His hiss draws a few eyes. He bends toward me. "We don't know anything for sure."

"You were sure enough to resign." I spin my chair around and sit forward.

TJ folds himself gracefully into the chair next to me.

Everyone's at the table now, ready to eat. Dixie says grace and we start passing dishes, but something feels off. After a few bites, she clears her throat. "The children have informed me that they're ready to share their mission with us." She nods to Fez.

Fez puts down his fork. "We're sorry for our deception. We didn't lie to you, but we have withheld much."

"What now?" I put down my fork.

Eddie shushes me.

Nairobi clears her throat and nods. "Our ages, for one. Our English is not so good that we may sound younger and with our small size, we thought it best to let you continue to assume.... I'm nine and Fez is eight."

I shake my head, trying to reconcile their size with their ages. In praenex terms, they're still a few years from petitioning for majority. Some praenex gain adulthood as early as twelve; by then they're fully grown. These two wee creatures look more like toddlers than pre-teens.

Nairobi continues. "You described how the nulls—"

"They like to be called Couvies," Fez interrupts. "They don't like *nulls*. It's like a swear."

Sheriff Arson chuckles before May kicks him under the table.

"Stop interrupting," Nairobi tells Fez. "The *Couvies* have so many sapiens ancestors that their praenex traits have started to fade, like their gem tone, and their gifts. Our society is the opposite. Spherans are *more* praenex than any others. Our gifts are still strong—many hear the Creator's voice like your generations of old."

I lean back in my chair. "How is that possible?"

Dixie shrugs. "They live in a closed society. We haven't been in contact with them very long, and even then, only by comm."

"For seventy years." Nairobi aims a disapproving squint at Dixie.

"Seventy years is *not that long*?" I nudge my plate away.

Nairobi turns to Mercy. "You told the story of the Verge and Mr. Samuelson. Do you know too, the stories from the same time that tell of disappearances?"

Mercy sits up straight. "Oh, you mean the secret exodus of 2105? That story's so incredible, I can't believe it. You see, in 2105, maybe even earlier actually, no one can be sure.... Well, it's really more myth than any historical record, so it could have been going on for years, you know, and no one noticed—"

"Cricket?" I swirl my finger for her to move it along.

"Oh, right. Sorry." She cringes. "People began to disappear. Whole families. Brilliant scientists, distinguished architects, and other people too—teachers, carpenters, technicians. Everyone. All around the world."

"Kidnappings?"

Mercy shakes her head. "No, that's the strangest part. In every case the people tidied up their lives, packed, converted their credits into currency—some even sent farewell letters. Then they vanished. No one was ever able to trace them. Years later, after the Call, people started to look at the disappearances as a bigger part of the whole. The *Secret Exodus* theory was born, suggesting that these people had been called by God on some secret mission. No one ever learned what happened to them."

I push back in my chair. "Until now."

Fez giggles and turns to me. "Is this a good time for a swear?"

"Hell, yeah." I nod.

"So your mission is what?" Mercy asks. "To come here and reintegrate with the rest of Scorch?"

"Not exactly—" Nairobi stops to listen to what Fez whispers in her ear. She nods to him. "We need your help, but it's really up to our teacher, Dr. Varela to explain."

"It's a good thing we plan to rescue him then," I say.

"A mission followed by a mission." Mercy shakes her head. "It's a lot of responsibility. I'd feel a lot better if my parents were here to weigh in."

Eddie slaps a hand on the table. "One thing's for sure—we need to protect the children."

Dixie nods. "They'll be safe here. We'll see to it."

"Aye, then let's get to work. We've a whole lot of figurin' to do if we're gonna take on SciCorps and save a secret society, too."

CRANE ELDER

In the past...
August 2, 2110; 591 years ago
Fermont Compound, Quebec, UCA

Crane sometimes marveled at the friendship that had grown between herself and Sophie LeRoux. As her counterpart and the chief architect of the cooperative agreement between Fermont and Versailles compounds, Minister LeRoux had been a fierce negotiator with definite ideas about how their two societies should interact. Where Crane's prominence as the mother of the first praenex gave her status, it was nothing compared to Sophie's position as French Ministère de l'Économie. Yet after all the negotiations were finished and documents signed, the connection between them had blossomed into a warm and meaningful relationship.

"I don't know what I'll do now." Crane shrugged at the hologram of her friend sitting across the table from her. Sophie looked fashionable and sleek as usual in her fancy office inside the Palace of Versailles.

"*Chèrie*, it will take some weeks to complete all the plans, no?"

"*Oui.* The details of the ramp up still need to be added to long-term roadmaps and government plans, but in thirty-two years, I'm confident our obstetrics training will have a strong restart. They'll be ready for new babies when they arrive, but in the meantime my profession as midwife is finished. I'm completely obsolete."

Her friend scoffed. "This you say to the economic minister of a post-apocalyptic France?"

"You're right, I'm sorry. That was insensitive."

They were quiet for a moment, each reflecting on their own troubles.

"Come," Sophie said. "This self-pity is unattractive. Instead, you should be proud of this, how do you say, *réussite?*"

"Ah, *achievement.*"

"*Oui,* this achievement. And don't forget, you promised to send me a copy of this plan, yes? I believe my colleagues will be interested in adopting such procedures for our own people in Versailles." Sophie tipped her head to one side. "That is, of course, if we survive the next thirty years."

"Don't say that!" Crane rubbed a hand across her forehead. "You're going to survive. You're in a fortress, after all."

Sophie turned around to look at the bright pink wallpaper and ornate fireplace behind her. "This place?" She shrugged. "I would gladly trade the Mars Salon for my modern office back in Bercy, but as the English say, beggars cannot be choosers, no?"

Crane sighed. "I'll be begging soon too—for more work. I enjoy my time in the school with the children, but I need something more."

Brym entered the room at the same moment that the hologram of Sophie's praenex daughter Pauline climbed into a chair in France.

Brym raised a tiny palm. "God's grace with you, Madame LeRoux. *Bonjour, Maman*," Brym said. "We're ready."

Crane pulled out a chair for Brym and helped her settle her tablet on the table before half-lifting her into the seat. At two-and-a-half, the praenex girls had the physical maturity of kindergarteners, but it was clear that they would all be diminutive in stature when compared to their sapiens peers. But small as their bodies were, their brains were slightly larger given the added mass of the novitas lobe. More remarkable still, some studies suggested as much as fifty percent of their brain capacity was available for focused activities. Add to that their mature behavior, and you get a degree of precociousness that their sapiens caregivers were taking time to adjust to.

Crane greeted Pauline. "Tell us which project you're presenting today please."

Brym spoke up. "Last week you asked us to look at animals we like who can live in our warm world."

Pauline leaned toward them. "We picked two meat eaters and two vegetarian animals, but we liked many birds too."

Crane nodded. "Can you tell me the word we sometimes use for—"

"Carnivores and herbivores," Brym interrupted.

"*Oui*," Sophie agreed. "But I can see, *ma petite*, that I must remind you, as I often must my own daughter, that interrupting when someone is speaking is rude and will not make you any friends."

Brym glanced at Crane. "*Désolée, Maman.* Sometimes I hear the voice in your head like you're speaking out loud."

Crane smiled. She could only imagine how confusing telepathy made interacting with sapiens. "It's alright. Go on then."

Brym shared her presentation and a holo screen appeared. "The first animal is the Mexican wolf, Canis lupus baileyi…"

Crane and her friend watched as their daughters conducted a short but thoughtful presentation that she figured she herself could have managed perhaps by third grade. They were just finishing the first herbivore when something started to nag at Crane.

"Excuse, Brym, but what are the other two animals you plan to present?"

Brym clicked ahead to a summary slide toward the end. "The tropical pocket gopher, Geomys tropicalis, and the key deer, Odocoileus virginianus clavium. Why, *Maman?* Don't you like these animals?"

A slight hum started at the back of Crane's head and goosebumps rose on her neck. "No, it's not that…. It's just, well, aren't these animals extinct?"

"*Quoi?*" Sophie picked up her own tablet and started scrolling. "Why would you pick extinct animals, Pauline?"

Pauline looked at her mother with wide eyes. "They could live here now, *Maman.*"

"But they're gone." Crane lifted both hands.

Brym giggled. "Oh, yes, they *are* gone now." She grinned at her friend's hologram. Pauline giggled too. "We're too little now, but in a few years we can help with that."

"Help?" Crane asked.

"*Oui*," Pauline nodded. "With de-extinction."

Crane shook her head. "Scientists tried for nearly a century before the Call. They never found a viable solution of scale to reintroduce a species."

"Oh, but we know how," Brym said.

"And which ones," Pauline added.

The hum in Crane's brain had grown to a persistent buzz. She was almost afraid to ask the question. "How do you know, Brym?"

Her daughter smiled and patted her tiny hand on Crane's shoulder. "The Creator explained it to us."

"We'll have it all written down for you," Pauline chimed in. "In a few years."

"The Creator told you?" Sophie asked.

The girls nodded.

"How?" Crane asked.

Brym scrunched her forehead together. "What do you mean, how?"

Crane sat back. "I mean, how did the Creator tell you?"

The two girls thought for a moment, then Pauline lifted one small shoulder, looking very much like her mother the Minister. "Your question is strange to us. We did not think our way of talking with the Creator would be different than yours."

"Oh!" Sophie covered her mouth, then abruptly stood and

moved away from the table, her hologram fading out.

"*Maman!*"

"It's okay," Crane assured her. "Just give your *maman* a moment, Pauline. She'll be okay. Listen, both of you. I don't know how to explain this, but sapiens don't talk to God, at least not in the way I think you mean. Can you tell us more about your communication, how you do it?"

Brym raised an eyebrow. "I don't know. We talk, in my head. Sometimes when I'm quiet, or when I pray—"

"Sometime when I sleep," Pauline added.

Brym tipped her head to the side. "And sometimes I just know things I didn't before."

"Does it hurt you?" Crane asked, remembering the Call.

"No, *Maman.*" Brym squeezed her arm. "It doesn't hurt like that. My gem just feels funny," she said, gently rubbing a finger on the bump of black skin between her eyebrows. "Don't worry."

Sophie's hologram slid back into her chair, more composed. She hugged Pauline's shoulders then looked back at Crane, eyes glassy with unshed tears.

Crane took a deep breath and stared at her friend. She knew from months of collaboration that Sophie was adept at compartmentalizing issues.

They didn't move for a few minutes, but just sat in thought, letting things distill.

"*D'accord.*" Sophie cleared her throat. "Let's set the Almighty aside for a moment and talk about this." She waved a slender hand toward the presentation. "We asked them about animals they like, and they brought us this."

"Yeah."

"I don't know about *your* system, *mon ami*, but our educational structure is going to need, how do you say, *réaménagement?*"

"A complete overhaul," Craine agreed. "My thoughts exactly. We need to rethink the whole learning process if we're going to keep up with them."

"*Bon!*" Sophie pushed back in her chair. "I think you have found your next calling, no?"

"What? Me?"

"*Oui.* I look forward to your initial report." Sophie turned her attention to the children. "You did well, both of you. Unfortunately, we have much to do now, and will have to continue later, *s'il vous plait.*"

Crane rubbed the back of her neck and closed her eyes. Why hadn't she been more careful about what she wished for?

Brym nudged her elbow. "Here you go, *Maman.*"

Crane looked down to see her own tablet opened to the PSI entry screen. She exhaled through her nose. She didn't know which event to log first, *de-extinction procedures* or...

"It'll be okay, Mother Crane, I promise." Brym hugged her arm and planted a soft kiss on her cheek. "The Creator told me so."

"Oh, sweetie." She kissed the top of Brym's head and indulged for a moment in the sweet smell of her daughter's hair. Then she exhaled, rolled her shoulders and started typing: *PSI 5321: Conversations with the Almighty.*

13
MERCY

Current year: 2701
Thursday, 7 PM
The Verge

Some people are so convinced of their own strength that they have to be reminded that sometimes people fail for the simplest of reasons. Attila the Hun died of a nosebleed, for God's grace! I am not one of these people. I'm constantly aware of my weakness, my smallness, my peculiarities compared to those around me.

My rem is approaching. I can feel the heaviness behind my eyes. My breath is turning into involuntary sighs. "I need sleep soon."

My friends are gathered together, just the four of us from the mainland and the dogs. May's dog Piper is a sweetheart who lies contentedly as I stroke her long white fur. She's named after a twentieth century astronaut; I looked it up. May and TJ, I've learned, share a common interest in exploration. I think they might share more than that too.

I shift closer to Eddie. "What do you think of May?"

Across the room, TJ straightens, pretending not to listen.

Eddie glances at him before she answers. "She's interesting… independent, smart, kind of forceful, I think." She turns to TJ. "Have you known her long, bro?"

"Um…" TJ squints at the control panel on the device he's updating.

I look more closely. "Is that the configuration she helped you with? The program to fool the trackers?" He begins uploading into his implant.

Eddie huffs. "TJ? How long have you known May?"

Van holds up a hand. "We've known her about four years now. TJ, how much longer on your upload, man?"

"I'm done, now it's Mercy's turn." He straps the maintenance panel to my arm.

Eddie leans toward me. "She's kind of odd, don't you think?"

"Like we can talk. Although…never mind."

TJ squirms as he works on the panel. He sighs. "Although what?"

"Oh, well…the gloves?" I look at Eddie for confirmation.

"Yes, the gloves are strange. She even ate with them on. Do you think—"

"Aye, she's odd. So what?" Van rubs his arm as if he can feel the device buried deep beneath his flesh. "There's bigger things to be thinkin' on." He looks over TJ's shoulder. "Are ye sure they can't track us?"

"No, they'll track us, but we made some configuration changes. The program will report back tracking from this same time last year, with a few logical edits. You won't go to your apartment in the Hab," he says to me. "You'll go to Eddie's. It'll look perfectly natural."

I imagine what that means. "What if they try to find us and we're not where we should be?"

TJ keeps working. "Most people use their own comms to locate people. May coded in a routine that checks the user's location and adjusts *our* reported location to make sure we're never where the user is.… It'll take a while for anyone to notice. By then, we'll have your parents back." He squeezes my arm as he removes the panel and attaches it to Eddie's.

I find myself rubbing my skin, just like Van did. I smile to myself, but I can't look at him. I'm embarrassed to have said anything about May, and there's still some awkwardness after being apart so long. But here he is—larger than life, sitting in the chair next to me. I can smell the earthy warmth of his skin, hear his stifled sighs as he waits for something to happen.

Across the small table, Eddie's still in her serious mask, like she's trying to stay aloof even though it's just us.

"Eddie, are you well?" I ask.

She startles a little when I say her name, then lets her shoulders relax. "Of course. Why do you ask?"

"I don't know. You're so quiet today. The more exciting things get, the more you seem to step back."

"Aye, I noticed that too." Van shifts forward. "What's that about, lass?"

Eddie takes her time looking at each of us. "First, I would also observe that no one *needed* more action on my part today. From the moment we stepped onto the pier, Mercy's taken the lead for all of us."

I don't know what she's talking about. The lead? Me? "I…

No. I haven't done anything. It's because it's *my* parents who were taken, that's all."

"Pfft! It's not just about your parents. You're taking the lead. *You* got us here. *You* confronted Mayor Henderson. And your posts… Your posts have driven your rating up over 100 positions. And they're just the reflection of what you've been telling us. Don't you see?" She leans toward me, lowering her voice to a loud whisper. "You're the center of all of this, Cricket. TJ, Van and I, we all have roles but we're more like…like trajectories. Bozan. Fighter. Annoying geek." She points around our circle.

"Hey!" TJ pinches her.

She pushes his hand away. "You're the center—the moral center, Mercy. You keep us grounded and on the divine path."

"Huh." Van shrugs. "I never thought of it that way, but aye, I can see that."

My jaw drops. "See what?"

Van shrugs. "I always think of what you'd have me do, how you'd see my actions, before I do something big. Isn't that what Eddie's gettin' at?"

I shake my head. It's ridiculous. Moral center? What kind of skill is that?

"There's more." Eddie looks over her shoulder at the Couvies at the other end of the room waiting for us. "There's still a great deception here. Maybe more than one."

"You still don't trust them?"

"Not exactly. I trust what they've *told* us, and what they *intend,* but they're hiding something. Something big. Van, you've been here before; do have any idea what it is?"

Van scrunches his brows together. "Not a clue."

When our uploads are complete, we follow May, Sheriff Arson, and Dixie deeper into the building and down to a bank of elevators. The silence is heavy as we wait for the elevator.

"How are the children?" I ask Dixie.

"Fine, fine. Settled in like little ambassadors, asking questions and soaking in knowledge like sponges. They'll be happy here."

"Good, thank you."

We lapse into silence again. I turn to May. "Can I ask you something personal?"

She seems a little surprised but tips her head and smiles for me to go on.

"I'd heard that nulls…sorry, I mean Couvies, have unusual naming traditions like Farmers, only instead of plants and flowers, you have a different subject—"

"Sins and weaknesses," Dixie offers. "We name our babies after the most reprehensible sapiens characteristics we can think of. Helps us remember."

Sheriff Arson sniffs. "And keeps us humble, *t'est pas d'accord?*"

The way he grins—that lazy smile. It makes my cheeks burn, and I can't tell if he's sincere or playing with me. I turn back to May, trying to hide my blush.

"It certainly worked for you, Sheriff." Eddie's sarcasm gets a chuckle from Dixie.

The elevator arrives and we all file into the large compartment, the dogs circling between us. The sheriff presses a button low on the panel—B something—and we start our descent.

"But you all have such simple names. I mean, Sheriff Arson's is the most unusual, but you can hardly fault someone for their surname."

"Oh, no" May laughs. "Arson is his *first* name. Best to call him Sheriff, anyway. The cowboy persona is only *part* act."

"I'm right here, girl." Arson protests.

"We use nicknames," May continues. If you want the whole of it…well, I'm Mayhem Rose, *enchanté*." She gives me a saucy little curtsy.

I turn to Dixie and lift an eyebrow.

"Addiction Charity Ramirez Henderson, likewise." She extends her hand to me.

"Mercy Abigail Adams." I shake her hand, her firm grip reminding me of my father's. "You took your husband's name?"

"Yes, it's a sapiens custom we sometimes follow."

I nod. "I'm named after Mercy Otis Warren, a political writer and friend to John and Abigail Adams, my ancestors. She was the first woman to write a history of the American Revolution. She hosted Sons of Liberty meetings in her home. Many years later they named a battleship after her. I think she'd like that you're a mayor and play down your role as general." I smile. "Thank you for the meal, by the way. You've been very kind. I'm sorry I'm rambling. It's because I need to sleep soon."

"Ha!" She slaps me on the back so hard I think I feel a rib crack. "Now I understand why they call you Cricket."

The elevator doors slide open. We enter a lobby walled by windows overlooking a massive natural cavern filled with light and activity—an underground city whose purpose is immediately clear.

TJ gasps. I guess this is news to him too. Van steps forward silently, staring in wonder at the military aircraft—no bigger than children's toys from our great height—arranged in neat columns on the cavern floor below. With an audible thud, his forehead meets the glass.

Several huge doors glide open on the opposite side of the cavern, creating a wide opening through which a large plane could easily pass. Beyond the doors, two separate strips of pavement lead away from a field of concrete. They stretch, long, gray and endless, into the night.

"How did you build this?"

"We didn't." Dixie joins us at the overlook window. "This installation was originally built in the twentieth century as a secret military base. The town was built at the same time as a resort to camouflage the base. They used it to house the large number of people it took to build this place. Its true purpose was masked by the clearly commercial and residential nature of the town. Dr. Samuelson, our founder, bought the whole thing from the UCA."

TJ touches a hand to the glass. "This isn't anything like the airstrip we use for scavie runs."

"No, that's on the public end of the colony."

I turn to face her. "But how do you hide this from SciCorps? From everyone?"

"It's screened—"

"More Spheran tech?"

Dixie nods. "I know you have a lot more questions, but this is only part of why I brought you here." She turns to TJ. "Tern Journey LeRoux." Dixie sounds all General now, as she steps up to TJ. "Through the divine within and by recommendation of TAC command, I hereby offer you the commission of Major in the Terran Army Corps."

TJ's mouth falls open. He turns to his sister.

Eddie shrugs one shoulder. "What's an officer without an army?"

Sheriff Arson chuckles. "That's true, plus it wouldn't hurt to firm up your commitments in the Verge, now would it?"

I catch May glaring at him.

TJ turns to me next, but I don't know what he expects me to say. "I...I..." I take a deep breath to stop my stuttering. "I think they can help us find my parents. I think it's the right side to be on." I rest my hand on his shoulder and squeeze.

Dixie sighs. "Do you accept this commission, son?"

It's only a second before TJ stands taller, takes a breath and answers, "I do."

May hands Dixie a weathered kihle platter on which rests a Haida ceremonial knife, its grimacing face and leather-wrapped bone blade look ancient and mysterious. Dixie takes the kihle and holds out in front of TJ.

After a short hesitation, he picks up the knife, opens his left palm and presses the tip into his flesh. A small pool of bright red blood appears.

Dixie holds out the wooden kihle; it's stained in the center with the dark shadow of thousands of blood vows that came before. "What do you pledge to the Legion of Scorch, Major?"

Eddie's skirts rustle as she glides closer and places a hand over mine on her brother's shoulder.

Van does the same.

TJ clears his throat. He holds the blade across his heart and slowly turns his cut palm flat on the slab of wood. "I, Tern Journey LeRoux, do hereby affirm that I will support and defend the people of Scorch against all enemies in truth and faithfulness to the Creator; that I bear allegiance to the same, and accept this duty freely and with peace in my heart, so help me God."

Dixie grasps his other shoulder. "Congratulations, Major."

"Amen," Sheriff Arson laughs.

May makes a little whooping sound before wrapping TJ in a hug. He clenches his cut hand in a tight fist and slowly wraps his arms around her. His eyes close.

It's the most natural thing in the world, and I'm sure then—they're a couple. Before I can dwell on it, the dogs start barking and dancing around, trying to get in on the fun. It's a spontaneous party and absolutely sincere.

"First Lieutenant Elder!" Dixie's command silences everyone. Her expression is serious as she moves to stand in front of Van. "Through the divine within and by recommendation of TAC command, I hereby promote you to the rank of Captain in the Terran Army Corps. Do you wish to renew your oath to the Legion of Scorch?"

Van blinks.

"Well?" Dixie asks.

"Van." TJ lifts Van's left hand and punctures Van's palm

with the ceremonial blade, then grasps Van's bleeding hand with his own so their blood mixes. "Brothers."

Van nods and his Adam's apple bobs uncontrollably for a moment before he speaks in a raspy voice. "Brothers." He squeezes TJ's hand before taking the knife and laying it over his heart. "I, Sylvan Cré Elder, do hereby reaffirm that I will support and defend the people of Scorch against all enemies in truth and faithfulness to the Creator; that I bear allegiance to the same, and continue to accept this duty freely and with peace in my heart, so help me God."

"Congratulations, son."

"Thank ye, General," Van murmurs and bows his head shyly.

"Congratulation, Van." I want to reach up and kiss his cheek, but it's too awkward, so I smile with all the warmth I can muster.

Dixie takes my elbow. "That's the end of ceremony for today, friends." The smallest smile curves on her lips and I think she's holding back a laugh. "Let's find you a bed before you collapse, Dr. Adams."

Her comment reminds me how much I need my rem and I realize I'm surprised I'm even standing at this point.

When she guides me back into the elevator, I wave to Van, but he's still standing there motionless staring down at his palm.

When the elevator doors close, Dixie chuckles. "That was fun, but I think Van might be in shock."

"Don't worry, he's extremely durable."

She smiles and pats my hand. "I'm sure he is."

MAY

Current year: 2701
Thursday, 10 PM
The Verge

May knows it takes the Couvies thirty-five precious labor rotations a month to maintain twenty kilometers of highway running east into the wilderness beyond the Verge. Valuable resources. She's done the work herself—it's one of her favorite shifts. Despite the high-tech fixes and hundreds of hours, the pavement is still uneven in places—great scars run here and there, reminding them of the ever-changing earth beneath their feet.

May drives the truck with confidence, as familiar with this road as she is with any in town. The dogs press their heads around her seat toward the open window, jockeying for the best position as the truck speeds along, headlights cutting a sliver into the moonlit night that surrounds them.

Beside her, TJ sighs and leans his head back against the headrest.

She feels his eyes on her. "Have you told your sister about us?"

He's studying her in that peculiar way he always does. It makes her nervous and content all at once.

"I don't need to. She knows."

"Maybe she does know, but I wonder how she *feels* about us. Sometimes I catch her staring at me with that fierce look she gets like she's trying to read my mind, but then she acts like nothing happened."

"Hmm…that's my fault, I think. I can guard my thoughts when she's around, but not my emotions. She doesn't have to read my mind to sense how happy I am when you're with me."

A thrill runs through May. TJ seldom puts his love for her so plainly into words.

They lapse into silence as the road stretches on.

"I can't quite place it," he says a moment later, "but there's something about this drive that always makes the rest of the world seem, I don't know, less breathable."

"It's the temperature—the coolest place in the Verge. Try to enjoy the ride. We're almost there."

TJ reaches over and twists the non-functional radio knob on the dash. "This truck is an antique." He looks around the spartan cabin, poking at the compartments.

"It's not *antique,* that's for like furniture and jewelry. It's *a relic!* A 2072 Pinzgauer—older than the praenex." She caresses the dash and gives it a little pat.

"2072? *Non, tu te moques de moi.*" TJ shakes his head.

"I'm not kidding you. It's old, but it's retrofitted with new technology. A reformed halocarbon engine, for example. The tires are newly recycled. Most of the body's been replated. It's like that old expression—it's the same ax I've had for forty years, I've only replaced the head twice and the handle three times."

TJ laughs. "Still, why keep it?"

May slows the large truck as the flashing barriers marking the end of the maintained pavement appear ahead. There's no such thing as traffic here. This is the end of the passable roadway. And no one comes here except her.

"Because it can do this…." Carefully she turns the vehicle off road, down the steep ditch and up the other side. A rough—very rough—trail runs alongside the old highway. The Pinzgauer climbs and descends over obstacles, across a small stream and on into the wilderness.

TJ presses one hand to the ceiling, the other grips his seat as they bounce along.

After a few minutes, May stops in a clearing, cuts the engine and shoves open the creaky door. She jumps down, letting the dogs out behind her. The vehicle's lights fade and go out.

"Whoa," TJ whispers as he exits the truck.

She can hear him perfectly in this quiet, velvet world.

Insects chirp. Rodents scurry away into the night as the dogs spread out to investigate. A cool breeze brushes her cheek as she walks back around to where TJ has come to rest against the front bumper, bathed in the light of a full moon.

Her foot catches on a branch growing across the trail and she bends to pry it free.

He bends down to look at her face. "So?"

"So, this is it." She uses the twig like a wand to indicate the blackness of the forest ahead of them.

"*What* is it, exactly?"

"The reason I brought you here. All of this. Out there." At his blank look, she blows out a long breath. "Don't you ever wonder what could be out there? How many possibilities there are for people willing to work hard and take risks?"

TJ presses his lips together, scrunching his face in concentration. The moon slants silvery shadows along the planes of his jaw, his cheekbones, making him look even more serious than usual.

He shrugs. "To be honest, no. When I look out there"—he motions to the trail and the dense forest beyond—"I see the past, not the future."

May pushes away from the truck to face him, twisting the twig between her fingers, fighting the nervous energy buzzing through her. "But think of all the closed sites just waiting to be explored. We could…I mean…*people* could start new settlements almost anywhere north of the great storm. Maybe even cross the eastern sea to Greenland."

"Why?"

May throws up her hands in frustration. "Just because we can! To be somewhere else. To grow beyond the Verge and New Juneau. To explore again—the new world beyond what satellites tell us. To experience it."

"May, I know what you feel." He touches her hair and tucks a loose braid behind her ear.

A shiver raises goosebumps on her neck when he pauses to play with the shell of her ear. Her chin dips even lower. "I don't think you truly do know what I feel."

"I do. It…calls to you."

She lifts her head to gaze straight into his violet eyes. "Yes. Always…like a constant cry behind everything else. Sometimes it's all I hear."

He smiles out of one side of his mouth—that cocky smirk that makes her forget their differences, that adds a whole new kind of tension to the restlessness she's been fighting for weeks.

"Come on." He pulls her toward the back of the truck. "Let me show you what calls to me."

She laughs as she trips along behind him. "I'm not that naive, TJ LeRoux. If you think I'm going to climb in the back of this truck with you, then you're—"

"I'm what?" he challenges, as he jumps gracefully into the back, ducking just in time to keep from bashing his head on the roof bars.

"You're soft in the head, that's what." She stands, hands on hips, looking in at him.

TJ laughs. "It's not that, or…not only that. Look at this." He reaches around to the front seat and pulls a cube from his bag to open a small device inside. Instantly a universe of stars covers the dome of the truck's roof and races along the sides of the bed.

Without a second thought, she's suddenly lying back in the truck's bed beside TJ to get a better view. "It's amazing!"

"Eddie gave it to me. To help me find my way, she said." He turns his head to watch May's wonder as the star chart changes and moves.

Pressing up on an elbow he moves closer. "Come with me." His face fills her vision, his breath's a caress on her cheek as the stars swirl behind him. His eyes reflect the cosmos cast across the walls as she focuses on him.

She sees her own silhouette in the center of his pupil, the specks dancing around her too.

"Come with me," he whispers again before moving closer to eclipse everything else from her sight.

His lips are warm and soft. They're an answer unto themselves as energy rushes through her and into their kiss.

14
VAN

I woke with a sense of excitement for Addition Day. On this day in 2372, the human population began to claw its way upward for the first time since the Call. Our pop banners proudly show the increase, inspiring everyone. Celebrations abound in Alberta Farms, in New Juneau, at the Hub. In orbit above us, SATO Space Station supposedly projects the image onto the planet, so that you never see Scorch without the number emblazoned on it. I'd be annoyed to have that digital noise block my view of our beautiful planet.

Yet here in the Verge I've seen nothing to mark the day. No celebration. No recognition. The faded fabric banner at the marina is just part of their ruse. I wonder if Mercy's noticed.

As I lift weights in the gym to work out some of my pent-up energy, I can't stop thinking about the massive air fleet I saw yesterday. About the size of army it would take to man so many planes. The numbers buzz around in my brain like pesky mosquitos worrying my neck on a hot summer night.

There were times growing up in our busy house that I felt like my folks took it as their personal mission to repopulate the planet, and maybe they have. My mam has eleven children. My da has five more by surrogate. Humans are good breeders. It's one of the few things we do just as well as the praenex. So why is Addition Day, a celebration of growth, a major holiday in the largely sapiens Alberta Farms, just another day in the Verge where sapiens customs reign?

"Good morning." Mercy holds a single palm out to me, still shy, as she enters the gym.

Heat rushes to my face to be caught thinking about family, about children. and I'm thankful that my dark skin hides most of my embarrassment. I wonder again about the gift of her vision for me—three sons. Will she know that joy with me?

I press my palm to hers. "Divine grace."

TJ and May follow her, sharing a quick grin with each other before they untangle their held hands.

Everyone's attention seems riveted to the mat where Sherrif Arson spars with Eddie to assess her mission readiness.

It's a strangely graceful dance—Eddie's fluid martial arts against Arson's more brutal combat technique. The advantage constantly switches between the two. Eddie's signature skirts fly like flags across the mat, no longer confusing Arson, who's learned fast where the strike will come from. Clearly Eddie's been training harder since I last saw her spar. All the Legion are trained in martial arts, but I wonder if that's how she's working out her motherhood issues, with sweat and strikes.

I turn back to the newcomers. "Happy Addition Day."

"Oh, I forgot. To you too." Mercy looks around. "Where's the cake?"

May laughs, while TJ just rolls his eyes.

"Training or assessing?" Mercy motions toward the fighters.

"Aye, both. Performing for that group." I point to observers gathered at the side of the gym. "Come on, I'll introduce you."

Eddie and Arson stop their session and join us, both sweating and breathing hard, but clearly energized.

"This is Dr. Avarice Henderson, *pronoms fem*, leader of the Verge's bio engineering division. She's Sheriff Arson's wife. She's May's..." I dunno what to label her exactly. She raised May, but I've never heard May call her mother.

"Aunt," Ava explains. "May's lived with us since she was seven, after her parents passed."

"Oh, it's nice to meet you, Dr. Henderson." Mercy raises a hand.

"Please call me Ava." They press palms.

"You have fewer rings than the others." Mercy turns over Ava's hand to admire them.

"They interfere with my work."

I finish the introductions and we reconnect with Commander Vi Garcia, recently arrived from New Juneau with Bozan Kahinu.

"Are ye well, Bozan?" I ask them.

"Well enough to get back to work." They cringe a little when they smile—an indication that that might not be entirely true. Their jaw is still bruised—a purple cloud on ebony skin—I have a few just like it—and the cut over their eye is still red and swollen, but their spine is straight. Seeing anyone like that makes me angry, but knowing the same bastards tried to kill my da makes me wanna rip someone's head off.

Mercy must sense my tension; she nudges my elbow and I unclench my fists.

"Is there any further news on my parents?"

Garcia hesitates, shifts uneasily. "You know about the statement from SciCorps?"

"Aye, we heard. Do ye have any real information?"

"That's all. You're not going to like this, but once their whereabouts were confirmed, the investigation stalled. We don't believe they went willingly, but there's not much we can do without more evidence."

Mercy takes a step toward Garcia. "There was blood in my kitchen!"

"Mercy?" I tip my head toward the group. "Maybe it's time to share the disk?"

"Oh, right!" She pulls the photo from her bag and waves it toward Garcia. "My father wanted me to have this." She pulls the disk from behind the photo frame. "I think it's important somehow, but we haven't had a chance to look at it."

Commander Garcia and Dixie exchange a look, but it's Ava who speaks. "May I?" She holds her hand out expectantly.

No way I would turn that over. I'm about to step in when I feel Eddie's hand at my elbow gently holding me back.

Mercy looks at Ava's hand, then curls her fist around the disk. "I'm sorry. I need to be there when we read this. Can you understand?"

Ava smiles, but it doesn't reach her eyes. "We'll need to do that soon then. TJ, May, you'll join us?" When they nod, she turns to Eddie. "Bozan LeRoux, last night the children told me about your resistance to the Trade. I know more than a couple of doctors here who would love to talk with you, perhaps get a vial or two of blood?"

Now they want a piece of Eddie? I open my mouth to protest, but she squeezes my arm again.

"Of course. It's only blood, after all."

"No rest on Addition Day, I guess." I'm not sure what makes me say it, but the effect is immediate.

"Oh, yes." Bozan Kahinu lifts a hand to their forehead. "With everything else, I forgot. Happy Addition Day." They grin, but their smile starts to slip as they look around.

The Couvies shuffle and look away. So, it's *not* my imagination, this celebration is a problem for them.

Dixie clears her throat. In the set of her jaw there's a lie forming.

"Hold on." Mercy searches the faces of these nulls she's just beginning to trust. "This isn't Addition Day at all, is it?"

"What?" Rumesa's head swivels like Mercy's. As a powerful cleric, I bet they're not often surprised.

In a flash of movement, Mercy clamps a hand around Dixie's wrist. "Tell us. When is it truly? What's the *real* Addition Day?"

Dixie exchanges a look with Ava, then sighs. "July 20."

A growl forms low in my throat. "What *year*?"

Everyone stares at the mayor now. I think she knows it's well past the time for lies.

Dixie takes a deep breath. "2211."

Eddie hisses and it's my turn to restrain *her*. I put my hand over hers where she still holds my arm. "But that's—" I close my eyes as I try to do the math.

"160 years earlier than we thought, give or take," TJ blurts.

160 years of underestimating our population growth? I can't believe they managed to keep this secret, but if they can hide an air fleet, they can hide the pilots, too.

"But the trackers?" Mercy asks.

The mayor shakes her head. "Most of us have 'em. Sometimes parents request to skip the implant. We feel it's a choice they should make."

"How many?" My voice sounds far away to my ears. "How many are we *truly*?"

Ava steps forward. "We've approximately 24,000 in population not counted in census." At our gasps, she hurries on, "Don't blame Dixie, or any one of us, it's a social outcome of decisions made hundreds of years ago."

"Your deception makes us fools!" Eddie wrenches her arm away from me, breathing hard.

"Peace, sister." Rumesa raises a palm. "I admit that I'm surprised that you could hide so many from us, but is this not good news?" They look at us now, one by one. "We are thousands stronger. In this time of aggression, is it not helpful to have more in our legion?"

After a few breaths, my blood starts to cool. 24,000 people— no, not *people…Couvies*! They're right of course. Couvies are nearly all Terrans, though some are neutral, like May. I've never met a Pilgrim in the Verge.

"Are we done with this irrelevant argument?" Sheriff Arson interrupts and cracks his knuckles loudly. "We need to finish the combat assessment."

Eddie swings around to face the sheriff. "Do I pass?"

Arson smiles that crooked grin of his and wipes some sweat from his face. "*Oui*, Princess, you pass. And I know TJ and Van." He turns that lazy, wolfish grin of his on Mercy and she freezes in place like spooked animal. Her cheeks color.

"I can pass. I *need* to pass. I have to save my parents." Her voice is quiet but determined.

I step into his line of sight, breaking their eye contact. "She'll hold, ye have my word."

Arson shakes his head. "Look, this is a military op. I'm sorry Lieutenant. I need to know if she's qualified."

"It's *Captain*," I remind him, but my voice betrays me and cracks.

He smirks and plants his hands on his hips. "So it is. Well, *Captain*, last I checked *I'm* in charge of troop readiness, so if Dr. Adams wants to be part of the mission, *I* need to know what to expect."

"Van, son." Dixie shakes her head and I know I've lost this round.

I turn to Mercy, whose eyes flicker from fearful to annoyed.

"Don't worry about this, lass." I step onto the mat. "How about we all go through some exercises together and ye can assess the group at the same time."

Arson wraps a towel around his neck, shifts his balance to one hip. We wait. *"D'accord. Allons-y."* He waves for us to take position.

Commander Garcia steps onto the mat in front of me and immediately begins a sequence of tai chi movements for warmup. Rumesa surprises me by getting in line too.

"I'm sure you don't have to—"

But their long slender limbs are already moving with restrained strength and fluid grace. Rumesa's hobby is dance, Eddie once said. I dunno what kind, but the training has given them smoothness in even the simplest movements.

Thirty minutes later, Mercy's shoulders have rolled forward in defeat, a streak of sweat stains the back of her shirt and she's favoring a leg that must throb from the last throw. Rumesa was as gentle as possible as her partner, but Mercy just isn't a fighter.

"That's enough." Arson walks over to speak to Dixie, seated with May and Ava at a table off the matt. When he walks back to us, I can see his decision in the pinched creases at the corners of his eyes.

"We don't know yet exactly what this operation's going to entail, but hand to hand's definitely a possibility. Anyone who can't hold their own risks becoming a victim, or worse yet, a bargaining chip." He moves directly in front of Mercy, stares her in the eye. "You understand that, don't you?"

Mercy's eyes begin to fill and I'm there, between them, before I even think to move. "Ye're wrong."

Arson blows out a breath. "I can't see how."

I turn to Mercy. "Show them." When she finally looks at me, I straighten my spine and say it again. I let my pride show in my smirk. "Show 'em what ye can do."

"But that's different—"

"Aye, but just as valuable. Don't weigh yer strength in only muscle. Instinct and cleverness weigh equally in battle."

She stares at me for a few seconds, and then her eyes clear and she nods.

"Okay. You and you"—I point to May and Garcia—"ye guard the exits with yer backs to the room, eyes closed. Sheriff, Mayor, Dr. Ava, if ye'll please, follow me?" I lead them behind a storage locker, one of the few pieces of furniture in the room. "Will ye stay here please, cover yer ears and don't look?"

"Now, Captain—" Dixie begins.

"Please! If ye're not convinced after this, she'll stay behind. I'll make sure myself that she doesn't make a fuss."

"Fine," she agrees.

With some grumbling, she and Arson do as I've asked.

I walk quickly back to Mercy. "Now!" I whisper. While Mercy does her thing, I space the others on the mat where I want them, further back on the mat with passing room between them.

"Alright, ye can come out now," I shout.

Four minutes later, they still can't find her, even after searching their own waiting space. I give them credit for that one—it was an imaginative spot.

Arson shakes his head. He turns to Garcia and May for a second time. "You swear she didn't leave?"

May stabs a hand in the air for emphasis. "No one left this room."

Garcia nods in agreement.

"Well now, do ye give up?"

Arson shrugs.

"Come out Mercy." I know she must be close; I don't have to shout.

Garcia startles as the table shakes beside them and Mercy gracefully lets herself down from under the table's apron. With only inches of depth, even I'm impressed that she fit so neatly and held for so long. I chuckle as Vi and Dixie peer under the tabletop in disbelief.

Stretching her limbs and rolling her neck, Mercy walks to stand beside me, the audience fanned out in front of us, the mat and other trainees behind them.

"Nice trick, *chèrie*." Arson grins. "But hiding isn't enough."

She looks at me and smiles.

"Naw, it's not," I agree. "Take her into custody."

Arson chuckles, but motions May and Garcia to get Mercy.

In a flash of color, Mercy cartwheels into a back flip and tuck that takes her right between them. Her next move connects her heel perfectly with Arson's chin. It was probably a lucky hit, but he doesn't need to know that.

His teeth clack on impact and his eyes roll back in his head before he crashes to the mat. Garcia and May spin around and rush to his side. Dazed, he shakes his head and rubs his jaw when he gets to his feet. Cold anger burns in his violet eyes.

"Aye, and you still don't have her."

"Go!" he commands, but Mercy's gone.

May lifts a shoulder. "Where?"

"I didn't see," Garcia admits.

They wander through the trainees standing motionless on the mat.

I take a breath and wait for the perfect moment. "Mercy, strike!"

"Gah!" Garcia shouts as they stumble forward—their knee collapsing from a strike behind. May moves quickly, grabbing for Eddie. Mercy emerges from under the folds of Eddie's skirts and darts away on hands and knees. She uses TJ's legs next to evade May and Garcia's grabbing hands.

Arson lunges forward. Mercy sees him coming, her eyes wide. She slams her arm into the back of TJ's knees, forcing him to fall into Eddie. Both of them land on top of May and pull Garcia down too.

"I've got her!" Arson shouts. It's just a pile of people on the mat now, limbs sticking out everywhere. He pulls on an ankle and holds up a foot like a prize. Everyone starts standing up.

"Let go of me!" Eddie kicks at Arson's hand clamped around her ankle.

"Ouch! What the—?" Arson releases his grip and sits back on the mat, rests his arms across his bent knees.

Mercy giggles and pokes her head out from behind Rumesa's legs, a few meters away on the mat.

"*Bon!*" Mayor Dixie claps and whispers something to a laughing Dr. Ava.

"Girl!" Arson shakes his head, unable to stop his smile now. "How did you get so squirrelly?"

Eddie snorts. "She was born that way, far as we can tell."

Mercy stands up, walks over to Arson and holds out a hand.

"Want help up?"

He smiles, grabs her hand and heaves himself to his feet. "Alright, you're in."

Her grin nearly splits her face as she bounces on her heels. "Van!" She rushes over and hugs my arm. "I'm going to get my parents!"

"Aye, ye are, Cricket." I give her a one-armed hug, the most relaxed I've felt since arriving in the Verge. Things are looking up.

Arson clucks his tongue. "Can you shoot?"

Her face falls. "Shoot?" She looks at me and I can't think of anything to say to make it better.

"We're planning traditional rounds, no stun guns on this one," Arson confirms.

"Aw, hell." I should have known it wouldn't be this easy.

CRANE ELDER

Crane squeezed a towel around the thick cord of Brym's newly washed hair. The automatic motions of motherhood were like moments of meditation in her busy life. She squeezed and combed, and then squeezed again, working through tangles and letting her mind drift as she went.

She felt her life looping like yarn through the history of the world she knew. She remembered when the United Countries of America formed in 2098. By then, the world population had shrunk to two billion. The equatorial band around the planet was already a sweltering wasteland, lost to climate change. War and lawlessness covered the globe. Canada, her home, like other countries in the northern hemisphere, had created self-sufficient compounds farther and farther north. Crane met and married her husband, Jon Sr.—an Army officer. His unit was among the first to arrive in Fermont, Quebec—Crane in tow. After the Call, she watched as compounds like theirs became civilized havens for the survivors of the restless world.

Crane hadn't intended to get into politics—it sort of happened by accident, just by doing what needed doing. It wasn't until later that she realized where it was all headed, like the yarn of her life might have inadvertently spun into a metaphorical noose.

By Brym's second birthday, Crane had helped to forge an alliance between the compounds in the UCA and an unusual compound in Versailles, France, UCE. After that, *Mother Crane,* as the praenex children called her, pioneered an accelerated curriculum that could be taught at breakneck speed to the highly intelligent and endlessly curious, the praenex. Crane had a large team to help her. She turned out to be a good boss. People liked her. She was open and creative. She noticed things.

The fast-maturing praenex children loved her and considered her their sapiens leader. Her peers paid attention and her social media rating continued to rise. Her elevation to the Council was inevitable, and soon she found herself occupying one of the thirteen council seats that governed the allied compounds.

"Are you nervous, *Maman?*" Brym asked.

Crane startled as her daughter's voice brought her back to the present. She let the final section of Brym's smooth brown braid slide through her fingers as she wrapped an elastic around the end. She met Brym's amethyst eyes in the mirror in front of them. "You know I am."

"About being a councilmember?"

"Some," Crane admitted. "Also about other things."

Brym concentrated for a moment. "You think I should stay

behind. Why?"

Crane blew out a long breath. "Well, you're very young—"

"How old do I look to your eyes?" Brym straightened her spine and smoothed down her simple tan jacket.

Crane smiled into the mirror. "To me you look like a precocious eight-year-old."

"Precisely. Our caregivers have accepted our rapid growth—we're not like sapiens children. I go to school with your nine-year-olds, and in six months I'll be moving up another grade. They'll accept me."

"Yes, they will. I'm only worried that bringing you and the others along on my first day as councilmember makes too much of a statement—"

"I will make a statement. I will help them understand." Brym folded her arms across her chest and spread her feet.

Crane turned Brym away from the mirror to face her. "Brym, you really must work on not interrupting."

"Yes, *Maman*."

"What will you tell them?"

Brym pulled a small tablet from her jacket pocket. "Here, I've prepared a proposal. I'll explain that we praenex need to begin to participate in the council government, in order to prepare for the day that we become adults and join the sapiens in running things. Our brains are quite efficient—we can solve many of your problems for you."

Crane covered her face and sighed.

"Don't worry. I'll also explain that we're far too young to know how to run things now, and so we've chosen you to help represent us."

Crane uncovered one eye and stared at the beautiful child that had come into her life so unexpectedly. For years she thought that the occasional visits with her nephew were as close as she would get to motherhood. Those visits ended long ago, when she became a mother to Brym. Until her husband returned from overseas, she would raise her daughter alone.

"We better move along then." She reached for Brym's small hand. "It wouldn't be very novus of us to be late for our first council meeting."

Brym smiled in agreement.

Outside in the corridor, they met two praenex girls waiting for them.

"Siblings." Brym held up both hands, palms out. The first girl mirrored her gesture, touched Brym's palms, and then leaned forward until their foreheads met. She repeated the process with the second girl. This familiar, yet unique greeting had developed with the praenex children's earliest motor skills. Crane'd been there to watch it evolve, but it still made her throat tighten with emotion.

Once they crossed the short distance to the council chambers, Crane opened the door and ushered the girls in ahead of her. Distracted by the logistics of getting them all settled, Crane didn't notice the silence until she looked up and found that all fifty-odd people assembled in the chambers were staring at them.

"Oh, I'm sorry. We—"

"No problem." Dr. Laurens waved them in. "Nurse Elder, Brym O'Dell, and all of you, welcome." Her smile was bright but forced.

"*Bonjour*. Peace with you," Brym said in her high voice. She raised her hands, palms out to the room. Crane and the praenex girls did too.

After an awkward hesitation, the sapiens raised their hands. Brym waited.

A woman next to Dr. Laurens whispered in her ear.

"Oh, uh," Dr. Laurens stuttered. "Divine grace with you."

Brym beamed. "It's Brym Elder, if you please, *madam*, not O'Dell."

Crane moved them to the open seats at one end of the large conference table at the front of the room. It was like being on stage, she thought. One wall held three images of smaller rooms in Versailles, New Juneau, and Vancouver Colony. At least one praenex girl sat with the sapiens leaders at each location. Each one had followed Brym's lead and had dressed as prim and grownup as possible. The girl in New Juneau even wore a junior-size lab coat. Crane recognized the girl in Versailles as Brym's long-distance friend, Pauline LeRoux.

Crane smiled at all of them and began to relax. She tried not to look at the other wall with its always-descending population banner and large grid of peer ratings. She'd have to look eventually, she knew. To watch trends. To gather ideas. But here, only those thirteen who held council seats were allowed to speak; all the others had to content themselves, as she had for many years, with written comments, blog feedback, electronic votes, and other social media responses.

Dr. Laurens cleared her throat. "It's our tradition on this

council to give new members the opportunity to provide the opening remarks. Do you have anything you wish to say?" This last question was directed not so much at Crane, as at Brym.

Crane squeezed Brym's hand under the table. "Yes, I do," she said. "My daughter, Brym Elder, would like to read a statement explaining her presence here, along with the other praenex, and then we have a short proposal for their inclusion in future meetings."

A murmur rose among the audience and Crane noted with astonishment that her peer rating jumped two positions in a heartbeat—a clear indication that the council and advisors agreed with the inclusion of the praenex.

Brym smiled and turned to one of her companions. Without a word, the other girl bent and extracted a small stool from the bag she carried. She set it up next to Crane's chair and Brym stepped up onto it. Brym straightened her jacket and looked down the table at Dr. Laurens. She smiled, took a deep breath to speak, but suddenly jerked and gripped the table.

Crane reached to help her daughter, but Brym lurched to the side and spun around to face the Versailles video screen.

"No!" Brym grimaced in pain.

All the other praenex, both local and in the remote meetings, jumped to their feet.

An alarm sounded in the Versailles conference room connected by video. Everyone watched the image on the screen. The praenex girl there, Brym's friend, Pauline, turned to the window behind her and let out a high, piercing scream.

An explosion shook the Versailles conference room. Pauline

stumbled. Then another, louder explosion showered the room with dust. Plaster rained from the ceiling.

Pauline screamed and ran toward the camera. "Help us!"

Versailles erupted in chaos just before the video feed blurred with static, and then went out completely.

Crane and everyone else at the table were on their feet. She couldn't remember moving, but suddenly she found herself in front of the pop banner, the arms of three praenex girls wrapped around her middle. Her heart pounded in her chest, and her skin prickled with icy shock.

She held the girls while they watched in horror as the pop banner plummeted, by tens at first, and then by hundreds, and then thousands as the satellite over Europe subtracted the life signs that'd gone dark.

Crane sank to the floor and sat cross-legged in front of the screen. Brym clamored into her lap, her chest shaking with sobs as Crane looped her arms around her. The other two girls squirmed in on either side, linked their arms through Crane's elbows and reached out for Brym's hands. They stayed like that, holding each other close, as Versailles Compound fought for survival six thousand kilometers away.

15
MERCY

Sometimes I wish I'd been there 593 years ago when the world ended, which sounds crazy, I know. But I wonder how I would have reacted to hearing the Creator's voice so clearly in my mind. Would I have gone mad like so many did? Would I have taken my own life? If not, would I have been clever enough to survive the ensuing chaos that took millions more worldwide? Humans killed one another all the time before the Call, before the Collapse, but when the drama of the Call settled, humankind finally came to agree on one thing. Life is precious.

Now Sheriff Arson is trying to explain to me why it's not. As if killing is no big deal. "We've got eyes in the Hub. We know the Pilgrims are prepared to use lethal force if we come knocking."

"You can't be serious."

Van looks as surprised as I feel, but TJ doesn't. I nudge him. "You knew about this?"

He shrugs. "Not exactly, but I just remembered something. A few months ago, I piloted a Pilgrims-only scavie crew to a warehouse in Montana. I didn't think much of it at the time—"

May scoffs. "A scavie crew without Couvies? That didn't strike you?"

I hold up my hand. "Why is that unusual?"

May thinks for a second. "Scavenging is one of our things. Crews are mostly civilian Couvies with a few SciCorps or TAC participants mixed in, not the other way around."

"So it didn't seem strange to you, TJ?"

"No. Not on its own." He runs his hands through his hair. "It was a small crew. People I knew. We'd all been on crews together before. They told me the scavie captain had come down with some kind of virus or something—you Couvies do get sick occasionally. I didn't question it."

"Wait, I remember that." Dr. Ava presses two fingers to her temple. "A scavie captain came into the hospital. A colleague of mine treated her. She asked me to review some irregularities in her blood work, but by the time I got around to it, she was feeling better. They discharged her the same day, and we let it drop."

"That was only the first unusual thing," TJ continues. "Even though I'm along as the pilot, I usually also participate in the scavenge operations, at least peripherally. It's a perk. If I find something I like, they usually let me keep it. But this run was different. When we touched down, the commander told me to stay with the plane. It was his command; I couldn't really argue. They were gone less than an hour before they returned with munition crates, and we left."

"Did you tell anyone?"

"Who? It was an official op. Logged and everything. That's probably how the Couvie informants noticed in the first place."

"My brother, friends." Eddie rolls her eyes and goes back to pacing.

"Okay." Arson raises a hand to cut off TJ's response. "We know they have real guns with real bullets, but there're more reasons we're going in hot. For one, their attacks on Terran leadership had deadly intent. By divine grace, no one died, but it doesn't change the fact that whoever's behind this is willing to take a life."

"This is M.A.D." The history lesson pushes its way to the front of my thoughts. "Mutually Assured Destruction—only on a micro scale." I scan faces to make sure I have their attention. "In the twentieth century, some of the greatest military powers on Earth were locked in the Cold War, constantly wasting resources and building new machines of war in order to match one another's destructive capabilities. One side, the Soviets, poured so much energy into countering their enemies' strengths that their own people starved. Some say it was a war without a single shot fired, but we know that the ramifications, though delayed, were just as bad as any long-term war. The weapons used against the United Countries of Europe that cost millions of lives all originated in the Cold War."

Mayor Dixie, who's been quiet until now, exhales loudly and I know she's going to support Sheriff Arson. "History teaches big lessons but look at the small tactical scenario we have now. The mag tether carries what, 100, 120 people at most? We're going to have to keep the team small just to blend in. Disguises. Tech hacks for your trackers. Six people, maybe seven. No dogs." She gives TJ a pointed look. "Then let's say you get there and find a bad guy on the way to rescue the doctors. You stun him. What are you going to do, tie him up and hide him? In his own place? If not, twenty minutes later the same bad guy's going to be on your tail again."

"*Bad guys.*" I click my comm rings, tap in and expand a small virtual display. The book loads. "That reminds me of something." I begin to read.

May 11, 2113; Fermont Compound
Dear Jon,
The Versailles survivors arrived today, and so I know for sure what I've feared for the last six months. You're dead. A hero, they tell me, but I knew that already. The soldiers have been briefed. I know what you did, what you sacrificed to save them, to save the children they guarded. The warrior doctor, *they call you. Always showing off.*

I promise to talk of you often with our beloved nephew, Jon Jr., and Brym as well, although you won't meet her in this life. You've sent us 35 praenex and more sapiens than I know. We'll hold each life precious. We will love you always.

Your wife, your friend, your love,
Crane

I look up from the display. "It's signed Crane Elder. It's about your ancestor, Van. It's about Brym Elder too, why she never met her adopted father." I turn to Dixie. "The enemies he killed, they had families too. Wives. Children. They wrote letters just like this one. To them, Jon Elder Sr. *was* the bad guy."

I close the display. Everyone is quiet. Thinking. Rumesa wipes a tear from their cheek and smiles at me. Nods.

When I look at Van, his eyes are tracking mine. The fierce determination I see in the set of his jaw, the way he holds his body ready, gives me the strength I need to face the others.

I turn to face Sheriff Arson. "My parents would not want this. We will not participate in any operation that uses deadly force. This is not negotiable. We'll just have to find another way to get into the Hub and find the prisoners without being noticed."

I catch Dixie and Ava exchanging a look. I can tell they don't like sharing control. Eddie nudges me and gives me a thumbs up. She believes in me. A lump forms in my throat. I swallow to clear it.

Arson shifts on his feet. "And how do you propose we do that, *ma chère?*"

"A diversion, a ruse." I close my eyes and think for a second. "TJ! They'll let TJ in anywhere. He's the admiral's son. With any luck, few know about his resignation, and no one knows about him joining TAC except us."

TJ stares at the floor as we await a response. After a second, he nods.

Arson exhales loudly. "Okay, some of that might work. The attacks on the council and the open aggression toward all of you are the only public violence so far. The rest has been political and economic."

Dixie leans forward. "As far as Scorch's concerned, it's your word against SciCorps'. Your posts have been dramatic, but for the most part, it'll read like fiction until citizens see something for themselves."

"I'm still not sure TJ can just waltz in to see dear old dad," Arson says.

"Yes, I need a pretense. One that allows several people to travel with me."

Eddie steps into the circle. "*Un ami*, perhaps? A friend?"

"They suspect your friends." May shakes her head.

I hold up a finger. "Just give me a second…I think…I know, a *prisoner!*"

"Oh, aye!" Van's excitement is obvious. "TJ escortin' a suspect. Someone SciCorps really wants to get their hands on."

"It has to be someone believable. Someone recognizably valuable to the Terrans."

"I believe I can help with that." The woman's voice behind us has us all turning. The Gran Bozan stands a few meters away with her entourage forming a semicircle around her, silent and ready. Her bandages are gone. She dressed in full regalia, her petite frame heightened by a tiered zucchetto. She wears her red sash banded around her tiny waist and a fierce expression I've seen before.

"I think I can make a convincing prize, don't you?" She smiles and lifts her chin.

"Yes!" I clap my hands. "Let's go get my parents."

MAY

Current year: 2701
Thursday, 10 PM
The Verge

When the icecaps melted and the Earth's sea level rose 75 meters hundreds of years before anyone predicted, it transformed the planet. Coastal cities were lost. Giant inland lakes grew where farm fields once flourished. Inland lakes became vast fresh and saltwater seas, many polluted beyond hope by the towns and industry that they consumed, but others, clean and new.

May traces a finger along the edge of the topographical map displayed on her tablet. She's chosen just the place. With the help of a few like-minded friends, she's even drafted a plan for a new colony far east of Alberta Farms on the northern edge of Lake Claire. All she needs now is supplies and 500 adventurous souls. And TJ.

Piper whines and gazes up at May from where she rests across May's toes, impatient and alert. They've been waiting like this in front of TJ's door for nearly five minutes. Waiting for the courage to knock.

Her nerves buzz, heat rises on her skin. "Here goes," she whispers to the dog, then raises her fist and knocks.

TJ opens the door almost immediately. "Hi. I'm glad you're here." He drags her into his room and closes the door. "I need you to keep working on the ID hack. I think we're going to need to apply it globally. This war could be dangerous for everyone. And we should put in a few more hours on Mercy's data chip later. I think we're close to cracking that code."

May follows him into the hotel room and stands awkwardly by the counter of the kitchenette. The dogs greet each other before running off to wrestle over a toy. TJ continues packing his small bag, scrutinizing each item he places inside. His old SciCorps uniform is pressed and waiting on one of the beds.

"Uh, sure." May smooths a gloved hand over her hair. "Um, there's something I want to show you."

"What?"

She closes the space between them and holds out her tablet. "This is Lake Claire. She's clean and blue and vast. There's potential for excellent fishing—even access to the Hudson Ocean."

TJ creases his brow. He looks at the map and then shrugs. "Yeah, I guess. I mean, this war can't go on forever. Maybe we could work in a short trip next year."

May frowns. "I'm not talking about a vacation. I...I want to live there."

TJ tips his head to the side and studies her face. "That would get pretty lonely, don't you think?"

"Argh!" May throws up her hands in frustration. "Not alone,

you Neanderthal. With you! And about 500 other settlers. I want to start a new colony…. And I want you to come with me."

TJ's expression is blank, like his brain can't even begin to comprehend what she said.

May takes the tablet from him. "Look, there are closed sites here and here." She points to two locations on the map. "I can't be sure what's there without the manifest, but the region was known for forestry, agriculture, and energy. I'm sure we can build—"

"May." TJ wrestles the tablet away from her and tosses it on the bed. "I'm not a Terran. You know I'm not."

When she tries to turn away, he pulls her flush against him. His breath is hot on her face. "We may well be colonists one day, but not here. Not on Scorch."

"No." Her voice is a hoarse whisper. She shakes her head.

TJ puts a finger under her chin and forces her to look him in the eyes. "Yes, I feel the truth. I dream it. I know it. We're leaving. Together. I love you."

"If you love me, you'll stay!"

"I have to go, you know that…and I have to go on this current mission very soon. I need to get ready, and you need to finish the hack on the ID implants."

"This mission is madness!" May insists, fear rising to the surface to mix with her nervousness. "It's too dangerous. You could be killed. You could be—"

TJ cuts her off with a soft kiss. It only lasts a few seconds before he pulls back to search her eyes. "Okay now…. Better?"

"No! Let Van handle the mission."

"They'll never let him in alone, he's too well known." TJ goes back to his packing.

"He could trick them. *Au petit bonheur la chance....* Um, he could pretend to turn traitor and deliver the GB to your father."

TJ laughs and gives her a pitying look. "Captain Van Elder, traitor? *Bon chance!* They'd never believe it." He slides another perfectly folded shirt into his duffel. "Van is Terran from his smooth sapiens forehead down to the dirt under his fingernails. I'm the only one who can get us in."

"Once they realize—they're not null, you know. They'll figure it out. They'll—"

In a blur of movement, TJ grabs her and tips her onto the bed. May squeals as he rolls so that she's on top, pinning him with her weight. His lips are urgent at first, pushing against her fears, her worries. Then they soften and she feels his confidence pouring into her, pushing aside uncertainty and infusing her with a lightness she only feels when she's in his arms.

"Better, *ma colombe*?" he whispers in her ear a moment later.

"Cheater." She shoves him aside and rolls off the bed to straighten her clothes.

He stares up at her with a self-satisfied grin. "I couldn't help but notice you didn't say 'I love you' back."

May stills and focuses on his face. "Come back in one piece, and maybe I'll tell you then." With a shrill whistle, she gathers the dogs and sweeps out the door.

16
VAN

Mercy's not the only one with famous ancestors. My kin, Jon Elder Sr. joined the army and deployed to Europe in 2108, just months after the Call. His legendary wife, Crane, was a nurse midwife then, living in Fermont compound, doing what she could to prepare for the first generation. Their nephew, my forefather Jon Jr., was a young man then.

Brym and Jon Elder Jr. are famous folks for a lot of reasons. Theirs was the first marriage of a praenex to a sapiens. They were the first praenex-sapiens parents. They were also the first to divorce. Jon Jr. went on to father a lot of babies, though all through artificial means. Some say that his popularity among the hopeful mams-to-be at the Fermont fertility center was the Creator's work—a way to reward the Elder family who'd given so much to Scorch. But Mercy tells me historians suspect that his donor number was leaked. Folks knew him, they liked him, and lots of sympathetic lasses requested his paternity for their babies.

That was in 2148, after the forty years of infertility ended. Whatever the case, five hundred years later, here I am, one of his descendants. And I have lots of kin. There are Elders everywhere, but few are praenex. If Mercy and I marry, our children will be a whole new generation.

If Mercy survives.

I pull on my left boxing glove.

If I can protect her.

I tighten the laces.

If she can dodge bullets.

I pull on my right glove.

If we make it back alive.

I yank the laces tight with my teeth.

If she'll still have me.

I pound my fists together.

If.

Punch! The bag shudders.

If.

Punch! The bag swings wildly.

If.

Punch!

The punching bag soars away and smacks into the ground with a thud a few meters away. The empty chain swings over my head.

"Whoa!" TJ claps as he walks over. "Working out some aggression there, Van? Sure you don't want to save that for the Pilgrims?"

A half smile pushes up one side of his face. "Aye, yer Pilgrim enough." I raise my gloves. "Wanna go-round, flyboy?"

"No thanks." He raises both hands and takes a step back. "I just thought you'd like to know that the hack worked. We know exactly where the doctors are being held."

"That's great." I use my teeth to loosen my glove strap.

TJ sighs and grabs my wrist. "Teeth are not tools." He's quiet as he pulls back the straps and helps me loosen the laces.

As I start on the second one, I feel his eyes boring into me.

"What's going on?" he murmurs.

"Not a thing."

"Really? Does this not-a-thing have to do with that little praenex woman over there sparring with the enigmatic Sheriff Arson? The one about to throw herself into the middle of a military operation?"

I blow out a breath and grab my water. I hear Arson and Mercy laugh about something and refuse to look their way. One of the men from the GB's entourage heads their direction. I squirt some water on my face before swallowing a mouthful.

"It might," I admit.

"Look, I didn't grow up in an affectionate home like you did. It's always been just me and Eddie, for the most part, and them, our parents—more interested in their careers and ambitions than anyone else in the house. After Eddie left for the Legion, I was alone with them a lot. They're quiet people, cold even. They're passionate about pilgrimage, but not much else. But over the last few years I've noticed that they have a devotion to one another that I hadn't fully recognized before. It doesn't matter how long they're apart, that connection is always there. They...I don't know…orbit each other maybe. Like some part of their brains is always aware of the other, orients to the other subconsciously. They never say it in front of me, but I know they love each other.

"It's that way with you and Mercy too. The orbit-thing. You just need to tell her. That's all it'll take."

"Oh, that's just grand. Tell her what?" I growl. A few folks glance our way and I struggle for control. "Divine grace, tell her what?" I pitch my voice lower. "That I don't want her to go on the op? That I want her to trust me to bring her parents back safely? That I can't stand the thought of her in danger? That it'll be a distraction? Do I look like an eejit? It'll only make her feel like a child."

"No. Tell her you love her. Tell her you'll wait for however long it takes."

I take a deep breath to tell him why I can't admit to that vulnerability. Why I want her to *know* how I feel without having to say it again. But nothing comes out.

We both feel and hear the thud as Arson hits the mat a few meters away. As I look over, Mercy reaches out a hand to help him up. They're laughing again and when he takes her hand to stand up, she has to lean with all her weight to keep from falling on top of him. The other man grabs her around the waist and together they heave the sheriff up.

"How old would you say Arson is?" TJ asks.

"I dunno. Old… forty?"

"Ha! No, not forty, Van. Not nearly forty." TJ shakes his head.

"He's married!"

"That he is."

"His wife's right over there." I point toward Ava, working at a table with Dixie and the clerics.

"Yes, she is. The sheriff's a hopeless flirt. I know, because I used to be one too. I'm sure he has no interest in Mercy aside from her sweetness, her peculiarity. And maybe how it irks you."

"She's not peculiar."

TJ snorts. "She is, and you know it. And pretty too. But I've never seen any of the guys on the Farm or at the Hab pay her any special attention. Everyone there knows you're promised. But here, well, here I'm not sure they know your personal history at all, and since you've barely touched her in the few days we've been working through this whole thing, it's not like they can tell."

"Aye, it's a good thing *she's* not a flirt then."

As I say this, Arson twirls a finger in the air and points. Mercy nods and flies into a series of flips and twists, ending with a short, cocky bow. Arson and the other man applaud.

TJ chuckles. "Yes, a good thing."

May bursts into the room and rushes over to Dixie, the children fast on her heels. After a short conversation, she looks up and waves us over. "TJ, Van, come here!"

"What?" I wipe my sweaty face with a towel as we join her.

"We did it." She wags the data disk in the air. "The information that Mercy gave us from her father. The children helped me; we broke the code."

"What is it?" Mercy asks from behind me. I back up to extend our circle so she and the others can join.

May grins. "It's the solution, I think. Or part of one; the data's incomplete."

"We agree!" Nairobi interrupts. "The issue your scientists have been having with the ozone loom, we think your father found the answer."

At our blank looks, Fez clears his throat. "We're scientists too."

"I'm ozone. He's botany," Nairobi adds, as if that explains it.

"These Spherans just get weirder and weirder," Eddie says *sotto voce*.

"Okay, slow down." I put a hand on May's shoulder. "It's information about the loom?"

"Yes, I think he was working on a way to solve the cohesion issues. If his data's correct, then we'll have an operable mend for the ozone layer when he finishes this work."

"That's great news, right?"

"Yes, of course," Ava agrees, but she frowns and gnaws her lip.

"Not if you're a Pilgrim," TJ adds.

"What do ye mean?"

"If you're a Pilgrim building a space colony transport ship, you control over half the *known* population and you've just frozen the world banking system, hearing that we're close to closing the hole in the ozone that keeps this planet from healing—"

"People might change sides," Eddie blurts.

I wipe sweat from my brow. "Aye, they won't want *that* to get out."

"Worse, I'm afraid," Dixie says.

Mercy looks up at me, her eyes wide and beginning to fill. "They won't want him to finish. They'll kill him."

I'm a Farmer and a Terran—I love the land, but I can appreciate the water. Old Earth built cities on the ocean. They fished. They traveled. They played. The shore was a paradise, until a few hundred years ago, anyway. Then global warming melted the ice caps, and the sea swallowed the land. The cities weren't just lost, they were infected. Pandemics and plagues raged, finding easy victims among populations struggling to find food and safe shelter and dodge chemical leaks and other hazards in the floodwaters. Global collapse wasn't far behind.

While some scientists focused on healing the ozone, another group prepared for evacuation, ultimately forming SciCorps. As the ozone problem persisted, more and more resources were diverted to the Pilgrim ships. Earth's population survived by moving inland and toward the poles. The UCA built and planned for new population centers—quasi-military compounds filled with folks living with one purpose: to survive. Other wealthy countries did the same.

After the Call, only the strongest and best prepared survived. Forty years without new sapiens births meant the end to whole civilizations, whole cultures. In those years the praenex flourished. Fully mature at ten years, having babies with sapiens husbands or through cloning at twelve, their numbers grew. That was the novus experience—nurturing and expanding. But for sapiens, it was different. Forty years of no sapiens births meant that only the youngest sapiens could hope to have sapiens children themselves someday. It was a long wait.

The world changed quickly with the praenex in charge. Their novitas lobe gave them special gifts—telepathy in the first few generations, along with increased brain activity made them all as smart as the most brilliant sapiens. Add their resistance to sapiens illness and disease, and the praenex quickly became the dominant race.

I've always admired their drive and energy, pushed myself to match it, to keep up. I've seen the vids of their greatest achievements—the SATO Space Station for one. I've studied the plans and specs of the colony ships, but what I see before me today, with my own eyes, is equally astounding.

Deep underground, the Couvies have a massive science building, and Ava's giving us the grand tour.

In all my years visiting the Verge, I never suspected this. I knew there were places I hadn't been, work I hadn't witnessed. But this…. It's like another underground city beneath the streets and shops of Vancouver Colony. From our vantage point on a mezzanine overlooking the loom construction area, I can see hundreds of folks at work. The cavern is only slightly smaller than the military hangar we saw yesterday—it feels like a week ago— but here the open floor plan has been transformed into cohesive work areas, labs, and cubicles.

At the center of the space, a large, illuminated ring, as big as a building itself, rises off the concrete floor on temporary legs. It's just one piece of the ozone loom and it's hard to understand how such construction could have gone on so quietly for years. Mercy's da has been working on the chemistry and the design, but I doubt he knew about this either.

"Nearly a hundred of these make up the loom," Ava explains. "They each have a range of several hundred miles." She points to an area at the far side of the cavern. "Those are the rockets that will take them into the stratosphere, where they can rest with minimal power. Four rockets per ring."

The cone-shaped rockets look tiny compared to the ring. "They're so small."

She smiles. "It's a one-way trip."

Mercy raises her hand, like she's in a classroom. "How does my father's research help any of this? I'm not aware of him having any interest or skill in hardware."

"You're right," Ava answers. "Dr. Adams's work was chemical, based on marine biology. See those ports on the side of the ring? Those are the ejection ports that emit the chemically infused lasers that connect to other rings to create the grid of ozone-rich fabric in our stratosphere like hundreds of threads pulling at the edges of the hole. That's why we call it a loom. We're going to weave a new ozone layer to accelerate the planet's natural repair process.

"Perhaps equally important, however, is the filter in the ring itself. The ring will collect the CFCs caught in the stratosphere. After a year or so, we'll have removed enough to let the planet take over."

"What happens then?"

"Then the engines nudge the rings into orbit where they're programmed to connect into one long column like a giant tube. They'll remain there until we can finish the tech to do something more."

Mercy humphs. "Space garbage."

Ava laughs. "I'm afraid so."

"SciCorps can't like that much—more debris to track."

"No, but SciCorps never expected us to get this far either."

"Amazing. Eddie would like to see this," Mercy says.

Ava nods. "I'll make sure she gets a tour when her rem's complete."

"Aye, 'tis fascinatin', but what does this have to do with the mission to save Mercy's folks?"

Dixie steps away from the Gran Bozan's side. Turns out they're old friends. "The GB offers a ruse, as you suggested. But if we can launch the loom at the same time, we're sure to create a diversion as well."

"Launch?"

Dixie nods. "This is the last ring. The rest are spread across the valley, hidden from SciCorps' eyes thanks to the screening technology the Spherans shared with us. It'll take a few weeks once the chemical composition is tested and confirmed, but we'll be ready to launch a single prototype ring in two days. That'll be enough to get their attention." She turns to me. "You have one more day to get the op ready, Captain, then it's time to make for the tether."

The Gran Bozan joins us. "Mercy Adams, I'd like to meet with you in my quarters at 08:00 tomorrow morning." She looks up at me then. "You may join us if you wish, Captain Elder, as this concerns you too." With a regal nod, she sweeps away down the corridor. The others follow in her wake, leaving Mercy and me in stunned silence.

This is the opportunity I've been waiting for. We're alone. Eddie and her sharp tongue are asleep somewhere far away. I'm free from TJ's critical gaze.

I open my mouth to speak. I hold Mercy's gaze, watch the question form in her mind. I reach for her hand at the same instant that she raises it to tuck a strand of hair behind her ear. She doesn't see me reach for the empty space at her side. I tuck my hand in my pocket and look away, across the mezzanine.

When I find the courage to look back, she's stepped away from me. Her eyes trained on the floor.

"Mercy, I—"

"We better go." She quickly walks away, and the moment is lost.

CRANE ELDER

In the past...
March 10, 2113; 588 years ago
Fermont Compound, Quebec, UCA

Crane sat with her eyes closed, head back, enjoying the cool night breeze from her tiny, converted balcony overlooking Fermont Harbor to the east. She no longer waited for news of her husband, Jon Sr.; she'd lost hope long ago. Now she used this place as a temporary haven when she needed to let her emotions flow freely, when she needed to be alone with her thoughts, away from Brym's telepathy. A moment without questions.

She fell back into childhood memories, as she often did, drifting away to another place, another time. Before the Collapse, before the Call.

She felt Brym's presence like a tingling at the corners of her mind before she heard the rustle of her clothing. "What's that noise, Mother Crane?"

Crane knew without asking that Brym meant the noise Crane'd been remembering in her mind, not any noise in Fermont.

"It's a freight train." Crane kept her eyes closed.

"It sounds loud and mean. Why do you like it?"

"When I was a child, I spent many summers on my grandparent's farm in Ontario. My parents couldn't always take me with them when they went away—closing sites was a dangerous business, especially in the summer when the Great Storm was at its worst."

"I remember you told me about them, your grandparents. Did they own the freight trains?"

Crane laughed. "No, the trains were part of national commerce. They ran all day and all night back then, moving supplies north. I would lie in my bed in my grandparents' house and listen to the rhythmic sound of the freight trains passing through town. Even miles away you could hear them and feel their rhythm. I would wonder if my parents could hear it too, wherever they were."

"Now you wonder if your husband hears it?" Brym whispered.

Crane opened her eyes and glanced toward Brym. It was always a shock at moments like this, to see the growing pre-teen, so much larger in real life than in her mind's eye.

"I have a deep memory too." Brym bit her lower lip.

"You do? What is it?"

"It's a song, but, I don't know…"

"I want to hear it." Crane rocked forward, encouraging her daughter.

Brym hesitated, cleared her throat, then gently sang.

"I know dark clouds will gather 'round me
I know my way is rough and steep."

Crane gasped. Brym's voice was higher than Phoebe's, but Crane recognized the song. It was the one Phoebe sang at Brym's birth, just before she died.

"But golden fields lie just before me
Where God's redeemed shall have their sleep.
I'm going home to see my mother
And all my loved ones who've gone on
I'm only going over Jordan
I'm only going over home."

Crane wiped a tear from her cheek and tried to smile. She swallowed past the lump in her throat and tried to keep from breaking down into a weeping mess.

Brym touched her shoulder. "I miss her too."

Crane took a deep breath and reached for Brym.

They hugged for a long moment. When they finally broke apart, Crane leaned back and sighed. "I think you've grown another inch this week! Tell me what news you have."

Brym rolled her eyes, a mannerism she'd copied from her French friend, Pauline. "How do you know I have news? Maybe I just wanted to cheer you up."

"Ha! If it were Elsa sneaking up on me, I would believe it, but you? For all your kindness, Brym, you always have an agenda."

Brym opened her mouth to disagree, then snapped it shut.

From behind her back, she drew two tablets and held them out to Crane.

"What's this?" Crane took the tablets.

Brym sat in the chair beside her. "The first is a detailed outline for our new government along with work assignments and educational plans for the people of Fermont Compound. My siblings and I have been working on it for a while now."

Crane exhaled loudly, scanning through the first list. "Wait, this is… this is nearly twice the number of residents."

Brym nodded. "That's because of the second list."

A chill ran down Crane's spine. She gazed into Brym's amethyst eyes and for the first time, noticed the sadness there. "What's the second list?"

Brym frowned. "A detailed plan for the massive rescue operation we're about to begin…. Europe is lost."

Crane could hear the freight train again. Its rhythm had changed to match her heartbeat and it made her ears ring. "If it's lost, then why is there a rescue?"

"He saved them." Brym choked on the words. She didn't say who, and she didn't need to. "He sent them to us, *Maman*. So brave…" Brym reached for Crane's hand and squeezed it tightly. A single tear tracked down her cheek. "I wish I could have met him. I wish I could have called him *papa*, even once. He saved her—my friend, Pauline LeRoux. She's with all those he got out."

Crane shook her head. So, her husband, her love, truly was lost. No, not lost…dead.

Brym took a breath and sang again.

"I'm only going over Jordan
I'm only going over home."

With a stab of pain, Crane filed away the grief for a different moment, and focused on Brym. "I need to enter the PSI. We've got to wake everyone up and get to work."

Brym nodded in agreement. "We'll need more soldiers… sailors. They come by sea."

17
MERCY

I find myself unusually at peace this morning, as if I'm simply watching my life tick from one moment into the next, waiting to see what it will bring. The old Mercy Adams stayed behind in New Juneau a few long days ago. I am who I am now, regardless of what anyone else believes. I am who I am, and I don't think anyone else needs to weigh in on that.

That's why I'm contemplating the door to the Gran Bozan's office instead of going through it. This strange peace I feel, I don't know what it is. I'm not sure if it's what I need, or more likely, something that will get me in trouble.

I'm five minutes late for an appointment. A praenex who is breaking our rule of punctuality. Inaction, in this case, is a statement in itself.

The door before me flies open. Eddie darts out and pulls up short when she sees me. "What're you doing out here?" She pulls me into the room.

Everyone's here. Waiting. For me.

When the Gran Bozan stands, everyone else jumps to their feet.

I barely hold back an eye roll. Oh yes, this is something that will get me in trouble.

"Divine peace, Dr. Adams." The GB's fingers rest on the desk in front of her. She waves me to the single chair set in front of the desk. Bozan Kahinu sits to her left.

"May the Creator's hand guide you," I reply.

She flashes the slightest smile and sits. Clothing rustles around the room as everyone else relaxes too. I feel Van's eyes on me, but I refuse to look at him. *He* may be unsure, but I'm not. I don't plan to act like an insecure child anymore.

I slide into the chair, straighten the hem of my jacket, and fold my hands lightly in my lap, waiting.

This is not what the GB expected. She sends a sideways glance at Rumesa, and I can feel Rumesa gently probing my thoughts.

It's extremely rude. I snap my gaze to them and narrow my eyes, their probing stops immediately. They look away. I'm not trained in the Legion's art of telepathy, but I *am* a gifted praenex.

The GB clears her throat. "You're late."

"Yes, I was deciding whether to enter."

"I see. You've been making a lot of decisions lately. That's one of the things we want to talk to you about, actually."

"Oh?"

"We don't normally anticipate such strong ideas, challenge even, from a minor. Yesterday, you dictated terms of the operation Sheriff Arson and Captain Elder are planning. To what can you attribute this sudden forcefulness?"

A chair scrapes the floor behind me and I know that it's Van, struggling to stay put. The way he leaps to my defense like he thinks I'm a child used to annoy me. But today I find it revealing. It's more about him than me, I realize. I'm simply sitting here being spoken to. He's the one fighting with himself over something that has nothing to do with him at all.

"I've been thinking about this insignia." I point to the circle-rocket pin on my collar. "It's meant to symbolize the belief that our society can be both at home and in flight. We can be Terrans and Pilgrims and still be kin. *All nature's difference keeps all nature's peace.* That was John Adams's favorite line from an Alexander Pope poem. It's based on the concept of *concordia discors*—TJ?" I turn to my linguistically gifted friend.

"Ah…*differences harmonized.*"

"Exactly. Thank you." I turn back to the GB. "You can see how this philosophy pairs nicely with my insignia, but I've been thinking that it applies more broadly here."

I stand and pace in front of the desk.

Rumesa opens their mouth, but I raise a hand to stop them, and they close it again. The GB watches me intently.

I stop pacing and look directly at her. "Later generations simplified the concept as *I'm okay, you're okay.* You'd like to judge me based on your opinion of how I perceive my gifts. I can see the future—just glimpses. It's more of a parlor trick than anything. My deep understanding and pursuit of history has always been viewed by the Legion as a peculiarity, but I've decided *it's* my true gift.

"Yesterday, I directly influenced a major decision in this civil war. John Adams said that statesmen will always lean to vanity, pride, and ambition. *Nothing but Force, Power, and Strength can restrain them.*" I look at Van, Eddie, and TJ in turn. "My friends listen to me. I'm not a child in *their* eyes. I'm the conscience of this group, the moral center"—I smile at Eddie—"and I've decided I don't need you or anyone else to *award* my majority. I am who I am, and who I am is an adult citizen of the legion of Scorch."

The room is so quiet, I don't think anyone's even breathing. I can't read the GB, but when she stands and rolls her shoulders back, I know she's decided. She picks up her skirts and comes around the desk to stand directly in front of me.

I force myself to maintain eye contact. I really have no idea what's going to happen, but truly I don't care.

"Congratulations, *Citizen Adams.*" She holds up her palms.

I press my palms to hers. "Thank you."

It sounds like a rush of wind as everyone else exhales. Someone chuckles, another says "amen." The GB curls her fingers through mine and smiles—a broad grin this time. "Your parents will be so proud."

"*Bon!*" Dixie claps a hand on my shoulder.

After that everyone closes in. Bozan Kahinu squeezes my other shoulder and Van rests his hand on my back, large and firm. Eddie grips my forearm and TJ reaches over all of them to put his hand on my head. We all laugh and the joy that follows is a cacophony of voices in a moment of true peace.

"What a morning." Eddie pats my back as we follow the others out of the GB's office and down the hall to the hotel lobby. "Let's go spend time with the Spherans and see if we can learn a little more about them, hmm? I'd like to know more before I have to go into rem again."

I nod. My face hurts from smiling. I try again to stop, but it's hopeless. Then I think about my parents, wherever they are, missing this, and it's not so hard to stop smiling after all.

As we pass the threshold into the lobby, Van pushes off the wall to catch me.

"Mercy?" One side of his face is bathed in bright sunlight streaming through the tall windows. Sharp shadows play across his other cheek making him even more handsome than usual—one brown eye's bright with flecks of gold, the other's intensely dark.

"Van." I start to automatically lean toward him, but I catch myself, give myself a mental shake. Not even half an hour's passed since I decided not to fall into his orbit again. To be my own person.

He drops the hand he'd reached toward me and looks at Eddie, standing behind me, waiting.

"Uh, I'll just wait over here—" Eddie scurries away.

He takes my arm to guide me toward the windows. "Listen, Cricket, about yesterday...." He lets go of my arm and looks down at the floor.

Should I give him an easy way out? Make everything fine? It

would be so easy to touch his arm now, smile and reassure him, but too much of the new Mercy is still pinging around in my brain—the one who arrives late, tells adults she doesn't need their approval, and calls herself a *moral center.*

"I'm listening, Van, but I just don't hear anything. You're a grown man. You have been for a while. If you have something to say to me, whatever it is, just say it."

He runs a hand over his mouth and for just a second, meets my eyes. He shifts his weight from foot to foot and his Adam's apple bobs up and down as he swallows.

Still, no words.

I tip my head to the side. "Or don't. Tomorrow's extremely important. I don't think we want to go into it like this...unresolved." I straighten my back and lift my chin. "Sylvan Elder, I release you from your promise. You're free of me." Ice slides down my spine. I've never felt something so absolutely contrary in my life.

Van's eyes whip back to mine, intense, confused. "Mercy, what? Released? What are ye talkin' about?"

Now I'm confused. If this isn't about breaking off our promise, what is it about? "You don't have to cushion it for me...I—I'm..." I stutter.

"You think I'm...But that's not...I mean..." He growls at the ceiling and runs his hand across his mouth again.

This time he turns his head slowly toward me, a muscle flexing in his jaw, heat I've never seen before in his eyes. Suddenly his arm is around me. He pulls me tight against him.

My breath squeezes out in a puff, and I don't have time to

inhale before his mouth is crushing mine. Warm. Demanding. Sure.

I don't move. I don't know what to do. And I think I might be on fire. His other hand finds its way along my neck into the hair at the back of my head. I can't connect my thoughts enough to move in any way, but even if I could, his strength is all around me. I'm cocooned in his embrace.

His lips soften against mine and he changes the angle of the kiss, pressing small, slow kisses from one corner of my mouth to the other.

Finally, some deep instinct within me starts to answer his kiss. My hands struggle to rise from where they're pinned to my sides. Then just as suddenly, I'm hugging air.

Van steps back and looks at me. His nod is short. Satisfied. With one final swift movement, he kisses my forehead and storms away.

The room is a little tippy, maybe because I'm not breathing. I inhale like a swimmer coming up for air. I take a step, but my knees don't seem to be hinged properly. I stagger a little, and then Eddie is here, helping me into a chair.

"Oh, no!" Eddie rubs my back. "Don't you pass out on me. Um…put your head down." She pushes my head between my knees.

It's ridiculous, but I feel better right away.

"Yep, big morning," she says.

In 2108 when the first generation praenex girls were born, their caregivers at the compounds invented a special system to identify, investigate, and communicate discoveries they made about the new human subspecies. *Potentially Significant Incidents* or *PSIs* could be created by anyone, submitted through the global system and triaged. Some of the most important PSIs were submitted by Crane Elder. As adoptive mother to the legendary Brym Elder and a nurse/leader in Fermont Compound, she had a unique perspective on and position with the first generation. History considers PSI 4218 one of the most pivotal and controversial theories she ever submitted—that the praenex were telepathic.

As I listen to Fez and Nairobi describe their home, watch their silent interactions before they speak, I wonder how the Spherans turned out so different from us. It's our last chance to visit with them for a while, and I'm thankful Eddie suggested we try to learn more about them.

"And the biosphere, is it physical, like an enclosure?" Eddie quizzes them.

"In some ways," Nairobi answers.

Fez continues, "Terra Faire's walled to keep out the worst predators and other destructive animals, but we have small gates that allow us to pass through, to the fields and jungle beyond."

"The largest gates are like walls themselves, for moving equipment and large things, but these have not been used for generations," Nairobi finishes.

"What else, besides the walls, creates the biosphere?" Eddie asks.

The children exchange a look and Fez nods.

Nairobi thinks for a moment. "There's a dome—a screen of artificial atmosphere created using magnetic technology similar to the tether or your magrail. It shields us from the UV-B, so our environment is more stable, cooler, but it allows rain and air to move through it."

"Like ozone," I say. "Amazing." This secret is too big to have been kept from us—from the technology we possess. "How did Terra Faire hide from SciCorps satellites?"

"The screen shields us from your technology. We've shared it with the Couvies, now they use it too." Fez smiles at me and I notice a small scratch near his eye and the beginning of a bruise.

I touch his chin to turn his face to the light. "What happened here?"

His smile turns to a grin. "I had a fight! I met a Couvie boy. He said I looked strange and talked funny. I called him null for saying so. He curled his hand like this." Fez holds up a fist. "I pushed him, then he hit me right in the head. It was glorious."

Nairobi is bouncing and smiling too. "Sheriff Arson knows many swears. When he pulled the boys apart, he said—"

"No! Stop." I hold up a hand to silence her. "We don't want to know what he said."

"But it was a very inventive name for part of an animal we've never even heard of—"

"Nairobi!" I hiss.

With a humph, she finally stops.

"Huh," Eddie mumbles and shakes her head. "I must truly need some rem because this is actually starting to be funny."

"What was it like when Captain Elder kissed you? Did it

hurt?" Nairobi asks me.

"What? I—"

"It looked like it hurt," Fez agrees. "Could you breathe? I thought maybe you would fall down when he let go."

"Was it wet? Did you like it?" Nairobi asks. "Did he taste good?"

"Your toes barely touched the ground." Fez giggles.

Nairobi points her toes and stiffens, making a funny startled expression to imitate me. They both giggle.

I can picture it again with the help of their questions. Heat flares in my cheeks. I wish I could escape all the teasing, but this information about Terra Faire is important. There's so much more to discuss.

Eddie takes their hands to get their attention. "Let's get back to the biosphere."

"Where is it?"

"Chileru," Nairobi answers.

"That's in the Andes Mountains?" I ask. "And you speak Portuguese?"

They nod. Nairobi holds up a finger. "Until the last generation, we only spoke Portuguese. Most of our builders came from Brazil. It made sense for the others to learn their language."

"But last generation," Fez adds, "we knew for certain that the time would come when we'd need you, all of you, and so now we speak English too."

"Your English is much improved already," Eddie observes.

"Yes," Fez agrees. "It helps to hear so much."

It strikes me that the children haven't truly been around that much conversation in just three days. "Nairobi, I want to ask you a personal question, if I may?"

She nods slowly.

"A few in our society are still somewhat telepathic, like the early praenex. These people, like Eddie, get special training. She's remarkably good at it. For many others, it develops over time within family members. Sometimes, when I'm with people I know well, who know me, we can hear each other's thoughts a little. Do you and Fez share that kind of gift?"

"No, not me and Fez."

"But sometimes it seems you finish each other's sentences or communicate without words."

Fez sits up. "She means not *just* me and Nairobi.... We hear everyone's thoughts."

Eddie gasps. "How is that possible?"

"All Spherans are telepathic." He shrugs.

CRANE ELDER

Crane often thought that some of the anatomical changes in the praenex were so logical, sapiens doctors would have recommended them themselves. No appendix or gall bladder, extra kidneys, larger lungs, and smaller, more efficient liver and spleen. One of the most exciting changes was the redundant heart design—the cardiologists were giddy.

But it was the new organ—the nova—that truly caught everyone's attention. Two centimeters wide, the square of rough skin rested on one point, like a diamond, between the eyebrows at the top of the nose bridge. It connected directly to a new lobe in the center of the brain dubbed the *novitas* lobe. The nova and novitas lobe created the Extrasensory System.

Crane's paper, *Living with Telepathy – a Parent's Journey Through Praenex Childhood*, had just been published through the network. Her inbox was inundated with questions and comments from the community, many from other parents of praenex. Many of them asked the same question that Crane herself had been wondering about—just when would the fast-maturing praenex hit puberty and what would that be like?

"Are they worried about our behavior?"

Crane jumped with surprise. Even after all these years, Brym still had the ability to sneak up on her.

"Sorry, *Maman*." Brym stood next to Crane at their small kitchen counter. "Didn't mean to startle you."

"*C'est bien.* Have you eaten?"

Brym was already reaching for an apple. Taking a huge bite, she asked around the lump of apple in her mouth. "Do they think we'll become uncontrollable or something?"

Crane shook her head and wondered why her daughter, who already had the educational equivalent of a twelfth grader, could not master simple manners.

"Sorry." Brym reached for a napkin to wipe the juice from her chin. She finished chewing, swallowed, and asked again. "We fail to understand what the sapiens fear from puberty. It's a simple biological growth process. Why are they so worried?"

Crane sighed. "Probably because they remember their own experiences. For sapiens, puberty lasts several years, sometimes longer. It can be a confusing and painful process."

Brym considered this. "Ours will last only nine months. After that we'll continue to grow in size for a few more years, but we'll never reach your kind of height, no matter how tall our parents are."

Crane threw up her hands. "How do you know this?"

Brym shrugged. "The Creator explained it to us. We

understand all about ourselves; in fact, that's what I want to talk to you about."

"What specifically?"

Brym handed her another tablet. "This is some research on which we'd like to collaborate with the doctors, but…"

Crane looked up from the analysis to meet Brym's eyes. "But what?"

Brym sucked in a breath and let it out slowly. "We want the immunizations to stop."

Crane pushed off her stool. "Not this again. We've been through this—"

"*Oui*, but this time we have medical proof to explain our…what do you call it? Aversion…our aversion to the shots. Look at the data." Brym pointed to the tablet.

Crane reluctantly leaned against the counter and reopened the file. She was no scientist, but her medical training gave her enough understanding for the information she was reading to send ice through her veins.

"My God…is this right? Is this…" She covered her mouth with her hand, swallowed past the lump in her throat.

"Yes, it's not good, but we hold no one to blame. None of you could have known. We'd like to work with the doctors to confirm, but we're fairly sure." Brym reached for her mother's free hand. "It's no one's fault, *Maman. We understand that the immunizations are lifesaving for sapiens.*"

Crane shook her head again. "If this analysis is right, the immunizations have done irreparable damage to the praenex. I'm so sorry, Brym. But this analysis also explains why none of you ever get sick."

"Yes, our blood has unique filtering properties, but there's a tradeoff. Each illness we encounter depletes our natural ability, reduces our reserves, and…shortens our life span."

Closing her eyes, Crane let her mind race ahead. When she opened them again, she knew which questions to ask.

"When will you reach puberty?"

Brym grimaced. "Next month."

Crane blew out a breath. "But…you're only eight years old."

When Brym opened her mouth to reply, Crane held up a hand to quiet her. "And full maturity?"

"At ten years." Brym didn't hesitate this time.

Crane sank onto the stool and let her head fall forward. "Full life expectancy?"

Brym sighed beside her and rubbed Crane's back.

Instead of comfort, she felt a spike of anger. "Life expectancy?" she repeated through clenched teeth. She waited for what seemed an eternity before Brym answered.

"Perhaps fifty years."

Crane tried to control her emotions—knew that she failed when she felt Brym's hand clench against her back. Involuntary empathy was a side effect of telepathy that the praenex were helpless to avoid, and Crane knew the emotions she was broadcasting at that moment were difficult to endure.

"I'm sorry." Crane reached for Brym's hand, unrolling Brym's clenched fist and sliding her own fingers into Brym's small grasp. "I'm okay now."

Brym took a deep breath. "I…appreciate your sadness…and

your anger, but there is something more we've learned which may help."

Crane doubted it, but she tried to muster some optimism. "Go on."

"Do you remember the Call?"

Crane flicked her eyes up to meet Brym's. "The Call? *Oui*, of course. It's not something you forget, hearing the Creator's voice in your head, watching the world fall apart around you as it repeats hour after hour. Why do you ask?"

"The Creator said *no human-born for forty years*." Brym returned Crane's intense stare. "We believe he meant it literally in the terms of the day. We know sapiens women cannot conceive or carry children, but…"

"But what?"

Brym straightened her back and cleared her throat. "We believe we novus can."

"But…my God." Crane's thoughts stuttered for a moment. "Wait, how?"

Brym laid a steadying hand on Crane's shoulder. "Through procreation with sapiens or IVF, and one other way that we're just coming to comprehend."

Crane experienced a wobbling sensation like balancing on a very thin plank. Somehow, she knew that her world was about to transform—again. She closed her eyes, and then took Brym's hand from her shoulder and held it to her cheek for a moment.

"Just give me second, *mon couer*." She breathed in and out until the air moved smoothly through her. She opened her eyes and pulled out the stool next to her. "Alright, tell me."

Brym climbed onto the stool and swiveled to face Crane. "Are you familiar with the biological process of parthenogenesis?"

"Yes, it's a form of asexual reproduction found in simple life forms like germ cells and some fish and lizards, usually in the absence of males. Never among mammals. Why?"

"We're certain that we'll be able to procreate with sapiens; we're sure about that. But we've been forming an idea over the last few months about a private meditation—a ritual almost—that we don't find in any sapiens texts."

"What do you mean that the idea's *forming*?"

"It started quietly as some shared dreams among a few of our medically inclined siblings, but soon we all started to have the dreams. We prayed on it, we spoke with the Creator, and over time we've come to understand that this process—the meditation, some specific foods, isolation, heat, and other techniques—are designed to prepare our bodies for a very unique gift."

Crane's mouth gaped, she shut it sharply. "Parthenogenesis?"

Brym nodded. "We're calling it *aeterna-sui rituali.*"

"My Latin isn't that good—"

"It means 'the ritual of the eternal-self.' The offspring will be clones, basically. We'll call them *aeternas.*"

"That's…that's incredible!" Her mind raced through the possibilities, the complexities. "Controlled, not spontaneous then?"

"Yes, controlled. The thoughts and feelings we have surrounding the process are peaceful and safe—we're sure it'll be completely voluntary regardless of the lack of male novus. We've come to think of it as an option unique to the praenex. We have a team working on the specifics of the ritual, the details of the nutritional requirements, et cetera. We'll be ready."

"That's amazing really, both the timing of maturity and the parthenogenesis. If your calculations are correct—"

"We'll be having babies in a few years," Brym said, finishing Crane's sentence for her. "My siblings and I discussed it. We've decided that in our tenth year, when we're the sapiens equivalent of approximately twenty-three years, we'll begin to choose our mates among sapiens, consider IVF, or attempt the ritual."

Crane was stunned, but her mind was keeping pace with the radical change that clicked into place, altering her understanding of the world. A strangled laugh escaped her. Finally, she shook her head and sighed. "I'll start on the PSIs—this is going to take more than one."

Brym smiled and squeezed her hand. "I was hoping you would. We think the ideas might take some getting used to."

18
VAN

Current year: 2701
Sunday, 6 AM
The Verge

We're almost the only ones at the Verge station, and that suits me fine. One sleek mag-rail car will carry us and everything we need and allow a few to catch some rest as we travel five hours to the tether base east of New Juneau. It was a simple matter to get the supplies we needed, and creating our costumes was easy—the Couvies seemed to know just what to do. It makes me wonder how long they've been thinking about this, or more to the point, how long they've been planning a little rebellion.

I'm thankful that the praenex are so organized, otherwise loading supplies and passengers while disguised and in character would be like milking cows in my dress uniform.

The diplomacy of our mission is tricky, especially with so many of the Legion's folks involved. Avoiding public conflict is necessary—to show our hand now would jeopardize our chance to rescue Mercy's folks by putting SciCorps on high alert.

"Captain, a word?" The GB waves me aside as the final

medical supply crate's secured in the hold.

"Yes, Yer Grace?" I pass a hand gently over my artificial gem, careful not to knock loose the glue.

She glances around, inclines her head to her two guards, dressed like me as SciCorps police. "I understand how important it is for us to stay in character. My guards will stay close. Though to others they will appear to be guarding a prisoner, they will, in fact, protect my life as best they can. You and your team must focus on the rescue. I'll not have you distracted by any real or imagined danger to me."

"Aye, as ye say, Yer Grace."

"There is another matter.… Bozan LeRoux!"

"Your Grace?" Eddie joins us, her swirling skirts replaced with a tether worker's uniform. She's so skinny even I wanna feed her—no one's going to suspect how lethal she truly is if it comes to a fight. Her face is caked with makeup to tone down her paleness, and her hair is covered by an ugly hat. She looks almost plain as she tugs on rough cotton gloves. It's disturbing—like looking at a bad copy of my friend.

"Eddie, are ye okay with this?"

She shrugs one shoulder. "*Oui*, I'm ready."

The GB straightens. "Bozan Kahinu spoke to me before we left town. There are people at the Hub who'll recognize you. Your makeup helps, but that albino skin is too difficult to mask completely. You'll have to stay at the base." The GB raises a hand to stop her argument. "You'll serve as our link to the Verge and provide backup if we need it."

Eddie's nostrils flare and she clenches her jaw. She's tryin' hard not to broadcast her annoyance to all the praenex here.

"Aye, 'tis a good idea. We need someone at the base who's ready to make adjustments to our plan, respond to issues, and, if necessary, intervene."

Eddie nods. "As you wish."

The doors to the waiting tram car finally open. "Let's go then. *Allons-y!*" The GB enters the tram car and heads straight to the front bay, her guards keeping pace.

The sheriff and Commander Garcia move past me, but I put out a hand to stop them. "Excuse me. Yer rings?"

They both look down at their hands, reluctance clear on their faces.

"I understand yer commitment to yer culture, but those rings will immediately place ye as Couvies."

"They're hardly noticeable," Arson argues.

Mercy steps up next to me. She's dressed as a SciCorps clerk in a plain jacket and pants, only the chain of her icicle necklace showing. "It was one of the first things I noticed about Officer Vi when I met them."

"Aye. Ye've dyed yer gems black." I point to their foreheads where gleaming black dye covers their flesh-toned gems. "Why hold to these rings?"

"They're not simply jewelry," Vi explains. They shoot Arson a questioning glance, and at his nod of assent, they continue. "They're tech." They pull off a silver ring encrusted with jewels of different shapes and sizes and hold it up to the light. "This one contains special compounds—sedatives, a truth serum, one paralyzing agent. This one." They point to a ring on their left hand, made of more ornate metals, but no jewels. "It records everything it hears and transmits it to my tracker where it's downloaded into the Verge core for safe keeping."

I wipe a hand across my face, amazed at my own blindness—in all the years I visited the Verge, I never suspected, never asked. "Well, regardless of their usefulness, they'll have to go."

Reluctantly they pull off their rings, securing them in small fabric pouches to store in their cargo pockets. When they're finished, even I'd believe they're SciCorps police.

"Good." I motion them inside and wave TJ, Eddie, and Mercy ahead of me. All together we make nine. With Eddie planning to stay behind at the base, that's eight for the tether. I think we can make it without suspicion, but only if the diversion and various tech hacks work.

The four of us take seats closest to the door and after a short wait, the magrail pulls out. One of our Couvie guides further up the car slouches down in his seat and starts playing the harmonica. The sound is sad, almost mournful.

Eddie leans toward the music like someone's pulled an invisible string attached to her chest. When I catch her eye, she shrugs and sits back. She thinks her bottled-up passion for music is a secret, but really, it's a secret we all agree to keep. To dwell on all we've sacrificed for Scorch, for saving the species—giving up our talents, our youth—it's too much, but at the same time, it has to be enough because it's all we have. What would our lives mean if we didn't do all we could to save our planet? We really have no choice.

"I don't like leaving Cousteau behind." TJ shifts restlessly in his seat.

"Aye, but he'll be fine. May'll take good care of him."

"It's not that….I'm just used to having him around. It's helpful to gage his sense of a situation. He's remarkably intuitive."

I raise my eyebrow at him. "Huh. I guess I never thought of that. Ye know, because he's a dog."

TJ shoves my shoulder, but joking like mates is wee comfort.

"We leave some strengths behind," Eddie says as she pulls a strange looking pack from her bag and shoves it into her travel case. "And add others. This is Dr. Varela's magic medicine pouch." She points to the pack and rolls her eyes. "The children made me bring it along. If the Spherans have been isolated for six hundred years, how good do you think their medicine could be?"

"They're praenex." Mercy replies.

"True." Eddie gives a one-shouldered shrug.

"I left all my books," Mercy states flatly.

We all stare at her.

"Ye did, Cricket?" I notice for the first time how light her bag looks. "Why?"

She shrugs. "Just didn't need them."

We lapse into silence, thinking our own thoughts. I don't mind the moment to balance myself, to practice inaction, to reach for the state of calm, no matter how fake.

TJ squirms beside me. Mercy sits up suddenly, then tries to hide her discomfort with a lazy yawn. They don't fool me. I can tell they're getting twitchy. I concentrate for a moment, and feel something wrong too, something more than the obvious tension.

"What?"

"I'm sorry." Eddie hangs her head. "I'm broadcasting. I apologize."

I look at TJ, but he won't meet my eye. "Someone care to fill me in?"

Mercy touches my knee. "Eddie's…worried. About the war… About her children."

I blow out a breath. I'm still getting used to the idea that any of us are parents.

"It's not that exactly," she explains. "I mean, I *do* worry about them. But I also worry about what they represent."

"I still don't understand, lass."

She lifts her head and looks at me. "I'm trying extremely hard to find *normal*. Me. An albino. A bozan. A LeRoux. *Tu comprends?*"

TJ exhales loudly.

I'm not sure what to say. "Eddie—"

"Don't!" she hisses. "I don't need to be soothed or…or reminded of my qualities. It all comes down to one thing in our world. Survival. Or more specifically, procreation. I'm almost nineteen! Unless *all* of my children are to be raised by others, what man…" She looks me in the eye. "How eager would *you* be to mate with a praenex sister who already has a hundred kids?

"It's not a hundred!"

"Not yet, but it will be. Sometimes I wonder, is this what I give up for the world? A normal life, I mean."

We're all quiet again.

"That's depressing." TJ shakes his head. "You truly don't

want to hear about all your qualities?"

Eddie scoffs, shakes her head.

TJ's comm buzzes, and not in the usual way, more like an alert. He flicks it open and reads. "Holy…Eddie, what did you do?"

"What?" I ask.

She looks away and I get the impression she knows exactly what.

"Aye, what now?" I wave to TJ's display. "Let me see that."

He holds the virtual display in his palm so that I can read it.

"Well now, yer rating just jumped into the top 100, but ye dunno why?" I scramble to open my own comm so I can read for myself.

"It's not a big deal," Eddie insists. "People hover in and out of the top 100 all the time. It's temporary."

I blow out a huge breath and look at her. "Ye just jumped to 42."

We're all staring at her now.

For just a second, there's shock in her eyes, in her stiff back. Then she shrugs.

I flip through more information on my screen. "Well, that's just grand. Ye posted about the Spherans. Ye published every bloody thing we know about 'em."

Eddie kicks at a bump in the floor. "So?"

We all just wait.

"Fine! I did. I had permission, if you really want to know."

"Permission?" I bristle. "Since when do citizens need permission to post information?"

TJ sighs. "You mean that they *told* you to post it...the Legion. It's good publicity."

Eddie looks up. "I'm not their puppet if that's what you think. It was my idea. We've become de facto experts on the Spherans, you know. Leadership just suggested the time was right."

I laugh. "Aye, another diversionary tactic."

"Something like that."

"Well, it turned out good for ye..." I stand and check that everyone in our train car is part of our team—no public stragglers mixed in—and then I clear my throat. "Ladies and Gentlemen," I announce in a stadium voice, "allow me to present the newest, brightest, and by far palest Advisory Committee member, Bozan Edelweiss Renee LeRoux." I sweep her an exaggerated bow.

"Be quiet!" she hisses and tries to pull me down to my seat.

Folks mostly ignore us, but Commander Garcia claps in a short staccato, and Arson tips his SciCorps cap toward Eddie, his white teeth gleaming in the shadows.

"Can we change the subject please?" Eddie whispers.

"I love hearing your full name," Mercy whispers back. "It's so regal."

TJ chokes a little and earns a glare from his sister.

"Seriously, though." Mercy squeezes Eddie's knee. "Congratulations."

"Thanks." Eddie shakes her head.

"Ye know what this means don't ye?"

"What?"

"Responsibility."

Eddie scoffs.

"Oh!" Mercy sits up in excitement. "That's right, it's like a job. You have to give your opinion about all kinds of things now. Even stuff you know nothing about."

TJ laughs. "Hey, this is my sister we're talking about—she knows everything."

Eddie socks him in the arm.

"Ow! Wait until they learn about your violent outbursts."

Eddie collapses back in her seat. "Can we please talk about something else?"

"Okay then. I have just the thing." I pat my pocket.

"Now?" TJ asks.

"Oh!" Eddie perks up. "Yes! Now is perfect."

"What?" Mercy asks, peering at me all nervous-like. Ever since our kiss she's been jumpy around me. And I like that fine, too.

"This." I hand her the small cotton pouch I've been carrying around since forever.

She takes the sack. "What is it?"

"A gift, from all of us. To celebrate yer majority. I did the research, TJ scavenged it and Eddie gave up the credits we needed to pull it off."

TJ sniffs. "We've been carrying it around for a while now."

Eddie punches him again. "Open it!" She nudges Mercy.

Mercy's tiny fingers tremble as she opens the ties holding the top shut and shakes the coin into her hand.

"It's a 2007 Abigail Adams mule," I explain. "Abigail on one side and—"

"Louise on the other," Mercy finishes. She turns the coin over and over in her hand. Rubs her thumb across the surface. "I can't believe you found this." Her voice is hardly more than a whisper. When she looks at me, her eyes shine with unshed tears. "It's perfect. Thank you! Thank you all!"

She jumps up and slides into my arms like it's the most natural thing in the world, like it's something we do all the time, instead of just in my dreams.

As I relax into Mercy's hug, Eddie stands and wraps her arms around us. When TJ grabs ahold, we sway with the added weight. I'm pretty sure I've never had a more perfect moment in all my life.

We laugh, and for just that moment, I feel the kind of peace I did years ago, before we really were adults. Someone shifts and we crumple onto a bench in an awkward, laughing heap.

The sun's rising as the tether tube lifts off from Tether Base, all of us safely aboard. The tether and its carriage remind me a bit of an ancient building I once saw on a vid, the Seattle Space Needle, if the needle extended to the edge of the atmosphere and was powered entirely by magnetic energy.

The tube's compartment is functional and right boring; the engineers who designed it didn't give a dust about style. Most importantly, it has all the tech needed to protect our fragile human bodies as we travel into space. The tube gets its name from its circular shape, wrapping around the magnetic tether at its center. I can walk the full circumference, though I have to duck to fit through the four hatches that join the quarter sections. There's room for about a hundred passengers, arranged in pods and groups of rows facing out toward the ring of windows that runs all the way around the craft. Only the control room and cargo areas are enclosed, but I've no interest in those. We want the short tether flight to the orbiting Hub to go as smoothly as possible—just another day of work, another SciCorps assignment for us workers.

I'd felt a moment of panic when we went through the boarding procedure. The efficient little clerk paused when they got to the GB. They checked the ID twice, staring at the GB a long moment until finally calling a security officer over to review their tablet. I was about to act when I remembered that the GB's ID wasn't hacked—it was her true identity they were dealing with. A moment later the officer nodded to us, their chest swelling with pride as they waved us through. They believed the GB was our prisoner. So far so good.

My appreciation for TJ's tech skills grows daily. His is the most convincing disguise of all of us because, like the GB, he's a version of himself. He's back in his old uniform—the one he wore daily as a member of SciCorps' military. We bet that few folks know about his resignation. It's something his da would try to keep quiet, in hopes he could change TJ's mind. They need men like TJ. They'll be extremely unhappy when they find out he's joined TAC.

I slide into a seat next to my best friend and watch as he continues working on his tablet. "What's that?" I point to the small black strip that runs along the tablet's edge.

"That's the best disguise of all," he says without looking up. "It's sending all kinds of normal data and queries through the network along with my specific requests, making me look like any typical tech officer on this flight."

"Gettin' anything good?"

"I'm connected to May's network in the Verge, they're at t-minus 20 minutes. Should work out perfectly. I'm also transmitting everything by vid to Eddie. She'll know what's happening as it happens."

I notice a small video running in one corner of his screen. The sound is muted, but Mayor Dixie is standing at a podium in the middle of the public square in the Verge. "What's goin' on?" I point to the image.

"Demonstration."

"Another one? Turn it up."

"I can do better than that." TJ throws his comm hand toward a wall screen. Dixie's image appears large as life.

"Some people think that we harbor animosity toward our Pilgrim cousins…" The camera pans back, revealing hundreds of brightly dressed Couvies sitting on the pavers, their attention focused on Dixie. *"That's simply not true. We respect them, we admire their ingenuity, their focus, and their dedication to their mission. Our frustration lies with Pilgrim leadership, specifically SciCorps councilmembers who insist on perpetuating two mistaken ideas.*

"First, they refuse to recompute the mathematical, statistical, and social equation that hundreds of years ago suggested that the human race lacked the population and resources to pursue both responses—

fight or flight—so fiercely at work in our population.…Fight or flight? We Terrans want to fight for this world, to heal it. The Pilgrims want to flee, to find a new world and start again. An equation hundreds of years ago told SciCorps we can't do both. Simply put, the math is wrong. We can *do both. I call on SciCorps leadership to run the numbers and see for themselves. We* can *do both. And truly, we* must *do both in order to survive."*

The crowd cheers. Dixie has to raise her hand to quiet them before she can go on. The folks around us in the carriage are watching intently now, their postures tense. Nearly all the folks around us are Pilgrims on their way to work.

"The second misconception, which seems to be shared more broadly among the Pilgrim population, is that forced conformance— forced compliance—*with an evacuation order will be met with reluctant agreement at worst. We are Terrans. Since the first generation, the Verge has distinguished itself for its dedication to Mother Earth. Alberta Farms stands at our side, as do many scientists in New Juneau. It's our shared calling, it's our mission, and we will not ignore the work that the Creator has put before us simply because a majority stands opposed. We are Terrans, and we are many. We have no desire to waste our energies, sacrifice our blood and resources, in armed defense, but we will* not *be forced from our homes, our farms, our environmental mission. We are Terrans, and here we stay."*

The crowd in the Verge erupts. Folks surge to their feet. The camera cuts to a larger crowd of sapiens filling the park in Alberta Farms. They raise their arms and shout in agreement. The image splits to a similar, though smaller crowd on the steps of the train station in New Juneau.

"I'd say our diversion has already started."

"*Oui. Vive la Terra*," TJ mutters.

Just then the automated voice announces our approach to the Hub. The folks watching the vid shake themselves, some begin packing up their bags and stowing tablets. Everyone sits, as a precaution mostly—tether flight's known for its smoothness. I feel the small lurch as we brake and attach to the tether barge. Now comes the truly risky part. For the short flight from the tether to the Hub, we're in flight in outer space. The only serious accidents in tether history have been in this short space. I hold my breath as the Gs increase—I've been through many sims, and this part's not my favorite.

For just a moment, I see the planet, mostly brown and blue, below us. The angry eye of the great storm at the center of the North American continent slowly spins—its image an ever-present reminder of the destruction of global warming. Finally, the docking mechanism engages, loading us into the bottom side of the structure and the view changes to the metal walls of the docking port. Just like that, we're in the Hub. The SATO Space Station is visible now, a massive spiny disk glinting in the void to starboard. Showtime.

We wait for all the other passengers to disembark. When it's our turn, those dressed as police exit in a formation around the GB. I stay to the back, near TJ, still tapping away on his tablet, and Mercy, who looks convincingly bored as a clerk going through a process she's repeated many times. In truth, it's her first time at the Hub too.

The processing area is all tech and glass. As we move toward the receiving lane, I see a group of officers across the large room on the other side of security. One figure is immediately familiar—wavy gray-blond hair spiking up from a head connected to a long, thin frame. Admiral Yuri LeRoux is so much like TJ in appearance, I sometimes wonder if my friend sees his da like a mirror in time.

"Uh oh." TJ moves behind me.

His da suddenly straightens and steps free of the group, his chin high as his eyes scan the crowd.

Mercy gulps at the sight of him.

"He senses ye?" I whisper.

"Not yet. I think right now, it's just a vague sense of familiarity. Once he sees any of us though, I think he'll know I'm here. He certainly won't expect to see the GB."

We've just passed through the queue and into the station proper when the GB glances back at me, clearly aware that meeting the admiral this soon was not in the plan. Behind her, my eyes refocus on the admiral. Just a few more meters and he'll scan our group. I reach for my stunner, but the station erupts in chaos.

Alarms sound, lights flash overhead. A computerized voice announces an unauthorized launch from the surface. The crowd turns to look toward the planet below.

I see it then—just a speck of silver with a tiny white trail behind it. We watch as the ring rises into orbit and immediately jets off toward the southern pole, out of sight.

At the station, troops rush off in all directions, responding to orders directed into their comms. By the time I look back toward the admiral, the top of his head is moving away with the officers in his earlier group, and he vanishes down a corridor.

Large screens on the walls show a close-up of the ring entering orbit before they go black.

"That worked perfectly!" TJ slaps me on the back.

"Aye, it worked. Let's go. Which way to the doctors' chamber?"

"This way." TJ leads us quickly down a corridor opposite the direction that his da went. Our group moves in an organized formation, with better synchronization than I would have imagined from a group of Couvies, Legion, and Terrans. Only Mercy is out of step, nearly jogging to keep up with our longer steps.

We stop in front of a plain white door about halfway down the long hall.

TJ closes his display. "This is it. From the moment we breach this door, we have about four minutes to get out and back to the tube before someone figures out what we're doing."

I nod. "Ready?"

The others nod in agreement, stunners drawn, they're crouched for action.

The GB steps regally up to the door, the rustle of her skirts the only sound. "Open the door please, Major."

TJ enters a command on the side panel and the door pops open with a click.

The GB presses a hand to the door and steps inside. We all follow, quickly fanning out along the inside wall.

The scene before us is not at all what I expected. The white walls are completely covered with writing and equations. Two men sit at computers arranged on a small table at the center of the room—Dr. Parker Adams, and the ambassador, Dr. Varela. They stare at us in surprise.

"Father!" Mercy rushes forward and hugs him.

"Cricket?" Dr. Adams gazes around, confused. "This truly isn't a good time, my dear."

"What? Where's Mom?"

"Dr. Adams, we're here to rescue ye," I try to explain.

Dr. Varela stands and moves around the table to Mercy and her da. "He's drugged. We think your mother is at SATO station. We haven't seen her since we arrived, but we heard the guards talking. They removed her tracker."

The ambassador is younger than I expected, maybe a few years older than us. His gem has the distinctive rim of pale skin that indicates the disease, the Trade. I wonder how long he has left.

"Dr. Varela, I'm relieved that you're safe." The GB walks forward. "We need to remove you from this facility immediately."

Dr. Varela shakes his head as if to clear it. "Of course." He bends down to talk closely into Dr. Adams's ear. "Come friend, we'll finish this work later." He pulls on one of Dr. Adams's elbows while Mercy pulls on the other.

She turns to me. "My mother?"

It kills me to have to shake my head. "There's no time."

"Three minutes, twenty seconds," Commander Garcia adds.

"Come on, Papa," Mercy begs, pulling on his arm, but he

doesn't budge.

"It's the medicine." Dr. Varela waves a hand. "It affects him more than me. Come friend, we'll finish in your office at home."

"Oh, that's good, yes." Dr. Adams finally stands. "But what about our notes?" He motions to the walls.

"We'll record them," Dr. Varela suggests. "You, you can record this, yes?" he asks TJ.

"Two minutes fifty-five seconds," Vi announces.

I wave an arm. "TJ, just do it. Fast!"

TJ immediately moves to pan the room with the camera in his tablet. We all hustle out of his way as he continues his sweep.

We're bunched at the back of the room as he finishes. I grip the GB's elbow to guide her out when I hear a distinctive click—the sound of a weapon activating.

Admiral Yuri LeRoux stands in the doorway. Caesar Naveen and three soldiers press in around him, weapons drawn, but pointing downward. We're trapped.

"Or not quite four minutes," Vi mumbles.

"Gran Bozan." The admiral smiles. "What an honor. Imagine my surprise when I saw your entourage on the security feed." The admiral turns to TJ. "Hello, son. You've been avoiding my calls." He wags a long knotty finger at TJ.

TJ takes a step forward and away from the rest of us.

"Stop!" Naveen shouts at TJ.

"It's fine, Lieutenant," the admiral assures him.

"Naveen." TJ smiles. "I can't say I'm surprised to see *you* here."

Naveen's eyes turn to slits. "Nor I, you."

That knife-wielding bastard. "Aye, it's like a reunion. How's the arm, lad?" I grind my teeth to keep from growling out loud.

"Healing. You?" Naveen replies.

I take a menacing step forward. "Oh, fine, fine. This is craic, but we've got to go. We're returning to the surface."

The admiral's expression changes in an instant. Teeth clenched, hands fisted, he edges toward TJ. "You will *not* disobey me."

"I'm not your soldier anymore." TJ's voice is cold as he peels back the collar of his shirt and tosses his rocket insignia to the ground. "I'm a TAC officer. Now let us by!"

Naveen raises his weapon, an old-fashioned, vicious-looking gun, and points it at TJ.

"Lower your weapon!" the admiral shouts and pushes Naveen's arm.

The crack of the shot surprises me.

MAY

Current year: 2701
Sunday, 9 AM
The Verge

Deputy May Forge has wicked tech skills—it's a talent that melds well with her occupation in law enforcement. It's also the first thing that brought her and TJ together. He was sent by SciCorps to investigate the possibility that the Couvies were spying on SciCorps communication. Instead of exposing them, TJ became an ally—SciCorps lost their spy to the secret attractions of Vancouver Colony.

May's connection with him, which began when they were both still barely more than kids, was a major part of TJ's life-changing decision to befriend the Couvies. She's never forgotten that.

"How's it coming?" May's grandmother Dixie pulls out a chair and sits with a huff. It's just the two of them in the lab.

"I think I'm finished. I found a way to adapt TJ's hack to the whole network."

"How did you get past security?" Her grandmother leans

forward to look at the screen.

"Well, first I found a backdoor in a lesser system used for server maintenance, then I—"

"Never mind. I won't understand it anyway." Her grandmother leans back in her chair. "So, how's this going to work? Can you isolate who gets hacked and who doesn't?"

May blows out a breath and runs a hand over her gem. "Well, no. I mean, how do we even know who's who? It's not like our personal data includes a metadata element like *'Are you a Terran revolutionary? Yes/No'.*"

"Ha! I guess that's true. And clearly, we can't assume anything based on geography." Her grandmother points to May's circle-rocket insignia. "So, what're you suggesting? That we apply this to everyone?"

"*Oui.* It seems fair. Besides, it won't take long for people to realize the data is garbage. Then everyone will ignore it."

"True privacy." Her grandmother stares at a point behind May's head, absently rubbing her forearm where the implant rests below her skin.

When she refocuses on May, her expression is serious. "What do you think of Mercy Adams?"

May presses her lips together and thinks about Mercy. "Well, she's fairly transparent, I think. Honest. A little too serious maybe." May laughs and shakes her head. "Divine grace, she's got Van Elder tripping over his own boots, doesn't she!"

They both laugh. Her grandmother nods in agreement. "I've always liked that boy—good judge of character."

Instead of going on, her grandmother fiddles with one of her rings, twisting it this way and that.

May's seldom seen her grandmother nervous. Worried, yes, but never nervous. "*Grandmere*, what's going on?"

Her grandmother blows out a slow breath. "Before she left with the rescue team, Mercy filed a formal request with the Couvie council—not the full Terran council, mind you, and that says a lot. She wants us to divulge our true population here for census."

"Oh, well, maybe she's right. After all, it'd give all the Terrans a bit of hope—"

"And add pressure on SciCorps," her grandmother interrupts. "I'm not sure that's such a good idea right now. We need to know what's in that transmission we intercepted—the one that set SciCorps in motion. We have to know what motivated them to start this whole thing. Trying to assassinate councilmembers? It's radical. That transmission *must* hold the key."

May waits quietly for her grandmother to say more. Is this secret something she needs to add to her list of troubles? Her grandmother seems to think so.

Their peaceful silence is interrupted by the sound of footsteps pounding up the corridor toward them.

"By all that's holy, what's this?" Her grandmother stands.

Ava rushes past the lab window and flings open the door. "We have a problem. TJ's ID just stopped transmitting. It's completely dead."

CRANE ELDER

In the past...
August 5, 2118; 583 years ago
Fermont Compound, Quebec, UCA

From the moment she became Council Leader, Crane began to prepare for a general election. The new government created by the praenex was in place. It included four branches: scientific, spiritual, agricultural, and preservationist. Elements of these branches existed in all the compounds and communication between them was good, both technically and politically; Crane could see an easy path to democracy.

The compounds continued to operate within the governance of the United Countries of America, but a time would come when that government would cease to exist. The world population was about to fall below one billion. From there, more and more independent communities would find their way to the safety and quality of life that the compounds offered. Adding to her certainty was the fact that all 86,152 surviving novus humans had migrated to the compounds. Where the praenex lived, so lived the future.

Her nephew Jon had just completed a two-year assignment on the medical team at Alberta Farms, which was quickly becoming a full-fledged compound. As a grown man of twenty-four, he was tall and broad like his uncle, Crane's late husband, with an easy smile and a booming laugh. He didn't stay with her anymore when he visited Fermont—he hadn't since Brym was born. And though this current visit was a longer work assignment, she rarely saw him herself. When they were together, he seemed almost shy of Brym. So she'd been surprised to hear from her daughter that their paths were crossing at work. Brym had even visited the Farms a few months ago with a medical delegation.

These days Crane's apartment was at polar extremes—either completely quiet or a hive of activity—now that Brym was all grown up. Crane only saw her when she came home to sleep and sometimes eat. Brym went to work each day, worked her own community labor shifts, and did her share of the housework. Though serious and responsible, Brym's curiosity meant a nearly constant stream of conversation and questions when she was at home.

Now, in a moment of peace, Crane sat on the sofa in their small apartment with drawings, maps and her tablet arranged on the coffee table in front of her. A small headache threatened at the base of her skull. She was treating it with one of the few self-medicating chemicals still available—caffeine.

Taking a long sip of hot tea, she considered moving to her office in the council building. But no, she decided, right now she just needed the privacy and quiet of her own space to think and mend.

"*Tante?*" Jon shouted as he slammed the apartment door. Like a kid, he never looked for her first, but just shouted.

The loud noise sent a spike of pain through Crane's head. She shut her eyes and rubbed her neck. "I'm here." She sighed as she shut down the analysis she'd been reading. So much for quiet privacy.

Placing her teacup on the table, she listened to Brym chatting animatedly in her sweet high voice, as she and Jon hurried down the hall to the living room. A waft of warm air rushed in with them from the interior hall.

Jon and Brym dropped into chairs opposite the coffee table. They were out of breath and smiling like fools but trying not to show it. Crane sat back and narrowed her eyes. Jon squirmed a little when he met her glare and stopped smiling—or tried to. It seemed nearly impossible for him to keep a straight face for more than three seconds.

Brym fussed with her skirt, then plumped the pillow on her chair, blushing madly every time she glanced toward Jon, though Crane noticed they never actually made eye contact.

Brym broke the uncomfortable silence first. "Is that the latest population map?" She pointed to the map on the table before picking it up.

Crane nodded and waited, trying hard to keep her headache-induced temper in check.

"The migration into Winnipeg is just what we expected…" Brym observed. She cleared her throat and put the map down. Sitting back, she reached toward Jon, then snatched her hand back at the last second like she'd been burned.

Jon coughed into his hand and squirmed a little more.

Crane rolled her eyes and threw her hands in the air. "Okay, what's up? Should I open the PSI application and get ready for a new entry or what?"

She looked back and forth at them, rubbing her neck as she waited.

"Oh, it's nothing like that—"

"Well, you see—"

They talked over each other, then stopped awkwardly.

"I'm sorry," Jon said to Brym, finally meeting her eyes. "Please go on."

"Oh...oh, no, *I'm* sorry," Brym said, smiling again, her shoulders relaxing as she stared at him.

Crane waited a moment, but nothing else happened. They just stared at each other like she wasn't even there.

"Well." Crane slapped her knees, making them both jump. "You let me know when you're ready." She stood up, pushed her glasses into her hair, and gathered her teacup.

"Oh, no, wait!" Brym stood. "I'm sorry, *Maman*, we're just so distracted and..." Brym looked to Jon as if for help.

He stood and ran a hand through his messy blond hair, then noticed what he was doing and shoved his hand in his pocket instead. "Um, you see...Well, you know that Brym and I have been getting to know each other—"

"But not like adopted cousins, really—" Brym interrupted, shaking her head and making a face.

"Oh, right no, not like that...more like..."

Brym snapped her fingers. "Friends!"

"Yes, like friends," Jon agreed, pointing at Brym. "We've become close *friends*. And then we saw each other in Alberta, and then more recently and we didn't know, I mean…we didn't realize—"

"Until recently," Brym interrupted again.

"Right, until recently," Jon agreed. He nodded and blew out a huge breath.

Brym laughed nervously.

Crane waited again, standing there like an idiot holding her teacup, listening to…nothing really. They hadn't actually *said* anything. She sighed and took a step toward the kitchen. Her headache was getting worse.

"Wait!" they both shouted.

Crane cringed and shut her eyes. Pivoting slowly on her heel, she faced them and allowed her pain to show. "What?" She squeezed her temples with her free hand.

"We're trying to tell you," Jon insisted.

"Tell me what?" Crane looked back and forth between them.

When they simply stared at her, she sighed and inched toward the kitchen.

Jon took a step closer, stopping her. He looked at Brym, standing close beside him now. He groped for her hand, found it, and held it.

Brym turned back to Crane. Her smile was all teeth. "We're getting married!"

19
VAN

Last year I went with TJ on a routine scavenge near the Billings ruins. The warehouse had been tagged and sealed by closers five hundred years ago. The seal was tight, and everything seemed fine with the site. He'd flown us in a light transport. Our assignment was simply to open the seal, extract some residential building materials and hardware, and move them outside for later crews to transport to the local airstrip.

Nothing inside interested TJ. He stayed with the chopper. I worked with the other scavies transferring small loads to the concrete lot outside.

We were inside, securing the final load when we felt the ground shake, heard the brutal crash of metal and concrete. We raced outside, but the chopper was gone, along with all the lumber and steel we'd moved so far, swallowed whole by a giant sink hole.

We called for TJ, thought we heard his voice. When the

cloud of dust finally cleared enough to see the chopper, there he was, waving at us as he sat on its roof with a cloth over his mouth.

I asked him later if he was scared, if he thought he might die. I'll never forget what he told me.

"I never worry about dying in a crash," he'd said. "I've always known I'll die in battle."

We laughed at the time. After all, we live on a peaceful planet. Our greatest cause of death is the Trade, a disease which'd become the praenex equivalent of old age.

TJ's not waving now—in fact, he's not moving at all. No one is. We're all paralyzed, staring at his body slumped on the floor.

"My son!"

Bursting into action, the admiral and I reach him at the same time.

Our rush of movement starts everyone firing weapons. It's madness—shouting and shooting.

TJ groans and rolls over. "It's just my arm." He clutches at the wound oozing blood from his forearm.

"Thank the Creator." The admiral hangs his head, oblivious to the bullets and paralyzing laser fire flying around us.

I turn back to the room. More troops have entered. Arson knocks over the table and pushes the doctors down behind it. Commander Garcia is firing their stun gun at everything that moves, but the troops keep coming.

They look at me. "The GB!"

Somehow the GB's been pressed back against the far wall. She has no cover. I stare at Naveen, the only one in position to take a shot, decision clear in the set of his jaw. I lunge for her just as Naveen aims his weapon. I see a flash of tan in my peripheral vision, hear Mercy's unholy battle cry as she cartwheels into Naveen's arm.

The bullet's impact is like a sock to the gut. I crash to the ground, sliding a few feet until I stop in front of the GB. My hands are wet when I pull them away from my stomach, and all the noise sounds distant now.

Vi dives in front of me. "Get down!" they shout. Their arm swings out, and the small ring they threw lands right in the center of the troops storming the room.

Mercy's running toward me now. Her lips move, but I can't hear her. I can't hear anything except a steady buzz.

She launches herself over the desk. Behind her a tremendous flash of arching electricity spreads through the attacking soldiers. A flash stun. Brilliant. The streams of blue and white light are pretty, but they grow smaller and smaller as the black fringe edging into my vision grows.

It's gratifying to see that bastard Naveen crumple to the floor. I can't believe he shot me.

The room is just a pinpoint of light now. It's Mercy's face. Then the tunnel closes, and everything goes dark.

The first Gran Bozan foretold a time when all of the Creator's plans for reshaping the world would converge in a great culmination of events. Clearly, the GB places great importance on what's happening now. So much importance that she's taking risks that put her folk in danger.

"They're dead." I hear her say as I fight back to consciousness. I'm lying on my good side staring into the lifeless violet eyes of the fallen guards.

It's a struggle to stay conscious. Everything's disjointed. I see the GB reach toward me. She has my stun gun now. It's covered in blood—*my* blood, I realize.

"He's awake," she says.

"Good. Up we go!" The sheriff bends to get under me, enough to sit me up.

The room spins, then settles. "Aye, I'm okay."

He chuckles.

"Van! Oh, Van. I'm so sorry…I shot you!" Mercy babbles. "Well not me, I didn't shoot you, but you know what I mean. My kick—"

"It's okay, Cricket," I slur. "I deserved it anyway…for the kiss."

"Oh Van, don't joke."

Somehow, I find myself standing, braced by the sheriff on one side and Dr. Varela on the other.

"We've got to move!" Vi grabs TJ, but the admiral stops them.

"I'm not leaving his side."

Sheriff Arson points his stunner at the admiral "Then I guess you're coming with us."

I put all my energy into my voice. "The GB?"

"I'm here," she says, her warm hand at my back. "Let's go."

Mercy's ahead of me with her da. She glances at every door we pass as we move back along the corridor. I know she's thinking of her mam. TJ and the Admiral are here too, arguing as usual.

"Stay *here* with me, *mon fils*," the admiral pleads.

"I don't belong here, not like this," TJ mumbles.

"I can take care of all this. It's just a misunderstanding. We don't need any more bloodshed—you could stay here with me and your mother, and together we can work it out with the Verge, with your friends in TAC."

The tube carriage is ahead of us now, just a few more meters. The reception area's abandoned. Security is wide open. Everyone must be at their emergency posts.

The sheriff leans more heavily into me and gives the admiral a nudge with the barrel of his stunner. "Keep movin'."

"Actually." The admiral turns to face us. "I think perhaps not—"

"Actually," the sheriff imitates, "I think you will. Seems only fair we host our own *guest*, since Mercy's *maman's* staying behind. So, keep moving or we'll stun you and drag you, *comprenez-vous?*" He gives him another shove with the barrel of his gun to make his point.

"Father, if you truly want to end this diplomatically, then come with us and talk it out in the Verge." TJ points with his head toward the carriage.

"Aye-ye, let's go den." The words are clear in my head but sound all slurred coming out of my mouth.

The admiral considers for a second, and then nods. "As you

say."

He takes TJ's uninjured arm as they enter the tube. Commander Garcia's right behind them, sweeping left to right, watching for danger. Mercy and her da go next. I'm aware that our group has changed. We're leaving folks behind, good folks. Now dead.

I feel the pain in my gut now. My bandage is tight and wet. I'm still bleeding. I look down to see if it's soaked through and I realize I won't be able to tell because the fabric wrapped tightly around my waist to hold my wound is the GB's red sash.

"Oh, no." I try to pull the knot loose, but my fingers are weak as a baby's. "Sacred. Can't ruin this—"

"Hush, Captain!" The GB touches my head like my mam would. "It's only a piece of cloth."

The crack of gunfire erupts behind us. At the same moment the GB crashes into me. I lose my balance and fall forward taking them all down with me. More shots ring out.

Even as I fall, I see Mercy turn toward the sound. See the fabric of her shirt explode. Hear her yelp of surprise as the shot's impact throws her like a rag doll against the tube's wall.

"Mercy!" I scramble up and over the pile of folks collapsed on the floor. The pain is nothing now. If Mercy dies, what will it matter? What will any of this matter?

Commander Garcia fires out the door behind me. "Her legs!"

I'm vaguely aware of the sheriff scrambling up to pull the GB all the way into the tube.

Mercy's face is gray. I think she's in shock. "Am I shot?"

I peel back her jacket where it's torn. Her shirt's clean, no blood.

"I...I dunno." More slurring words.

She reaches up and touches her jacket. Her finger pokes through a hole in the pocket and she pulls out the mule. It's dented. The squashed slug clatters to the floor.

"Oh, no." She turns the coin over in her hand. "It's ruined. Your perfect gift. It's ruined now."

I let out a huge breath and try not to laugh. "Mule saved yer life."

"Yes, but it's ruined now. I liked it better not ruined."

I try to hug her, but my arms aren't working right; they just hang at my sides.

She sniffs. "I think Abigail Adams would appreciate the irony. Oh, Van, you're bleeding so much!"

I fall to one side to lean against the wall. The room is getting fuzzy, but I see Commander Garcia reach into their little bag of rings.

"Last one!" they shout, before hitting the door mechanism and throwing it.

I hear a soldier shout. I think it's Naveen. There's a bright flash just as the door closes.

The sheriff takes one fast step over to the admiral and smashes his fist into the admiral's face. "Now you'll give the order to let us go safely or I'll hit you hard next time." His voice is as cold as I feel.

I don't hear the reply. The world is a narrowing pinhole again, and then it's nothing at all.

CRANE ELDER

In the past...
October 08, 2119; 582 years ago
Fermont Compound, Quebec, UCA

Crane wondered what the NASA people saw when they looked at the praenex leaders assembled for the conference. Introductions the day before had been cordial, but tense. The praenex women looked professional, mature, and serious. Some, like Brym, portrayed their adulthood in just-showing pregnant bellies. Still, the sapiens were older, nearer Crane's age, and they hadn't been around praenex very much. It had to be hard for them.

Brym raised a hand, palm out, to call for silence. As elected leader of the praenex council, she managed these first meetings. "Colleagues, let us begin."

Everyone from the compound bowed their heads in silent prayer. The NASA team at first looked around, then awkwardly bowed their heads too.

"Now then," Brym said a moment later, "I'd like to thank you all again for agreeing to meet with us. You've seen the agenda, so you know we'd like to begin with a review of the deep space colonization program."

A gray-haired man cleared his throat. All the other attendees looked at him. "Excuse me, Sibling Elder—"

"*Brym* is fine, Admiral. Or doctor, if you prefer."

"Of course, *doctor*, the deep space program is classified. We can't share information with you about that program. However, if you wish to submit any materials or suggestions, we'd be happy to receive them."

Crane watched impatience flit across Brym's face. Two praenex scientists raised their hands and looked at Brym. Crane understood that a short telepathic communication took place during the pause.

Brym nodded. "Certainly." She waved to several clerks who began distributing tablets to the NASA people. Brym pointed to the panel on the wall. A project dashboard appeared. "We've analyzed the reported issues, timeline, and scope of the program and determined—"

Chairs screeched on the floor and several of the NASA team, the admiral included, were on their feet. The admiral's face turned a brighter red as she watched. Jon, Brym's husband by then, slowly stood as well.

"How did you get this information?" the admiral demanded. "This is classified material! You can't—"

Brym silenced him simply by standing. After a moment, she pushed back her chair, rubbed her back and slowly paced around the room toward the admiral. Jon slid silently into her wake. When she reached the first NASA man standing, she smiled sweetly, held out her hand and shook his. She said a few quiet words and patted his shoulder. She stepped aside so that Jon could reach the man, shake his hand, and wait for Brym's words and her natural aura of command to reach the man's senses. After a moment, the man let out a tense breath, rolled his shoulders, and sat.

Next, she reached the admiral, held out her hand, and waited.

Reluctantly, he took her hand and shook it.

Brym smiled. "I'd like to teach you something please, sir."

The admiral nodded.

"This is how *we* greet one another." She held up two palms, tipping her head to indicate that he should do the same.

Slowly, he let out a breath and placed his palms to hers. They made a funny pair—Brym's small, feminine frame compared to the admiral's tall sapiens form. He bent slightly at the knees and waist to decrease the difference in their height. Crane wondered if he realized it.

"Very good." Brym's smile was warm and open. "When we have a special bond with someone, or if someone is family to us, we do this." She threaded her fingers through the admiral's and squeezed. He mirrored her automatically.

Staring eye to eye, she continued. "In 29 years, more sapiens will be born, but by then, the world will be praenex. The UCA shall cease to exist, replaced by the Scorch government. We'll have a popular democracy with four branches: scientific, spiritual, agricultural, and preservationist. I'm currently Council Leader, representing the science division. I'd like to combine our efforts to reduce your deep space project timeline from twenty-five years to four years. I have 1,800 praenex scientists, all with genius IQs—we need a new test, it seems—ready to join your brilliant group of scientists and astronauts in Alaska. 12,000 trained sapiens workers are prepared to accompany them."

The admiral took a shuddering breath and flexed his fingers, still gripped in Brym's, as if to test his own strength. "Why?"

"Why?" Brym repeated.

"Yes, why? If you're so much smarter than us, so much more...well, everything..." He released his grip and gently pulled his hands from hers. He rubbed his hands together before dropping them to his side. "Why don't you start your own project? Why join ours?"

Brym smiled and made a little hiccupping noise. "Well, because the Creator told us to join you, of course."

At this, the admiral slowly slid back into his chair, his shoulders slouched. His colleagues reluctantly sat.

Brym seemed not to know what to do next. She looked at Crane in confusion.

"Admiral," Crane said, "you and I, we won't live forever. We've got to pass the torch. I've lived with the praenex since Brym was born. I've learned to trust them. If you don't believe me, just think of the Call. We were *meant* to follow them. I've found it's best to do just that."

The admiral closed his eyes briefly, then opened them and pressed his palms to the table in front of him. "It'll take weeks just to move that many people to the site. We'll need provisions, housing—"

"We have plans for all that." Brym nodded encouragingly.

The admiral blew out a breath. "Of course you do."

"Now, if you'll turn your attention to the next slide, our torporics leader would like to discuss several breakthroughs in long term stasis technology..."

20
MERCY

In my studies, I learned that before the Call, over 300,000 babies were born each day on Old Earth. History shows that doctors around the world expected this many praenex to be born in the first generation. *"All children conceived yesterday will be my New Order."* But it took only weeks to understand that the numbers didn't mesh. Too few pregnancies occurred. Some regions of the world seemed to expect no praenex at all, while others predicted half the usual number of conceptions.

In the end, less than 100,000 praenex were born. With the chaos and warfare that surrounded many, only about 86,000 lived long enough to reach a safe compound. It took years for some to reach safety, their parents and guardians struggling to find a way through the madness and disease all around them.

They called the forty years following the Call "The Great Death," as the world population plummeted daily. The pop banners were invented then. They recorded the steady, dismal decline. Most of Asia fell around 2109, crippled by the Second Pandemic and the Indo-China war. Africa followed in 2112. By the time the first praenex were four years old, each life had become precious. The survivors clung to life.

In stable regions, there were no homeless who wanted a home, no orphans who wanted a family. Humanity suddenly understood what it had lost, and peaceful people banded together.

In unstable regions, angry sapiens prepared for war. They fought to take what they did not have. Some fought against the basic idea of matriarchy; their culture of gender inequality making them unadaptable, even to save themselves. They would not accept the Creator's judgment, and they wanted no peace for anyone who did.

Now, 600 years later, I cradle the GB's head in my lap and understand that kind of violence for the first time in my life. My tears wet her hand as I press it to my lips. My father sits silently behind me, his palm on my shoulder, giving me strength. He's not entirely himself yet, but I'm so glad he's here now where I can see him, touch him.

"You'll be alright. You'll be fine," I murmur.

The GB smiles weakly at me, then grimaces in pain. A trickle of blood trails out of her mouth.

Dr. Varela slides to his knees beside us and begins examining her wounds. There are many. "I'm a medical doctor. Commander!" He looks for Commander Garcia. "I need a med kit now!"

Turning back to the GB, he pushes her straight black hair off her forehead and tucks it behind her ear. Her Asian features are stronger than mine, and I'd never noticed before how young she is—probably my father's age.

Dr. Varela leans over her. "Do you know how to slow the bleeding? How to slow your heart?"

She nods.

"Then pray with me." He covers her forehead with his palm and looks at me. "Put your hand on mine and pray with us."

He closes his eyes and I do as he says, focusing all my thoughts on our Creator's love, the beauty of the world the Creator gave us, the certainty of my path in following divine will. I hear the GB's breathing begin to even out and sense the calm emanating from her, from Dr. Varela.

It happens in this moment of connection with him—the noises around me are replaced by others. In my mind I see another place, another time.

"Minha flor?" Dr. Varela emerges from a room and crosses to another door.

We're in a large, beautiful apartment filled with exotic plants, plush white furniture and musical instruments of every kind strewn about, waiting to be played. Outside a breathtaking view of an unfamiliar city glitters far below the floor-to-ceiling windows. He's searching for someone, growing more frantic by the second.

"Hello?" He stops in the center of the room. Waves of emotion emanate from him: panic, anger, and the sharp edge of regret. He fists his hands in his hair, then drags them down his face. His jaw grinds, and he turns to open another door.

"Ms. Rios, where is she?"

There's a squeak and thump of furniture moving in the hallway outside. Clicks of footsteps on the tile.

"I'm sorry, Ambassador. I thought you knew.... She's gone, sir. She left with the rest of them hours ago."

Dr. Varela turns from the door and quietly shuts it. He steps back to lean against the wall and slowly slides to the floor. He covers his face with both hands as his shoulders begin to shake.

"Here!" says Commander Garcia, jolting me from the vision when they sit next to me.

I open my eyes and find Dr. Varela staring at me. His expression is intense, even angry.

He shakes himself and takes the kit from Vi. "Thank you."

He opens the med kit and riffles through the supplies. He selects a pre-filled pressure syringe and quickly administers the shot to the GB's neck.

"For the pain." He tells her.

I remember then what the children told us, that all Spherans are telepathic. So, he saw it too. I'm sorry for this. I'm sorry to add to his troubles. Usually my visions are joyful—only rarely is one tragic. At least that's how it used to be. These tragic visions are the hardest to recover from. I always carry some of the sorrow with me, even find I replay the vision in my mind more frequently, reliving the pain.

Who is this *Minha Flor* he was looking for? And why would I see his future—a man so loosely tied to me? I force myself to stop thinking of it. To stop pushing these thoughts on him.

At that moment the tube carriage shakes as we disengage from the barge and begin our descent on the tether.

"Will she live?" I ask.

Dr. Varela shakes his head. "Even if I had the right medicines… Gran Bozan Li?" The GB opens her eyes. "I knew you only hours in all, and in each hour the Creator held your hand. I am honored to have known you. May your next journey bring you peace."

The GB releases my hand and holds her palm up to Dr. Varela. "Divine grace with you, doctor."

"May your soul embrace the glory, Your Grace."

The doctor turns to me then. "I must see to Captain Elder now. Will you stay with her?"

I'm torn. I want to follow him to Van's side, but the GB is dying and I can't leave her alone. Plus, my father is here. I look over at Van where he's stretched out on the floor a few meters away. He's watching us.

"Van?"

He waves at me to stay. "I'm good. Stay… stay with her." He turns his head and stares up at the ceiling.

Dr. Varela collects the med kit and moves to Van's side.

"Dr. Adams," the GB wheezes, turning her face toward my father. "You must convince Bozan LeRoux that her life is destined to be far greater than she knows." She coughs and struggles for breath.

"Rest, Your Grace," my father says. His voice is deep and slow—he's still feeling the effects of the drug.

Vi returns and hands me the red sash, stiff with blood, but folded as neatly as possible. "Doc applied a wound patch. He thought you might want this."

I take it from her hands. With a jolt, I realize that I'm living the vision I had five days ago. Good God, is it only five days since I sat paralyzed by this vision? I can almost feel the bench beneath me, hear the sounds of the station, feel the bruise Naveen had just given me.

I stare at the sash, rubbing the hem, unsure what to do. I raise my arm and watch it unfold like a long red flag—a flag marked with blood. Van's blood. I wonder if I would have acted differently if I'd known that five days ago.

The GB squeezes my hand again. "Mercy." She's never used my first name before. It sounds strange coming from her lips. "The sash. You must see it safely into Eddie's hands. It's hers now. It's always been traveling to her…through this Culmination. You've done well so far, Mercy Adams, and you'll all play a part. You will…all…do the Creator's…" Her head tips to the side as her eyes take on a far-off expression.

The sash may be marked with Van's blood, but his is not the only sacrifice. What is a praenex society without the Gran Bozan? Without this fearless woman? What is Eddie? What am I? The ache of loss throbs deep inside me—that kernel of ice again, only this time edged with the heat of knowing exactly what we've lost.

Tears streaming down my cheeks, I reach over to gently close her eyes. I say goodbye to Gran Bozan Li, our spiritual center. And then I pray and pray. I send her to the Creator on a bed of prayers.

My sobs fill the room, but no one tells me to hush.

MAY

May thinks it must the oldest cliché known to humans, that you don't know what you want until it's gone. She hopes it isn't gone.

It's been over two hours since TJ's implant stopped transmitting. Her grandmother Dixie's been sitting with her at home for the last hour, waiting for word, trying to help contain her panic, while Ava tries to get some information.

Her grandmother sets a steaming cup of tea in front of her. "When a person dies, their transmitter keeps transmitting. It's just a malfunction."

May peers into her grandmother's sad eyes and sees that she wants to believe this as much as May does.

"We don't know anything yet." Her grandmother squeezes her hand, then pulls it away quickly, like she's been burned.

"Sorry, Grandmére." May shakes out her hand. "I can't help it. This energy…it's been a problem for a while now, but usually I can run it off or share during worship."

Her grandmother waves a hand in the air. "Don't fret, it's nothing. Although…"

"What?"

"Well, I was thinking we could talk it through. It might help—to talk through your conflicted feelings for TJ."

May sighs. "My feelings for TJ are not conflicted—I love him with all my heart. The conflict is that he wants to leave, and I want to stay…and now I don't even know if he's alive.…" She can't speak around the lump that's grown in her throat. The thought of a life without TJ is unbearable.

"Alright." Her grandmother sets aside her drink and reaches both hands across the table to May. "Let's get through this then. Let's take a look."

May tips her head to the side, considering. Her grandmother wiggles her fingers in encouragement. If her grandmother's willing to link with her frantic energy, why not try?

Reaching out, she closes her grip around her grandmother's waiting hands. At first, she feels her grandmother's struggle to accept the brunt of the force ripping through her, but then her shoulders relax and her breathing evens out. Eyes closed, her grandmother explores the future her gift opens to her.

"I see.…" Her grandmother opens her eyes and smiles. "I see a baby still. A healthy baby with a gleaming black gem, just like Mercy told you."

May exhales loudly. "That's good."

"Good? What more assurance do you need that TJ'll return. The baby proves it."

May shakes her head. "No, *Grandmére*. The baby isn't proof.

I could already be carrying it."

She waits while her grandmother processes this information. Watches as surprise, joy, and finally understanding move through her grandmother's expression. "Alright, let's try again then."

Her grandmother closes her eyes and concentrates. Minutes pass. Slowly, she opens her eyes and slides her hands from May's grip. "I'm sorry, I can't see more."

"What now?"

Her grandmother drinks her tea and stares into the cup. "What does your heart tell you?"

May forces herself to think. She closes her eyes and breathes.

What does her heart tell her? It's the same heart that's been torn these past days, knowing that she loves a man who wants the opposite of what she wants. But when she concentrates on TJ, when she pictures him in her future, she doesn't see the setting in distinct detail. Only TJ—his face, his voice, his laugh—resonate in her mind. Could it be so simple?

She feels it then—the energy converging around this simple truth. All her doubts and struggles compartmentalized as non-essential. All her love and hope and life centered on one single truth.

She opens her eyes. "I love him. If he lives, I'll follow him anywhere."

21
MERCY

Though smaller, praenex are naturally much stronger than sapiens. The bigger sapiens athletes have never had an unfair advantage in feats of strength, but I've seen Van in those rare moments of athletic freedom use his size to simply overwhelm his praenex opponents. Last year I watched him score in a game by simply carrying two men clinging to his back as he ran down the field.

To my annoyance, the respiration mask obscures Van's face, but I don't dare take it off. We've ten minutes left before we land at Tether Base, and I know Van's fighting for his life. My struggle to control my sadness, my panic is equally difficult. My tears stain everything.

"The bullet nicked his lung," Dr. Varela explains. "I think it's collapsed. The wound patches have slowed the bleeding we see, but his lung is filling with blood. He needs a surgeon."

"Are there surgeons at the base?" I ask TJ, wiping my face

with my already damp sleeve.

Vi is just tying off the wrap around TJ's wounded forearm. He grimaces and looks at his father.

The admiral shakes his head. "We've never had much need…"

"Don't worry." My father pats my shoulder. "Dr. Varela is a good doctor. He'll help Van."

Dr. Varela blows out a breath. "If I had my own kit—"

"We have the kit!" I cry.

My excitement jolts Van awake and he groans.

"Sorry! We have your kit. The children insisted that we bring it with us. It's with Eddie at the base."

"We'll need blood too—sapiens, whatever his type."

TJ flips on his comm link and starts awkwardly typing in commands one-handed. "She's got it. She'll meet us when we land."

"How long?" the doctor asks.

TJ checks his comm. "Four minutes."

"Really four minutes this time?" Commander Garcia motions to TJ and they wander away arguing quietly.

"Well, Admiral." Sheriff Arson straightens in his chair and lays his stunner across his knees. "What kinda reception can we expect when we arrive?"

"Are you always so distrustful? Is it a Couvie trait?" The admiral sucks his teeth. "It goes well with stubbornness and secrecy, I suppose."

"Oh, that's rich—"

"Stop it, both of you." My voice is sniffly and rough.

To my surprise they do as I say.

"Mercy?" Van's voice is muffled by the mask. He reaches for me. "Mercy."

I take his hand and move closer to his head. "Shh. Don't talk. You need to save your energy."

"I'm sorry. I shoulda been there for ye. I shoulda…"

"Shh." I brush my fingers over his curly hair. "It doesn't matter. Just be still."

He winces as the tube lurches a little. We've entered the enclosed section of the tether, the last 1,000 meters to the surface. Only moments now.

Dr. Varela looks around. He motions the sheriff over. "When we arrive, we need to get him up onto a table. I can't do this on the floor."

The sheriff signals Commander Garcia and they hurry deeper into the tube.

A second later, they're back. "Around the corner, there's a table, and it's a better defensive position too." The commander slants a look at the admiral. "Just in case we need it."

"Good. Now how're we going to lift him?" Dr. Varela asks.

We all look down at Van. Simply put, he's huge. Even with our praenex strength it's going to be tough.

"I can lift him." My father steps closer, eyes clearer. Either the gravity of what's happening has reached him or the drug's wearing off. "I can get him up, if you know where you want him."

I'm relieved to see some of his normal practicality returning. I forget sometimes how strong my father is. I'm so used to thinking of him in the laboratory where he flexes different muscles entirely. But he's right. Among the praenex my father is a contrast—taller and wider, with more the stature of his seafaring ancestors than the narrow, wiry build of the others. My mother calls him *sailor* as a term of endearment. I hear her voice calling him that now, the shadow of a laugh behind her words. The memory brings a surge of missing her, an ache like a huge empty hole deep inside me.

Suddenly the tube stops with a gentle hiss and barely audible thump as the docking clamps engage. We all turn back to the glass doors to see what awaits.

It's Eddie. Both palms pressed to the doors, not in greeting, but in urgency. She has the doctor's strange looking medical folio looped around one wrist, two more kits across her shoulder, and bags of blood in her grip.

"Let's go!" Dr. Varela shouts.

"Wait. I need a second." I can't let it go like this. Without having some control over this, over what happens next.

I look down at Van's brown eyes staring back at me, waiting. Before I lose my courage, I lift his mask aside and press my lips to his. His lips are soft and warm with rough edges, just like him. I watch through slitted eyes as his pupils expand. I press harder for one second before pulling away and replacing his mask.

I sit back so my father and the others can lift Van. At the same moment the outer and inner doors peel back to let Eddie in. The base behind her is vacant, but I sense many eyes watching us.

A wave of sorrow hits me as she steps inside. The other praenex blanch—she's broadcasting her emotion so clearly that I know she knows the GB is gone.

Eddie peels the shouldered kits over her head and hands them to Vi. She doesn't look at the body draped on the floor a few meters away. Still, I have to steel myself against the emotions pulsing from her in waves. It's nearly overwhelming. It helps to focus on something else—I read the words on the medical cases.

Wound Care.

Transfusion Kit.

Not so helpful in settling my emotions after all.

Eddie starts to follow Vi, then comes up short when she sees the admiral standing opposite me, also waiting for this moment.

"Father."

"Omag Gran LeRoux." The admiral smiles, a tight, almost painful expression. They don't touch palms.

Eddie breathes loudly, straightens her back and lifts her chin. I both see and feel the moment she wins the struggle for composure—she's intentionally closing off her emotions to us now. "It's *Bozan* LeRoux, sir."

"Bozan!" Now the admiral's smile is sincere. "Congratulations, my dear. I'm extremely proud. Your mother will be delighted."

"I very much doubt that…. Father, what have you done?"

The admiral's expression changes instantly to angry resolve. "What I must. What every Pilgrim must—"

"*Power always thinks it has great soul,*" I say.

Eddie tips her head toward me thoughtfully. "Machiavelli?"

I try to smile at the slight, but it feels brittle and false. "No, my forebearer, John Adams, of course."

Commander Garcia rushes from around the corner. "The doctor needs us…now!"

"Of course." Eddie strides after them.

As I follow her quickly around the corner, the doors softly hiss closed behind us. We huddle around Van where he lays on the long table and the admiral joins our group.

Dr. Varela's already started surgery. Van's wound is framed by a fabric drape. The bullet hole seems so small for having caused so much trouble. I know there must be a matching wound on his back where the bullet exited.

I stare at the angry red hole—I can't seem to look away. I wonder where the bullet is now. Embedded in a wall? My vision wavers and my ears begin to buzz. I think I'm going into shock again. I know I have to fight it, to stay focused, to stay here.

Dr. Varela unrolls his folio next to the other kits lined up behind him and begins administering shots. "These will prepare him for surgery, help with infection."

I turn to my father. "Do you think you can help the doctor? Do you feel sober enough?"

My father nods. "I can prep, but you'll have to start the line, doctor."

"Thank you," Dr. Varela answers. They work quickly together to start the transfusion. When that's done, Dr. Varela pulls a long silver case from a sleeve in his folio. It's high-tech and sleek, a dramatic contrast to the simple bundle in which it was transported.

"What's that?"

He presses a button that flips back the lid to reveal a long, dangerous looking syringe. "This syringe is filled with microscopic robotic tools. I'll inject them into the wound, and they'll perform the internal repairs."

"That's impossible." My father shakes his head.

"No, it's possible. I've performed this procedure many times. The bots are programmed to take my direction, but they use the body's natural healing properties to help with the repairs. But I do have one problem…. I've never performed this procedure on a sapiens before."

Of course he hasn't. For all I know, Van is the only sapiens he's ever met. "What do you need us to do?"

Dr. Varela looks at me. He takes the needle from its case and pauses just above Van's wound. "Hold him, all of you."

The men hold Van down while I frame his head in my hands. Dr. Varela slides the needle into the wound slowly. After an initial jerk, Van's body relaxes. Dr. Varela depresses the plunger as he slowly withdraws the needle.

"Sheriff, Commander Garcia, you've done this before. I need you to assist me. To show the others how to direct their energy."

The sheriff shakes his head. "Sorry, doc, we've never done anything like this before."

"But you have." Dr. Varela presses his palm to Van's bare chest. "You've done this many times with…" He closes his eyes briefly. "Dixie! You pray with her. Lend her your energy so that she can use her gift more fully."

Arson and Vi exchange a look.

Vi shrugs. "Okay, we can do that." They elbow the sheriff lightly. "Stop being so stoic. Later you can say you saved his life.

That'll annoy the hell out of him."

Arson scoffs and turns back to the doctor. "How do we start?"

With the doctor directing, and Arson and Vi coaching, we all place our hands on Van. It's like meditation, only we're not focusing on Van, but on the doctor, sending all of our energy into his mind, his hands. I wish my mother were here to add her energy to this group. To add her love.

A moment passes in silence. Van coughs suddenly and a line of blood drips from his mouth.

"What's happening?" I ask.

"It's working, but too slowly. His anatomy confuses the bots, it's taking too long. We need more energy, I need more…strength of purpose."

I turn and look at Admiral LeRoux where he's leaning against the far wall, watching us with a vaguely bored expression. "Admiral, we need you."

His head snaps up and he meets my eyes. He shakes his head slightly.

"Father?" TJ holds out his good hand.

The admiral doesn't move.

"He's like a brother to me."

After a few seconds, the admiral clenches his teeth and pushes off the wall. "I don't know how *I* can help. I'm no friend."

TJ grips his shoulder. "We may have our differences, but you've always had more strength of purpose than anyone I know."

"Except for mother," Eddie adds.

TJ and the admiral exchange a look, and then the admiral

steps into our circle and wraps his hand around Van's wrist. We all shuffle to make room. The doctor closes his eyes, and we focus.

I focus on the doctor. On giving him all my strength. On giving him all my peace and resolve.

I focus on Van. On sharing all my histories with him. On giving him all my future life. On giving him all my love.

CRANE ELDER

In the past...
April 23, 2124; 577 years ago
Fermont Compound, Quebec, UCA

Crane often wondered what it was like to have God whispering in your ear, leading you through your dreams. Over the past sixteen years, much bad news had reached the people of Scorch via the Creator's messages to the praenex, but even the worst could not compare to this.

Her son-in-law's face was red, his eyes puffy. Though only thirty years old, Jon looked much older now—beaten down by the news that his family was about to be torn apart.

"It's too much." He mumbled into his hands. "Too much."

The twins, though only a year old, showed a high degree of empathy. They scampered into his lap, wriggled their way under his arms, but didn't stay long. With so many of their loved ones in pain, they flitted back and forth between the adults and their older brother, Odell, who was named to honor Brym's birth mother, Phoebe O'Dell.

Odell was the first male praenex born, the twins were the first twins. Brym had a habit of being the first at everything. But not only everything *good.*

"It's too much." Jon leaned back in his chair and grimaced at the ceiling.

Brym leaned toward him. "Jon, husband, it can't *be* too much—it must be just the right thing, though it feels so wrong to us. The Creator showed me a long line of sapiens Elders spreading across Scorch. Shaping it. Healing it. Feeding it. They're important. Imperative. And they're *yours* Jon, not mine. They're sapiens. You must stay and wait for this woman who will help you build this future—" Brym's voice cracked.

"Stop!" Jon shouted. "How can you even say such a thing? How can you…? I love you, Brym." He stood and pulled her up with him.

Crane watched them hug. She saw what Jon did not—Brym's face contorted in pain, her eyes filled with tears she refused to let fall.

"You'll raise Odell and the twins. Talk of us often, and I'll tell this one"—she pulled back and rubbed her still-flat belly—"I'll tell her all about all of you."

Jon shook his head and reached for her again. With a wave, he gathered all the children to them. Crane stood and stepped toward the mass of crying people—the family she would have fought anyone to keep from this pain. But what use was it to fight the Creator's will? Where Brym would lead, they all must follow. Instead of struggling, she wrapped her arms around them.

"We will live long lives; I have seen this for all of us.…" Brym took another breath. "We must find what comfort we can in knowing that our love for one another, for this family, will survive, no matter how many kilometers, how many years separate us."

"Tell me where you're going. Tell me!" Jon demanded.

"I can't tell you, *mon cœur*. It's not meant."

Jon stared at Brym, his beloved wife. "I can't do it. I can't voluntarily let you go." He turned to Crane. "*Tante*, what can I do?"

Crane swallowed. It took her a moment to fight back the tears and answer. "You're a strong man, Jon, just like your uncle. When the time came, he took the risk the Creator asked of him. He took the risk, and he helped save thousands of lives. Your sacrifice is just as painful, but at least you know that I'll keep her safe, her and the baby."

"I can't do it!"

Brym stepped back from the group just as a knock sounded at the door. "You need *do* nothing, husband, except stay here for now. In two days, my office will broadcast my farewell message. And every day you need only love our children and raise them well. God will do the rest."

Brym hugged Odell then, kissed the top of his golden head, before reaching for the twins. Crane did the same, and then led the children, weeping, to their rooms.

At the second knock, Crane stopped next to Jon and bent to grab one of her bags. "I'm proud of you, Jon. You're the best son-in-law, the best man, I could have prayed for. I trust Brym's vision. I believe it, all of it...I know you will be so much more. I wish I could stay to see it happen. You're my family. You'll always be my family. I love you and I'll miss you." She hugged him quickly, nearly overcome by the silent sobs shaking his body, and then she walked briskly through the door and into the hall.

Two praenex stood in the dim hallway waiting—both of them clearly distressed. On Crane's signal, they entered the apartment and returned with the rest of the bags. Brym was quick on their heels.

She faced one of them, her friend, Pauline LeRoux. "You'll file these papers after my statement is released the day after tomorrow." She shoved the papers at Pauline.

"Yes, sister." Pauline's voice shook and tears slid down her face in an endless stream. Rolling her shoulders, she took the sheaf of papers that Brym held out to her.

Divorce papers, Crane knew. They'd discussed it. Brym refused to leave Jon without the freedom to remarry. The idea seemed ludicrous to Crane, but Brym had insisted.

Brym paused a moment, clenching her hands until her knuckles were white. A tremor shook her whole body, and she grimaced through clenched teeth. Crane had seen people in a similar state collapse on the spot—passing out from sheer emotional trauma. But Brym reeled it in, and with nothing left to do, turned on her heel and paced quickly away from the apartment. Away from her children. Away from her beloved husband. Because it was the Creator's will.

The two praenex carrying the bags were crying openly now. As telepaths they shared Brym's grief, as would those around them. They followed quickly after Brym, and as Crane steadied herself to move, she saw doors opening all along the hallway—

crying faces of praenex neighbors peering out.

Crane paused and looked back down the corridor. She could hear Jon's mournful cries and felt as if her heart were truly torn in half.

She looked to the ceiling and spoke to God. "This had better be worth it."

22
VAN

I never really took Mercy to be a superstitious lass, but she insists that if we don't get married right now, something bad is going to happen. Suits me fine, of course. My only regret's that my mam and the weans can't make it here in time. Though truth be told, that was never going to be easy. Even if they could make the trip from the Farms, squeezing all of them into this hospital room would be impossible.

"Are you comfortable?" Mercy leans over me and tries to fluff my pillow for the tenth time. She's so tiny and I'm so big, her fussing has no effect.

"Aye, leave be, Cricket. I'd much rather be up outta this bed instead of lyin' here like a dosser, but if ye won't let me do that, then least ways stop fussin'."

"You're not leaving that bed, Captain," the doctor says, looking up from my chart. "Don't start with me again."

I take a deep breath to argue, but the stabbing pain it causes changes my mind. "Aye, doctor. I'll stay put."

The doctor steps aside as the door swings open and May enters, dragging TJ by his good hand. "We've got a surprise." She grins and waggles her eyebrows.

"No exertion," the doctor warns again before leaving.

TJ raises his hand. "Don't worry, it's nothing bad." He follows May and the door swings in again, bumped by a small cart Mercy's father is pushing.

"Maybe we should remove the door," I suggest.

Dr. Adams waves off my remark. "I got it!"

"Got what, Papa?" Mercy moves to hold the door. I can see her full outfit now—a red satin tunic that leaves her arms bare and sets off her pretty hair. Her shoes are graceful little slippers with intricate designs; they wink out from under her cropped white trousers, making her feet look incredibly small.

For a moment, I can't breathe at all. She's the most beautiful creature on Scorch, I'm sure of it. It's some kind of luck that she's finally mine, that all the years I've waited are finally coming to an end.

"Not that one!" TJ points to the electronics May's assembling on the cart. "Do you want to fry the entire relay?"

May drops the cable and stands with hands on hips. "Listen, flyboy, I can connect a simple amplifier without your help, thank you. Why don't you go sit over there? Rest your arm."

"I don't need to sit—"

"TJ?" I hold up my hand. "Maybe you can fill us in like?"

TJ slaps his thigh. "Sure, okay. So, the holo capacity in this suite is good for about two, maybe three images—"

"Fifteen siblings!" Dr. Adams exclaims. "Mercy, you're going to have more siblings than you ever imagined once you're married. How will you remember all their names?"

Mercy grins. "Oh, well, I worked out a system, you see...." Mercy opens her comm and they bend their heads together over her holo.

"Are you ready for this?" TJ sits on the stool beside my bed.

"Ready? Aye, they even let me put on trousers." I kick one leg out from under the hospital sheet. "And a clean shirt, though it's still the hospital type with no buttons."

"You're getting better then? The ceremony won't be too much?"

"I should be fine as long as I don't have to get up to go to the jacks. Takes forever."

"Knock, knock." A familiar head peers around the door.

"Captain Souza!" Mercy hurries over to hug her old friend.

"I hope you have room for one more," Souza says, his white teeth gleaming.

"Aye, it's jammers in here, but since yer officiatin', I guess we better make room."

"I'm so glad you could do this for us. It means so much." Mercy's still holding his hand as they come around to the empty side of my bed.

Captain Souza holds up one finger. "*Love is all we have, the only way that each can help the other.*"

Mercy taps a finger on her chin. "Rumi?"

Souza chuckles. "Euripides, my friend."

"I don't care who ye quote, as long as ye marry us." I hold out my hand and he squeezes it gently.

Souza's face falls. "Any word on Coral?"

Everyone quiets at the mention of Mercy's mother.

Her father shakes his head. "They insist she can't be disturbed, but they promise to share the vid with her to watch when she's free. We really don't know what it means, whether she's safe or—"

"Don't think it, Papa!" Mercy hugs his arm, before turning back to Captain Souza. "Eddie is trying one more time to get a holo connection."

"Here we go!" May says. She taps in a few final commands and holograms start to appear.

First a group of children, tall and small, on the right, then another on the left. They wave and shout and giggle, and it's almost like coming home. Finally, in the middle, my mam and oldest siblings stand before me, and then I am home.

I sigh. "God's grace, it's good to see ye, Mam."

"Oh, aye." My mam grins and clasps her hands, joy sparkling in her pale blue eyes. Her ginger hair streaked with bits of grey is pulled up higher than most days and her dress is crisp and clean—her best linen, I'm sure. "Ye look even better than yesterday, Van, and ye were right…this is just perfect now." She spreads her arms to encompass the room.

I shake my head. "It's the same as yesterday, Mam."

"Well, I always say the only decoration a weddin' needs is a lovely bride, and Mercy, my dear, yer the loveliest bride to be for sure."

"Thank you, Mrs. Elder." Mercy makes a little bow toward

my mam and my throat constricts.

"Best ye call me Mam now, daughter, for that's what I'll be to ye, I promise. But where's yer da, Sylvan?"

There's a commotion at the door as Eddie and my da wrestle their way through carrying an enormous shallow tray piled with greenery. They lay it crossways at the bottom of my bed.

"Any luck, Eddie?" Mercy steeples her fingers below her chin.

Eddie shakes her head. "I'm sorry, Cricket."

"Aye, it's disappointin', but wait until ye see this!" My da spreads his massive arms, taking up what's left of the space in the room.

Eddie takes one end of the garland and Dr. Adams takes the other. Between them, they cross the lasso over Mercy's head and mine to make an infinity loop.

"It's gorgeous!" Mercy brushes the colorful garland.

"Aye, and heavy." I lift a section off of my ribs and notice it's a tidy bunch of bright red radishes and white turnips. "And edible, apparently."

Mercy giggles. "It's cabbages!" She laughs as her fingers play over the plate-sized face of a pink ornamental cabbage.

My father puffs up his chest and grips his lapels. "Aye! I finally got 'em here. 'Twas a mission in itself, which we started long ago, if ye remember, Van."

"I do, Da. Thank ye." I swallow past the knot in my throat and glance at Mercy. "Are ye ready then, Cricket?"

She grins. "I love you, Van Elder. I've never been more ready in my whole life."

I take her hands. "Aye, let's do it, then."

EPILOGUE
EDDIE

Current year: 2701
Two weeks later
The Verge

My home—the Legion's Enclave—is technically part of New Juneau, but instead of clinging to the sea cliffs, it nestles tightly into the mountains northeast of the city, connected by magrail but little else. It was built three hundred years ago in a location once covered by massive glaciers. A quietness and coldness still persist there. It's a place that inspires whispers and light footsteps. A place of deep contemplation. A good place for questions. A good place for my father to contemplate his role.

A good place for a funeral, as it turned out.

It's where I, Bozan Edelweiss LeRoux, intended Gran Bozan, should be. Not here in this noisy community in the Verge, so full of normal life. So full of people—people sneaking glances at me, whispering to each other. I feel their eyes, their questions press on me. It was in the Enclave that my natural talent was honed into telepathy, and usually I'm glad for the advantage. But not right now.

After our recent mission, the Legion decided it was time to release information about my resistance to the Trade, the disease that until now killed us all. Now the population knows there could be a cure. They know about my abundance of offspring, also naturally resistant. Add to that the fact that my parents have essentially started a civil war, and it means that far too many thoughts are focused on me, on the name LeRoux. It's difficult to ignore a fame that's pushed into my head telepathically.

I take a deep breath and reach for calm to quell the nervousness growing inside me. I try to see the notes of my newest composition, but the melody eludes me. My drumming fingers can't find the right cadence. I'm annoyed instead of soothed.

The door on the opposite side of the lobby opens and Mercy walks in with her entourage. They're talking animatedly, pointing at their tablets, then she sees me and halts them with a word. She waves toward a group of chairs set up in a corner near the door, and the small group immediately steps away and gets right back to work.

She strides toward me, head high. "Van's joining us shortly." Her cheeks flush a little when she says his name. So cute.

"Good." We press hands and sit. "You're busy, I see."

She glances back at the group deep in discussion. "Yes, the Spherans have shared some information about their educational system and asked me to review it. My team's working through a strategic approach at this point."

"Any word about your mother?"

Mercy shakes her head and looks away. "How are you?"

I look down, not sure how to answer. I touch a corner of the red sash neatly folded in my lap.

"Will you wear it, do you think?" Mercy murmurs.

I can sense that she's trying not to pry. The quiet sadness that's been hovering behind her eyes these past weeks remains. Her mother is still missing and diplomatic efforts to get information about her health have failed.

I rub my thumbs across the red sash—freshly laundered, all traces of the blood and sacrifice removed. *Will I wear it?* "I don't think so. Not yet. Rumesa will manage things, while I…decide. It's not…"

"Urgent?"

I nod. "When people found out that Bozan Li passed the sash to me… Well, suddenly I'm a councilmember and an even greater curiosity, but I think they understand that I need some time and space."

"Do you think they'll give you time?"

"Time, yes…a little. It's the space that I'm worried about."

Mercy grimaces. "What'll you do now?"

"I don't know."

She exhales loudly and closes her eyes, thinking. *"Living at risk is jumping off the cliff and building your wings on the way down."*

"E. E. Cummings?"

"Good guess…Ray Bradbury."

"Did anyone ever take him up on it?"

"I don't know." She chuckles, then squeezes my arm. "But if *you* do, I know you'll soar."

"Or plummet to my death trying."

We laugh. Granted, it's short, ironic laughter, not the joyful type, but laughter just the same.

She's the only one I've laughed with since the GB's funeral. I still feel the pain like a hollow place inside my chest. Gran Bozan Li was the closest thing this world had to royalty, the closest thing to a mother for us all. The events leading up to her death have been analyzed in excruciating detail these past weeks. Everyone knows where she was, who she was with, how she died. She's a hero, perhaps even a martyr, because of the circumstances.

Oddly, for all we *do* know, there's one key fact that we *don't*… We don't know who killed her. We don't know the name of the soldier who shot Gran Bozan Li. But we know who to blame, and as a LeRoux, my family's shame threatens to overshadow everything.

Mercy nudges my knee and gestures to the population counter hanging on the wall.

"It's time." We wait, holding our breath despite everything that's led to this point. A hush falls over the hall.

As planned, the counter subtracts three numbers, one at a time, to recognize the GB and her guards who died during the SciCorps coup. We pray—the world prays—as we wait for the moment of silence to pass. Then we watch again as the counter flutters and some forty thousand lives are added—as unregistered Couvies, and the secretive Spherans join the human race.

Mercy squeezes my knee and I blow out my breath. 264,292. Such a huge change, and yet such a small number for what's to come.

I turn to Mercy and watch a tear slide down her cheek.

She sighs. "My mom would've loved this."

"She *does* love this! She's watching somewhere, I know she is."

Mercy meets my gaze and smiles, just a little, and then squeezes my knee again before letting go.

A fresh shaft of sunlight bounces off the wood floor, temporarily blinding me as the door across the lobby opens. I shield my eyes to see Van enter. His gait is still delicate, like he's steeling himself against pain when he moves. I first noticed the pinched lines at the corners of his eyes at the GB's funeral. I understand that he blames himself. He's an officer and the GB was carrying his gun when she was shot. She shielded him from bullets. She saved his life. A life my father's people were trying to take.

I shake out my skirts and stand, trying to swallow the hard lump that keeps forming in my throat when I think too long about the mission, about what we've lost. I ignore the curious stares locked on me. Let these strangers look—I'll show them nothing.

Mercy stands beside me. "I've got to go."

Van reaches us and holds out a hand to her. She grips it.

I look into his eyes and see reflected back at me my pain, my conflicted relief to be alive. I nod and lift my chin. I hold one palm out to Van. He presses his free hand to mine, but before he can pull away, I curl my fingers through his and squeeze. I can be brave for both of us.

"Captain."

Van raises a brow in surprise, and then he takes in the

audience of curious Couvies around us. When his eyes come back to me, he studies my face, then relaxes, just a little. He curls his fingers with mine. The corner of his mouth lifts and I'm glad to bear this weight, to let him take a break from the sorrow.

I squeeze his hand hard before we both let go.

Van smirks. "Well now, what's my luck yer both waitin' here for me to make yer lives more interesting?"

Mercy sighs and gives him a little shove. "Oh, the ego. Have I ever told you the story of a man named Caligula…"

They leave me, walking away, hand in hand, Mercy leaning against him while she talks animatedly. They have their new life as a married couple. I wonder what it will be like, given the war and upheaval all around them. Whatever comes, I know they'll meet it head on. Together. She's just that kind of Adams, and he's just that kind of sapiens. I think their ancestors would be proud.

So, the question now is, what kind of LeRoux am I?

I smooth the sash one last time, then slide it into my bag.

I turn away from the crowd before anyone can approach, and head back into the corridor leading to the Couvie stronghold. I pass many couples as I wind my way deep underground to the laboratory that has become my brother's home. I return their greetings briefly and hurry along, trying to avoid any conversation. Has the Verge always been this way—so filled with pairs—or are people responding to the strain of war in a very human way, seeking comfort from one another?

Nearing the elevator bank, I round a corner and collide with a stranger.

"Umph!" Their breath ruffles my hair and I realize I was almost running.

I grab their arm to steady us—their tablet clunks to the floor. "Oh, I'm so sorry."

They shake their head. "No, no, it was entirely my fault, I…" They scan my face.

I know the moment they realize who I am. I also know my blush is probably shocking against my albino skin. It only makes me blush harder.

"Divine grace! You're…I mean…"

"Greetings." I raise my hand in hopes that the formality will help us both gain some composure.

The stranger straightens and holds up their palm to mine. "Greetings, Bozan LeRoux. I'm most blessed to meet you—"

The introduction is interrupted by the small crowd that's formed around us—people first wanting to make sure we're alright, and then hoping to gain an introduction themselves.

"Bozan LeRoux!"

"Divine grace, Bozan."

"Peace with you, Bozan!"

Hands thrust into my space, palms raised. I hear my name repeated over and over again, as I'm jostled through this crowd of eager Couvies. My heart races as I shuffle backwards. Their questions press on my mind, vague but insistent. When I feel the wall at my back, I twist to press the button that calls the elevator. My smile is brittle. My pulse, a deafening drum. When the elevator door slides open behind me, I can't hold back the impulse to push them away.

Back! My mind gives them a mental shove before I can restrain myself.

They gasp and step back from me, looks of shock and awe spreading through the small crowd.

"Forgive me. I…I have an appointment."

The doors slide closed and I'm alone again. I concentrate on the low hum of the elevator and gather my wits. The hum is nice. I try humming myself, Pachelbel's Canon.

God, but that was close. Am I so out of control?

I'd like to drift away now, follow the chords in my mind.

Is that what it's like to be GB? If it is, how in the Creator's name could I manage it?

I descend to arrive at the lab where TJ, May, Dr. Parker Adams and Dr. Varela have taken up a partnership of sorts, struggling through their loosely related projects together. TJ and May are working on deciphering the communication that the Verge intercepted a few months ago, the message that set SciCorps' offensive into motion. Mercy's father, Dr. Parker Adams, is completing his work on the chemical engineering for the ozone loom. And Dr. Varela—*Cai* Varela, as he wants to be called—is working on a cure for his people. My people too. A cure for the Trade. I bet you'd never guess what *his* work is based on.

As the lab door slides open, I'm unsurprised to see them there, all four of them, huddled over their workstations. I breathe in the calm, the focus. On the desk next to Dr. Adams's workstation, I see the now-familiar framed photograph of his family—the same photograph that Mercy smuggled out of the

Hab, the photograph behind which Dr. Adams hid a clue to the events driving this civil war—his breakthrough in ozone repair.

I stare at the group busy at work, but only May raises a hand in greeting. She's not wearing her gloves today, so her Couvie rings send a rainbow of prisms dancing around the lab. It's like confetti, and my heart warms a little.

The others all know I'm here, but as is typical, they don't feel the need to disrupt their work to greet me.

On this thought, Dr. Varela—*Cai* Varela—looks up and smiles at me. A knowing smile.

I'm not sure how I feel about his telepathy, but there's nothing I can do about it, except try harder to control my thoughts.

"Bozan LeRoux." He gestures for me to come over.

I'm standing next to him before I think of moving. I wonder for the hundredth time whether he has this magnetic effect on all women, or just me. His dark curly hair and violet eyes make a handsome contrast with his olive skin and noble jaw. From the first moment I saw him in the rail station, he's had this unspoken pull on me. But what use is it for me to want this man? A Spheran. His home is as far as possible from mine.

I should be back there, in my apartment in the Enclave. Safe from judgement. Safe from hope of a normal life. What man could want me and all my offspring? And now this red sash and all *it* represents?

A quiet voice in my mind whispers *this one*.

He wants me right now, but not for the same reason. So much for controlling my thoughts. I look him in the eye.

A crease forms around his gem. "Are you alright?"

I suck in a breath and try for a neutral expression. "Yes, of course. I'm ready for another half-liter if you need it." I roll up my sleeve and take my place in the chair next to the phlebotomy station.

He smiles, but it doesn't reach his eyes. Silently, he gathers the supplies and gets ready to start the line.

I feel the sharp pinch.

"My research is going well." He looks up through his lashes as he turns the valve and lets the blood flow from my arm into the tube. We watch as the pouch begins to fill.

We wait in silence.

"You're wrong, you know." He speaks without looking at me.

"Wrong about what?" I'm not sure if we'll be direct about this or continue to dance around our attraction as we have for the last two weeks.

He looks me straight in the eye now. "Many men—the *best* men, perhaps—would only have to see you here...." He lightly touches my hip where my incision and bruises from my ovarian surgery are still healing. I'm surprised by the jolt of sensation I feel through my clothes. My breath catches.

Cai continues. "They'd only have to see the scar to understand your conviction, your purity of heart. They would not be marrying the woman you see of yourself. They would be marrying a hero, a leader. What man would *not* want you and all your gifts?"

I'm saved from answering when TJ jumps up, knocking his stool backward onto the floor with a huge clang, sending

Cousteau into a barking fit.

"That's it! We've got it! Come see!" He motions all of us over.

Cai disconnects the tube from my arm and presses a gauze pad to my skin. "We're done…for now." He doesn't look at me again.

That's fine with me. I bend my arm and press the bandage hard as I slide out of the seat. We walk over to TJ and May's area together. Dr. Adams is already there. They're looking over the virtual displays arranged above TJ's desk, chatting excitedly.

"It's impossible." Dr. Adams shakes his head.

"What is it?" I can't see anything noteworthy on the displays.

"This part—" TJ points to the database listed in the corner of one display. "This is still garbage. It's encrypted, and I can't break the code. It's unlike anything I've seen before—"

"Unlike anything *either* of us have seen before," May interrupts him. "It's not code, it's not language—"

"But this—" TJ points to the main section of the image containing a message format. "This proves that the Nina didn't fail her deep space test five hundred years ago. She wasn't dismantled and used as components for the Pinta and the Santa Maria like history tells us."

Cai squints at the data. "Your pilgrim ships?"

"Yes, only two remain," I explain. "But how can this secret transmission have anything to do with the Nina? And what does *that* have to do with our current conflict with SciCorps?"

TJ turns to me. His eyes are wide, his cheeks flushed. Excitement and fear emanate from him. "Because…because this transmission is from outer space…it's from the Nina."

"What?"

May nods. "She wasn't lost. She *left*!"

Dr. Adams sits heavily into a chair. "If this is true, then why're they communicating with SciCorps now, after all this time?"

"That's the best part." TJ grimaces when May smacks his arm.

I raise a hand to stop their argument. "Focus! What aren't you telling us?"

TJ looks me in the eye, and I feel him pull a small measure of strength from me, from our twin connection. He straightens his shoulders. "The Nina's nearing direct communication range, but best we can tell this message was sent several months ago."

Cai shifts next to me. "So, they're on their way back. That's good, right?"

May shakes her head. "It would be if…"

"What? What's the problem?" I ask.

TJ lets out a huge breath. "They're running out of fuel."

CAI

Current year: 2701
Tuesday, 12:45 PM
Over the Albuquerque ruins, North America

"Beep, beep, beep…beeeep, beeeep, beeeep…beep, beep, beep."

In the moment it takes me to understand what I'm hearing, TJ has already started trying to locate the signal. "We have a distress signal. Bearing…on screen."

"What's going on?" Van Elder's bulk fills the remaining space in the cockpit. For a large man, he moves incredibly fast. I wonder if that's true of all sapiens, or just him.

I look at the screen. "That can't be right. Check your inputs."

It only takes a heartbeat for TJ to answer. "Confirmed. Signal originates approximately 804 kilometers due east."

I shake my head. "That's impossible. We've never picked up any kind of signal before. Maybe it's a sensor glitch."

Van snorts. "A sensor glitch that sounds out S-O-S? Where are we?"

I check our heading. "About 520 kilometers east of Humphrey's Peak. Best to ignore it—"

"Aye, that puts us over Old New Mexico—near the Albuquerque ruins." Van crouches down so he's level with our screens. "Are we off course then? Why're we so far east?"

"We adjusted course to avoid a thunderstorm," I tell him. "That's the only adjustment we're making."

TJ turns to Van. "They closed Albuquerque to scavenging years ago. No one flies here anymore."

"Let's not get distracted—"

"Sure as that would explain why no one else has intercepted the signal." Van interrupts, ignoring me again. "So then, what are we waitin' for?"

I can't believe his question. "What do you mean, what are we waiting for? We can't afford this distraction; we've got to get to Terra Faire. We can't go 800 kilometers off course after some unidentified signal."

Van tips his head to the side. "It's not unidentified, it's an SOS. That's quare specific. I dunno about yer little city, but in the Farms, when someone sends up a flare, we run toward it, not away."

"Even if we had the power reserves, we can't do it. It would lead us directly toward the eye of the Great Storm. The Agulha's sturdy, but even *she* can't withstand those winds."

"We can't do nothing."

TJ checks the readings again. "Look at these figures on storm activity. The storm's almost in a lull—these are nearly the best conditions we could hope for, and that's probably why we heard the signal."

I shake my head. "No, no, no. We've got to stay on course."

A warmth that I know well is spreading through my limbs. If I were to check my moral compass right now, I know I'd find myself a bit off course myself. But I'm more stubborn than that, I *will* stay focused on the goal of reaching Terra Faire, of seeing Giza before it's too late.

"What's going on?" Eddie's muffled voice comes from behind Van. "What's that noise? What's the problem?"

I blow out a breath. "Do you have the controls?"

TJ nods.

I've got to control this whole situation or I'm going to lose everything. "Okay, let's go."

I motion Van back into the main cabin and unbuckle my harness to follow him. Bending slightly under the overhead compartments, I look at the concerned faces of my passengers. I can do this. I can. I've convinced a tougher audience than this to see my way of things. I can do this.

Van tucks himself into the area surrounding his seat. "We've encountered a distress signal due east, near the eye."

This announcement meets with silence as the women absorb the information.

I clear my throat. "There's no way of knowing whose signal it is or how long it's been active. We need to stay on course or risk running out of power."

"What? We can't ignore it!" Mercy tries to stand, but her seatbelt holds her down.

"We know nothing. Where would we land? How would we take off again?"

May points her hand toward the floor. "The Creator put this

in our path."

She's a woman of few words, and I've learned that when she speaks, others listen.

I turn to Eddie in frustration, hoping that she'll see reason, but her face is turned away from me, her eyes closed in deep concentration. When her eyes fly open and pin mine, I know she's made some kind of decision. "We have to go. We have to see what's at the end of that signal."

"What? No!" No, no, no! I want to scream at them. I've got to get control of this! Everything is at risk. If we somehow survive the landing and get stranded, my people continue to die. If by some miracle we only get delayed, Giza dies alone. If, God forbid, Eddie is lost to the world completely, how much longer will our world have to wait for a cure?

Mercy raises a hand. "This is a democracy—"

"I vote yes!" TJ shouts from the cockpit.

"Yes," Eddie says.

"Yes!" Mercy and May shout.

"I'm sorry, yer highness." Van clamps his beefy hand on my shoulder. "Majority rule."

Immediately the plane banks east and accelerates. TJ shouts from the cockpit. "I've got it, I'm locked on the signal! New heading, on course."

These people! So frustrating, so unfocused! I close my eyes and push down the anger rising in me. I *don't* have control of this. Because they're like children at times, chasing after a shiny red balloon! But what are my options? They already understand this mission, that my people are suffering from the Trade at a far

more aggressive rate than theirs. I could tell them about Giza....
No, that's like emotional blackmail. Eddie'd never forgive me or
herself if I told her and then she chose to follow the signal
anyway. She's already straining against the many labels her people
have tried to put on her. How would she react to so blatantly
adding *savior* to the list?

Van drops back into his seat. "Don't worry, princess, we'll get
ye back to yer adoring masses somehow."

"Don't call me that!" The heat in Eddie's eyes as she stares
across the aisle at Van tells me I'm right.

She shifts her attention to me. "Well? I'd really rather not die
today so maybe you could help TJ fly your plane?"

I grit my teeth and stride back to the pilot seat to strap in.
The sky ahead of us is menacing. It's a permanent storm so large
it can be seen from outer space, turning part of our once blue-
green planet into an orb with a big splotch of swirling red and
brown. The Great Storm may be nearing a lull, as TJ called it,
but it's still a sight I never imagined I'd intentionally fly into. It
matches my mood perfectly.

Both of the dogs start whining in the back. I know how they
feel.

"If we're doing this," I say, "here's how it's going to
go—"

Beep, beep, beep.

"Now what?" I check the new warning blinking on my virtual
display. "Proximity alarm!"

"Proximity?" Eddie asks.

"Everybody buckle up."

TJ swivels between controls. "I've got signals coming in from the west. Approximately…. God's grace! Twenty aircraft flying in formation."

"Have they seen us?"

"I don't think so, not yet. They're staying on course heading south of our new course east."

"I'm tracin' 'em," Van calls from behind me.

"What are you doing? Get back in your seat!"

He's crouched in the aisle, his TAC combat communication kit open on the floor. A tiny virtual screen projects a map of blinking lights over his controls. "Holy hell! It's SciCorps. Twenty class three unmanned drones on course to…. It has to be South America."

I turn to TJ. "They must have gone around the storm like us. What are they doing?"

He shakes his head. "The only thing that fits is that they're looking for us, and maybe trying to find Terra Faire."

"Aye, fits fine I'd say." Van settles on the floor with his tech spread around him.

I take a deep breath. It makes sense. "I agree."

"Yer shielding technology, is it on?" Van asks.

"No, I turned it off shortly after departure to save energy."

Eddie leans forward. "If those drones see us, they'll follow us, now or later after we reach that distress signal. Mother won't just lose interest once she realizes they've found their target."

TJ nods. "I agree, she'll sink her teeth in."

"Mother?" I ask.

Eddie sighs. "We discussed it. The name on everyone's minds

while you were captive on SATO Station? That *LeRoux* wasn't our father; it was our *mother*, Fleet Admiral LeRoux. She's pulling the strings."

TJ swears under his breath. "We should cloak."

I tap in the commands. "Cloaking now." The interior lights dim as my jet diverts energy to the technology that shields it from both sight and radar. Now we should be safely invisible.

"God's grace!" Van's big hands run over the controls.

"What?"

"They've found us. The drone at the tail end of the convoy just changed course to intercept us." He pounds a fist on the wall. "We're bloody eejits!"

"Why? What happened?"

TJ banks left. "Still following?"

The dogs are barking now; May tries settling them but without much luck. We wait for Van's reply.

"Aye, course adjusted. Eejits, like I said."

"It's chance, has to be." I turn to TJ. "It picked us up right before we cloaked."

TJ shakes his head. "More like right after. SciCorps's smart. They must've found a way to identify the energy signature of your cloaking tech. The second we cloaked we lit up like a beacon."

"Bollocks." Van taps furiously into his control board. "Confirming, drone is unmanned. I'd bet good credits those drones don't have independent operators yet, but that won't last long."

"We need to put distance between us and that drone. It

doesn't matter now if they see us. Dropping cloak. Prepare for acceleration," I warn them.

"Go, now!" Van shouts. "Drone accelerating. That little gobshite just got a pilot."

"Get in your seat!" I can't wait for Van to comply; I increase speed, the jolt pressing me back. I hear the dogs yip and May's answering gasp.

"Van!" Mercy cries.

Van's kit crashes against the wall with a loud thud, knocking Van down with it.

The wind picks up and TJ and I fight for control. We're flying fast, the tempest buffeting us from all directions reducing visibility to less than a kilometer.

"There it is!" TJ points to starboard just as a flash of light passes in front of the windshield. A new alarm blares.

"What was that? Quiet those dogs!" I shake my head. "Are they shooting at us?"

"Tracker!" Van shouts.

I risk a glance back to see he's juggling his kit again, trying to operate his combat tech.

"Get in your seat!"

"Nah, got better things to do. That one missed us, but they'll try again. Stand by to bank left on my mark."

The plane shakes violently. Turbulence pushes us up and down within dusty clouds of pale orange. The dogs are absolutely crazed now.

"I see it! There!" TJ points ahead of us.

The drone is a black shadow in the haze. I catch the flash of light and bank hard left even before Van gives the command.

"Left! Gah!" Van groans as his head smacks Eddie's seat.

"Missed!" My joy is fleeting. Like a surreal image from a nature vid, I watch the drone swirl past us again caught in the funnel of a small tornado. One of its wings rips away before it's sucked into the core.

"The drone is down!" TJ shouts.

"Brace for impact!" I don't even have time to pray before the edge of the funnel catches our nose and tosses us like a skipping stone toward the ground. "Creator help us all."

Read the rest of Eddie and Cai's story in
Flare *(Scorched Earth Series: Book Two),*
coming January 2025.

ACKNOWLEDGMENTS

I began writing this book in 2016 based on a simple question: *What if God is real and knows what we're doing to the planet?* I loved the idea of a new human species being born through a deliberate and undeniable act of God. How would old and new humans interact? What skills would humans 2.0 have? Soon Mercy Adams and her world took shape in my mind.

It took six years to complete the first three books in this series; book four is underway. Through those years numerous people supported me, either directly with critiques and suggestions, or by sharing craft tips and a sense of community.

I'd like to thank my beta readers, Megan Nostrand, Adam Quinn, and Rebecca Schleuning. Without the excitement and encouragement of these young people, I might never have made it to subsequent stories. When I think of how much my manuscripts have improved from those early drafts, I'm even more grateful for their perseverance and love of story. Thanks also to my BFF Kim Murphy who has no interest in sci-fi, but was always game to ride shotgun during my writing sabbaticals. When I reluctantly dragged myself out of Scorch and back to reality, it was awesome to find her there waiting for me, usually with a gourmet meal and a beverage on ice.

Along with them, I'd like to thank all the hosts and writers involved with my local Society for Children's Book Writers and Illustrators (SCBWI) chapter as well as writers and staff at my local library, all of whom provided priceless critiques and feedback over the years. The camaraderie I experienced with these energetic and thoughtful people—and their generous guidance—kept my spirit strong as I continued through endless revisions and rewrites.

Everyone knows that writers consider their books like children. Entrusting my manuscript to an editor was a big step and I couldn't have been any luckier than to find my fantastic editor Laurel Garver. Her insights into the craft of storytelling improved my books beyond my expectations. Laurel, I can't thank you enough for helping me send my work out into the world.

A huge thanks to my cover designer Sarah Hansen for taking my vague yet wildly complicated ideas and turning them into amazing images of Scorch. Partnering with an artist who could make my words come alive in imagery was an amazing experience.

Thanks to fellow author Clara Kensie for connecting me with Snowy Wings Publishing. Scorch and its inhabitants may never have reached readers if it were not for Lyssa Chiavari and the team at SWP. Lyssa's guidance on all things publishing made a complicated process manageable. I'm grateful that she always had time for one more question.

Of course readers hold a special place in my heart. Thank you to all of you for eagerly seeking new worlds and challenging environments in which our imaginations can explore new possibilities. I'm proud to be part of your list.

Right up there with readers, I must thank the many teachers who influenced my life, especially Dee Johnson who somehow managed to convince my spastic teen self to read for pleasure and write for fun. Without her enthusiasm, the kindred spirits she connected me with, and the many skills she taught as our school's devoted literary magazine manager, I may never have realized my fundamental need to create.

Many thanks to my siblings who showed me how to use my imagination back in a time when television was limited to channels 2, 5, 7 and 9. Whether we were tramping through the woods looking for witches' graves or jumping on the furniture in a game of lava, they taught me that the worlds we create in our minds can be inspiring as well as entertaining. And of course, thanks to my parents who supported my education without once asking me about the job prospects of a Rhetoric major. Allowing me to find my own way was a gift.

Finally, thank you to my family, Steve, Parker, and Rebecca, for supporting my decision to fulfill my dream and allowing me the time and space to be a wife, mother, and writer. I would apologize for all the missed meals if I didn't know how much you enjoyed the takeout. You believed in my talent without question and gave me the confidence I needed to keep going. Thank you.

ABOUT THE AUTHOR

Sandra Macek is the author of the young adult sci-fi series Scorched Earth, which includes the novels *Kindling*, *Flare*, *Magma*, and *Firestorm*. After graduating with a degree in rhetoric, she dreamed of becoming a novelist; instead she got a job so she could eat. Now she's an IT professional by day and a writer by night—surviving suburbia on a continuous diet of girl-power fiction. Given the chance to be anyone else, she'd be Buffy, Bella, or any woman in Paris.

You can find her online at SandraMacek.com.

www.ingramcontent.com/pod-product-compliance
Lightning Source LLC
Chambersburg PA
CBHW020901060726
47591CB00004B/1025